大亨小傳
The Great Gatsby

中英雙語典藏版

史考特·費茲傑羅——著

邱淑娟——譯　成惠英——圖

晨星出版

導讀

爵士年代的絢爛大夢

文字工作者 李曉菁

一九二二年的美國長島西卵鎮，已經聞不到第一次世界大戰的煙硝氣息。

勞斯萊斯車駛入仿法國諾曼第市政建築的豪宅，通宵的狂歡派對鼓噪著各式樂器聲，義大利歌劇融合美國百老匯戲劇，爵士樂的慵懶穿插其中，交織出繁星般的燦爛與俗麗。不知道彼此姓名的男女，爭妍鬥豔，只要擁有一輛名牌跑車，彷彿握有一張擠入蓋茨比豪宅的通行證，豪宅裡有穿越國界與時空的幻想——挑高的歌德式藏書室牆壁鑲嵌英國雕花橡木的裝飾；有人性的墮落與欺騙——捧著酒杯入書房的客人，語氣嘲諷地確認著書櫃上陳列的是如假包換的書，而不是充當壁飾的假磚塊書。

夜裡的蓋茨比豪宅是一九二零年代紐約上流階級的縮影。那時世界大戰方休，對大戰採取孤立主義的美國年輕一代，移轉對戰爭的恐懼與無助，沉醉在美女、美酒與舒軟爵士樂生活中，需要更多的金錢作後盾。

費茲傑羅極盡物質奢華的《大亨小傳》於是生成。讀者從小說聞到資本社會的銅臭味。讀者自小說感受爵士年代的恣肆氛圍。讀者也隨小說進入酒品禁制的時空。那時美國禁止販賣私酒的法律行之有年，極端的管制卻導致更大的慾望，私釀酒的販子更形猖獗。《大亨小傳》中無數飲酒作樂的場面，不免讓支持禁酒法律的讀者扼腕搖頭，然而小說主人翁蓋茨比的神祕成功，卻可能肇因於他私酒走私犯的身份，矛盾的是，蓋茨比的豪宅夜夜款待賓客，斗酒十千恣歡謔，他卻滴酒不沾。

不喝酒這點使蓋茲比不同於其他賓客。他總是站在外面，冷眼看狂歡，一副眾人皆醉我獨醒的姿態。那些賓客有相仿的來歷，來自中西部，移民東部追求「美國夢」。所謂美國夢，就是相信不管任何人，無論出生貧富，只要透過努力都可以獲得成功與財富。在淘金這層次上，蓋茲比成功了！可他的美國夢卻不僅只有金錢，他還憧憬愛情，一股年輕時對愛情的憧憬，引導我們進入《大亨小傳》的浪漫動人之處。不同於周旋於酒色的賓客，蓋茲比不談股票、保險與汽車，他要的是一個女人，五年前熱戀的黛西，然而當時的蓋茲比，還是個一文不名的軍官，只能成天穿軍服，掩蓋自己沒有像樣便服的窘困。

費茲傑羅巧妙揣摩蓋茲比陷入情網的矛盾心態，無非也是自身經歷的投射。一八九六年，出生於明尼蘇達州一古老保守家族的費茲傑羅，移民東部，進入普林斯頓大學，學生時代便開始創作，還沒畢業就從軍，參與第一次世界大戰。在軍中，他愛上珊爾妲。珊爾妲出生富有家庭，父親是阿拉巴馬州的法官。兩情相悅而後訂婚，珊爾妲卻在費茲傑羅決定前往紐約接下一份低薪工作後毀婚。為了贏回心愛女人，費茲傑羅重操舊業，書寫普林斯頓大學的學生生活，文中摻入都會男女的速食愛情觀。一九二零年，《塵世樂園》（The Side of Paradise）暢銷，讓他一夕成名，大賺版稅，贏得美人歸。為了享受上流社會生活，他開始在《星期六晚郵報》（The Saturday Evening Post）《時髦人士》(The Smart Set) 大量發表短篇小說，同時搬進長島豪宅，這裡遂成為《大亨小傳》西卵鎮的靈感來源。可惜的是，蓋茲比的故事雖受評論家所青睞，卻不為讀者接受。夫妻生活拮据起來，爭吵不斷，費茲傑羅開始酗酒，珊爾妲更因精神問題，頻頻進出醫療診所。對婚姻絕望的費茲傑羅，在一九三七年搬到好萊塢，從事電影劇本創作，著手關於電影的新作。可惜的是，作品還沒完成，他就在一九四零年死於心臟病。

《大亨小傳》在費茲傑羅生前雖不受青睞，卻在作者死後大受重視。關於小說的研究在一九四零和五零年代達到顛峰，成為大學英美文學的教材，導演傑克·克萊頓在一九七四年更將小說改編成電影，搬上大螢幕。

　　小說以第一人稱敘述。敘事者尼克是參加過「世界大戰」的耶魯大學生，自中西部移民東部，投入名不見經傳的股票公司工作，意外成為蓋茨比的鄰居和傾聽者，旁觀蓋茨比、表妹黛西和大學同學湯姆的感情糾紛。尼克是說故事高手，當所有角色以自我為中心，只關心自己的感覺和欲望，不負責任地道聽塗說，尼克卻能從各家八卦中，條理分明地爬梳線索，道出蓋茨比的半生。

　　從尼克眼中，我們看到中西部的樸實、狹隘甚至沉悶，強烈對比東部的眩惑與不協調的拼貼感，難怪尼克「總覺得東部的生活有一點畸形。尤其是西卵鎮，在我許多古怪的夢中總有它。」它，是紐約，夜晚漲滿不安、放縱和冒險的浪漫情調，白天則屬於股票、名車、豪宅與名牌服飾。從尼克眼中，我們更看到蓋茨比讓人無比安心的笑容、紐約客一夕致富的特質：與生俱來的樂觀、羅曼蒂克的希望、無比神祕的力量——可能殺過人？在戰時當過德國間諜？否則「一個年紀輕輕的人，怎麼可能莫名其妙冒出頭，在紐約長島購置一座宮殿式的別墅？」

　　讀者一直透過尼克的眼睛在偵探蓋茨比，直到第三章，終能一睹蓋茨比的風采。就像《基督山恩仇記》的基督山伯爵一樣，蓋茨比的神祕，在於當時無人知其巨大財富從何而來，然而不同的是基督山伯爵帶來復仇的緊張；蓋茨比帶來愛情的悸動。

　　從蓋茨比對黛西的執著看來，《大亨小傳》是部浪漫的都會愛情小說。在充滿戀物情結的社交圈談情說愛，讀者不禁要質疑，被物欲綑綁的黛西，到底懂不懂真愛？黛西是不是真如蓋茨比的理解：「她當初嫁給你（湯姆）只不過是因為我很窮，她累了，不想再等我了！」蓋茨比追求的，到頭來是不是只是物化的愛情，冰冷而缺乏溫度？

　　蓋茨比二度追求黛西，構成《大亨小傳》的主軸。五年前，蓋茨比第一次親吻黛西，兩人發生親密關係，他雖離開，卻將對她的熱望轉化成賺錢的動力。在蓋茨比眼中，黛西是無可取代的珍寶；可從尼克眼中，黛西沒有蓋茨比的夢想美好：黛西善於編織謊言，說話響著金錢碰撞的叮噹聲，散發奇妙吸引力，富有的老公與美麗的小女兒是她炫耀的題材，還會抱著衣料號啕大哭：「從沒見過這麼漂亮的襯衫。」不小心開車撞死梅朵後，卻什麼事也沒發生似的一走了之，甚至在蓋茨比的葬禮上，連一個字、一朵花都沒有。

湯姆，黛西的丈夫，有強健肌肉供炫耀、用珍珠項鍊收買女人心。他不頂聰明，可是對自己的健康、財富與地位極端自信。他性格的矛盾表現在他的大男人主義愛情觀：他對於自己與情婦梅朵的逢場作戲，可以堂而皇之接受、誇耀；蓋茨比與黛西的相愛則罪不容赦。當他發現老婆的背叛，他也展開一連串反擊，加入調查蓋茨比身世的偵探行列。

湯姆與情婦梅朵的戀情乍看沒有重要性，卻為小說埋下伏筆。最後，梅朵的老公威爾森，輕信湯姆的錯誤分析，以為梅朵是蓋茨比撞死的，闖入豪宅用槍殺死蓋茨比。蓋茨比成為無辜犧牲者，而威爾森的愚昧、湯姆的煽動與黛西的無知，都是這場謀殺的共犯。讀者為蓋茨比的死喊冤，又該如何理解費茲傑羅用「偉大」形容蓋茨比？顯然這是尼克的說法，若是從湯姆口中說出這字眼，必定充滿嘲諷與挑釁；而站在讀者的角度，蓋茨比的偉大在於他的神祕與執著，在賺進大把鈔票後，還信念單純，不遺忘愛情。

故事並不隨蓋茨比的死去而落幕，之後的章節，毋寧說是另一場偵探小說的開始，尼克鍥而不捨地追究蓋茨比身世之謎，揭露的卻是紐約都會人的無情與冷漠，當初夜夜入豪宅狂歡的賓客，竟無一人參加蓋茨比的葬禮。當蓋茨比的老父穿著廉價大衣出現葬禮時，眾人更是一陣錯愕，那偉大的財富或許只是蓋茨比一手策劃的巨大騙局，在無情的紐約社交圈中，踏進圈中的人比圈外人更孤獨。

第 1 章

　　在我年紀還輕，涉世不深的時候，我父親曾經訓誡過我一段話，至今我還放在心上反覆思考。

　　他對我說：「每當你開口批評別人，請記住，世界上不是每個人都像你這樣，從小就占盡各種優勢。」

　　他沒有繼續多說——我們父子之間雖然話不多，但總有些事情異常相通，所以我當時知道他話中有話。由於這個教誨，我養成了不妄下斷語的習慣。而這種態度吸引了很多性情古怪的人把我當成知己，什麼心事都對我說，甚至有些面目可憎、言語無味的人也來糾纏我。大概那些心理不正常的人見到正常人有這種性情，就會馬上伺機接近。所以，我在大學時代就被視為政客，這很不公正，因為總有冒冒失失的陌生人找我傾吐心事，其實我一點都不想知道，一旦情況不對，發現有人要把我當知己，準備向我坦露心事，我就會裝睡或藉故忙碌，一副事不關己的模樣，說幾句玩笑話；因為年輕人把你當作知己所傾吐的隱私往往千篇一律，而且有所隱瞞。不對人妄下斷語代表一種無窮的希望。我提起父親的話，似乎顯得我們父子都有點瞧不起人，但他其實是要提醒我，待人寬厚是一種天賦，並不是每個人生來都相同，我時時提醒自己記得這個準則：責人過苛，而有所失。

　　雖然我如此強調對人寬厚，但不得不說寬厚也有限度。人的行為，有基於磐石、有出於泥沼，可是過了某種程度，我也不管它的緣由了。去年秋天剛從東部回來時，心情的確非常沉重，巴不得全世界的人都穿上制服來向道德觀念立正致敬；我再也不想放縱自己涉足他人的內心，讓人家對我推心置腹了。但是只有蓋茨比——本書的主人翁——例外，這位大亨代表了我所鄙夷的一切。假使一個人的個性是一連串不間斷的成功姿態，那麼他一定有其迷人之處；他對於生命具有超高敏感度，像是能夠偵測萬里以外地震的精密儀器。這種能力與一般美其名為「創造型人格」的那種軟弱的多愁善感完全不同，是一種異乎尋常、與生俱來的樂觀，一種浪漫的希望，是我在別人身上從未發現過，以後也不可能再遇見。沒錯，蓋茨比最終也沒有令我失望，使我對人世間虛無的悲歡暫時喪失興趣的，就是蓋茨比內心所受的一切折磨，以及在他的幻夢消逝後隨之而來的污濁灰塵。

　　我們卡拉威家三代住在中西部這個城市，家境富裕，也算是當地名門望族。據說我們原本是蘇格蘭博克祿地方的公爵世家，而我這個支系的直系先人是我的伯祖父。他在一八五一年移居到這，在南北戰爭期間買了傭兵替他打仗，他自己則創辦了一家商行，專做五金批發買賣，如今我父親還繼續經營這項祖業。

　　我從未見過這位伯祖父，但我應該長得像他——從父親辦公室牆上那幅稍嫌冷酷的肖像畫就可以看出來。我在一九一五年從紐哈芬市的耶魯大學畢業，剛好比我父親晚了四分之一個世紀。不久後我參加了稱之為世界大戰，但我視之為條頓民族大遷徙的

延續。這場反侵略的仗，我打得興致高昂，退伍回家後仍靜不下心來。中西部家鄉不再是我心中溫暖的中心，而是宇宙邊緣的荒漠，因此我決定到東部去學債券生意。我的朋友全進了這一行，所以再多收容我一個也無妨。為了這件事，我的叔伯姑嬸討論了好久，就跟決定送我到哪所私立中學去一樣緊張。最後，個個臉上露出嚴肅而且猶豫的神情說：「那麼，好吧。」父親答應資助我一年。耽擱了一陣子後，我終於在一九二二年的春天來到這裡，當時我還以為這一去就不再回來了。

在大城市生活最現實的問題就是找到棲身處，那時已是溫暖的季節，而我又離開了花木扶疏、綠草如茵的家園，所以當一位年輕同事建議一起去近郊租房子同住時，我馬上答應了。不久就找到了一間飽經風霜的木造平房，月租八十元。但正要搬進去時，公司忽然把他調到華盛頓，我只好一個人搬進郊外這間房子。與我作伴的還有一隻狗——雖然沒幾天牠就跑了——和一部道奇老車，還有一位芬蘭籍的女傭人，她每天來替我整理床舖、準備早餐，每次她站在電爐前，總會自顧自叨唸著芬蘭人為人處世的道理。

頭一兩天我覺得很孤單，直到有一天，我在路上碰到一個比我對這地方還陌生的人。

「請問到西卵鎮該怎麼走？」他一臉無助地問我。

我指點方向後繼續往前，頓時不再感覺孤單。陌生人把我當成嚮導、拓荒者、定居者。他無意間認定我為這地方的一份子。

這個時節陽光普照，綠樹倏然成蔭。就像在縮時電影裡一

樣，花草在一夜間繁茂了起來。夏天接著來臨，我也再度有了生命復始的信念。

要做的事不少，有許多書要讀，憑藉著清新的空氣，也有許多有益健康的活動。買了十幾本有關銀行學、信用貸款和證券投資的書籍，一本本燙了紅金的書本擺在書架上，就像造幣廠製的新鈔一樣，等著為我揭露邁達斯國王、金融家摩根和羅馬巨富梅賽納斯等人的致富祕訣。除此之外，我打算要讀更多其他種類的書。我大學時頗有文藝氣息，曾經替《耶魯新聞》寫過一系列內容嚴肅而淺顯的社論。現在我打算重新在這些方面下功夫，使自己成為「通才」，換句話說，就是最膚淺的專家。這並不是什麼俏皮話，畢竟專心致志的人生總是要成功多了。

我租的房子在北美最怪異的一個地方，這純屬巧合。這個小鎮位在紐約東方一個延伸出來的細長怪島上，除了天然奇景外，還有兩處不尋常的地形，像一對碩大的雞蛋，離城裡有二十英里路，一束一西，中間隔著一道小灣，兩邊地角伸向西半球直到長島海灣恬靜無波的鹹水裡。這兩處隆起的地形一點都不圓滾，倒像哥倫布故事裡的雞蛋一樣，在觸地的那一端都有點壓扁了。在天空翱翔的海鷗看見了，一定驚訝不已；而對於插翅也難飛的人類來說，這兩個地方除了形狀大小之外，並無絲毫相似之處。

我住在西卵，是比較不漂亮的區域，但只是表面上的區別，實際上兩邊的差異宛若隔著一條古怪又險惡的鴻溝。我租的房子座落在雞蛋的頂端，離海邊只有五十碼，擠在兩棟每季要一萬二到一萬五租金的大別墅之間。右手邊的那棟，不管用什麼標準衡

量都稱得上是富麗堂皇。是仿造法國諾曼第省的市政廳的建築，一邊聳立著嶄新的古堡式塔樓，覆蓋著一層稀稀落落的藤蔓，有四十多英畝的草坪和庭園，還有一個大理石砌造而成的游泳池。這就是蓋茨比的豪宅。其實我還不認識他，只曉得住在這棟別墅裡的是叫蓋茨比的先生。我租的那間房子實在難看，不過幸好只是小小的難看，並不會太引人注意，因此我常有機會欣賞海景，欣賞隔壁鄰居的一小塊草地，此外，能夠和百萬富翁比鄰而居更叫人欣慰，而這一切只需付出每月八十元的代價。

從我住的地方眺望海灣對岸，只見東卵瓊樓玉宇林立，映照在水面上閃閃發光。這年夏天的事，要從我應邀到東卵湯姆·勃肯納夫婦家吃晚飯那天開始。黛西是我遠房表妹，我和湯姆則是在大學就認識，戰後我曾到芝加哥找過他們，住了兩天。

湯姆是位成就斐然的運動員，曾經是紐哈芬市耶魯大學難得一見的足球健將，可說是聞名全國的風雲人物；像他二十一歲就登峰造極的人，日後不論做什麼，總有點走下坡的況味。他的家境極其富裕，他在大學時代揮霍的程度就已經頗令人側目，現在他從芝加哥搬到東部來，搬家排場更是令人咋舌，例如：他從森林湖市家裡把打馬球的馬匹全部運送過來。在我這一代竟然有人這麼闊綽，實在令人難以置信。

他們為什麼要搬到東部來，這我倒不知道。之前他們沒來由地到法國旅居了一年，後來又四處遊走，只要哪裡有人打馬球、哪裡有富人，他們就往哪裡去。黛西在電話上告訴我，這次他們要在紐約定居下來，可是我還是不信。我猜不透黛西的心思，不

過我覺得湯姆這輩子會像這樣抱著些許的期盼飄蕩下去，追尋著過去在球賽激戰中的興奮。

於是，在一個溫暖有風的傍晚，我開車來到東卵探望這兩位幾乎陌生的老朋友。他們的房子比我想像中還要豪華，面臨著海灣，宜人的紅白相間，是喬治王殖民時代風格的別墅。草地從海灘往大門延伸了四分之一英里長，一路跨過日晷臺、磚道和幾處花朵盛開的庭園，最後到了房子前，索性變成綠油油的藤蔓，沿著牆往上爬升。房子迎面立著一排落地玻璃窗，此刻正敞開迎著暖風，被金黃色的夕陽照得閃閃發亮，只見湯姆‧勃肯納一身騎馬裝扮，跨開雙腳站在前門陽臺上。

和大學時代比起來，湯姆變了很多。他現在已經三十歲，體型壯碩，頭髮淡黃，談吐舉止間充滿傲氣，嘴角略帶冷酷。在他臉上最突出的，是他那雙炯炯有神而傲慢的眼睛，總是給人一種盛氣凌人的感覺。那身騎裝雖然華麗得有點女子氣，卻掩蓋不了他魁梧的身軀——他穿上那雙皮靴時，似乎要把鞋帶從上到下綁得緊緊的，肩膀轉動時，一大塊肌肉在他薄薄的外套下互相牽動著，這是一個孔武有力的健壯身軀。

他說起話來聲音高又粗啞，更讓人感覺他暴躁乖僻，言談間還如同長輩教訓人的口吻，即使對他喜歡的人也是如此，在耶魯大學唸書時有不少人恨死了他。

「喂，你別因為我力氣比你大、比你更像個男人，就凡事都順從我。」他似乎就是這麼說的。我跟他加入同一個社團，雖然我們沒有成為知己，但我總覺得他很欣賞我，而且帶著一種想親

近又不屑遷就的神氣，希望我也瞧得起他。

我們在陽光照耀的陽臺上聊了一會兒。

「我這裡很不錯。」他說，焦躁的眼神閃爍不定。

他單手把我轉過來，然後用他寬大的手掌畫過我們眼前的那幅景致，引領我望向遠方的義大利式凹型花園、占地半畝、氣味濃烈的玫瑰花圃，以及海上一艘隨著浪潮起伏的汽艇。

「這塊地原來是石油大王狄曼的。」他又把我轉過來，相當客氣卻也突兀。「我們到裡面吧。」

穿過一道挑高的走廊，走進玫瑰色調的明亮客廳，兩頭的落地窗把整個房間玲瓏地嵌在這屋子裡。窗戶微開，外頭碧綠的草地彷彿要延伸到室內，在清新綠意的烘托下，落地窗更顯得光亮。一陣風輕輕吹進來，把窗簾吹得像一片片虛無飄渺的旗幟，從這一頭吹進來，那一頭吹出去，又吹向天花板上婚禮糖霜蛋糕似的裝飾，然後輕拂過酒紅色地毯，就像風吹拂過海面一樣。

屋子裡唯一靜止的東西是一張龐大的沙發，沙發上坐著兩個年輕的女子，活像熱氣球般繫在繩上。她們都穿著白色衣裳，衣裙被風吹得飄飄鼓鼓的，好像隨風在屋外飄了一圈，剛被吹回來似的。我呆立了好一會兒，在那裡傾聽窗簾吹動的聲響和牆上一幅掛畫的吱嘎聲。忽然砰的一聲，湯姆‧勃肯納把後面的落地窗關上，室內的餘風漸漸平緩下來，窗簾、地毯和那兩位年輕女子也冉冉降落地面。

比較年輕的女子與我素昧平生。她舒展著身子坐在沙發的一頭，一動也不動，下巴稍微仰起，好像頂著什麼東西，生怕它掉

下來似的。我不知道她有沒有瞧見我，因為她不動聲色，反倒是我吃了一驚，幾乎要為自己進屋驚動了她而囁嚅地說聲抱歉。

另外一位是黛西，她看見我來了，作勢要站起來，她的身子略向前彎，表情正經，但忽然噗嗤一笑，滑稽卻又迷人的一笑，我也跟著笑了，然後便走進客廳。

「我高興極了！」

她又笑了，好像自己說了什麼詼諧的話。她握著我的手，仰起笑臉望著我，似乎在說這個世界上她最想見到的人就是我。黛西一向如此。她輕聲地對我說，那個下巴頂著東西的女孩姓貝克。我曾聽說，黛西說話之所以小聲，是為了要讓人靠近她一點；這是不相干的閒話，然而並不損其迷人之處。

不管怎樣，貝克小姐仍只是稍微顫動了一下嘴脣，輕輕地朝我點了點頭，輕到幾乎看不出來，然後連忙又把頭抬高。她頂在下巴上的那件東西顯然晃了一下，才會讓她嚇了一跳！我忍不住又要開口向她道歉。凡是可以無視他人存在而自得其樂的人，總能讓我佩服得五體投地。

我將目光移向表妹，她開始用那低沉、迷人的聲音向我問話。她那種聲音總能令人側耳傾聽，好像每句話都是一經演奏就成絕響的音符。她的臉龐略帶憂鬱，五官亮麗，有著明眸皓齒，以及充滿熱情的雙脣，但追求過她的男人都說，最使人神魂顛倒、難以忘懷的，卻是她那令人銷魂的聲音：一會兒是引吭高歌，一會兒是喃喃低語的「你聽」，像是在說她剛做了一些令人歡欣鼓舞的事，而且下一刻還有更刺激快活的事在等著她。

　　我告訴黛西，我到東部來的途中曾在芝加哥待了一天，那裡至少有一打朋友託我問候她。

　　「他們想我嗎？」她欣喜若狂地大叫。

　　「整個芝加哥都想妳想得好悽慘。所有的車子都把左後輪漆成黑色，作為哀悼的花圈，城北湖邊一帶整夜慟哭聲不斷。」

　　「太美了！湯姆，我們回去吧，明天就走！」忽然她又沒頭沒腦地說：「你應該見見我女兒。」

　　「我是想看看她。」

　　「她已經睡了。她兩歲了，你還沒見過她嗎？」

　　「還沒。」

　　「你非得看看她不可，她真是……」

　　湯姆・勃肯納不耐煩地在屋子裡晃來晃去，但忽然間停了下來，把手放在我的肩膀上。

　　「尼克，你現在在哪兒做事？」

　　「我在做債券投資。」

　　「哪家公司？」

　　我告訴了他。

　　「我沒聽過。」他直截了當地說。

　　我有點不高興。

　　「你早晚會知道的，」我也不客氣地回他。「只要你留在東部，以後就會知道了。」

　　「你放心，我一定會在東部住下來，傻瓜才會再搬到別處去住。」他一面說一面瞥向黛西，又朝我望了望，好像防著什麼。

就在這時，貝克小姐突然插話：「對極了！」因為太突然，我不禁嚇了一跳。這是我進客廳後她說的第一句話，她可能也吃了一驚，因為她打了呵欠後，熟練敏捷地站起了身來。

「我全身都僵了。」她抱怨道，「我不知道在這沙發上躺了多久了。」

「不要看我，」黛西回嘴說，「我一整個下午都想把妳弄到紐約去。」

「不用了，謝謝。」貝克小姐婉拒了從廚房裡剛端出來的四杯雞尾酒，「我這一陣子在鍛鍊身體，很節制的！」

男主人向她瞧了一眼，非常地詫異。

「真的嗎？」他一口氣把酒喝光，彷彿杯裡只有一滴酒。「我真難以想像妳做得成什麼事。」

我看向貝克小姐，心想她「做得成」的是哪些事。我很喜歡看這個女孩子，她的身材修長筆直，胸部小小的，像個年輕軍校生一樣挺起胸膛。她用那雙被太陽照得瞇起的灰色眼珠回望著我，同樣帶著禮貌性的好奇，她的臉龐蒼白、迷人，又帶點不滿。此刻我忽然覺得在什麼地方見過她，或者是見過她的相片。

「你住在西卵，」她輕蔑地說：「那邊我認識一個人。」

「我一個人都不認識……」

「你一定知道蓋茨比。」

「蓋茨比？哪個蓋茨比？」黛西問道。

我還沒來得及說他是我的鄰居，管家就來通知開飯了。湯姆‧勃肯納用他強而有力的胳臂插在我肩下，硬把我推出客廳，

好像是把一顆棋子推到另一格去似的。

兩位年輕女子懶洋洋地將手輕輕搭在腰上，先行走到外面玫瑰色調的陽臺上去。陽臺向著落日，餐桌上點了四根蠟燭，燭火在微風中搖曳不定。

「點蠟燭做什麼？」黛西皺著眉不高興地說，她用手指把燭火捻熄。「再過兩個禮拜就是一年裡白畫最長的一天。」她神采飛揚地看著大家，「你們會不會老等著一年裡白畫最長的一天，結果還是錯過呢？我就老是盼著那一天，結果卻錯過。」

「我們應當計劃做點什麼。」貝克小姐邊打呵欠邊說，她坐下的樣子就好像要上床睡覺一樣。

「好啊，」黛西說。「我們要計劃什麼？」她無助地面向我問道，「大家都計劃些什麼？」

還沒來得及回答，就見她神色驚異地盯著自己的小手指頭。

「你們看！」她抱怨道。「我的手指頭受傷了。」

大家都看著她的手——關節處有點瘀青。

「湯姆，都是你害的。」她指控道。「我曉得你不是故意的，但是就是你害的。這是我的報應，誰叫我嫁了一個野蠻人，一個又粗笨又蠻橫的……」

「我最恨妳用這個笨字，」湯姆一臉不高興地說，「開玩笑也不可以。」

「粗笨。」黛西故意又說了一次。

有的時候黛西和貝克小姐無意間同時開口，說的都是一些無關緊要的玩笑話，稱不上嘮叨，而是清淡地跟她們的白色衣裳，

以及冷漠、清心寡慾的眼神一樣。她們兩人在這裡禮貌性地敷衍著湯姆和我,說一些無關痛癢的應酬話。她們知道晚餐很快就會結束,再過一會兒夜晚也會結束,一切都無所謂了。這點跟在西部截然不同,西部的晚宴總是緊鑼密鼓,一個階段接著一個階段,大家總是聚精會神,期盼後頭會更精采,但是希望總是落空,要不然就是每一個時刻都令人感到緊張不安。

「黛西,跟妳在一起,我覺得自己很不文明。」在我喝著第二杯略帶軟木塞味,但味道卻還相當不錯的葡萄酒時,不打自招地說。「妳不能談談農作或其他的事嗎?」

我這句話根本沒有什麼用意,想不到卻引來一番長篇大論。

「文明就快瓦解了。」湯姆突然激動地說,「我近來越來越悲觀。你有沒有看過那本高達德寫的《有色帝國的興起》?」

「沒有。」我回答道,同時對他的口氣感到震驚。

「這是一本好書,每個人都應該讀一讀。書裡的大意是說,假如我們白種民族不小心一點,就會……就會被澈底消滅。這個理論是有科學根據的。」

「湯姆的思想變得很深奧,」黛西說,表情流露出不經心的憂傷,「他老是在看一些很深奧的書,書裡的文句又長又難懂,上次那個……」

「這些書都是有科學根據的,」湯姆強調,同時不耐煩地看了她一眼。「這傢伙把整套理論解釋得很清楚。雖然現在我們占優勢,可是如果不小心提防,有色人種就會控制一切。」

「我們非打敗他們不可!」黛西小聲地說,眼睛朝著燦爛的太陽不安地眨個不停。

「你應該到加州住住──」貝克小姐才一開口,湯姆就在椅子上重重地挪動身子,打斷了她的話。

「書上說我們都是北歐民族,我,你,妳,妳……」他猶豫了一下後點點頭把黛西也算在內,黛西隨後又對我眨眨眼。「而且人類文明全是靠我們打造的……科學、藝術等等。懂嗎?」

他專注地論述大道理,神情顯得有點可悲,雖然那種自命不凡的態度更甚以往,但似乎已經滿足不了他。這時屋子裡的電話響起,管家走進去接電話時,黛西就趁這空檔朝我靠過來。

「我告訴你一個我們家裡的祕密。」她小聲卻興奮地說。「是關於管家的鼻子。你想知道管家的鼻子怎麼了嗎?」

「這就是我今晚來拜訪的目的。」

第 1 章

「其實，他本來不是擔任管家職務；他以前在紐約某戶人家裡專門負責擦拭銀器，那戶人家有一套兩百個人用的銀器。他從早到晚擦個不停，擦到後來鼻子受不了——」

「後來情況越來越糟。」貝克小姐插了一句。

「沒錯。情況越來越糟，最後他不得不辭掉那份工作。」

夕陽的餘輝一時映在她紅撲撲的臉龐上；她的聲音讓我不由自主地湊上前屏息傾聽。然後光芒漸漸退去，每一絲光線都依依不捨地離開她的臉，就像黃昏時孩子們在街頭捨不得離去一般。

管家回來後在湯姆耳邊輕輕說了幾句話，湯姆聽了皺起眉頭，把椅子向後一推，不發一語地走進屋子裡。他的離去似乎刺激了黛西，她再次傾身向前來，聲音聽起來熱切而悅耳。

「唉呀，尼克，我真喜歡你來我家做客。你使我想起……玫瑰，真真實實的一朵玫瑰。對不對？」她轉向貝克小姐，希望她認同。「是不是像一朵實實在在的玫瑰？」

這不是真話，我一點也不像玫瑰花。她不過是隨口說說，可是她身上流露出一股激動的氣憤，似乎想透過胡言亂語來向你傾訴。忽然間她把餐巾往桌上一甩，說了聲抱歉便走進屋子裡。

貝克小姐和我互看了一眼，故意不做任何表情。我正想開口說話，她卻忽然凝神直起身子，發出「噓」聲警告。後面的房間傳來兩人激動卻刻意壓抑的說話聲，貝克小姐毫不避諱地傾身向前，想聽聽他們說些什麼。細語斷斷續續傳來，時而低沉，時而激昂，隨即便陷入一片沉默。

「妳剛才提到的蓋茨比先生是我的鄰居——」我開口說話。

「別出聲，我想聽聽發生了什麼事。」

「出了事嗎？」我天真地問。

「你難道不知道？」貝克小姐十分訝異。「我以為大家都知道了。」

「什麼事？我不知道。」

「嗯……」她猶豫了一下，「湯姆在紐約有個女人。」

「有個女人？」我困惑地重複了一遍。

貝克小姐點點頭。

「這女人應該要懂規矩，居然吃飯時間打電話來找他，你說是不是？」

我還沒聽懂她的意思，就聽見裙擺拂動和皮靴軋軋的聲響，湯姆和黛西又回到餐桌上來了。

「對不起，沒有辦法！」黛西故作歡笑地大聲說。

她坐下之後朝貝克小姐和我看了一眼，然後接著說：「我到外面看了一下，外面非常浪漫。草地上有一隻鳥，我猜一定是搭著『庫那號』或『白星號』郵輪過來的夜鶯。牠在那兒不停地唱歌……」她的聲音也像在唱歌：「很浪漫對不對，湯姆？」

「的確很浪漫。」他說，然後苦著臉對我說：「吃完飯後如果天色還夠亮，我帶你到下面的馬房看看。」

屋裡的電話又響了，大家都吃了一驚，黛西朝湯姆堅決地搖頭。於是，關於馬房，或者該說是所有話題，都煙消雲散了。在餐桌上的最後五分鐘裡，我依稀記得蠟燭無緣無故又被點亮，我感覺到自己很想正視每一個人，同時又希望避開所有人的視

線。我看不出黛西和湯姆在想些什麼，我想貝克小姐也未必能把這位客人尖銳、急迫的電話聲完全拋到腦後。對某些人而言，這種局面或許很有意思——我的直覺卻是想立刻打電話叫警察。

不用說，看馬房的事就沒人再提了。湯姆和貝克小姐隔著幾呎寬的夕陽餘暉一同走進書房，那副神情，好像裡面躺了個死人要去守夜一樣。我則盡量保持高興的樣子，一面裝聾作啞，跟著黛西穿過一連串的走廊，來到前門的陽臺上。在蒼茫的暮色中，我們並肩在一張藤椅上坐下來。

黛西把臉埋在手心裡，好像在感受她那美麗的輪廓，然後她慢慢抬起頭望著柔和的黃昏。我看得出她內心的激動，因此故意問了一些關於她女兒的事，設法緩和一下她的情緒。

「尼克，我們彼此並不太熟，」她忽然說。「雖然我們是表親，我結婚的時候你也沒來。」

「當時我在戰場上還沒回來。」

「是啊。」她遲疑了一會兒。「尼克，有一陣子我很不好過，但現在我對人性已經看透了。」

顯然她會看破一切是事出有因。我等著她說下去，可是她並未開口，過了一會兒，我很勉強地把話題轉到她女兒身上去。

「我想她大概會說話了，會……吃東西，什麼都會吧？」

「是啊。」她心不在焉地看著我。「尼克，我想告訴你我女兒出世的時候我說的一些話，你想聽嗎？」

「當然想。」

「你聽了之後就會明白為什麼我會這樣看待……一切。她出

生還不到一個鐘頭，湯姆就不知道跑到哪裡去了，麻醉藥退後我醒了過來，有一種被遺棄的感覺，我馬上問護士是男孩還是女孩。護士告訴我是個女孩，我轉過頭眼淚就流了下來。『也好，』我說，『女孩也好，希望她長大後是個傻瓜，在這世界上女孩子最好是傻瓜，一個漂亮的小傻瓜。』」

「我知道多說也沒用，事情已經無法挽回了。」她語氣肯定地繼續說。「大家都這樣想……那些思想前衛的人也這麼想，我就是知道。我什麼地方都去過，什麼世面都見過，什麼事情都做過。」她的眼中閃現出不服氣的神色，和湯姆很像，接著便發出令人毛骨悚然的譏諷大笑。「飽經世故……天曉得，我真是一個飽經世故的人！」

她的笑聲停下後，我不再勉強去注意和相信她的話，我覺得她所說的根本不是真心話。這使我很不安，似乎這個晚上的一切只是個圈套，要逼我去附和她的情緒。我不說話等著，果然，她一直看著我，那張可愛的臉上露出一抹假笑，好像她剛才的話正足以表示她和湯姆都是屬於高人一等的貴族祕密集團。

屋子裡那間通紅的客廳此刻正燈火輝煌。湯姆和貝克小姐坐在長沙發的兩頭，她正為他大聲讀著《週六夜間郵報》，聲音低沉，語調平順，一連串的字組成了舒緩的音調。燈光照亮了他的皮靴，照在她秋葉般的黃髮上卻顯得黯淡無光，又照在雜誌的紙張上一閃一閃的，她每翻一頁，手臂上纖細的肌肉也跟著動一下。

我們走進屋子時，她舉起手來示意我們先別說話。

「欲知詳情，」她說著，把雜誌扔在桌上，「且看下期。」

　　她不安地移動了一下膝蓋，然後站起身來。

　　「十點了。」她邊說著雙眼邊往上看，彷彿天花板上有個時鐘似的。「我這個乖女孩該上床睡覺了。」

　　「喬丹明天參加比賽，」黛西替她解釋，「在威徹斯特。」

　　「哦……原來是喬丹‧貝克。」

　　現在我知道為什麼她很面熟了。在報導阿什維爾、溫泉市或是棕櫚灘的報刊體育欄照片上，我經常看到這張漂亮而稍帶傲氣的面孔。我還聽過一些關於她的閒話，是對她不利的傳聞，但詳細內容我早已忘了。

　　「晚安，」她輕聲地說。「明天早上八點叫我好嗎？」

「只要妳起得來。」

「我一定起得來。晚安，卡拉威先生。改天見。」

「你們很快就會再見面的，」黛西肯定地說。「老實說，我還想替你們做個媒呢。尼克，你多來幾趟，我就⋯⋯撮合你們兩個。唔，像是不小心把你們關在衣櫥裡，或者讓你們搭同一條小船送你們出海，像這一類的⋯⋯」

「晚安。」貝克小姐從樓梯喊著。「我一個字也沒聽見。」

「她是個好女孩。」過了一會兒湯姆說。「他們不應該讓她這樣到處亂跑。」

「你說誰不應該？」黛西冷冷地問。

「她家裡的人。」

「她家裡只有一個老得不能再老的姑媽。何況尼克可以照顧她，是不是，尼克？她今年夏天會常到這裡來度週末。我想這裡的家庭環境對她會有好處。」

黛西和湯姆默默地互看了一會兒。

「她是紐約人嗎？」我問。

「她是路易維爾人。我們在那裡一同度過了純潔的少女時期，美麗純潔的⋯⋯」

「妳剛才在陽臺上是不是對尼克說了一些內心裡的話了？」湯姆忽然問道。

「我有嗎？」她望著我說。「我不記得了。我記得我們談的好像是北歐民族問題。沒錯，我們的確談到那個話題，不過好像不知不覺就談起了⋯⋯」

「尼克，別聽到什麼就信以為真。」湯姆勸告我。

我很輕鬆地回答說我什麼也沒聽到，幾分鐘後我就起身告辭了。他們送我到門口，兩人背對著燈光並肩站著。我發動車子引擎後，黛西突然高喊了一聲：「等一等！」

「我忘了問你一件很重要的事。聽說你在西部跟一個女孩訂了婚。」

「是啊，」湯姆和善地補充一句說。「聽說你訂婚了。」

「那是謠言，我太窮了。」

「可是我們真的聽說了，」黛西堅持地說，我很詫異她再次像花朵般展開笑容。「聽過三個人這麼說，所以一定是真的。」

我當然知道他們指的是什麼，但是訂婚這件事根本連個影子都沒有。事實上，我決定到東部來的一部分原因，也是因為傳說我要和某位女士訂婚。我不能因為謠言就不跟老朋友來往，但是一方面我也不會遷就謠言而去結婚。

不過他們的關心倒令我感動，這讓他們不像一般有錢人那樣難以親近；然而，我開車離去時，心中還是不解，同時有些厭惡。我覺得黛西應該抱著她的孩子立刻離開這座房子——可是她顯然毫無這個意圖。至於湯姆這人，老實說，他「在紐約有個女人」我倒不奇怪，奇怪的是他竟然會因為讀了一本書而沮喪。不知道為什麼他這樣的人會去從無聊的學說中找尋安慰，除非是他發覺自己那壯碩的體格還不夠維持他一向唯我獨尊的心理。

一路開車回家，眼前所見已經是仲夏的景象，路旁只見招徠過往客人的飯館和汽油站，漆得鮮紅的加油機一個個蹲在電燈光

圈裡。當我回到位於西卵的住處,把車停進車庫後,在院子裡一架棄置的剪草機上坐了一會兒。風已經停息,只剩下嘈雜而清亮的夜,樹上鳥翼撲撲,大地吹響了青蛙,發出連續不斷的風琴聲。月光下有一隻貓的黑影在移動,我回過頭去看,發現並非只有我一個人在那裡——大約五十呎外,隔壁別墅的陰影中出現一個人,他雙手插在口袋裡,站在那兒仰望滿天銀色的星斗。從他悠閒的步伐和雙腳穩踏在草地上的姿態看來,那應該就是蓋茨比先生,他到外頭來看看我們頭頂上的天空哪一部分是屬於他的。

　　我打算向他打一聲招呼。剛才吃飯時貝克小姐曾提起他,我可以藉這個話題跟他攀談。但是我沒有出聲,因為忽然間他給我一種感覺:他目前寧願一個人——他以一種怪異的方式朝幽暗的海面伸出雙臂,雖然我離他很遠,但我十分肯定我看見他在發抖。不知不覺地,我的視線也轉移到海面上去,除了遠處一盞微弱的綠燈,什麼都看不見,那可能是某一家碼頭上的標誌。我回頭再去看蓋茨比時,他已消失不見,只剩下我一個人在這不平靜的黑夜中。

第 2 章

　　西卵到紐約的中途，公路跟鐵道忽然在此會合，並行了四分之一英里，為的是避開一個荒涼地帶，一個布滿塵土的山谷。在這裡，塵土像小麥一樣堆成了田野、山丘和奇形怪狀的花園；也堆成了房屋、煙囪和裊裊的炊煙，最終經過一番努力，還堆成一個個滿身灰土的人，隱約走在布滿灰塵的空氣中，漸漸粉碎化為塵土。有時可以看見一隊灰色車輛沿著隱形的直線緩緩前進，然後車子喀答一聲停下來，一群黑灰灰的人馬上拖著深灰的鐵鏟一窩蜂包圍上來，搞得灰塵滿天飛，根本看不清楚他們在做什麼。

　　在這片永遠被塵土籠罩的灰色地表上，多看片刻，就會發現兩隻龐大的藍眼睛，光是瞳孔就有一碼長，那是「艾珂爾堡醫生」的眼睛。這雙眼睛沒有臉，也沒有鼻樑，卻戴著一副巨大的黃色眼鏡。顯然是皇后區某個眼科醫師異想天開地豎立了這樣一座廣告招牌來招攬生意，後來要不是進了棺材，就是搬走了，這雙大眼睛卻遺留在這裡。由於久未重漆，加上風雨的侵蝕，這雙眼睛已變得有些黯淡，卻仍靜靜地注視著這個陰鬱的垃圾堆。

　　這個布滿塵土的山谷地帶有一條骯髒的小河，每當吊橋拉起讓駁船通過時，如果火車湊巧來到這就得停下，車上的乘客便可盯著這片淒涼的景象看上半個小時。平常火車開到這一站至少都

要停一分鐘，因為如此，我第一次見到了湯姆‧勃肯納的情婦。

認識湯姆的人都會一再強調他有情婦。他們都看不慣他常帶她出入熱鬧的酒吧，把她單獨留在餐桌上，自己則到處跟熟人打招呼。我雖然對這個女人感到好奇，可是我並不想見她——最後還是見到了。有天下午我跟湯姆一起搭火車前往紐約，火車開到垃圾堆那一站，他忽然站起身，抓住我的手臂硬把我拉下車。

「我們這一站下車，」他堅持說：「見見我的女朋友。」

我想他中午喝了不少酒，因此幾乎是暴力地堅持要我陪他。他自以為是地認為禮拜天下午我絕對不會有什麼要緊的事可做。

我跟著他跨過火車鐵道旁一排低矮的白漆柵欄，在艾珂爾堡醫師目不轉睛的注視下，沿著馬路往回走一百碼。四周只有一排矮小的黃磚房，孤單地佇立在這片荒地的邊緣，算是供應當地居民生活所需的商店街，附近什麼都沒有。這裡的三家店鋪有一家待租，一家是通宵營業的小餐館，門前有著一道道顧客留下的灰色足跡；另一家則是修理汽車的車行，招牌上寫著：「喬治‧威爾森——修車；二手車買賣」。我隨著湯姆走進這家修車行。

車行裡四壁蕭條，看起來毫無生意的樣子；只有一輛布滿灰塵的破舊福特車蹲在陰暗的角落裡。我心想，這個車行可能只是個偽裝，豪華浪漫的公寓也許隱藏在樓上。這時車行老闆從他的休息室走出來，拿著一塊破抹布不停地擦手。他是一個頭髮淡黃、臉色蒼白的人，長相倒還不錯，可是一臉的無精打采，看見我們進來，那雙淺藍的眼珠露出了一絲希望。

「你好啊，威爾森老傢伙！」湯姆愉快地拍拍他的肩膀說：

「最近生意如何？」

「還不錯。」威爾森缺乏說服力地回答。「你那輛車子到底什麼時候才要賣給我？」

「下個禮拜，我已經叫人把車子送去修理一下了。」

「他動作可真慢，是嗎？」

「一點也不，」湯姆冷冷地回道。「你若是不高興，我賣給別人好了。」

「你誤會了！」威爾森連忙解釋：「我的意思是……」

他話還沒說話聲音就逐漸消逝，湯姆只是不耐煩地往車行四處亂瞟。不久，我聽見有人走下樓梯的聲音，一個身材結實的女人擋住了休息室的燈光。她大概三十五、六歲，體型略顯豐腴，卻流露

出某些女性特有的肉感。她穿著一件深藍色縐綢圓點洋裝，雖然長得不是很特別也不美，可是一眼就感覺到她有一股活力，彷彿全身的血液都在不停地燃燒。她先慵懶地一笑，然後視若無睹地從她丈夫身邊走過，跟湯姆握手時兩眼發亮直看著他。接著，她用舌頭潤潤嘴脣，頭也不回便低聲粗氣地對她丈夫說：

「還不趕快拿椅子過來請客人坐。」

「喔，馬上來。」威爾森趕緊到休息室裡搬椅子，他的人影一轉眼就融進了水泥牆壁中。灰白的塵土籠罩著他深色的衣服和淡黃色的頭髮，籠罩著屋子裡的所有東西，除了他老婆例外。她此刻走近湯姆身邊。

「我想見妳。」湯姆急切地說：「搭下一班火車。」

「好。」

「我在車站地下室的報攤旁邊等妳。」

她點點頭，從他身邊走開，威爾森才從休息室裡搬了兩張椅子出來。

我們在公路旁沒人看見的地方等她。再過幾天就是七月四號美國獨立紀念日了，一個滿身泥土、骨瘦如柴的義大利小孩在火車軌道旁放了一排魚雷炮。

「你看這裡多糟。」湯姆說，同時對著艾珂爾堡醫生的眼睛皺了一下眉頭。

「糟透了。」

「離開這裡對她有好處。」

「她先生不反對嗎？」

「威爾森？那個人笨得連自己是活人還是死人都搞不清楚了。他還以為她是到紐約去找她妹妹呢。」

就這樣我和湯姆·勃肯納以及他的情婦一起到紐約去了，也不能說一起去，因為威爾森的老婆坐在另外一列車廂，以免引起注意。湯姆還算顧全大局，怕萬一在火車上被東卵的鄰居看見。

那女的在離開前換上一件棕色連身紗裙，到了紐約，湯姆扶她下車時，衣裳被那肥闊的臀部繃得緊緊的。她在報攤買了八卦雜誌《紐約閒話》和一本電影雜誌，又在車站藥房買了罐冷霜和一小瓶香水。我們走上樓梯，站在回音四起的陰暗車道旁，她故意略過四部計程車，最後選了一部裝了灰色椅套的淡紫色新車，我們搭著這部車離開車站的人潮，開進燦爛的陽光下。忽然間她似乎看見了什麼，馬上回過頭來敲敲前面的玻璃要司機停車。

「我要買一隻小狗。」她很起勁地說。「我要買一隻養在公寓裡，養小狗很好玩。」

我們的車子倒退到街邊一個頭髮灰白的老人那裡，沒想到他竟荒謬地神似煤油大王洛克斐勒。他的脖子上掛著一個籃子，裡頭有一打剛出世、難以確定品種的小狗。

「這是什麼狗？」他一走到計程車窗旁，威爾森的老婆便急著問。

「什麼狗都有。妳要哪一種呀，太太？」

「我要一隻警犬，我看這裡沒有警犬吧？」

老頭不太確定地朝籃子裡看看，伸手進去捉出一隻小狗來。小狗被他擰著頸背不斷地扭動身子。

「那才不是警犬。」湯姆說。

「對,不是純種的警犬。」老頭帶著失望的口氣說:「應該是艾爾谷狗。」他伸手摸摸小狗背上的棕毛,「妳看看牠這身毛,真是漂亮!養這種狗,妳絕對不必擔心牠會感冒。」

「好可愛啊!」威爾森的老婆很高興地說:「要多少錢?」

「這隻狗?」老頭以欣賞的眼光看著他的小動物。「這隻狗賣十塊錢。」

那隻艾爾谷狗——牠的確混了一些艾爾谷狗的血統,只是四隻腳實在太白了——就這麼完成交易了,坐到了威爾森老婆的大腿上,她很高興地用手撫摸著小狗身上的長毛。

「這隻狗是男孩還是女孩?」她細聲細氣地問。

「這隻狗,啊!是小男孩。」

「是隻母狗。」湯姆肯定地說。「錢拿去吧,拿了再去買十隻狗。」

我們的車開到第五大道上,在這夏季的週日午後,城裡空氣溫暖且柔和,像是充滿了田園風味,即使忽然有一群綿羊悠然走過來,我想我也不會吃驚的。

「停車,」我跟司機說:「我得在這裡下車。」

「不行。」湯姆阻止我。「你要是不到我的公寓坐坐,梅朵會難過的。梅朵,妳說是不是?」

「來嘛,」她也勸著:「我可以打電話叫我妹妹凱瑟琳過來。有眼光的人都說她是個大美人。」

「唔,我是很想去,但是……」

車子繼續往前開，又掉頭穿過中央公園，向西邊一百多街的方向走。車子在一百五十八街一大排白色蛋糕似的公寓前停下。威爾森的老婆下車時，一雙大眼睛環視著周遭，頗有皇后回宮的氣勢，雙手抱著小狗和她剛才買的東西，趾高氣揚地走進去。

我們乘電梯上樓時，她像在宣布大事般的說：「我要請麥基夫婦上來。」我們搭上電梯後，她繼續說，「當然囉，我也得打電話給我妹妹。」

湯姆的公寓在頂樓，有一間小客廳，一間小飯廳，一間小臥室還有一間浴室。客廳擺了一套織錦的傢俱，由於體積實在太大，都擠到門口邊了，在那裡走動，稍微不小心就會被絆倒在凡爾賽宮女在花園盪鞦韆的織錦圖上。牆上唯一的掛畫是一張放得特大的美術攝影照，像是一隻母雞蹲坐在照得模糊的岩石上，但是遠遠望去，母雞卻又化成戴著一頂軟帽的胖老太太，她和藹可親地看著客廳裡的人。桌上擺著幾份過期的《紐約閒話》，還有一本流行小說《彼得·西門傳》和幾份專門報導百老匯八卦消息的雜誌。威爾森的老婆最關心的是她那隻小狗，她請電梯小弟去找一個墊滿稻草的箱子和一些牛奶。那小弟心不甘情不願地照她的吩咐去做，又自作主張買了一罐又大又硬的狗餅乾，在倒滿牛奶的碟子裡泡了一塊，沒多久餅乾就泡爛了，但整個下午都沒人理會。這時，湯姆拿鑰匙打開壁櫥，取出一瓶威士忌。

我這輩子只喝醉過兩次，第一次就在那天下午，因此發生的一切就像雲霧般，游離而迷糊。雖然過了八點，屋裡仍充滿明亮的晚霞。威爾森的老婆坐在湯姆的大腿上四處打電話找人來。一

會兒發現菸抽完了，我便出門到附近的藥房去買。等我回來時他們兩人都不見了，於是我很識相地坐在客廳裡，打開《彼得‧西門傳》開始讀。若不是這本書寫得太糟，就是我喝了太多威士忌，我讀來讀去就是看不懂。

湯姆和梅朵——一杯酒下肚之後，我和威爾森的老婆就彼此直呼名字了——再度在客廳出現時，客人們也陸續到來。

梅朵的妹妹凱瑟琳是一個年約三十歲左右，看起來相當世故的女人，身材高瘦，一頭又硬又短的紅髮，臉上抹的粉白得像牛奶一樣。她把眉毛拔光，重新化上一個比較時髦的樣式，但是原有的眉毛又長出來，使得她的眉線更模糊不清了。她走路時，手臂上的許多陶製手環上下地晃動，不斷發出叮噹的聲響。她毫不

客氣地走進公寓四處看著,那種神氣好像她是這裡的主人,我還以為她就住在這裡。但是當我問她時,她卻大笑,把我的問題重覆了一遍,然後告訴我她跟一位女性友人住在旅館。

麥基先生是樓下的鄰居,一副小白臉模樣。他大概剛刮過鬍子,臉頰上還有一點白色肥皂沫。他禮貌地跟屋子裡的每一個人打招呼。他告訴我他是「搞藝術」的,後來我才知道原來他是攝影師,牆上掛的那幅梅朵的母親模糊不清的放大照片就是他的傑作,像是徘徊在牆上的靈異物質。麥基太太的聲音尖細,一副無精打采的樣子,長得不難看,可是有點讓人受不了。她驕傲地告訴我,打從結婚以來,她丈夫已經替她拍過一百二十七次照了。

梅朵悄悄進房換了另一套乳白色薄紗的午後宴客裝,拖著長袖,在屋子裡轉來轉去,不斷發出沙沙的聲響。衣服一換,人也跟著改變了。先前在修車行裡引起我特別注意的活力,此刻變成一副貴婦模樣的高傲神氣。她的言行舉止和聲調越來越做作,而且不斷膨脹,而周圍的空氣逐漸縮小,在煙霧瀰漫中她簡直像走馬燈似的,在嘎吱作響的木軸上直轉。

「親愛的,」她尖聲怪氣地向凱瑟琳嚷嚷:「這年頭一不留神就會上當。大家什麼都不在意,只知道向錢看齊。上禮拜我叫一個女的來看看我的腳,等她把帳單送來差點沒把我嚇一跳,割個盲腸也沒有那麼貴。」

「那個女人叫什麼?」麥基太太問。

「姓艾伯哈特,她整天到人家家裡替人看腳。」

「妳這件衣服真好看,」麥基太太說:「我很喜歡。」

　　威爾森的太太聽到這句恭維話，只不屑地挑了挑眉毛。

　　「妳說這件舊衣啊，我不想花心思打扮時就會拿出來穿。」
她說。

　　「不過妳穿起來特別漂亮，妳明白我的意思嗎？」麥基太太
接著說：「要是妳能讓奇斯特拍張照，我想效果一定很好。」

　　大家都默不作聲地望著威爾森的老婆，只見她撥開蓋住眼睛
的一撮頭髮，然後對著大家淺淺一笑。麥基先生側著頭朝著她仔
細打量，再接著用手在面前慢慢地前後移動幾下。

　　過了一會兒他說：「燈光要換一下，我想把五官特徵突顯出
來，因此要盡量在頭髮後面打光。」

　　「燈光不必調整了，」麥基太太插嘴道：「我覺得……」

　　麥基先生「噓！」了一聲，大家不禁又把視線轉回到他的模
特兒身上，這時候湯姆‧勃肯納大聲地打了呵欠，並且站起來。

　　「麥基，你們兩位要喝點什麼？」他說，「梅朵，趁大家還
沒睡著，再弄點冰塊和礦泉水來。」

　　「我早已叫那小弟去拿冰了。」梅朵豎起眉毛，對於下人辦
事不力頗有怨言：「這些人！非得隨時盯著他們不可。」

　　她說完看看我，無緣無故地笑了笑，然後突然衝到小狗旁，
抱起牠親個沒完，接著往廚房拂袖而去，好像裡面有十幾個大廚
師正等著她差遣。

　　「我在長島拍過幾張相當棒的照片。」麥基先生說。

　　湯姆茫然無言地看了他一眼。

　　「有兩幅我們裱了框，掛在樓下。」

「那兩幅是什麼照片？」湯姆問道。

「兩幅風景照。一幅我命名為『蒙托克岬──海鷗』，還有一幅叫『蒙托克岬──大海』。」

凱瑟琳突然坐到我的身邊來。

「你也住在長島嗎？」她問我。

「我住在西卵。」

「真的？我到那裡參加過一次宴會，大概一個月以前。在一個叫蓋茨比的家裡，你認識他嗎？」

「我就住在他隔壁。」

「有人說他是德國皇帝威廉‧凱撒的姪兒或親戚，所以才會那麼有錢。」

「真的嗎？」

她點點頭。

「我見到他有點害怕，一點都不想招惹他。」

關於我鄰居的這個消息頗令人感興趣，但卻被麥基太太打斷。她突然指著凱瑟琳對她丈夫說：

「奇斯特，你應該也替她拍一張。」她出其不意地說，可是麥基先生只是不耐煩地點點頭，然後又轉過頭去跟湯姆談話。

「要是有管道的話，我很想到長島多拍些照。只要他們肯給我起個頭。」

這時梅朵端了一盤東西出來，湯姆大聲一笑說：「問梅朵好了。她可以幫你寫一封介紹信，是不是，梅朵？」

「寫什麼？」她頗為驚異，滿臉疑問。

「替麥基寫一封介紹信，讓他替妳丈夫拍幾張照。」他喃喃說了幾句後，才又大聲說：「『加油站旁的喬治‧威爾森先生』什麼的，你們覺得好不好？」

凱瑟琳湊近我的耳邊，小心翼翼地告訴我說：「他們倆都受不了自己的另一半。」

「是嗎？」

「真是受夠了。」她看看梅朵，又看看湯姆。「既然婚姻關係都已經糟到這種地步，何必還在一塊過生活呢？要是我，我會離婚，然後馬上和對方結婚。」

「她也不愛威爾森嗎？」

不料回答的人竟是梅朵，她無意中聽到我的問題。一連串粗俗不雅的字眼，把威爾森罵得一文不值。

「這下你可相信了吧！」凱瑟琳得意洋洋地叫囂，然後又壓低聲音對我說：「要不是因為湯姆的太太，他們早就結婚了。他的太太是虔誠的天主教教徒，不可以離婚的。」

黛西並不是天主教徒；我對這樣的謊言不禁感到詫異。

「他們早晚會結婚的，」凱瑟琳接著說：「結了婚他們打算到西部去住一陣子，等事情平靜了再回來。」

「到歐洲不是更好嗎？」

「喔，你喜歡歐洲嗎？」她驚訝地問我。「我剛從蒙地卡羅回來。」

「這麼巧。」

「那是去年的事，我跟一個女性朋友同行。」

「待了很久嗎？」

「不久，只去了蒙地卡羅就回來了。我們是從馬賽去的，當時兩人身邊帶了一千兩百塊錢，可是不到兩天就在賭場被人騙光了。不瞞你說，我們在回來的路上吃了不少苦頭。我真是恨死那個地方了！」

一片晚霞在窗外展開，有如地中海蔚藍而甜蜜的海水──但是麥基太太的尖細聲音又把我喚回到屋子裡來。

「其實我也差點鑄成大錯！」她提高了嗓門說：「我差點就嫁給一個追了我好幾年的猶太小子，我知道他配不上我，大家都警告我：『露西，那小子根本配不上妳。』要不是後來遇到奇斯特，我一定嫁給他了。」

「沒錯，」梅朵直點頭，「但至少妳沒嫁給他。」

「我是沒有。」

「但是我嫁給他了。」梅朵說得語意含糊。「這就是妳和我不同的地方。」

「梅朵，妳當初為什麼要嫁給他呀？」凱瑟琳質問她。「又沒人逼妳。」

梅朵想一想，過了一會兒才說：「我當初會嫁給他是因為我以為他出身好，誰知道他連舔我的鞋都不配。」

「但是妳的確迷戀過他一陣子。」凱瑟琳說。

「迷戀他？」梅朵不敢置信地大喊：「誰說我迷戀他？要說我迷上他，還不如說我迷上那個男人。」

她忽然指向我，使得大家都轉頭過來望著我，並投以譴責的

眼光。我試圖用表情傳達我和這個人的過去毫無瓜葛。

「我承認我一時糊塗嫁給他,當下我就知道錯了。他向人借了一套很棒的西裝,準備結婚當天穿,卻把我蒙在鼓裡。後來有天他不在家,有人來要回這套衣服。」她環顧四周看有誰在聽她說話,「『哦,這套衣服是你的啊?』我說,『我從來沒聽他提過。』我馬上把衣服交還給他,然後跑到床上痛哭了一下午。」

「梅朵真的應該離開她的丈夫。」凱瑟琳又接著對我說。「他們已經在那車行住了十一年,湯姆可是她的第一個情人。」

那瓶威士忌酒——已經是第二瓶了——在座每個人都想喝,只有凱瑟琳例外,因為她說「什麼都不喝的感覺很好」。湯姆按鈴把管理員叫來,要他去買一些很有名的三明治回來,可以餵飽大家的肚子。我幾次想告辭,打算在柔和的暮色下往東邊的公園去走走,但每次起身要走,一陣嘈雜尖銳的抗議聲就像亂麻一樣把我糾纏住,將我拉回椅子上。我心想,如果有人站在暮色蒼茫的街道上往市區上空看,我們這排燈火通明的窗戶應該埋藏了一些人類的祕密吧。我和他一樣詫異地望著,我彷彿置身局內又好像置身局外,對這幕人生悲喜劇無預警的演變,既陶醉又厭惡。

梅朵把她的椅子拉到我面前坐下。忽然間,她吐著微醺的氣息開始向我訴說她跟湯姆當初相逢的故事。

「火車上總會有兩個位置沒人坐,那天我們碰巧面對面坐下來。當時我正準備前往紐約找我妹妹,打算在那裡過夜。湯姆穿著一身輕便禮服和一雙漆皮鞋;我看著他,眼睛捨不得從他身上移開,等他每次回看我一眼時我就趕快轉移視線,假裝在看他頭

頂上的廣告。下車的時候他走在我身邊，靠得很近，他那雪白、硬挺的襯衫輕輕磨擦著我的手臂。我跟他說我可是要叫警察來了，可是他知道我心裡不這麼想。當時我興奮得什麼都搞不清楚，結果跟著他上了一部計程車，我還差點以為是走進地鐵。我只記得心裡反覆對自己說：『人生苦短，人生苦短。』」

說到這裡她突然停止，又回過頭去跟麥基太太交談。整間屋子充滿了她那做作的笑聲。

「親愛的，」她喊道，「待會兒我就把這套衣服脫下來送給妳。明天我打算再去買一件。唉呀！我得把明天要做的事寫在單子上。我要去美容院享受按摩、整理頭髮，替小狗買條項圈，買一個那種有彈簧的煙灰缸，還要買一個結了黑絲帶的花圈，好在母親墳上擺一整個夏天。我一定要寫下來，不然會忘了。」

已經九點了——一會兒我再看錶時，已經是十點了。麥基先生在椅子上呼呼地睡著了，兩隻手握拳在腿上，頗有行動派的模樣。我掏出手帕，把他臉上那堆讓我一整個下午都不舒服的泡沫痕跡擦掉。

那隻小狗蹲在桌上，兩眼從煙霧中茫然地朝外看，不時汪汪地吠叫著。屋子裡的人時而消失，時而出現。本來計劃一起到什麼地方去，忽然又找不到對方，於是四處尋找，找了半天發現就在面前。快到夜半時分，湯姆‧勃肯納和威爾森的老婆氣呼呼地吵起架來，為的是威爾森的老婆有沒有資格提黛西的名字。

「黛西！黛西！黛西！」威爾森的老婆連聲叫嚷著。「我愛什麼時候叫就什麼時候叫！黛西！黛……」

　　湯姆‧勃肯納手稍微一揮，一個巴掌把梅朵打得鼻血直流。

　　起了一陣騷動，擦鼻血的毛巾扔得浴室滿地都是，屋子裡夾雜著女士責罵的聲音。在吵雜聲中還有斷斷續續痛楚的哀號。麥基先生突然醒了過來，恍恍惚惚摸索著要出去，快要走到門口時又回頭探望了一下屋子裡的情形——他老婆和凱瑟琳一面怒罵一面安慰，同時在擁擠的傢俱間跌跌撞撞地遞過藥來，而躺在沙發上的那位，神色哀戚，血流不止，還忙著把一份《紐約閒話》攤在凡爾賽風景的織錦上。後來麥基又轉過身，接著走出門去。我從燈架上取回我的帽子，也跟著離開。

　　「改天一起吃個飯。」電梯往下降時，他對我說。

　　「在什麼地方？」

　　「在哪裡都可以。」

　　「別再碰電梯開關！」電梯小弟毫不客氣地喝斥他。

　　「對不起，」麥基先生嚴肅地說：「我不知道我碰到開關了。」

　　「沒問題，」我答應他：「我很樂意。」

　　不久，我發現自己站在麥基先生的床邊，他坐在被窩裡，身上只穿著內衣，手裡拿著一本大相簿。

　　「『美人與野獸』……『寂寞』……『識途老馬』……『布魯克林大橋』……」

　　又過了一會兒，我發現自己半睡半醒地躺在賓夕法尼亞車站冰冷的候車室裡，眼睛瞪著《紐約論壇報》，等待清晨四點鐘的火車。

第 3 章

　　整個夏天的夜晚，經常都有音樂聲從隔壁的住宅傳來。在他那撒滿月光的藍色庭院裡，紅男綠女如飛蛾般，在喁喁細語、銀色香檳酒與燦爛的群星之間不斷穿梭著。下午漲潮的時候，只見他的賓客在海邊的高板上跳水嬉戲，躺在他的私人沙灘上曬太陽，或是搭著滑水板拖在他的兩艘遊艇後方，在海灣裡轉來轉去，破水急馳，弄得浪花四濺。每逢週末，他的勞斯萊斯轎車便成了公車，從早晨九點到午夜時分，不斷往來城鎮接送客人，而他的另外一部旅行車則像隻黃殼甲蟲，蹦蹦跳跳地去迎接每一班列車。到了星期一，則有七個傭人外加一個臨時僱用的園丁，拿著抹布、刷子、釘鎚、剪刀等等工具，辛苦地收拾前一晚客人狂歡後所留下的殘局。

　　每個星期五，紐約一家水果行會照例送來五箱柳橙和檸檬。到了星期一，這些柳橙和檸檬便成了一大堆果皮，從後門被運出去。他的廚房裡有一架機器，管家只要用大拇指在機器的一個按鈕上按個兩百下，就能在半小時之內榨出兩百顆柳橙份量的果汁。

　　每兩個星期都會有一天，一支籌辦宴席的隊伍，帶來幾百呎的帆布帳篷和數不清的色彩繽紛的燈泡，把蓋茨比偌大的花園布

置得像一棵聖誕樹。自助餐桌上擺滿了令人雙眼發亮的開胃菜，五香火腿緊靠著布置精巧的生菜沙拉，還有烤得色澤金黃的烤乳豬和烤火雞。大廳裡搭設了一個酒吧，吧台底下還有一條純銅的橫桿，除了供應杜松子酒和一般烈酒，更有各種甜酒，有些是早已不多見的珍品，大多數的女賓客都太過年輕，根本分辨不出來。

　　晚上七點鐘，樂隊來了。這可不是什麼簡簡單單的五人樂隊，而是個大樂團，有雙簧管、小號、長號、薩克斯風、簫、笛、喇叭、大提琴、小提琴、高音銅鼓、低音銅鼓等。在海灘游泳的男女客人現在都已經進屋來，正在樓上換衣服；紐約來的豪華轎車一輛輛停在車道上。屋子裡的玄關、客廳和陽臺上，到處是裝扮華麗的紅男綠女，女士們的髮型爭奇鬥豔，披肩的樣式更是連卡斯提爾王國貴婦都夢想不到的。酒吧的氣氛十分熱鬧，服務生不停地把一盤盤雞尾酒端到花園裡。空氣中充滿了談笑聲，大家輕鬆地打趣著，陌生的雙方才剛介紹認識，一轉身又忘得一乾二淨，女士們雖然親熱地擁抱打招呼，卻始終不知道彼此的姓名。

　　太陽漸漸從地平線消失，燈光顯得更加明亮，此刻樂團演奏起雞尾酒樂，使得眾人的聲音也提高了一個音。隨著時間的流逝，歡笑的聲浪愈來愈高亢，引起一陣陣嘩然大笑。到處都有圍成一圈一圈的小團體，隨著來來去去的人潮，散了又聚、聚了又散；有些自信滿滿的年輕女郎不斷來回遊蕩著，穿梭在比較固定不變的人群中，前一刻還是某一群人裡閃耀的焦點，下一刻又帶

著勝利的興奮情緒，游移到如潮汐般變換的面孔、人聲與色彩當中。

忽然間，其中一位周旋在人群中的吉普賽女郎走了出來，全身上下珠光寶氣，隨手抓了杯雞尾酒一飲而下，壯了膽之後，兩手開始學著佛里斯哥舞扭動的動作，獨自站在舞臺上跳起舞來，頓時大家都默不作聲；樂團指揮馬上相應配合為她伴奏，緊接著便是一陣竊竊私語，謠傳她就是百老匯當紅舞星吉爾達·葛雷的臨時替角。於是，這晚的好戲就此開場了。

第一次到蓋茨比家的那一晚，我應該是少數幾個正式受邀的賓客之一。一般人都不需要邀請函，便會自動前來。他們坐上汽車開往長島，不知怎麼的車子總是開上蓋茨比家的車道，到達之後總會有人替他們介紹蓋茨比，經過介紹之後，他們就

可以像在遊樂場一樣盡情地享樂。有些人甚至從頭到尾都不跟主人打聲招呼，純粹抱著玩樂的心態來參加宴會，這樣就足夠了。

　　沒錯，我的確是被正式邀請的。那天星期六一大早，一個身穿藍綠色制服的司機越過我的草地，為他的主人送來一封意外地非常正式的請柬，敬邀我參加他的舞會，還說我的到訪將是他無上的光榮。接著又說與我有數面之緣，早有心登門拜訪，但是俗務纏身，遲遲未能成行之類的客套話，最後面是傑伊‧蓋茨比的簽名，筆跡頗為雄渾。

　　到了晚上七點多，我穿上一套白色法蘭絨裝走進蓋茨比的花園裡，不安地周旋在陌生的人群中──不過我偶爾會碰到一兩個在火車上見過的熟面孔，但是最吸引我的是客人中夾雜著不少英

國青年，一個個衣著整齊，面有飢色，低聲下氣地跟美國富翁談話。我相信他們一定在推銷東西──不是基金、保險，就是汽車。他們心裡知道這裡有錢可賺，只要幾句中聽的話，大把的鈔票就是他們的了。

我一到就設法去找主人，可是問了兩三個人，他們都用極其詫異的眼光看著我，同時極力強調他們不知道蓋茨比的行蹤，我只好悄悄挨近雞尾酒吧──在這花園裡，也只有在那裡能夠一個人待著，而不至於顯得孤單無聊。

在我打算喝個酩酊大醉以擺脫侷促不安之際，喬登・貝克小姐正好從屋裡走出來，站在大理石臺階的頂端，身體斜靠著，用一種藐視的眼神俯瞰花園。

不管她歡迎與否，我立刻走上前去。我的確需要找一個人來作伴，不然就得開始問候身旁的陌生人了。

「嗨！」我大喊一聲，走上前去，我的聲音在花園裡聽來似乎大得很不自然。

「我正在想你也許會來的。」我走近她的時候，她心不在焉地說，「我記得你說過，你是他的鄰居……」

她無所謂地握著我的手，表示她待會兒再來找我，然後轉而招呼著臺階下兩個穿著同樣黃色衣裙的女孩。

「哈囉！」她們同聲喊著。「妳沒贏球真是可惜啊！」

她們指的是高爾夫球比賽，上個星期的決賽她輸了。

「妳不認得我們了吧？」其中一個黃衣女郎說，「我們一個多月以前在這兒見過的。」

「妳染了頭髮。」喬丹對她說，我覺得有點突兀，但黃衣女郎已經雙雙走開，喬丹這句話等於是對著月亮說的——天空中出現銀盤似的月亮，就像當晚的酒菜一樣，也是餐館師傅包辦的。喬丹用她金黃細瘦的手臂挽著我，我們走下臺階在花園裡散步。夜色蒼茫中，一盤雞尾酒向我們漂浮過來，我們找了一張桌子坐下，同桌的除了那兩個黃衣女孩外，還有三位男士，一一介紹之下，每個姓名聽起來都像是「唔噥」。

「妳常來參加這裡的宴會嗎？」喬丹問她旁邊的那個女孩。

「我上次來這兒就是見到妳的那一次。」女孩回答，聲音聽起來很機靈且自信。「露西，」她轉身問她的朋友：「妳也是吧？」

露西也是一樣。

「我喜歡來這兒，」露西說。「我向來不在乎到什麼地方，做什麼事，所以我總是能玩得很開心。上次我來的時候，不小心把禮服勾破了，他問了我的姓名、地址，不到一個禮拜我就收到『夸耶服飾店』送來的包裹，裡面是一套全新的晚禮服。」

「妳收下來了嗎？」喬丹問。

「當然。我本來打算今晚穿的，但是那套衣服胸口的地方尺寸太大，送去修改了。禮服是灰藍色的，上面鑲著淡紫色的珠子，定價兩百六十五元。」

「會做這種事的人還真是奇怪。」另外一個黃衣女郎急切地說：「他真是不願得罪任何人。」

「誰啊？」我問。

「蓋茨比呀！有人告訴我……」

那兩個女孩和喬丹神祕地靠攏身子。

「有人告訴我，他以前好像殺過人。」

我們幾個人不約而同地打了一個寒顫。那三位「唔噥」先生也湊向前來側耳細聽。

「那只是謠傳吧，」露西懷疑地說：「倒是他在戰爭期間當過德國間諜的可能性比較大。」

其中一位男士點點頭。

「我也聽人這麼說過。那個人從小跟他在德國一起長大，蓋茨比的事他都知道。」他很肯定地對我們說。

「不是，」第一個黃衣女孩又說：「戰爭的時候他在美國陸軍服役。」我們把注意力又轉回她身上，於是她便更加熱衷地說：「你只要趁他不注意的時候瞧瞧他，我敢打賭他殺過人。」

她把眼睛緊緊閉上，渾身發抖。露西也在發抖。於是我們大家轉身看看蓋茨比在哪裡。連這些認為世上任何事都該開誠布公的人，談論起蓋茨比時都只敢交頭接耳，鬼鬼祟祟的，可見他是如何激起人們對他的種種聯想和臆測。

第一次晚餐開始了——午夜過後還有一餐——喬丹邀我到花園那邊跟她同來的朋友一塊兒坐。這桌坐了三對夫婦，還有喬丹的護花使者，一個執拗的大學生，說話常意有所指，自認為喬丹早晚會委身於他。這群人不像其他人那樣閒聊，他們帶著驕矜的表情，有一種代表東卵鎮貴族階級蒞臨西卵鎮的神氣，同時保持著尊嚴，不像其他客人那樣恣意地喝酒玩樂。

半小時的光陰在這裡被無謂地浪費，喬丹輕輕對我說：「我們走吧，這裡太拘束沉悶了。」

我們兩人站起身來，她向其他人說她要帶我去見見主人——因為我還沒有見過他，所以覺得有點過意不去。那個大學生帶著嘲諷而抑鬱的神情點點頭。

我們先到酒吧間去看看，那裡擠滿了人，但蓋茨比不在那裡。喬丹走到臺階上，沒見到他的蹤影，陽臺上也沒有。我們看見一扇相當氣派的門，推開了門才知道裡面是一間挑高的歌德式藏書室，四壁鑲嵌著英國雕花橡木，可能是整套從國外某座遺址裡拆下運過來的。

書房裡有一個肥胖的中年男子，臉上戴著一副貓頭鷹似的眼鏡，醉醺醺地坐在一張大桌子邊，恍惚地盯著架上的書。聽見我們進來，他慌張地轉過身來，從頭到腳打量了喬丹一番。

「你們覺得怎麼樣？」他急切地質問。

「什麼怎麼樣？」

他指指書架上的書。

「這些。其實你們也不必看了。我已經確認過了，都是真的。」

「什麼都是真的？你是指這些書？」

他點點頭。

「如假包換的書，一頁不漏。我以為這些只是硬紙糊的假書，但是仔細一看，絕對是真的。不信你們來看看。」

他以為我們也跟他一樣對這些書充滿疑問，便急忙到書架

前，拿了一本《史達德講學全集》第一集。

「你們看！」他相當得意地嚷道：「這可真是貨真價實的印刷品，真把我唬住了。這傢伙神通廣大，簡直可以和舞臺設計大王畢拉斯哥媲美。太成功了，多麼仔細逼真！而且拿捏得恰到好處……你看，一頁都不缺，多麼棒！你還想怎樣？還有什麼話說？」

他從我手裡把那本書一把搶回去，急忙放回原處，說什麼如果一塊磚塊不見，整個藏書室就會垮掉了。

「誰帶你們來的？」他質問：「還是不請自來？我可是有人帶領的，大部分的客人都是有人帶進來的。」

喬丹神色愉悅但有所提防地看著他，沒有回答他的話。

「是一位姓羅斯福的太太帶我來的，」他接著說：「克勞德·羅斯福太太。你們認識她嗎？我昨晚不知道在什麼地方看見她。我已經醉了差不多一個禮拜了，我以為在藏書室裡坐一會兒酒便會醒。」

「有用嗎？」

「有一點吧，還不知道，我在這兒坐了不到一個鐘頭。我還沒有告訴你們這些書的事？都是真的。都──」

「你已經告訴我們了。」

我們認真地和他握握手，然後回到花園。

此刻花園裡已有人在台上跳起舞來；上了年紀的男人挽著妙齡女孩不斷轉圈圈；高傲的時髦男女彼此擁抱，在角落裡跳著最時興的舞步；還有一些落單的

女子自得其樂地跳著,有的跑到樂團中把五弦琴或爵士鼓搶過來耍弄。進入午夜,群眾的情緒興奮到最高點。一位有名的男高音歌手唱了一支義大利歌曲,還有一位聲名狼藉的女低音唱了幾段爵士曲子;其他客人趁節目空檔也在花園中到處「表演」。快樂、空虛的笑聲此起彼落,消散到夏夜的天空。一會兒舞臺上又出現了一對穿著打扮一模一樣的演員——原來就是那兩位黃衣女郎——她們換上了戲服,客串表演一齣「搞笑劇」。香檳不斷地端出來,杯子比洗手指用的玻璃盤還要大。月亮升得更高了,海面上飄浮著一個三角形的銀色倒影隨著五弦琴鏗鏘的聲響微微顫動著。

我仍然和喬丹·貝克在一起。與我們同桌的有一位跟我年紀差不多的男士,以及一位吵鬧的小女孩,動輒毫無克制地放聲大笑。兩大碗香檳喝下肚,現在我玩得也挺高興的,眼前的景色開始變得自然、一位深沉而充滿哲學意義。

餘興節目的間歇,同桌的那位男士看著我,面露微笑。他客氣的問:「您好面熟。打仗的時候您是在陸軍第三師服役的嗎?」

「是啊。我在第九機槍營。」

「我在第七步兵師，一直待到一九一八年六月。我就知道在哪兒見過您。」

我們交談了一會兒，聊的都是法國的一些陰雨潮濕的小村莊。他顯然住在附近，因為在談話中他告訴我他剛買了一架水上飛機，準備明天早晨去試飛一下。

「有沒有興趣一起玩玩，老兄？就在海灣沿岸邊轉轉。」

「什麼時候？」

「都可以，看您什麼時候方便。」

我正想問他的姓名，喬丹卻在此時回頭對我笑了笑。

「現在玩得開心一點了嗎？」她問我。

「好多了。」我又回頭對我的新朋友說：「今晚這宴會對我來說相當特別，我到現在還沒有見到主人呢。我就住在那邊……」我指著遠方模糊的一排多青樹，「蓋茨比先生今天早上派了他的司機送來一份邀請函。」

他望著我有一會兒，好像沒弄懂我的意思。

「我就是蓋茨比。」他脫口說道。

「什麼！」我大叫：「哎呀，真對不起！」

「老兄，我還以為你知道。看來是我這個主人不夠盡責。」

他體諒地笑了笑——不，不只是體諒而已。那是一種罕見的笑容，讓人看了就覺得無比安心，這一生中大概就只見得到四、五次。這張笑容注視過——或者看似注視過——全世界片刻之後，便不由自主地將注意力轉移到你身上，只對著你一個人笑。你彷彿可以感覺到它了解你，就如同你希望獲得了解一樣；它相

信你，就和你相信自己一樣；它對你的印象，就跟你希望給人的一樣。恰好在這個關頭，他收起了笑容，我眼前看到的只是一位年約三十一、二歲，說話時矯揉造作的魯莽男士，使人覺得有些荒謬。在他沒有自我介紹以前，我就已經察覺到他遣詞用字都經過刻意斟酌。

　　正當蓋茨比說出自己的身份時，管家匆忙跑過來，說是有一通從芝加哥打來的長途電話。他站起來微微躬身——很周到地向大家道歉。

　　「老兄，你要什麼儘管開口，別客氣。」他誠懇地對我說：「不好意思，一會兒後再來奉陪。」

　　他走開之後，我馬上轉向喬丹，急於要向她表示我的驚異。我原本以為蓋茨比先生是一位紅光滿面、肥頭大耳的中年男子。

　　「他到底是誰？」我問她。

　　「不過就是一個叫蓋茨比的人！」

　　「我要知道他是從哪裡來的，是做什麼的？」

　　「你也跟大家一樣對他產生好奇啦。」她微微一笑，回答道。「讓我想想，他曾經告訴過我說他是牛津大學畢業的。」

　　我聽了這番話，腦中開始勾勒起蓋茨比的身世，但是隨著喬丹接下來所說的話，一切又都推翻了。

　　「可是我不相信他的話。」

　　「為什麼？」

　　「我不知道，」她堅持道：「我不相信他會在牛津大學唸過書。」

　　她說話的口氣令我想起先前那位女孩說的話：「我猜想他殺過人。」這更激起了我的好奇心。若說蓋茨比的出身是怎樣的微寒我都會毫不懷疑；是路易斯安納州的沼澤地區也好，紐約東城的貧民窟也好，這都是可以理解的，可是一個年紀輕輕的人絕不可能──至少依據我這個鄉巴佬狹隘的經驗來看──莫名其妙冒出頭來，而且有能力在長島購置這樣一座宮殿式的別墅。

　　「無論如何，他常常舉辦大型宴會。」喬丹轉移話題，她和一般都市人一樣不喜歡討論實際問題。「我最喜歡大型宴會，感覺多麼舒服，不像小型派對一點私人空間都沒有。」

　　這時大鼓忽然轟隆一響，樂團指揮也提高嗓子，聲音蓋過花園裡眾人的喧囂聲。

　　「各位先生女士，」他高喊著：「應蓋茨比先生的要求，我們現在要為各位演奏音樂大師弗萊米爾‧托斯陀夫先生的最新作品，就是五月在卡內基音樂廳演出，大受歡迎的曲目。各位如果看過報紙就知道，那是樂壇的榮耀。」他笑容滿面同時又帶著諷刺的口吻加了一句：「真是轟動一時！」大家聽了都哈哈大笑。

　　「這支名曲，」樂隊指揮繼續用宏亮的聲音說：「叫做《弗萊米爾‧托斯陀夫的世界爵士音樂史》。」

　　我沒仔細去注意托斯陀夫先生這支曲子的風格，因為樂聲揚起時我看見蓋茨比一個人站在大理石臺階上，用滿意的目光觀望眾人。他臉上的皮膚曬得黝黑而緊繃，光滑而英俊，頭髮剪得短短的，像是每天都有修剪一樣，實在看不出他有什麼陰險的相貌。不知道是否因為他不喝酒的關係，使他跟他的賓客們有所差

別，似乎大家愈是玩得放浪形骸，蓋茨比就愈顯得得體。等到
《世界爵士音樂史》演奏完畢，有些年輕女孩像開心的小狗一樣
把頭依偎在男士的肩膀上，有的嬌聲嗲氣地假裝暈倒在男人懷
裡，有的索性朝後一仰，因為她們知道總會有人托住她們。可是
沒有人倒在蓋茨比懷裡，沒有法式短髮的女孩依偎在蓋茨比的懷
中，也沒有三缺一的四重唱來拉蓋茨比加入。

「對不起，小姐。」

蓋茨比的管家不知道什麼時候已經站在我們身邊。

「您是貝克小姐嗎？」他問道。「對不起，蓋茨比先生想跟
您單獨談話。」

「我？」她驚訝地問。

「是的，小姐。」

她慢慢站起來，向我揚了揚眉毛表示莫名其妙，然後跟著管
家走進屋裡。我發現貝克小姐無論穿任何服裝，都像穿著運動服
一樣，舉止輕快活潑，似乎她從小就是每天一早在空氣清新的高
爾夫球場上學走路。

我又落單了，當時已經快兩點了。有好一會兒，從陽臺上的
大客廳傳來一陣雜亂奇怪的聲音。陪伴喬丹前來的大學生此刻正
被兩個舞群女團員糾纏住，拚命央求我去幫幫他，可是我設法避
開了，趕快走到室內去。

大客廳擠滿了人。其中一個黃衣女郎正在彈琴，她身旁站著
一個身材高的紅髮少女正在唱歌，也是從某個知名合唱團來的。
她喝了不少香檳，唱著唱著忽然極度傷感起來，於是——一邊唱

歌一邊流淚，每唱完一段，她就用嗚咽抽噎的哭聲啜泣著，接著
又跟上歌詞，用她那女高音的尖細嗓子顫抖著唱下去。她的眼淚
慢慢流下來，沾染了眼睫毛之後變成黑墨水，沿著臉頰彎曲往下
流，好像兩條小黑河一樣。有人開她玩笑說，為什麼不乾脆唱她
臉上的樂譜，聽了這句話，她雙手向上一甩，整個人沉進椅子
裡，沉進醉醺醺的夢鄉了。

　　「她剛才跟一個自稱是她丈夫的男人打架。」我身旁一位女
孩向我解釋說。

　　我看看四周圍，多半還沒走的女客人現在都在跟她們所謂的
丈夫吵架。連喬丹的那群東卵鎮來的四位朋友，也為了意見不合
呈現分裂的狀態。他們之中的一位男客正聚精會神跟一個年輕的
女演員聊天，他的妻子起先還若無其事地置之一笑，沒多久便端
不起架子，別無他法下採取迂迴戰術──時不時走上前來在他耳
邊像是毒蛇一般地嘶聲：「你答應過我的！」

　　流連忘返的不只是那些酒醉後反覆無常的男人。玄關裡就有
兩位清醒得可憐的男人和她們憤怒不已的妻子。這兩位太太你一
言我一語的彼此訴苦。

　　「每次他一見我玩得開心就吵著要回家。」

　　「我這輩子沒見過這麼自私的男人！」

　　「我們每次總是最先離開的。」

　　「我們也是。」

　　「不過，今晚我們幾乎是最後一個離開的了，」其中一位先
生怯生生地說。「連樂團都已經離開半個鐘頭了。」

　　儘管兩位太太一致認為先生們不通人情、大殺風景，但這場糾紛終於在一陣掙扎中結束，兩位先生各自扛起太太走入黑夜中。

　　我正在玄關等管家替我拿帽子時，貝克小姐和蓋茨比一起從藏書室走了出來。他還在對喬丹說最後幾句話，但是剛好有幾位客人走過來和他告別，他原先熱切的態度又突然變得拘謹起來。

　　喬丹的朋友在陽臺上不耐煩地連聲催她，可是她還是逗留了一下和我握手。

　　「我剛才聽到一些不可思議的事，」她悄悄地對我說。「我跟他在裡面待了多久？」

　　「差不多一個鐘頭。」

　　「簡直……太不可思議了，」她愣愣地重複著說。「可是我剛才發誓不告訴別人，現在又吊你胃口。」她優雅地對我打了一個呵欠。「有空請來看我……電話簿上……雪歌妮·哈華德太太……是我的姑媽……」她匆匆忙忙邊說邊走，又向後揮揮她那隻曬得黑黑的手致意，然後就隱沒在門口等她的那群同伴中。

　　我覺得有點不好意思，第一次來參加蓋茨比家的宴會就待到這麼晚。其他幾位留下來的客人包圍著蓋茨比先生，我也擠上去，想向他解釋我稍早之前就到處找他，同時為自己在花園裡沒認出他而道歉。

　　「沒關係，」他懇切地安慰我。「請別放在心上，老兄。」他這樣熱絡地稱呼我，還用手拍拍我的肩膀，可是感覺上卻不是真的那麼親切。「別忘了，明天早上我們要去試試那架水上飛

機,早上九點。」

　這時候,管家在他背後說:

　「先生,有一通費城來的電話。」

　「好的,告訴他們我馬上就來……明天見。」

　「再見。」

　「再見。」他微笑著,讓人感覺到愉快而有殊榮,待到這麼晚才走,似乎是被主人特別挽留的。「再見,老兄……再見。」

　我走下臺階時,才發現這熱鬧的一晚還未完全結束。離大門不到五十呎遠,有十幾個車燈照著一個亂七八糟又奇怪的場面。一輛簇新的跑車,兩分鐘前剛從蓋茨比家門口開走,現在卻歪倒在路旁的水溝裡,一隻車輪已被撞落下來。原來是圍牆突出了一塊,開車的沒看見而出了這個意外。五、六個好奇的司機紛紛下車關心,可是他們把自己的車子停在路中間阻礙了交通,後來的車輛不耐煩地按了好幾次喇叭,一片刺耳的聲音使得整個場面更加混亂。

　一個穿著風衣的人從撞壞的車子裡走出來,站在路中間,看看車子、又看看車胎、看看所有的旁觀者,顯得有些興奮又困惑的樣子。

　「你看!」他解釋道:「車子開到水溝裡去了。」

　他對這件事感到無比驚訝。這聲音好熟悉啊,我仔細一看,原來就是稍早在蓋茨比家藏書室碰見的那位先生。

　「怎麼回事?」

　他聳了聳肩膀。

「我對於機械一竅不通。」他斷然地說。

「怎麼會出事？你把車子撞到牆上去了嗎？」

「不要問我，」貓頭鷹先生撇清責任道：「我不大會開車，可以說是完全不懂。我只知道車子出了事，其他什麼都不知道。」

「你要是開車技術不佳，就不應該在夜裡開車。」

「我沒有開車。」他氣憤地解釋。「我根本沒有開車！」

旁觀的人都十分驚異，一時鴉雀無聲。

「你真是活得不耐煩了。」

「算你運氣好，只撞壞一個輪子！開車技術那麼差，還不特別小心！」

「你們弄錯了，」肇事者解釋道：「開車的不是我。車裡還有一個人。」

聽了他的話，眾人更為吃驚，異口同聲地叫著：「天啊！」同時跑車的門被打開了。此時四周已經擠滿一大群人，大家不禁向後倒退一步，車門大開時，忽然有一種像是鬼魂即將出現的凝滯氣氛。接著，一個臉色慘白、身體不停搖晃的高個子從撞壞了的汽車中慢慢跨了出來，一隻穿著大舞鞋的腳還在地上試探了幾下。

這個幽靈般的人物，兩隻眼睛被車燈照得睜不開，又被不斷亂鳴的喇叭聲吵得發昏，站在那裡搖晃了一會兒，才認出穿風衣的那個人。

「怎麼回事？」他很鎮靜地問：「汽油用光了嗎？」

「你看！」

　　六、七根手指頭同時指向那個被撞落的車輪。他瞪眼看了半晌，然後抬頭往上看，好像輪子是從天上掉下來的。

　　「輪子撞掉了。」有人向他解釋。

　　他點點頭。

　　「我起先還沒發現車子停下來了。」

　　隔了一會兒，那人深深吸了一口氣，挺著胸膛，用堅定的口氣說：「有沒有人可以告訴我，哪裡有加油站？」

　　周遭至少有十幾個人——有的只比他清醒一些——七嘴八舌地向他解釋：車輪跟車身早已分了家了。

　　「倒車。」他提議。「把車子倒退出來。」

　　「可是車輪撞掉了啊！」

　　他遲疑了一會兒。

　　「試試也無妨。」他又說。

　　後面車子的喇叭聲在此刻達到高潮，我也轉身，穿過草地自行回家，一度又回頭看了看。一輪明月照耀著蓋茨比的別墅，夜色依舊美好，花園依舊燦爛，而歡笑早已消逝。一股空虛從大門與窗戶流瀉而出，烘托出門廊上主人遺世獨立的身影，此時一手高舉，做禮貌上道別的手勢。

　　我把以上所寫的重讀一遍之後，覺得可能會讓人產生誤解，以為那相隔幾個星期的兩三天夜裡，所發生的事佔據了我的思維。其實不然，那只不過是繁忙夏日中的兩三件瑣事，我一向十分專注於個人的私事，這些也是後來才開始留意的。

　　我花了大半的時間在工作上。每天一早，當太陽把我的影子

投射到西邊時，我匆忙沿著紐約下城摩天高樓間的縫隙快步走到
「正誠信託公司」上班。我跟公司裡其他職員和年輕的業務員混
得很熟，中午還跟著他們到陰暗、擁擠的小餐館吃些香腸、馬鈴
薯泥，喝咖啡。我甚至還跟會計課的一個女同事交往過一陣子。
她家住在澤西城，可是她哥哥後來對我不太友善，因此等到七月
她去度假時，我就趁機與她結束關係。

　　平常我都會在耶魯校友會吃晚飯──不知道為什麼我覺得這
是一天中最不快樂的時刻──晚飯後我會到樓上圖書室去看一個
小時的書，研究投資市場和證券交易。校友會裡不免有幾個無所

事事的人，但是他們不會進圖書室，所以那裡倒是可以安靜自習的地方。自修之後，如果天氣不錯，我就會沿著麥迪遜大道散步，經過老穆雷山飯店，再沿三十三街走到賓夕法尼亞車站。

我漸漸愛上紐約這個城市，大都市的夜晚有一種放縱和冒險的情調；街上男男女女和往來的車輛使你目不暇給而感到滿足。我喜歡走在第五大道上，在人群中看看美麗神祕的女人，幻想自己走入她們的生命，但是沒有人會知道，也沒有人反對。有時候，我會幻想跟著她們轉彎抹角走到她們的公寓，她們會回頭對我燦然一笑，然後消失在門內溫暖的黑暗中。迷人的都市黃昏有時也使我感覺到孤寂和惆悵，還以為別人也有同感——像公司那些年輕職員，下了班便在商店櫥窗前面徘徊，等到晚餐時間才一個人上館子吃飯——一群在黃昏時刻虛擲光陰的年輕職員，白白浪費了夜晚與生命中最寶貴的一刻。

到了晚上八點，當四十幾街旁的大街小巷擠滿了要趕到戲院的計程車，我忽然感到一陣空虛。車裡的人彼此依偎在一起，語聲曼妙，偶爾有人說了什麼笑話，引出一陣陣笑聲，車裡還隱約可見一圈圈點燃的香煙頭閃著紅光。我想像自己也正奔向歡樂，與他們共享著內心的興奮，我不禁由衷地祝福他們。

有好一陣子我沒有見到喬丹‧貝克，直到夏天過了一半時我才又遇見她。我陪著她東奔西跑，起初我很引以為傲，因為她是一位有名的高爾夫球健將。後來我對她的感覺卻似乎多了一些。我不能說我愛上她了，可是我漸漸對她起了一股溫柔的好奇心。她經常對人擺架子，態度驕傲，我想一定有什麼不為人知的隱

情——一般人裝模作樣多半是在隱藏一些事，即使起初並非如此——後來有一天我終於得到了答案。那天我們兩人一同到華威克一個朋友家去參加宴會，她借了一部車子，因為車蓬敞開沒關，被雨淋濕了，結果她撒了一個謊，不肯承認。這件事忽然令我想到那天晚上我在黛西家第一次和她見面時，似乎曾聽過關於她的謠言，但一時記不起來，現在我想起來了。她初次參加一場重要的高爾夫錦標賽時，在複賽中有人指控她在草地中移動球。當時她不承認，在裁判、選手和觀眾之間引起軒然大波，幾乎鬧到要登報。後來球童改了口供，而另一個唯一的證人也承認自己可能看錯，一場風波才平息下來。可是這個事件以及當事人的姓名，卻在我腦中留下印象。

喬丹·貝克本能地避免跟聰明、機靈的男人交往。我現在才明白，因為她覺得跟老實人在一起比較有安全感。她自己天性不誠實，無法改變。她凡事不甘落後於人，所以我想她應該從小就學會了耍花招，這樣一方面可以永遠對別人表現出傲慢的態度，另一方面又能滿足來自她那副自信活力身體的需求。

可是我並不介意她這個缺點。女人不誠實，是不可太過苛責的——我對於喬丹的行為只是稍感遺憾，過後也就忘了。就在我們去拜訪朋友的那一天，我們為了開車的問題有過一段奇怪的對話。因為她把車子開得太靠近路旁的一群工人，車子的保險桿不小心刮落了一個工人的釦子。

「妳開車太大意了，」我提出抗議。「最好小心一點，不然就別開車。」

「我很小心的。」

「妳一點也不小心。」

「別人會小心的。」她很輕鬆地說。

「這跟妳開車有什麼關係?」

「別人小心就會躲開我,」她堅持地說,「除非兩方面都不小心才會發生車禍。」

「萬一妳碰到一個跟妳一樣不小心的人呢?」

「我希望不會,」她回答道,「我討厭不小心的人。也因為這個緣故,我喜歡你。」

她那對灰色的瞇瞇眼一直目不轉睛往前看,但是她所說的話顯然把我們兩人的關係改變了,我還一度以為自己真愛上她。可是我的思路向來遲鈍,而且有許多自身守則,迫使自己壓抑感情的衝動。別的不說,第一步我得把家鄉的那段情感糾葛一刀兩斷才行。事實上我每星期還寫信給我那位女性朋友,信尾署名:「妳親愛的尼克」,但是我腦海中所能想到的畫面,卻只是那個女孩打過網球之後,嘴唇上邊沁出一道汗珠,像長了小鬍子一樣。儘管如此,我們彼此的確有過那麼點意思,非得好好地解除,我才可以獲得自由。

每一個人都相信自己至少有一項美德,我的美德就是誠實。在這個世界上我所知道的誠實的人不多,而我是其中之一。

第 4 章

　　禮拜天早上，當沿海每個小鎮的教堂鐘響時，凡夫俗婦重新光臨蓋茨比的別墅，在他的草地上快活地閒聊著。

　　「他是一個販私酒的。」年輕的女士們一面品嚐欣賞著他的美酒和奇花，一面這樣說道：「有一回他殺了一個人，因為那人發現他是德國馮·興登堡將軍的姪兒，是魔鬼的表親。喂，替我摘一朵玫瑰吧，親愛的，再替我倒些酒在那邊那隻水晶杯子裡，讓我喝一口。」

　　有一次坐在火車上覺得無聊，我拿了一張時刻表，在空白處把那年夏天蓋茨比別墅裡嘉賓的姓名一一寫下來。現在這張時刻表已經很舊，紙摺的地方快要解體了，上面印著一行字：「此表自一九二二年七月五日起有效。」但我還是依稀認得出我用鉛筆寫下的那些人名，也許對讀者來說，比聽我籠統地形容，這樣可以知道得更清楚一點，是哪些人當初接受蓋茨比的款待，到頭來對於蓋茨比的底細卻一無所知。

　　那麼，從東卵說起。來的客人當中有契斯特·畢克夫婦，有利奇夫婦，有一位我在耶魯認識的姓彭森的，還有韋伯斯特·薛維特醫師，就是去年夏天在緬因州溺斃的那位。還有侯賓夫婦、威利·伏泰爾夫婦，以及赫白克一家大小，他們在宴會裡老是喜

歡躲在一角，一看見別人走近，就像山羊一樣，一個個把鼻子翹得高高的。此外有伊士美夫婦、克利斯提夫婦（實際上是修伯特‧奧爾巴陪著克利斯提先生的太太同來的），以及愛德加‧畢佛，就是後來據說有一年冬天頭髮不知怎麼的一個晚上變得全白的那位。

我記得克拉倫斯‧安狄夫也是從東卵來的。他只來過一次，穿著一條半長的白色馬褲，還在花園裡跟一個姓艾提的無賴打了一架。從長島更遠的地方來的，有基多夫婦、史瑞德夫婦，和喬治亞州的史東‧傑克森‧亞伯拉姆夫婦，以及費士嘉夫婦和萊普立‧史奈爾夫婦。史奈爾在下獄的前三天還來參加過宴會，他那天爛醉倒在石子車道上，右手還被尤里西斯‧史威特太太的車輪軋過。那對姓丹西的夫婦也來過，還有年近七十的懷特貝特和莫理斯。福林克、韓慕海夫婦、做煙草生意的畢魯加，以及畢魯加帶來的幾位小姐。

西卵來的客人有波爾夫婦、莫瑞迪夫婦、西爾‧羅伯克、西爾‧項恩，以及州參議員顧立克，還有「卓越影片公司」的大股東牛頓‧奧吉德，和艾克豪斯、克萊德‧可享、唐‧史華茲（小史華茲）和亞瑟‧麥卡提——他們這幾個人多多少少是跟電影界有關係的。還有凱德甫夫婦、班姆堡夫婦和歐德‧莫頓——就是後來勒死妻子的那個莫頓的哥哥。投資房地產發財的達‧馮太諾也來過，還有愛德‧李格羅、綽號叫「酒鬼」的詹姆士‧菲萊特、德容夫婦和恩納士‧利里——這些人都是來打牌的。每當有人瞥見菲萊特一個人走到花園去，大家就知道他這晚又輸得精

光，第二天「聯合鐵路運輸公司」的股票又得大漲，他得把錢撈回來才行。

有一個姓克利史賓格的人因為常來，後來大家給他取個外號叫「食客」——我猜他真的是無家可歸。講到戲劇界，常來的有葛士·威茲、何雷士·奧唐納文、萊士特·邁爾、喬治·德克維德和法蘭西斯·布爾。從紐約城裡來的還有克羅姆夫婦、拜克希遜夫婦、丹尼寇夫婦、羅素·貝蒂、考立根夫婦、祈勒赫夫婦、杜瓦夫婦、司古利夫婦、比爾赤、史茂克夫婦，以及年紀很輕卻已經離婚的昆恩夫婦，還有亨利·巴爾麥多，就是後來在時報廣場地鐵臥軌自殺的那位。

班尼·麥克那亨總是左擁右抱帶著四個女孩子一起來。雖然每次都是不同人，但她們長得都是一模一樣，看上去都好像從前來過的。她們的名字我記不得了——好像有賈桂琳，也許有康雪愛娜，或是葛勞麗亞，或是茱迪或茱恩之類的，她們的姓不是美妙悅耳的字眼就是非常莊嚴的美國大企業家的姓氏，只要你逼著問，她們也會承認是某某大人物的遠親。

除了這許多人之外，我還記得浮士梯娜·奧白萊恩小姐至少來過一次，還有貝德克家姊妹、戰爭期間被轟掉鼻子的小布魯爾、阿伯爾堡先生和他的未婚妻海格小姐、阿迪泰·費茲彼得和一度當過「美國退伍軍人協會」會長的朱威德先生、克勞地亞·希普小姐和一個據說是她的司機的男伴，還有一位某某王子，我們都叫他「公爵」，就算我當時知道他的名字，現在也忘了。

以上這些人，那年夏天都是蓋茨比別墅裡的座上客。

七月底，有一天早上九點，蓋茨比的豪華汽車從崎嶇不平的車道一路顛簸到我的門口，車子喇叭放出一陣音樂聲響。這是他第一次來找我，雖然，我已經去過兩次他的宴會，乘過他的水上飛機，而且在他熱情的邀請之下時常光顧他的沙灘。

「早啊，老兄。既然我們今天約好一起吃午飯，我想就一起開車進城吧。」

他說話時一隻腳踏在擋泥板上，姿勢矯健──一種典型美國人的姿勢。我想這可能是因為從小沒搬舉過重物的緣故，而我們總習慣隨興而刺激的運動，因此就更加不習慣規規矩矩的姿態了。他總是坐立不安，不是抖著腳踩地板，就是手掌不斷地一張一合。

他看見我用羨慕的目光望著他的汽車。

「這部車子漂亮吧，老兄？」他跳下來好讓我仔細看一看。「你沒看過我這部車嗎？」

　　我當然看過，大家都看過。這輛車是乳白色的，金屬邊閃閃發亮，巨長的車身凹凸有致，還設有龐大的置帽箱、置餐箱和工具箱，擋風玻璃上方映射出令人眼花撩亂的陽光。我們坐在層層疊疊的玻璃後面，坐在綠色皮椅上，向城裡出發。

　　過去一個月中，我跟蓋茨比交談過幾次。我很失望，發現和他這人並沒有多少話說。我最初以為他是一位相當有聲望的人物，後來這種感覺漸漸消失，覺得他只不過是隔壁一家豪華夜總會的老闆。

　　可是這次跟他同車進城，倒使我相當窘迫。車子還沒有開到西卵鎮，蓋茨比已經支支吾吾，看起來似乎猶豫不決地用手拍著他淡褐色西裝褲的膝蓋。

　　「喂，老兄，」他突然開口，嚇了我一跳，「你覺得我這人怎麼樣？」

　　我有點不知所措，只好含糊其詞地支應過去。

　　他不等我說完就插嘴道：「我還是告訴你一點關於我的事吧。」他打斷我的話。「我不希望你聽信那些閒話，對我產生誤會。」

　　原來別人對他那些怪誕不經的指控，他並不是不知道。

　　「上帝做見證，我要跟你說的都是實話。」他忽然把右手舉起來發誓。「我出生在中西部一戶有錢人家，家人全過世了。我是在美國長大的，但是在牛津大學受教育，因為我們家世世代代都是在牛津唸書的，這是我們家裡的傳統。」

　　他一邊說一邊斜眼朝我望望——我這才明白為什麼喬丹‧貝

克會認為他在撒謊。他說「在牛津受教育」那句話時,似乎是含糊地快速帶過去,或是半吞半吐,好像這句話不大說得出口。由於我對他起了疑心,他那一大篇自我介紹隨之粉碎,我心想也許他真有什麼不可告人的隱私。

「你家在中西部什麼地方?」我故意很隨意地問。

「舊金山。」

「哦。」

「我的家人全過世了,我繼承了一大筆遺產。」

他的聲音非常嚴肅,好像想起家族凋零的悽慘猶有餘悸似的。我一度懷疑他是在開玩笑,但是看了他一眼之後,便相信他的話了。

「後來我過著像王公貴族般的生活,遊遍歐洲各國首都 ——巴黎、威尼斯、羅馬 ——到處收藏珠寶,我尤其喜歡紅寶石,打打獵,學學畫,不只是為自己消遣而已,一方面也盡量去忘掉好久以前令我非常傷心的事。」

我極力克制自己不要噗哧笑出來。他這樣信口開河,沒有一句令人感到可信,我聽了腦中不禁浮現一個畫面,那就是一個裹著頭巾的「印度阿三」,像塞滿木屑的傀儡玩具一樣,在巴黎的布隆涅公園裡追捕老虎。

「後來,老兄,歐戰爆發了。那對我來說倒是種解脫。上前線冒著炮火,很想一死了事,可是我這條命好像有老天保佑一樣。一開始,我被任命為中尉軍官。在阿爾岡森林一役中,我率領一個機槍營的殘餘部隊到最前線去,我們的位置全無掩護,支

援的步兵都趕不上來。我們苦戰了兩天兩夜，一百三十名士兵，十六架路易斯式機關槍，一直撐到步兵後援到來，他們在堆積如山的屍首中發現德軍三個師的旗幟。我後來晉升少校，盟軍的各個政府也都頒給我勳章——就連蒙特尼哥羅都頒給我一枚勳章，遠在亞得里亞海的那個小國！」

　　蒙特尼哥羅！他說這個名字時特別提高音調，向這個英勇的小國微笑致敬；這一笑表示他了解並同情蒙特尼哥羅民族動亂的歷史以及開國的艱難，同時感激這樣一個小國居然對他會有這種熱情的褒獎。我聽到這裡，心中對他的狐疑已變成驚奇；聽他述說這些傳奇故事，就像匆忙地翻閱十幾本雜誌一樣。

　　他將手伸到口袋裡，接著便有一塊綁著緞帶的金屬落在我的掌心中。

　　「這就是蒙特尼哥羅頒給我的那塊勳章。」

　　我很驚訝，這塊勳章看起來不像是假的。勳章上周圍刻著一行小字：「丹尼羅勳章——蒙特尼哥羅王尼古拉斯二世。」

　　「翻過來看看。」

　　我把獎牌翻過來唸道：「頒贈傑伊·蓋茨比少校——英勇無雙。」

　　「這裡還有一件我隨身帶著的紀念品。牛津大學時的照片。是在三一學院裡拍的，我左邊的那個現在已經是唐卡斯特伯爵。」那是一張合照，相片上有五、六個穿著運動服的青年，悠閒地站在拱門廊下，背後隱約看得見許多歌德式建築物的尖頂。我認出蓋茨比來，比現在顯得年輕，但差別不大，手裡拿著一根

打板球的球板。

　　這樣看來全都是真的。此時我彷彿看見他在威尼斯大運河旁的豪宅裡，牆上供著獵來的老虎皮；也彷彿看見他打開一箱紅寶石，讓那些珠光寶氣撫慰他破碎沉痛的心。

　　「我今天有一件要緊的事要請你幫忙。」他一面說，一面很滿意地把他的紀念品收回口袋裡。「因此我想應該讓你對我有所了解。我不想讓你認為我是一個來路不明的人。你曉得，我周遭老是圍繞著陌生人，因為我東飄西蕩的，為的是要忘掉很久以前那些教我傷心的事。」他猶疑了一下，「今天下午你就會知道了。」

　　「吃午飯的時候？」

　　「不，今天下午。我碰巧知道你約了貝克小姐喝下午茶。」

　　「你是說你愛上貝克小姐？」

　　「不是，老兄，不是。可是貝克小姐很願意幫忙，她答應我跟你談談這件事。」

　　「這件事」究竟指的是什麼，我毫無頭緒。而且我不但毫無興趣，還感到有點氣惱。我約貝克小姐喝茶並不是為了要討論傑伊‧蓋茨比的事。我敢保證他要請我幫忙的一定是什麼異想天開的事，這一刻我突然後悔了，自己根本不該認識這個人，更不該踏進他那個賓客如雲的大門。

　　他也沒再多說什麼。我們離城裡越近，他的態度也越拘謹。車子經過羅斯福港，我們瞥見停泊在碼頭上漆得鮮紅的船隻，又穿過一處貧民區，石子路旁一排排黑漆漆的酒館，裡面人頭鑽

動。接著,垃圾堆在我們面前展開,車子急馳而過,我瞥見威爾森的老婆在加油機旁氣喘吁吁地替人加油。

　　汽車的擋泥板有如插了翅膀一樣向前飛翔,為半個阿斯托利亞區帶來了光明——可是當我們正在高架鐵道的支柱間迂迴繞行的時候,忽然聽到熟悉的摩托車「突——突——突——」的聲響,接著一名警察氣呼呼地趕了上來。

　　「好了,老兄。」蓋茨比喊著,一邊將車子慢下來,從他皮夾裡掏出一張白色卡片,在那位警察的眼前搖晃了幾下。

　　「是,是!」警察連忙舉帽表示歉意,並說:「我不知道是蓋茨比先生,下次一定會認得了。對不起。」

　　「你給他看的是什麼?」我問他。「牛津拍的相片嗎?」

　　「我幫過警察廳長的忙,他每年都會寄聖誕卡給我。」

　　車子急馳過皇后大橋,陽光從鋼架中透過來,照在川流不息的車輛上一閃一閃的發光,對岸的都市驀然呈現在眼簾,一棟棟像白糖塊一樣的高樓,都是花了沒銅臭的錢,許了心願建築起來的。從皇后大橋上遠眺紐約市,那奇異的景觀永遠好像是初次看見一樣,充滿了世界上所有的神祕與瑰麗。

　　一輛裝著死人堆滿鮮花的靈車,從我們旁邊開過,後面跟著兩輛窗簾拉得緊緊的轎車,還有幾部氣氛比較輕鬆的車子載著親友。這些送殯的親友們透過車窗向我們張望,他們抑鬱的眼神和薄薄的上唇,看上去像是東南歐人,我不禁替他們感到高興,在這個慘淡的送行中還能看到蓋茨比這部華麗的汽車。我們的車子經過布雷克維爾島時,一輛豪華轎車從我們旁邊疾駛而過,開車

的是個白人，車裡坐著三位衣著時髦的黑人，兩男一女。他們向我們高傲地翻翻白眼，大有彼此較量的神氣，我忍不住笑出聲來。

「過了這座橋，只怕什麼事都有可能發生。」我心想，「什麼怪事……」

甚至遇上另一個蓋茨比，也毋須訝異。

酷熱的中午。我跟蓋茨比約好在四十二街一家電風扇林立的地下餐廳吃飯。因為剛從大太陽底下走進來，我眨了眨眼才隱約看見他正在跟另外一個人說話。

「卡拉威先生，這是我的朋友渥夫辛先生。」

一位個頭矮小、塌鼻子的猶太人抬起頭來端詳我，他的鼻孔裡面長著兩撮很茂盛的鼻毛。過了一會兒我才在昏暗的光線中發現他的兩隻小眼睛。

「──然後我看了他一眼，」渥夫辛先生說，一面很誠懇地跟我握手，「你猜我做了什麼事？」

「什麼事？」我很有禮貌地問。

顯然他這句話不是對我說的，因為他隨即放下我的手，把他那隻富有表情的鼻頭轉向蓋茨比。

「我把那筆錢交給凱茲保，然後對他說：『好吧，凱茲保，他要是不閉嘴，從此一毛錢也別想拿。』他馬上就閉嘴了。」

蓋茨比一手挽著他，一手挽著我走進餐廳，渥夫辛先生話到嘴邊只好嚥了回去，一時有些茫然。

「來杯威士忌加冰塊嗎？」餐廳領班問。

「這家館子不錯，」渥夫辛先生眼睛望著天花板的寧芙女神說。「但是我喜歡馬路對面那家！」

「對，威士忌加冰塊。」蓋茨比點頭回答，然後對渥夫辛先生說：「那邊太熱了。」

「不錯，又熱、地方又小，」渥夫辛先生說，「可是充滿了回憶。」

「是哪一家？」我問。

「老都會。」

「老都會，」渥夫辛先生若有所思地說。「充滿了逝去的面孔。充滿了一去不返的夥伴。我一輩子也忘不了那天晚上羅西‧羅森索被人開槍打死的事。當時我們有六個人，羅西整夜大吃大喝，天快亮的時候服務生跑到他身邊，表情奇怪地對他說，外面有人找他。『知道了。』羅西邊說邊站起來，我把他一把拉回到椅子上。」

「『羅西，那班混蛋要跟你講話，就讓他們進來。你絕對不要離開這裡，羅西。』」

「那個時候已經是清晨四點，要是掀開窗簾，就可以看得見晨曦。」

「他出去了嗎？」我天真地問。

「他當然出去了。」渥夫辛先生氣憤地向我甩了甩鼻子。「他走到門口還回過頭來說：『不要讓服務生把我的咖啡收走。』說完他就走到外面人行道上，那幫人對準他吃得飽飽的肚子射了三槍，然後開車跑掉。」

「其中有四個人後來坐了電椅。」我補充一句，忽然記起當年這條新聞。

「五個，還有畢克。」他的鼻孔又轉向我，似乎開始對我感興趣。「我聽說你也想搭線，找人做生意。」

他前後這兩句話毫不相干，使我聽得一頭霧水。蓋茨比連忙替我回答：

「不是這位，」他說，「是另外一個人。」

「不是他啊？」渥夫辛先生似乎很失望。

「這位只是我的朋友。我告訴你了，改天再談那件事。」

「對不起，」渥夫辛先生說，「我弄錯人了。」

這時，一道美味的茱餚送了上來，渥夫辛先生立刻將「老都會」的感傷往事拋到腦後，開始吃了起來。他一邊吃一邊轉動著雙眼把整個餐廳掃視一遍——巡視完了前方與左右，最後轉過身來看看我們背後的人。我心想，要不是我在場，說不定他會彎下身，連桌子底下也檢視一番的。

「老兄，」蓋茨比向前靠近我說，「今天早上在車子裡我恐怕冒犯了你吧？」

他臉上又堆起那種笑容，可是這次我沒有理會它。

「我不喜歡你故作神祕，」我回道，「我不懂你為什麼不直截了當地告訴我你要做什麼，為什麼一定要透過貝克小姐呢？」

「喔，這並不是什麼不可告人的事。」他向我保證。「你知道，貝克小姐是一位傑出的女運動家，她絕對不會做出什麼不正當的事。」

忽然間，他看了看錶，跳起身來，匆匆走出餐廳，丟下我和渥夫辛先生兩人。

「他得去打個電話。」渥夫辛先生目送他出去，一面向我解釋。「很不錯的一個人，你說是不？相貌出眾，又有紳士風度。」

「是啊。」

「他是牛津畢業的。」

「喔！」

「他在英國牛津唸過書。你曉得牛津大學嗎？」

「我聽說過。」

「那可是全世界有名的一所大學。」

「你跟蓋茨比認識很久了嗎？」我問。

「好幾年了，」他欣慰地答覆。「戰後不久，我有一個機會跟他認識。跟他談了不到一個鐘頭，我就知道他是個出身不錯的人。我當時對自己說：『像這樣一位青年，真不妨帶回家去見見母親和妹妹。』」他停了一下又說，「你在看我的袖釦嗎？」

我本來沒有注意他的袖釦，可是經他這麼一提我倒真看了起來。他那副象牙袖釦形狀很特別，好像在哪裡見過。

「這是高級的真人牙齒。」他告訴我。

「真的！」我又仔細看了一看。「很別緻。」

「是啊。」他雙手猛地一動，把襯衫袖口收回外套底下。「是啊，蓋茨比對女人向來很小心，朋友的太太他看都不看一眼。」

渥夫辛先生所賞識的這一位又回到座位上坐下。渥夫辛先生一口把咖啡喝掉，然後站起身來。

「這餐吃得很高興，」他說，「我得告辭了，讓你們兩位青年人談談，免得你們說我不知趣。」

「不急啊，梅爾。」蓋茨比淡淡地說。渥夫辛先生舉起手好像在替我們祝福。

「你不用客氣，我和你們是不同世代的人。」他正經地說。「你們再坐一會兒，繼續談談運動、談談女人、談談……」他揮

揮手代替沒有說出口的那個名詞。「我已經是五十歲的人了，最好不要再打擾你們二位。」

他跟我們握手告辭時，他那古怪的鼻子又抽動起來，我不知道自己是不是說了什麼話得罪了他。

「他這人有時很情緒化。」蓋茨比向我解釋。「今天不巧又是他很情緒化的一天。他是紐約出了名的怪人——百老匯的一個人物。」

「他到底是做什麼的，演員嗎？」

「不是。」

「牙醫？」

「你說梅爾・渥夫辛？不是，他是個賭徒。」蓋茨比遲疑了一下，然後冷靜地補充一句：「一九一九年世界棒球聯賽舞弊案的主使人就是他。」

「世界棒球聯賽舞弊案的主使人？」我重複了一遍。

這句話簡直把我愣住了。我當然記得一九一九年世界聯賽作弊的那宗案子，可是，我總以為這種事難免會發生，是不可避免的。我怎麼也想不到這樣大的騙局是單單一個人的勾當，把五千萬球迷玩弄於股掌之間——就像小偷在黑夜裡爆開保險箱一樣簡單。

我愣了一會兒之後問道：「他是怎麼辦到的？」

「他只不過是剛好逮到機會。」

「他怎麼沒被捉去坐牢呢？」

「老兄啊，他們捉不到他的。他是一個絕頂聰明的人。」

吃完飯後，我堅持付了帳。服務生找零錢給我的時候，我在滿屋子的人中看見了湯姆‧勃肯納。

「跟我來一下，」我對蓋茨比說，「我得和一個人打招呼。」

湯姆一見到我們，馬上跳起身來，朝我們走近了五、六步。

「你上哪兒去了？」他質問我。「這麼久不打電話來，黛西氣得要命。」

「這位是蓋茨比先生，勃肯納先生。」

他們隨意地握了握手，蓋茨比臉上忽然顯出很不自然、很窘迫的樣子。

「你最近好嗎？」湯姆問我。「怎麼會大老遠跑到這兒來吃午飯？」

「我跟蓋茨比先生一塊兒到這裡吃午飯。」

我說著回過頭來看蓋茨比先生，他人已經不見了。

那天下午，在「廣場飯店」茶廳裡，喬丹‧貝克挺直地坐在一張高背椅子上，這麼對我說：

　　一九一七年十月裡的某一天，我在家附近街上沿途一直走著，一半走在人行道上，一半走在草地上。我喜歡在草地上走，因為我腳上穿的是一雙英國鞋子，鞋底有一顆顆的橡膠顆粒，踩在軟綿綿的草地上很舒服。我穿的那條格子花紋的裙子也是新的，風一吹，裙角就輕輕飄起，路邊住家門前掛的紅白藍三色旗也跟著張得開開的，發出不贊同的嘖嘖聲。

　　街道兩旁的住宅中，就屬黛西・費家的旗子最大、草地也最大。黛西那時只有十八歲，比我大兩歲，她是整個路易維爾地區最出風頭的女孩。她喜歡穿著白色衣裳，開著一部白色小跑車，她家裡的電話一天到晚響個不停，全是「泰勒軍營」的年輕軍官打來的，每一個都希望跟她約會，獨占她一整晚。「不然一個鐘頭也好！」

　　那天早上我走到她家門口的時候，她那部車子正停在路邊，她跟一位我從未見過的上尉軍官一同坐在車上，兩人彼此注視著對方，一直到我離他們只有五呎遠的時候，她才看見我。

　　「哈囉，喬丹。」她出其不意地叫了我。「請妳過來一下，好嗎？」

　　她竟然想跟我說話，這讓我感到受寵若驚，因為在所有年紀比我大的女孩子當中，她是我最崇拜的一位。她問我是否要到紅十字會去做繃帶。我說是的。於是她問我可否帶個口信給他們，說今天她不能去。黛西跟我說話時，那位軍官一直看著她，那種眼神實在太浪漫了，每一個女孩一定都希望有一天也能有人這樣看著自己。那一幕動人的情景，我到現在都還記得。那位軍官叫傑伊・蓋茨比。往後四年多，我再也沒見過他——就連最初在長島碰到他時，我都還不知道他就是那個人。

那是一九一七年的事。一年後我自己也有了幾個追求者，我開始參加高爾夫球賽，所以我就不常見到黛西。與她交往的人年紀都稍微大一點——我是說如果她有交往對象的話。關於她的謠言簡直是滿天飛——聽說有一個冬天晚上，她母親發現她在收拾衣物，準備到紐約去跟一個正要遠征海外的軍人道別。她最後沒去成，可是她也好幾個禮拜不和家人說話。從那件事以後，她便不再和軍人來往了，只跟本地幾個因近視或者扁平足等因素不能從軍的男士來往。

到了第二年秋天，她又和從前一樣快樂了起來，停戰之後，她父母為她舉辦了一個盛大的舞會亮相，到了二月，據說她已經跟紐奧良那地方的某人訂了婚。但是到了六月，她卻嫁給了芝加哥的湯姆‧勃肯納，結婚時場面的闊綽是在路易維爾從來沒有見過的。他包下四節火車，帶了一百位客人，在希巴希爾頓飯店租了一整層樓，又在婚禮前一天送了她一串價值三十五萬美元的珍珠項鍊。

我是她的伴娘之一。婚禮前夕我們為新娘舉行了一個送別餐會。我在半小時前到她房裡，發現她倒在床上，身上穿著華麗的禮服，美得有如六月的夏夜，可是卻醉得不省人事。她一手拿著一瓶白葡萄酒，一手拿著一封信。

「恭喜我吧！」她喃喃地說。「我從來沒喝過酒，啊，想不到酒這麼好喝！」

「妳怎麼了，黛西？」

我真的被她嚇壞了，不瞞你說，我從來沒有見過女孩子醉成那樣。

「呃——親愛的，拿去吧！」她把一堆垃圾抱到床上，伸手

在裡頭亂找一通，最後掏出一串珍珠項鍊。「把這個拿下樓去，是誰買的就還給誰。告訴大家，黛西改變主意了。就這麼說：『黛西反悔了！』」

她開始哭了起來，哭了又哭，哭個不

停。我趕緊跑出去找到她母親的女傭人，我們一塊兒把門鎖上，讓她洗個冷水澡。她手裡還抓著那封信不肯放，一起帶到澡盆裡去，揉成一團濕球，到後來看見紙都爛了，像雪花一樣一片片散開，她才肯讓我把它放在肥皂碟裡。

可是她隨後也不再說話。我們拿了一瓶氨水精讓她聞聞，在她額頭上敷了冰塊，幫她把衣服重新穿回身上。半小時後我們走出房間，她脖子上戴了那串珍珠項鍊，這場風波才算結束。第二天下午五點，她若無其事地跟湯姆‧勃肯納完成婚禮，然後就出發到南太平洋，開始為期三個月的旅行。

他們蜜月旅行回來的時候，我在聖巴巴娜見到他們。我從來沒見過一個女人如此迷戀丈夫，他只稍稍離開她身邊一步，她就

會東張西望,不安地問:「湯姆上哪兒去啦?」接著就是一副失魂落魄的樣子,直到看見他進門來才放心。她常常在海灘上一坐就是幾個鐘頭,讓湯姆把頭枕在她的大腿上,她用手輕撫他的眼睛,帶著無限的喜悅神情看著他。看見他們夫妻那種恩愛的模樣,真教人感動——常常讓人覺得驚奇,忍不住會心一笑。那是八月裡的事。我隨即離開了聖巴巴娜。一星期後的某天夜裡,湯姆在凡圖拉公路撞上了一架農車,把自己的車前輪撞掉了一隻,跟他同車的女人也上了報,因為她撞斷了一隻胳臂——她是聖巴巴娜飯店的女服務生。

第二年四月,黛西生了女兒,隨後他們便到法國去住了一年。那年春天我在坎城碰到他們,後來又在多維爾相遇,接著他們就回到芝加哥定居。黛西在芝加哥人緣很好,這是你知道的。和他們來往的大多是同一群人,一個個年輕、有錢又放蕩,但是她的名譽始終很好。也許是因為她不喝酒,跟一夥喜歡喝酒的朋友來往而自己不喝,那是很佔便宜的。你可以保持緘默,也可以趁別人喝得醉醺醺的時候,偶爾放縱一下,反正沒有人真正清醒著。就算看見了,也弄不清是真是假。也許黛西從來不跟別人有什麼曖昧,可是她說話的聲音老是給你一種感覺……。

大概六個禮拜之前,她忽然聽見一個她已經有好多年沒聽見的名字——蓋茨比。就是我那次問你——你還記得嗎?——你認識不認識一個住在西卵的蓋茨比。你回去之後,她跑到我房裡來把我叫醒,問我:「是哪個蓋茨比?」我半睡半醒,把他形容了一番,她聽了之後,用奇怪的語氣說,一定是她以前認識的那個人。那時候,我才把蓋茨比先生跟當年坐在她白色跑車裡的青年軍官聯想在一起。

等到喬丹·貝克把上面這段故事講完，我們離開「廣場飯店」已經有半個鐘頭，兩人搭著一輛出租馬車在中央公園裡閒逛。此刻太陽已經落在西城五十幾街電影明星住的高樓公寓後面，在濕熱的黃昏裡，孩子們揚起清亮的嗓音，像草地上的蟋蟀一樣唱著：

　　　「我是阿拉伯酋長，
　　　　妳是我的唯一，
　　　　　夜裡趁妳熟睡，
　　　　　　潛入妳的帳幕——」

「真是不可思議的巧合。」我說。

「這絕對不是湊巧。」

「為什麼？」

「蓋茨比就是因為黛西住在海灣正對面，他才會買下那幢房子。」

原來如此。這樣說來，六月裡那天夜晚他熱切觀望的不只是天上的星斗。剎那間，我覺得他好像從墳墓裡走了出來，突然有了生氣。

「他想問你，」喬丹繼續說，「能不能找一天下午把黛西請到你家裡，然後讓他們見個面。」

　　他的願望不過如此，真使我吃驚。難道相思了五年，購置了這麼豪華的別墅，擺出這樣闊綽的場面，為的只是某天下午，到一個陌生人的家裡來「見個面」？

　　「為了這一點小事，有必要把他過去的一切都告訴我嗎？」

　　「他心裡害怕啊，他實在等得太久了。你瞧，說穿了他到底是個無賴！他擔心你會不高興。」

　　這件事我覺得有點蹊蹺。

　　「他為什麼不直接讓妳安排他們見面呢？」

　　「他希望黛西看看他的別墅，」她解釋說。「而你剛好住在他隔壁。」

　　「喔！」

　　「我猜他本來抱著一點希望，也許哪天他會無意間在宴會上遇見黛西。」喬丹繼續說，「但是她始終沒有來過。後來他就開始打聽有沒有人認識她，而我就是他第一個找到的人。就是那晚他讓管家請我進去談話的那一次。你真該聽聽他那晚兜了多大的圈子才說到主題。當然了，那時我立刻就建議他們上紐約共進午餐——可是他好像很緊張，馬上對我說：

　　「『我不想節外生枝！』他說，『只要在隔壁鄰居家見見她就好了。』」

　　「我告訴他你跟湯姆很有交情時，他就想把計畫取消。他對湯姆知道的不多，但是，他說好多年來，自己總會看一份芝加哥的報紙，希望偶爾可以在報紙上看到黛西的名字。」

　　天色漸漸暗了，我們的馬車從一座小橋底下穿過時，我將手

放在喬丹金黃色澤的肩膀上，把她拉到我身邊，問她能不能和我共進晚餐。在這一剎那，我腦中想的不是黛西和蓋茨比，而是輕偎在我臂彎裡的這個漂亮、結實、對事事都抱持著懷疑態度的女孩。忽然間，有個急切而興奮的聲音在我耳畔響起：「世界上只有追求者和被追求者之分；一個忙碌，一個疲憊。」

「黛西這輩子也應當得到一點什麼。」喬丹對我喃喃地說。

「她願意見蓋茨比嗎？」

「我們不能讓她事先知道，蓋茨比不想讓她知道。你只能藉著喝下午茶的名義邀請她。」

我們的馬車經過一排幽暗的樹木，然後來到五十九街，一棟建築物亮起淡淡的燈光，映射到公園裡來。我不像蓋茨比，也不像湯姆・勃肯納，沒有哪個女孩的面孔在陰暗的屋簷下或耀眼的燈光中，像幽靈一樣忽隱忽現地纏住我，於是我將身邊這個女孩拉得近一點，手臂摟得緊一些。她蒼白、輕蔑的嘴脣對著我微笑，我不由得將她摟得更緊一點，同時把臉迎上去。

第 5 章

　　那天晚上回到西卵時，遠遠地看，還以為我的房子著了火。那時已是凌晨兩點，半島上的那一頭燈火通明，燈光照在灌木叢中看起來像是假的一般，又照在路旁電線上映射出一道道細長的閃光。當車子轉彎後，我才發現原來是蓋茨比的別墅，從屋頂到地下室的燈全點亮著。

　　起初我以為他又舉辦派對，把整個別墅開放，大夥兒在玩什麼「捉迷藏」或是「沙丁魚」之類的遊戲。可是四下一點聲音都沒有，只有風吹過樹叢，搖晃著電線，使得燈光忽明忽暗，好像那座房子對著黑夜不斷眨眼。我搭的計程車離去之後，隨即看見蓋茨比穿過他的草地，向我這邊走過來。

　　「你的房子好像世界博覽會。」我說。

　　「是嗎？」他心不在焉地看了房子一眼。「我剛才到幾個房間裡看了一下。老兄，我們到科尼島去逛逛，好嗎？我開車。」

　　「太晚了。」

　　「那麼到游泳池裡去，如何？我整個夏天都還沒下去過。」

　　「我得去睡覺了。」

　　「好吧。」

　　他在等我開口，顯然抑制著情緒。

過了一會兒我說：「貝克小姐跟我談過了。我明天就打電話給黛西，請她過來喝下午茶。」

「喔，那件事不急。」他故意毫不在意地說。「我不想給你添麻煩。」

「你覺得哪一天好？」

「應該看你哪天方便。」他立刻糾正我說，「我真的不想給你添麻煩。」

「那後天如何？」

他考慮了一下，然後不情願地說：「我要把草剪一剪。」

我們兩人不約而同地往草地上看了看——很清楚的一條分界線，一邊是我的一小塊雜亂草皮，另一邊則是他那片顏色較深、整整齊齊的廣大草坪。我懷疑他指的是要割我這邊的草。

「還有一件小事。」他吞吞吐吐，欲言又止。

「你是不是想延後幾天？」我問他。

「噢，不是那件事。至少……」他結結巴巴，不知從何說起的樣子。「我想……我說……老兄，你的收入不太多吧？」

「是不太多。」

我的回答似乎使他放心一點，他這才比較大膽地說下去。

「我想也是，假使你不介意……是這樣的，我有一點小生意，算是副業，你應該明白我的意思？我在想，如果你的收入不多……老兄，你是做債券生意的，是不是？」

「我還在學。」

「那麼這個你應該會有興趣。不需要花太多時間，還可以賺不少外快，不過這件事相當機密。」

我聽到這裡才知道他葫蘆裡賣的是什麼藥。這些話若不是在這種情形之下說出，可能會是我人生的一個轉捩點。可是，現在他如此坦率地提議，顯然是因為要我幫他的忙，先賣我個人情。我別無選擇，只好馬上打斷他的話。

「我手邊有太多事了。」我說，「真的謝謝你，我已經沒時間再做其他工作了。」

「你別誤會，這件事和渥夫辛沒有關係。」顯然他以為我是為了午飯時所提到的「找門路」而退縮，但是我很肯定地告訴他是他誤會了。他又等了一會兒，希望我先開口說話，可是我太沉溺在自己的思緒中而沒有回應，他只好無奈地回家去了。

這個晚上我非常愉快，飄飄欲仙，一進門很快就進入甜美的夢鄉。我不知道蓋茨比究竟有沒有去科尼島，也不知道他是不是

繼續到各個房間去轉了幾個小時，因為他的房子依舊燈火通明。第二天早上，我在辦公室裡打電話給黛西，請她到家裡來喝茶。

「不要帶湯姆來。」我叮嚀她。

「什麼？」

「不要帶湯姆來。」

「『湯姆』是誰啊？」她頑皮地問。

我們約定的那天下著傾盆大雨。上午十一點的時候，一個穿著雨衣、拖著除草機的人過來敲我的門，說是蓋茨比先生派他來替我割草。我這才想起，自己忘了吩咐那位芬蘭女傭今天回來幫忙，因此我就開車到西卵鎮上，在那些濕淋淋的白牆小巷裡繞來繞去地找她，隨後又去買了一些杯子、檸檬和鮮花。

其實，我買花是多餘的，因為到了下午兩點，蓋茨比那邊送來了一大堆鮮花，還有數不清的花瓶容器，好像把整個暖房都搬來了似的。一個小時後，一隻慌張的手推開了我家前門，只見蓋茨比穿著白色法蘭絨西裝和銀色襯衫，繫著一條金色領帶，慌慌張張走了進來。他臉色蒼白，眼睛底下還有失眠留下的黑眼圈。

「一切都弄妥了嗎？」他一進門就問。

「你指的是草地嗎？看起來好像不錯。」

「什麼草地？」他茫然地問。「哦，院子裡的草地。」他從窗口往外看，可是從他的表情看來，我想他什麼也沒看進眼裡。

「看起來很不錯。」他含糊地說了一句。「有份報紙說雨四點左右會停，大概是《紐約日報》吧。關於茶點——都齊全了嗎？」

　　我帶他到廚房裡去，他以責備的眼神朝那位芬蘭女傭望了一眼。我們一塊兒把買回來的那一打檸檬蛋糕審查了一番。

　　「可以嗎？」我問他。

　　「當然可以，當然可以！很好的！」他說著，然後又心不在焉地加了一句，「……老兄。」

　　大概三點，雨漸漸轉小變成了霧氣，不時還有幾滴雨水像露珠一樣飄著。蓋茨比漫不經心地翻閱著克雷所寫的《經濟學》，每次廚房裡芬蘭女傭腳步走得重一點，他就會大吃一驚，不時朝被雨水弄得模糊的玻璃窗向外看，好像外邊發生了什麼驚心怵目的事。最後他站起來用不太確定的口氣對我說他要回家去了。

　　「為什麼？」

　　「我看沒有人會來喝茶了。已經那麼晚了！」他看了看錶，好像還有其他要緊的事等他去辦。「我不能在這裡等一整天。」

　　「別說傻話了！還有兩分鐘才四點！」

　　他苦著臉又坐了下來，好像是我用手推他一樣。就在這時候，我聽見一輛汽車的聲音轉進我家的車道裡來。我們都跳了起來，我有點慌張地跑到院子裡。

　　一輛大型的敞篷車從滴著雨水的丁香樹下開上了車道。車子停了下來。黛西戴了一頂淺紫色的三角帽，側著臉看我，對我露出一抹燦爛的笑容。

　　「我親愛的，你就是住在這裡啊？」

　　她那迷人的聲浪從雨中傳過來，聽了使人歡欣鼓舞。我隨著她抑揚的音調仔細傾聽，過了一會兒才聽清楚她在說什麼。她的

臉頰上貼了一撮濕髮，像抹了一撇黑墨一樣。我扶她下車時，才發現她的手也被雨水打濕了。

「你是不是愛上我了？」她在我耳邊悄悄地說，「不然為什麼要我一個人來？」

「這是《瑞克蘭古堡》的祕密。叫妳的司機走遠一點，一個小時後再回來。」

「費狄，一個小時後再來。」然後她一本正經地低聲對我說：「他的名字叫費狄。」

「汽油味道會讓他的鼻子不舒服嗎？」

「應該不會。」她天真地回答。

我們走進屋內。客廳裡竟然空無一人，我大吃一驚。

「真是奇怪。」我不禁大聲說。

「奇怪什麼？」

此時，大門上響起輕輕的敲門聲。她回過頭去看，我走出客廳去開門。蓋茨比站在一灘水裡，臉色慘白，雙手沉重地插在口袋裡，用無助的眼神望著我。

進門後，他雙手還是插在口袋裡，大步跨過我身邊，然後像走鋼絲一樣突然一轉身，走進客廳就不見了。他這副模樣一點都不好笑，我將大門關上，以阻擋愈來愈大的雨勢，我感覺到自己的心跳怦怦地響得好大聲。

約有半分鐘的時間，客廳裡毫無聲響。然後便聽見裡頭傳來哽咽似的笑聲，接著就是黛西清晰而做作的嗓音。

「見到你我真是高興極了。」

　　然後又是持續好久的靜寂。我在玄關沒事做，只好走進客廳。

　　蓋茨比斜倚在壁爐旁，兩手仍然插在口袋裡，裝出一副輕鬆甚至無聊的樣子。他的頭往後仰，靠在壁爐台上一架年久失修的鐘上面，一雙困惑的眼神從上而下凝視著黛西，而黛西則坐在一張硬背椅的邊緣，表情驚訝卻不失優雅的氣質。

　　「我們以前見過面。」蓋茨比喃喃地說。他的眼光不時向我飄來，嘴角似笑不笑。就在這個時候，幸虧那座時鐘被他的頭碰得搖搖欲墜，他連忙轉過身來抖著手把鐘穩住並放回原處。

他直挺挺地坐下來，把手肘靠在沙發的扶手上，手托住下巴。

「很抱歉，你那座鐘……」他說。

此刻我的臉漲得通紅，腦子裡裝滿了寒暄客套的話，可是一句也說不出來。

「沒關係，只是一座很舊的鐘。」我傻傻地告訴他們。

我們的樣子就好像那座時鐘已經砸在地上碎了。

「我們有好多年沒見面了。」黛西說，聲音倒是很自然。

「下個十一月就滿五年了。」

蓋茨比這句機械式的回答，使大家再度沉默了許久。我不知如何是好，便建議他們到廚房幫我準備茶點，正當他們應聲而起的時候，我那個像魔鬼一樣的芬蘭女傭卻把茶端了出來。

在一陣遞茶杯、傳蛋糕的忙亂中，大家漸漸恢復從容的態度，這才教人鬆了一口氣。蓋茨比躲到一邊去，我跟黛西談話時，他神情緊張而不愉地看看我，又看看黛西。可是維持靜默並不是我們的目的，於是一有機會，我就站起身來。

「你要去哪兒？」蓋茨比立刻慌張地問。

「我馬上就回來。」

「等會兒再走，我有句話要跟你說。」

他激動地跟著我走進廚房，把門關上，小聲地說：「天哪！」他的神情看起來很痛苦。

「怎麼回事？」

「這是個錯誤。」他搖著頭說，「真是大錯特錯！」

「你只是不好意思罷了。」幸好我補了一句：「黛西也有點

難為情。」

「她也會覺得不好意思嗎？」他不敢置信地重複我的話。

「跟你一樣不好意思。」

「你不要那麼大聲。」

「你簡直像一個小孩。」我不耐煩地向他說。「不但如此，你也很沒有禮貌，把黛西一個人丟在那裡。」

他舉起手要我別再說下去，用一種令人難以忘懷的責備眼神看了我一眼，然後小心翼翼地把門打開，又回到客廳裡去。

我從後門走出去──半小時前，蓋茨比也是慌慌張張地從這裡出去繞到前門──我奔到一棵又大又黑的樹下，層層濃密的樹葉把雨擋住。此刻雨又下大了，我那塊凹凸不平的草地，雖然經過蓋茨比家園丁的修飾，仍然處處布滿泥沼。我站在樹下，除了眼前蓋茨比那座宏偉的別墅之外，就沒有什麼可看的了，於是我就盯著它看了半個小時，像哲學家康德端詳教堂的尖塔一樣。這座房子是十年前一位啤酒製造商蓋的，當時正流行「仿古」建築，據說這位富商還答應替附近所有的小住戶出五年的稅金，只要他們肯用茅草來蓋屋頂。也許他們的拒絕讓他放棄了在這裡建立家族的計畫──不久他就離開人世了。悼念他的黑色花圈還掛在門上，他的子女就把這棟房子賣掉了。美國人啊！他們寧願成為農奴──甚至渴望──可是死也不願意被人家當做鄉巴佬。

半小時後，太陽又露臉了，送食品的卡車沿著車道繞到蓋茨比家後門，為他的傭人送來做晚飯的材料──我敢肯定主人今晚一口也吃不下。一個女傭人把別墅樓上的窗戶一個個打開，還站

在中間的大窗口邊探出身子，毫不在意地朝花園裡吐了一口痰。我該回去了。剛才還下著雨的時候，聽起來彷彿是他們在竊竊私語的聲音，他們的情緒偶爾也隨著雨聲而起伏不定。現在四周又是一片靜寂，我覺得屋子裡也跟著靜默下來了。

我走進屋裡──在此之前我先在廚房裡盡量製造各種聲音，只差沒把爐子給拆了，不過我想他們什麼也沒聽見。他們各自坐在沙發的一端望著對方，似乎有人問了問題，或正打算發問，所有尷尬的氣氛已經完全消失。黛西的臉上還有淚痕，我走進來的時候她跳起來，立刻拿起手帕對著鏡子將淚水拭去。蓋茨比的改變卻令我感到困惑，他顯得容光煥發，雖然沒有欣喜的言語或表情，身上卻散發出一種幸福的光芒，籠罩著這間小小的客廳。

「嗨，老兄！」他的口氣好像我們已經多年不見，我甚至以為他要來和我握手呢！

「雨停了。」

「真的嗎？」他領會了我的意思，又見到陽光照進屋子裡，便露出微笑，像個氣象播報員，欣喜地將這個好消息告訴黛西：「妳看看，雨停了！」

「傑伊，我很高興。」在她充滿痛苦與悲傷之美的聲音裡，說的只是令她意外的喜悅。

「希望你和黛西到我家裡來。」他說，「我要帶她到處看看。」

「你確定要我一塊兒去嗎？」

「當然囉，老兄。」

黛西上樓去洗臉——我忽然想起自己那些寒酸的毛巾，可是已經太遲了——我和蓋茨比在草坪上等她。

「我的房子不錯吧？」他問道，「整個正面採光很好。」

我承認，的確很好。

「是啊。」他的視線掃過每一道拱門、每一座方形閣樓，「我只花了三年的時間，就賺足了錢買下這棟房子。」

「我以為你的錢都是由繼承財產得來的。」

「是啊，老兄。」他很自然地說，「可是經過那次大恐慌，戰爭帶來的恐慌——我的錢幾乎都沒了。」

我想他大概不知道自己在說什麼，因為當我問他從事什麼工作時，他竟回答說：「那是我的事。」後來他才發覺這樣回答不妥當。

「喔，其實我做過不少生意。」他改口說，「起初是藥材生意，後來是石油買賣。不過現在都不做了。」他留神地看著我，「你的意思是，那天晚上我提議的事情，你已經考慮好了？」

我還沒來得及回答，黛西已經走出來，她衣服上的兩排銅釦在陽光下閃閃發亮。

「就是那邊那棟大房子嗎？」她用手指著大聲地說。

「妳喜歡嗎？」

「很喜歡，但是我不懂你怎麼能一個人住那麼大的房子。」

「我這裡一天到晚有客人，都是一些有意思的人物——他們做的都是有意思的事。都是有名望的人物。」

我們故意不抄近路沿海岸走，而是繞到馬路上，再從後門走

進去。黛西望著那座宮殿式的豪宅，用她那迷人的聲音稱讚這棟別墅，邊走邊欣賞著園裡的花草，有花香濃郁的長壽花、清香撲鼻的山楂花和梅花，還有「親吻花」散放出黃金色的香味。走到大理石臺階時，感覺有點奇怪，因為沒看見有紅男綠女進進出出，也聽不到什麼聲音，除了樹上的鳥鳴。

進屋子之後，我們經過了法國「瑪莉‧安東尼皇后式」的音樂廳，和英國「復辟時代」風格的幾個小客廳，我疑心每個沙發、每張桌子背後都躲著客人屏息不動，因為奉命要我們走過後才准許出聲。當蓋茨比關上那間「默頓學院式」的藏書室時，我發誓我似乎隱約聽到那位像貓頭鷹的客人在裡面咯咯笑著。

我們走上樓，穿過好幾間古色古香的臥室，裡面掛著粉紅和紫色的綢緞，擺滿鮮豔奪目的花卉。接著又穿過一些更衣室、撞球間和擺有澡盆的浴室。我們不小心闖進一間臥室，裡面有一個穿著睡衣、披頭散髮的男人正在地板上作體操，我認出他就是那個外號叫「食客」的克利史賓格先生。那天早上我就注意到他在沙灘上晃來晃去。最後蓋茨比帶我們到他自己的套房，裡面有臥室、浴室和一間書房。我們在書房裡坐下，他從壁櫥裡拿出一瓶酒來請我們喝。

在這一段時間裡，他的視線始終沒有離開過黛西。大概是希望依據她那戀戀不已的目光，再把他房子裡所有的東西都重新加以評估。有時候，蓋茨比也如醉如癡地環視著自己擁有的一切，彷彿因為黛西難以置信卻又實實在在地出現在這裡，使得這一切都變得不真實了。有一次他還險些從樓梯上摔下來。

他自己的臥室裝潢得最簡單，唯一例外的，是梳妝台上擺了一副純金的化妝用具。黛西欣喜地拿起梳子梳著她的頭髮，蓋茨比看了便坐下來，掩著臉忍不住笑了起來。

「真是太有趣了，老兄。」他笑個不停地說，「我沒辦法……我一想起……」

很顯然的，他在經歷了兩種心情的變化後，現在正進入第三種狀態。最先是不好意思，然後是喜出望外，目前則是充滿了驚喜，簡直不敢相信她的確出現在他眼前。為了這件事，他已經想了很久，也不知做過多少次夢，始終咬緊牙關地期待著。現在終於如願以償，他反倒像個發條上得太緊的時鐘，忽然鬆弛下來。

他很快地讓自己恢復正常，他打開兩個設計新潮的大衣櫥，裡面掛滿了無數的西裝、浴袍和領帶，還有非常多的襯衫像磚塊一樣一疊一疊地放著。

「在英國，有人專門替我選購衣服，每年的春秋兩季，他都會幫我選一些衣服寄過來。」

他拿出一堆襯衫，一件件扔在我們面前──純亞麻、純絲綢和高級法蘭絨襯衫，本來摺得好好的，現在都給抖散了，五顏六色散布在桌上。我們一面欣賞，他一面又抱出更多，又細又軟的貴重衣料堆積如山──條紋襯衫、花紋襯衫、大方格子襯衫，珊瑚色、蘋果綠、淺紫色、淡橘色，上面還用深藍色絲線繡著他名字的縮寫。黛西忽然把頭埋進襯衫堆裡，號啕大哭起來。

「這些襯衫真美！」她啜泣著說，聲音悶在厚厚的衣料裡聽不太清楚。「我覺得很難過，因為我從來沒見過這麼……這樣漂

亮的襯衫。」

　　參觀完房子之後，我們本來還要去看看草地、游泳池、水上飛機和仲夏的花卉，可是外頭又開始下起雨來了，因此我們就站成一列，遠眺海上的波浪。

　　「假如沒有霧，我們可以看到對岸妳家的房子。」蓋茨比說。「你們家的碼頭上每晚總會有一盞綠燈一直點到天亮。」

　　黛西突然挽著他的臂膀，但他似乎還沉思著自己方才說的話。也許他剛剛領悟到，那盞綠燈所象徵的重大意義從此就要消失了。他跟黛西之間一直隔著遙遠的距離，相較之下，那盞燈似乎離她好近，近得幾乎可以碰觸到她，近得有如月亮旁的一顆星。而現在，它不過又是碼頭上的一盞綠燈罷了，於是他所憧憬的事物又少了一件。

　　我在房裡走來走去，在昏暗的光線中看著幾樣模糊不清的東西。掛在書桌上方牆上的一張巨大相片吸引了我的注意，是一位穿著遊艇服裝的老先生。

　　「這個人是誰？」

　　「那張相片啊？那是丹‧柯迪先生，老兄。」

　　這個名字聽起來有點耳熟。

　　「他已經過世了。幾年前他是我最好的朋友。」

　　書桌上有一張蓋茨比的相片，他也穿著遊艇服裝，揚起頭來，一副傲慢的神氣，當時大概十八歲左右。

　　「我真喜歡這張相片。」黛西嚷著說，「你看，你把頭髮全向後梳！你從沒告訴我你會留龐畢度髮型，也沒提過遊艇。」

「妳看這個。」蓋茨比趕緊岔開她的話。「這裡有一大堆剪報，全是關於妳的。」

他們並肩站在一起仔細看著剪報。我正想請他讓我看看他所收藏的紅寶石，但是電話忽然響了，蓋茨比拿起了話筒。

「是的……呃，我現在不方便說話……老兄，我現在不方便說話……我說的是一個小鎮……難道他連小鎮都不懂？……如果他認為底特律是個小鎮，那就沒什麼好談的……」他掛上電話。

「快過來看！」黛西在窗前喊道。

雨還在下著，但是西邊天空的烏雲已經散開，海面上飄起幾朵粉紅帶金的浮雲。

「你看。」她低聲地說，過了一會兒又說：「我恨不得摘一朵那種粉紅色的雲，把你放在上面四處推著走。」

當時我想告辭，可是他們一定不會聽我的。也許有我在場，他們可以更安心地獨處。

「我知道我們可以做什麼了。」蓋茨比說，「我們叫克利史賓格來彈琴。」

他走出房門喊著：「艾文！」過了幾分鐘，一個神色窘迫、疲憊的年輕人跟著他回來。那個年輕人黃髮稀疏，戴了一副玳瑁邊的眼鏡。他此刻衣服整齊了些，穿著一件開領的運動衫、一條顏色灰暗的帆布褲和一雙膠底鞋。

「我們沒有打擾你運動吧？」黛西很禮貌地問。

「我在睡覺。」克利史賓格先生脫口說出，卻又忽然覺得不好意思。「我是說，我睡了一會兒，後來就醒了……」

「克利史賓格會彈鋼琴，」蓋茨比打斷他的話，「是不是，艾文老兄？」

「我彈得不好。我不會……幾乎不會彈了，我好久沒……」

「我們到樓下去。」蓋茨比又插嘴說。他撥了一個開關，整個屋子亮了起來，灰色的窗戶也都看不見了。

大家走進音樂廳，蓋茨比把鋼琴旁邊的一盞立燈打開。他擦了根火柴，抖著手替黛西點上一根煙，然後和她到房間那邊的一張沙發上坐下，那裡一片黑暗，只有地板上映著從穿堂裡射進來的一些微光。

克利史賓格彈完了一首《愛之巢》，從椅子上轉過身來，悶悶不樂地在幽暗中尋找蓋茨比的臉。

「你看，幾乎都已經忘了，我早就說我不會彈，很久沒練習了……」

「別說那麼多了，老兄，」蓋茨比以命令的口吻說。「彈吧！」

「於清晨，
　　於黃昏，
　　　只要開心……」

外面風颳得很大，海上傳來一聲隱隱的雷聲。此刻西卵鎮家家戶戶都已點了燈；電車載著乘客冒著雨從紐約返回家。這是人事變幻無窮的時刻，空氣中洋溢著興奮的氣氛。

「千真萬確，無須懷疑

　　　　富者更富，窮者更——

　多子多孫。

　　於此時，

　　　　於此刻……」

　　我走過去跟他們告辭的時候，發現蓋茨比臉上又浮現出惶恐的表情，似乎他對目前的快樂產生了懷疑。就快五年了！即使在那天下午，他一定偶爾也會覺得，現實中的黛西還不如他自己的夢想——這不能怪她，而是因為他的夢太過栩栩如生了，這幻想超越了她，超越了一切。他讓自己投身在虛構的夢境裡，而且不斷添加意想得到的色彩，還利用迎面飄來的每根彩羽為它妝點。無論什麼樣的熱情，什麼樣的新穎實體，都比不上一顆心靈長久堆積的幻影。

　　我觀察著蓋茨比，發覺他稍微調整了自己。他握著黛西的手，她在他耳邊輕聲說了些什麼，他轉身面向她，情緒激動。我想，最使他著迷的應該是黛西富有旋律又充滿熱情的聲音了，因為那是無論如何也幻想不出來的——那聲音有如一首不朽的歌。

　　他們顯然已經忘了我的存在，不過黛西抬起頭來看見了我，便向我伸出手來；蓋茨比則完全不認得我了。我又回頭看了他們一眼，他們也望了我一眼，但是感覺上好遙遠，彷彿兩人早已被生命的火燄包圍住了。我走出了屋子，走下大理石臺階穿入雨中，留下他們兩人在一起。

第 6 章

　　大約就在這段期間的某一天早上，紐約一位野心勃勃的青年記者來到蓋茨比家門口，問他有沒有什麼話要說。

　　「關於什麼事？」蓋茨比很客氣地問。

　　「嗯……任何公開的聲明都行。」

　　經過五分鐘莫名其妙的對話後才弄清楚，原來這位記者在公司聽人提起蓋茨比的名字——他不肯說為什麼有人會提到，也許他根本不知道。這天他剛好不上班，所以就很勤快地自動跑過來「打聽、打聽」。

　　這位記者當然只是碰碰運氣，但是他的直覺卻是對的。在蓋茨比所招待的數百名賓客的大力宣揚之下，這些人成了蓋茨比過去經歷的見證人，也使得他的名氣在這個夏天愈來愈響，只差一點就要成為新聞人物了。當時有各種傳奇故事，像是「利用地下管線從加拿大運送私酒進來」等等，據說都跟他有關。還有一個流傳很廣的說法，說他住的房子根本不在陸地上，而是一艘像房子一樣的船，經常沿著長島海岸上下祕密地遊走。至於這些謠言究竟為什麼能帶給北達科塔州的詹姆士・蓋茲滿足和喜悅，倒不是一個容易解答的問題。

　　詹姆士・蓋茲——這是他真實的姓名，至少是他法律上的

姓名。他是在十七歲那年改名換姓的,那也是他事業的開端——
當時他看見丹‧柯迪先生的遊艇在蘇必略湖最兇險的水域下錨。
那天下午,身穿破舊的綠色汗衫和粗帆布褲在沙灘上閒晃的還只
是詹姆士‧蓋茲,但是後來當他借了一艘小船,划向「多羅米
號」去警告丹‧柯迪先生趕快把船移到別處停泊以免再過半個小
時會被強風吹垮時,他就已經是傑伊‧蓋茨比了。

　　我想,早在那個時候,他就想好名字了。他父母是窮困潦倒
的農人——在他心裡,從來沒有真正把他們當成親生父母。事實
上,長島西卵鎮的傑伊‧蓋茨比是他自我幻想中的產物。他是上
帝之子——因此他必須繼承父親的志業,專心致力於一種廣闊、
庸俗與浮華之美。於是,他以一個十七歲少年的想像力創造了傑
伊‧蓋茨比,而且一直到人生終了,他始終忠於這個身分。

　　在那以前一年多的時光,他常在蘇必略湖南岸晃蕩,每天撈
蛤蜊、捕鮭魚,或是做些別的雜事換取溫飽。那地方天氣爽朗,
他的皮膚曬得黝黑,身體也變得結實,很自然地過著半艱辛、半
懶散的生活。他很早就識得色慾,由於女人對他的寵愛,他開始
瞧不起她們,瞧不起年輕的處女——因為她們愚蠢無知;其他的
女人他也瞧不上眼——因為他的自我意識,許多事都被他視為理
所當然,女人卻老是大驚小怪。

　　可是他的內心一直混亂不安。夜裡躺在床上,各種離奇怪誕
的幻想都來侵擾他。當洗臉台上的時鐘滴答響著,當胡亂丟在地
板上的衣服沉浸在暈潤的月光裡,一幅筆墨難以形容的繁華世界
便會浮現在他的腦海。每夜他都會加入更多的幻想,直到睡意籠

罩住某個鮮明的畫面，他才能忘卻一切而入睡。在那段期間，這些幻想使他精神上得到一種發洩，同時使他了解到現狀並不是真實的，他也安心地知道，未來的世界還是穩穩地根植在仙女的羽翼上。

幾個月前，為了追求飛黃騰達的未來，他來到明尼蘇達州南部一個路德教會辦的聖俄拉夫小學院。他在那地方待了兩星期，沒有人注意到他的遠大前程令他感到很失望，他不禁徬徨失措，為了付學費，他還得去做自己所蔑視的工友差事。後來他又漂泊了一陣子才回到蘇必略湖來。那天他正想找點什麼事做，卻剛好發現丹‧柯迪先生的遊艇在湖邊的淺灣下錨停泊。

柯迪先生那時已經是五十歲年紀，他曾經在內華達州採銀，阿拉斯加的育空河邊淘金，一八七五年以來凡是發現礦藏的地方他都沒有錯過。後來他在蒙他那州經營銅礦生意，賺了好幾百萬，雖然身體仍然健壯，可是腦筋已經開始糊塗。很多女人發覺有機可乘，便企圖拐他一筆。有一個叫艾拉‧凱的女記者，學著曼特儂夫人的手段一度把他迷住，慫恿他乘遊艇出海旅行，之後又鬧出一些風風雨雨，這些消息在一九零二那年所有的八卦報章雜誌上都看得到。在過去這五年中，他乘著遊艇四處遊歷，到處受人歡迎，那天他剛好出現在「女童灣」，因而成為詹姆士‧蓋茲的貴人。

年輕的蓋茲倚著船槳，仰望著遊艇圍起欄杆的甲板，在他眼中，這艘船代表了世界上一切的榮華富貴。我想他大概對柯迪先生笑了一笑——他很可能早就發現他笑的時候很討人歡喜。總

之，柯迪問了他幾個問題（在答覆其中一個問題時，他那個嶄新的名字便出現了），發覺這個小子十分機伶而且野心不小。幾天後，柯迪帶他到德魯斯城去，為他買了一套藍色水手服、六條白色帆布褲，還有一頂水手帽。當「多羅米號」出發朝西印度群島和北非巴巴利海岸線航行的時候，蓋茨比也跟著離開了。

蓋茨比先後做過很多事——他和柯迪在一起就得輪流擔任小弟、副手、船長、祕書，甚至監視人，因為丹·柯迪在清醒的時候知道自己喝醉酒時會做出什麼荒唐的事，為了防止這類事件發生，他對蓋茨比也就越來越信任了。他們之間這種關係維持了五年，在這段期間，他們的遊艇總共環繞美洲大陸三次——原本可能會無限期地繼續下去，要不是有一晚停泊在波士頓的時候，艾拉·凱忽然上了船。柯迪先生也真不夠交情，一個星期後就與世長辭了。

我還記得在蓋茨比臥室裡看見柯迪的相片，一個頭髮灰白、面色紅潤、飽經風霜、表情嚴肅的人，他可說是美國某一段時期的酒色先鋒，這班人曾把西部妓院和酒館的粗獷氣氛帶回到東部。蓋茨比幾乎滴酒不沾，柯迪先生算是間接的原因。有時宴會酒酣耳熱，總有女人把香檳往蓋茨比頭髮上抹，為了自己好他早已養成滴酒不沾的習慣。

蓋茨比也從柯迪那裡繼承了財產——一筆兩萬五千元的遺產。但是他一毛錢也沒拿到，他一直沒弄懂對方是用什麼法律手段來對付他的，總之那幾百萬的遺產最後統統進了艾拉·凱的口袋裡。他唯一得到的就是珍貴而實際的經驗；先前的傑伊·蓋茨

比不過是模模糊糊的輪廓，現在已經成為有血有肉，真真實實的
人了。

這些話是過了好久之後蓋茨比才告訴我的，我在這裡先說出
來是為了要替他闢謠——一開始大家對於他的出身就多方揣測、
道聽塗說，一點事實根據也沒有。而且當他告訴我的時候，我心
裡正混亂不已，關於他的事，我不曉得到底該不該相信。現在這
段期間可說是蓋茨比停下來喘口氣，準備邁入人生另一個階段的
時候，因此我趁這個機會澄清世人對他的誤解。

其實，在這段時間裡我也沒跟蓋茨比來往。前後好幾個星期
我都沒跟他見面，也沒接到他的電話——大部分時間我都跟著喬
丹搭馬車在紐約四處閒晃，同時還要努力討好她那位老姑媽。不
過，後來我還是挑了個星期日下午去他家。我還待不到兩分鐘，
就有人帶著湯姆·勃肯納要來喝酒。我相當驚訝，但是更令人詫
異的是，湯姆以前竟然沒有來過。

他們一行三人在外面騎馬回來——湯姆、一個姓史隆的男
人，還有一個穿著棕色騎裝的美麗女子，她以前來過。

「歡迎，歡迎，」蓋茨比站在陽臺上說，「真高興你們能
來。」

其實他高興與否他們才不在乎呢！

「請坐，抽根煙或雪茄。」他在客廳裡團團轉，忙著搖鈴。
「我馬上叫人拿點喝的來。」

湯姆的光臨使他很不自在。但不管怎麼說，如果不趕快給客
人喝點什麼，並隱約得知這些人上門並無其他目的，他是不會安

心的。史隆先生什麼都不喝。檸檬汁好嗎？不用了，謝謝。來點香檳如何？真的什麼都不用，謝謝……，對不起，招待不周……。

「騎馬還愉快吧？」

「這一帶的路很不錯。」

「我想汽車……」

「是啊。」

剛才介紹的時候，湯姆只當彼此是陌生人，此刻蓋茨比忍不住轉頭對他說：「勃肯納先生，我想我們在哪兒見過？」

「是啊，」湯姆保持生硬的禮貌說，但他顯然已毫無印象。「見過，見過，我記得很清楚。」

「大約兩禮拜以前。」

「對了。你跟尼克在一起。」

「我認識你太太。」蓋茨比接下去說，帶了點挑釁的意味。

「是嗎？」

湯姆轉過頭來問我。

「尼克，你住在這附近嗎？」

「就在隔壁。」

「是嗎？」

史隆先生並沒有參與談話，只是仰身斜靠在椅背上；那位女士起先也沒說什麼，兩杯威士忌酒下肚後才開始寒暄起來。

「蓋茨比先生，你下次舉行宴會我們都來，」她提議，「你說好不好？」

「當然，你們能來是我的榮幸。」

「太好了，」史隆先生說，似乎沒有感謝之意。「唔⋯⋯我想該回去了吧。」

「不急，不急！」蓋茨比挽留他們。他現在已經鎮定下來，而且

想多認識湯姆一點。「我看你們就⋯⋯留下來吃個便飯吧？待會兒說不定還有朋友從紐約來找我。」

「還是你到我家吃飯吧。」那位太太熱情地說，「你們兩位都來。」

這包括我在內。史隆先生站起身來。

「走吧。」他說——可是只是對她一個人說。

「我說真的。」她堅持說，「我真的希望你們來，地方很大的。」

113

　　蓋茨比向我投以詢問的眼神。他很想去，一點也沒看出來史隆先生絕不歡迎他去。

　　「我恐怕是不能去了。」我說。

　　「那麼，你來。」她對著蓋茨比再次邀請。

　　史隆先生湊到她耳邊低聲說了幾句話。

　　「我們現在馬上就走，一點都不晚。」她堅持地大聲說。

　　「我沒有馬，」蓋茨比說。「我在軍中經常騎馬，可是從來沒買過，只好開車跟著你們。對不起，等一下我就來。」

　　我們其餘幾個人走出來到外面的陽臺上，史隆和那位太太站在一邊開始氣沖沖地交談。

　　「天啊，這傢伙居然真的要來。」湯姆說，「難道他不明白她並不要他來嗎？」

　　「她說她真的希望他去的。」

　　「她那是大型晚宴，他如果去的話一個人都不認識。」湯姆皺著眉頭。「真不知道他是在哪兒遇見黛西。也許我的思想太古板了，不過現在的女人太愛亂跑了，什麼阿貓阿狗都認識。」

　　史隆先生和那位太太忽然走下臺階，各自騎上了馬。

　　「走吧。」史隆先生對湯姆說。「我們已經有點晚了，得走了。」然後對我說：「麻煩你告訴他，我們不能等他了。」

　　湯姆跟我握握手，其餘幾個人彼此只冷冷地點一點頭，然後他們就很快地沿著車道騎馬離去。就在他們的身影隱沒在八月濃密的樹蔭間時，蓋茨比手拿著帽子和薄外套從大門裡走出來。

　　湯姆顯然很不放心黛西一個人到處亂跑，因為接下來的那個

週末晚上，他就陪著她一同來參加蓋茨比的派對。或許是由於他在場，我感覺到那晚的氣氛非常彆扭，整個夏天的許多次宴會中，我對這一次的印象最深刻。宴會裡仍然有那些客人，至少是那一類型的人，香檳仍然是源源不絕，有著同樣五彩繽紛、情緒高昂的熱鬧氣氛，可是我覺得空氣中瀰漫著一種不愉快的感覺，彷彿一種前所未有的不舒服感正逐漸擴散開來。也或許是因為我已習慣了，習慣把西卵認為是一個完整的世界，有著自己的習慣和獨特的人物，並自認為獨一無二，而現在我卻透過黛西的雙眼重新去看待這裡的一切。要是你費盡了氣力才弄慣的事，現在又要透過另一雙眼睛重新看它，難免會感到難受。

　　他們夫婦在黃昏時分抵達，當我們大家穿梭在珠光寶氣的人群中時，黛西喉嚨裡不斷呢呢喃喃地作聲。

　　「這一類的場合實在太令我興奮了。」她小聲地說。「尼克，今天晚上如果你想親我，請隨時通知，我會很樂意為你安排的。只要說出我的名字就行了，或者可以出示一張綠色卡片。我現在到處在發綠色的……」

　　「到處看看吧！」蓋茨比建議說。

　　「我是到處在看呀。我玩得開心極了……」

　　「你一定會看到許多你聽見過的人物。」

　　湯姆用傲慢的眼光掃視著人群。

　　「我們很少交際，」他說：「老實說，我正在想我這裡一個人都不認識。」

　　「也許你認得那位小姐。」蓋茨比指著一位端坐在白梅樹

下、氣質不凡的女子。湯姆和黛西盯著她看，認出她是只在銀幕上才見得到的明星，眼前這畫面看起來大有真真假假的感覺。

「她真美。」黛西說。

「彎著腰在跟她說話的是她的導演。」

蓋茨比領著他們夫婦向客人介紹，一會兒向這一夥，一會兒向那一夥。

「這是勃肯納夫人……勃肯納先生……」他猶疑了一下又補充一句說「鼎鼎大名的馬球健將。」

「不敢當。」湯姆趕緊澄清，「稱不上。」

可是蓋茨比似乎覺得這個稱呼很配，於是湯姆就這麼當了一整晚的「馬球健將」。

「我從來沒見過這麼多名人，」黛西說，「我很喜歡那個人……他叫什麼名字？……就是鼻子有點發青的那個。」

蓋茨比說出那人的名字，又說他只是一個小製片。

「我就是喜歡他。」

「我寧願不做馬球健將，」湯姆很隨和地說，「我寧願在一旁看著這些有名的人物……當個被遺忘的人。」

黛西和蓋茨比跳起舞來。記得當我看見他姿勢挺不錯地跳著狐步舞時，心裡很是詫異──我從未見過他跳舞。後來他們漫步走到我家那邊，在門前階梯上坐了半個小時，而我則應她的囑咐，站在園子裡替他們把風。「萬一突然發生火災、大水，或是什麼的。」她這樣解釋。

當我們正打算坐下來一塊用餐時,湯姆從他被遺忘的角落冒了出來。「我想去跟那邊幾個人一塊吃飯,你們不會介意吧?」他說,「有一個傢伙在說笑話。」

「去吧。」黛西和顏悅色地回答,「如果你想要把幾個人的住址抄下來,我這裡有隻金色小鉛筆。」她隨即東張西望四處看了一下,然後對我說那個女孩「很庸俗,但滿漂亮的」。我知道,除了跟蓋茨比在一起的那半個小時之外,她玩得並不開心。

我們這一桌的人喝得特別醉。這都怪我不好——蓋茨比出去接電話,我和黛西就加入了這一夥人,因為兩個星期前我剛認識他們,覺得這些人怪有趣的,不料當時覺得新鮮有趣的話題,如今卻已變得腐臭了。

「您還好吧,貝迪克小姐?」

這位小姐試圖倒在我的肩膀上,可是一直沒有成功,經我這樣一問,她才坐起身來,睜大眼睛。

「什麼?」

一位身材肥大、昏昏睡睡的女人,剛才一直要黛西答應明天陪她去打高爾夫球,現在則來為貝迪克小姐說話。

「噢,她沒事了。她每次只要喝了五、六杯雞尾酒,就會這樣大聲嚷嚷。我早勸她不要喝了。」

「我沒喝了!」被指責之後,貝迪克小姐不太有力地申辯。

「我們一見妳嚷嚷,就跟這位席維特醫生說:『醫生,那邊有人需要您幫忙。』」

「我相信她一定非常感激。」另外一位朋友言不由衷地說,

「可是你把她的頭按到游泳池裡，她全身都濕透了。」

「我最恨人家把我的頭按到游泳池裡，」貝迪克小姐咕噥著說。「有一次在紐澤西，就差點把我淹死。」

「那妳就不應該再喝了。」席維特醫生說。

「你也不瞧瞧你自己！」貝迪克小姐大喊道。「你的手直發抖，我就是開刀也不要你動手！」

情形就是這樣。我所記得的最後一件事，應該是我跟黛西站在一起，遠遠望著那位導演和他的「大明星」。他們仍然待在那棵白梅樹下，他們的臉現在距離很近，幾乎要接觸了，中間只隔著一絲月光。我想他大概整晚都站在那兒，很慢很慢地彎下身向前接近她，就在我望著他的那一剎那，我看見他似乎又彎低了一點，然後在她的臉頰上吻了一下。

「我喜歡她。」黛西說，「我覺得她很美。」

但其餘的一切都令她感到不快，毫無疑問地──因為這種不快並不是一種裝腔作勢的表態，而是貨真價實的情緒。她厭惡西卵，這個由百老匯三教九流的人在長島某個漁村所衍生出來的絕無僅有的「市鎮」──因為在它看似傳統委婉的外表之下，有一股野蠻的精力隱隱躁動，而此地的居民也不知是從哪裡冒出來的，一下子就聚居在一起，命運這種乖張強悍的力量也讓她害怕。由於這裡的一切過於簡單，她無法了解，因此感到恐懼。

我陪著他們坐在門前臺階上等車子到來。前面很暗，只有明亮的門邊灑著十方呎的亮光，光線從門內往外射向柔和昏暗的凌晨。樓上更衣室的百葉窗後面不時人影幢幢，在那看不見的玻璃

窗裡塗脂抹粉的人影，有如跑馬燈一般，一個晃過一個。

「蓋茨比這傢伙究竟是誰？」湯姆忽然問道，「賣私酒的販子？」

「你從哪兒聽來的？」我問他。

「不是聽來的，我是自己猜的。你也知道，有很多這樣的暴發戶都是做私酒買賣的。」

「蓋茨比不是。」我有點不高興了。

他沉默了半晌。車道上的小石子被他踩得嘎吱作響。

「不管怎樣，他一定費了很大的力氣，才能請到這些三教九流的人物。」

這時吹起一陣風，吹得黛西皮衣領上的灰色細毛微微顫動。

「至少這些人比我們認識的人有意思。」她有點勉強地說。

「妳看起來好像不是玩得很高興。」

「怎麼會，我玩得很高興。」

湯姆大笑，轉過頭來對我說：「那個女孩叫黛西讓她沖冷水澡的時候，你有沒有注意到黛西臉上的表情？」

黛西開始用沙啞的聲音，跟著音樂的節奏低聲輕唱，把歌詞中的每個字句注入一種空前絕後的意境。當旋律高升，她女低音的嗓子也隨著曲調改變，跟著音節的上下，向黑夜傾注她溫暖的魅力。

「這裡有許多是不速之客，」她忽然說，「那個女孩也沒有被邀請。他們就是硬要進去，他那麼客氣的人自然不會拒絕。」

「我很想知道他到底是誰，是做什麼的。」湯姆還是不死

心，「我一定查得出來。」

「我現在就可以告訴你，」她回答說，「他是開藥房的，好多家藥房。都是他赤手空拳打拚出來的。」

他們的轎車緩緩地沿著車道開了過來。

「晚安，尼克。」黛西說。

她匆匆看了我一眼，便將目光移往臺階頂端的亮光處，《凌晨三點鐘》──當年流行的華爾滋小調，簡單又帶點悲傷──的樂聲從敞開的門縫中流瀉出來。畢竟，在蓋茨比的宴會裡，這種喧譁、不拘小節的氣氛蘊藏著無限羅曼蒂克的可能性，是她的世界中完全沒有的。在那首歌中，不是隱藏著某種說不出來的吸引力，似乎在呼喚她回去嗎？在這不可思議的昏暗時刻，又會發生什麼奇妙的事？也許會出現某位意想不到的新客人，一位難得又讓人驚訝的客人，或是一位容光煥發的年輕女孩，只要她對蓋茨比輕拋媚眼，或者來段奇蹟似的相遇，就可能使那五年來始終不渝的愛情化為烏有。

那天夜裡我待得很晚。蓋茨比叫我多待一會兒，等他招呼完客人後和我再談幾句，於是我就在花園裡流連了一下子，直到那些下水游泳的客人冷得渾身打顫、高高興興地從漆黑的海灘跑上來，直到每間客房的燈都熄掉了，他才走下臺階，臉上被太陽曬黑的皮膚較往常繃得更緊，眼神發亮但微帶倦意。

「她不喜歡這個宴會。」他脫口就說。

「她當然喜歡。」

「她不喜歡，」他堅持著說，「她玩得不開心。」

蓋茨比沉默不語。我猜他心裡有說不出的失望。

「我覺得跟她之間有很大的距離，」他說，「很難使她懂我的意思。」

「你是說關於宴會的事？」

「宴會？」他一揮手便把所有舉行過的宴會都化為烏有。「老兄，你知道，宴會並不重要。」

他只希望黛西能親口對湯姆說：「我從來沒有愛過你。」等她用這句話把過去四年一筆抹煞後，他們可以計劃一些比較切實的行動。其中一個計畫是：一旦她自由了，他們就立刻回到路易維爾去，蓋茨比要從她家裡把她娶過來──就像五年前一樣。

「可是她不懂我的意思。她以前很懂我的意思，我們常常兩人在一起，一坐就坐上幾個小時。」他說。

他忽然打住不再說下去，然後開始在一條荒涼的小徑上踱來踱去，滿地都是果子皮、丟棄的禮物和被踩爛的花。

「我若是你，就不會對她太過要求。」我大膽地勸他一句。「過去是不能挽回的啊。」

「過去不能挽回？」他不相信地大叫起來，「當然可以！」

他發狂似的環顧四周，彷彿過去正躲在他這棟別墅的黑影裡，觸手可及。

「我要把一切的事安排得像從前一樣，」他堅定地點著頭說，「她等著看吧。」

他接著又說了許多關於過去的事，我猜他是想找回從前愛上黛西時所失去的某種東西，也許是他自我觀念中的某一部分。從

那時候起，他的生活就變得一團糟，可是假如他能回到起點，慢慢重新來過，他就能發現他所失去的究竟是什麼……。

五年前的一個秋夜裡，他倆並肩沿著落葉滿地的道路往下走，最後走到一處沒有樹木的地方，只有皎潔的月光照在人行道上。他們停下腳步，面對面站著。那天夜晚已經有點寒意，空氣中有一種夏盡秋來，帶點神祕的興奮感。屋宅內黯淡的燈火嘤嘤地響入黑夜當中，星斗間有一種喧囂和躁動。蓋茨比從眼角覷見一條條的人行道像是搭成的梯子，直通樹梢天邊一個祕密的處所——他可以攀登到這個高處，只要他單槍匹馬勇往直前，就可登上那高處吸吮生命的瓊漿，大口吞下那神妙無比的玉液了。

當黛西白皙的臉蛋湊到他臉旁，他的心愈跳愈快。他知道只要吻了這個女孩，把自己無可形容的夢想寄託在她短暫的呼吸上，他的心便再也無法像上帝的心一樣輕盈自在了。因此他又等了好一會兒，以便傾聽他那已經注定在星球之間的命運。然後他終於親吻了她。在他嘴脣輕觸之下，她就像一朵含苞的花，為他一瓣一瓣地綻放，而他也就脫胎換骨，從此變成另外一個人。

聽了他這番追溯，雖然覺得他多愁善感，卻也讓我感到忽忽若有所失——也許是很久以前聽過的一段不可捉摸的音節或幾句片斷的歌詞。我一度想開口說話，但又像啞巴一樣，嘴脣動彈而出的只有驚嘆的氣息。於是我幾乎就要想起來的話，就再也說不出口了。

第 7 章

　　就在大家對蓋茨比的好奇心達到頂點時，某個星期六晚上，他別墅裡一盞燈也沒亮──他那大宴賓客的好客作風來得蹊蹺，如今也不明所以地結束了。

　　我起先還不知道，後來漸漸才發覺，那些興致勃勃開進他家車道的大小車輛都只待上一兩分鐘，就又垂頭喪氣地走掉。我心想他會不會是生病了，於是過去看看，來開門的是一個陌生的管家，他面目猙獰，滿臉狐疑地從門內看著我。

　　「蓋茨比先生病了嗎？」

　　「沒有。」過了半晌，他才不情不願地加了一句「先生」。

　　「我好久沒看見他了，有點擔心。能不能請你告訴他卡拉威先生來找過他？」

　　「誰？」那人粗魯地問。

　　「卡拉威。」

　　「卡拉威。好，我會告訴他。」

　　才說完，他砰的一聲就把門關上。

　　我的芬蘭女傭告訴我，蓋茨比早在一個禮拜前就把家裡的傭人都遣散了，另外請了五六個人來。這一批新傭人從不貪圖店家好處去西卵鎮採購，只以電話訂購一些日常用品。據店裡送貨的

夥計說，蓋茨比家的廚房髒得就像豬圈一樣，而鎮上的人也覺得那些新來的人根本不是傭人。

第二天，蓋茨比打了電話給我。

「你是不是預備出門？」我問。

「沒有，老兄。」

「聽說你把所有的傭人都解僱了。」

「我想找不會說閒話的。黛西現在常來……下午的時候。」

因為黛西不認同他那賓客如潮的排場，所以那樣的場面現在就像紙牌屋一樣全垮了。

「渥夫辛想替這些人介紹點事情做。他們是一家兄弟姊妹，從前經營一家小旅館。」

「我明白。」

是黛西叫他打電話來的——問我明天能不能到她家吃午飯，見克小姐也會去。半小時後，黛西親自打電話來，聽到我能去，她似乎鬆了一口氣。看來一定發生了什麼事。然而我還是不敢相信他們會挑這樣的場合做為舞臺——尤其上演的還是蓋茨比在花園裡所勾勒的那幅尷尬的局面。

第二天天氣酷熱——幾乎是夏季的最後一天了，但絕對是整個夏天裡最熱的一天。我搭的火車鑽出隧道進入陽光底下時，只有「全國餅乾公司」工廠尖銳的汽笛聲劃破了中午的寧靜。車廂裡的籐椅墊曬得燙手：坐在我旁邊的婦人汗水滲出了襯衫，後來手裡捏著的報紙也被汗水浸濕了，她不禁熱得嘆了一口大氣，對溽暑的熱氣深感無奈。忽然間，她的錢包啪的一聲掉到地上。

「我的天！」她喘著氣喊。

我彎下腰去替她把錢包拾起來遞還給她，手伸得遠遠的，小心拿著錢包的一個角，表示我沒有覬覦之意。可是四周的每個乘客，包括這位婦人在內，還是不免懷疑我。

「熱啊，熱！」列車長跟面熟的人說。「好熱的天氣！熱！您覺得夠熱嗎？您熱嗎？熱嗎？……」

我從他手中拿回自己的月票，上面留下了他手指的汗漬。試想這種大熱天，誰還有心思去管他跟誰親吻，管他是誰的頭髮緊貼著他弄濕了他睡衣的胸前口袋！

蓋茨比和我站在勃肯納家門口的時候，穿堂裡一陣微風把電話鈴聲吹入我們的耳鼓。

「要老爺去啊？」管家對著聽筒大聲嚷著。「對不起，太太，今天不行——今天中午實在太熱了！」

實際上他要說的是：「好的……好的……讓我去看看。」

他放下電話，滿頭大汗地朝我們走來，把我們的硬挺草帽接過去。

「太太在客廳裡等你們。」他一邊說，一邊多此一舉地替我們指了指客廳的方向。在這麼個大熱天，每一個多餘的舉動都教人看了覺得費力。

因為窗外有帆布篷遮著，客廳裡十分陰涼。黛西和喬丹躺在沙發上，像極了兩尊銀像壓在自己白色的衣裙上，不讓風扇給吹得胡亂飄動。

「我們動不了了。」她們倆異口同聲地說。

　　喬丹和我握了手，她原本古銅色的手指都上了粉，擦得白白的。

　　「運動家湯姆·勃肯納先生呢？」我問道。

　　才問完，我就聽到他低沉粗嘎的聲音，在穿堂上講電話。

　　蓋茨比站在棗紅色地毯的正中央，睜著大眼四處張望。黛西看著他不由得笑了，笑聲甜美動人。一陣細細的粉末從她的胸口飄入了空中。

　　「聽說是湯姆的那個情婦打來的。」喬丹悄悄告訴我。

　　我們沒有出聲。穿堂裡的嗓門拉高了，氣憤地說：「好極了，那我車子就不賣你了……我可沒欠你什麼……以後要是為了這件事在午飯時間來煩我，我可受不了。」

　　「電話已經掛了還要裝腔。」黛西諷刺地說。

　　「他不是裝腔。」我向她保證，「這椿買賣是真的，我聽他們談過。」

　　湯姆猛地把門打開，他粗壯的身體一時把門堵住了，然後匆匆走進客廳。

　　「蓋茨比先生！」他伸出寬大的手掌來歡迎，並未顯露出內心的嫌惡。「很高興見到你……尼克……」

　　「幫我們拿些涼的來喝吧！」黛西喊著。

　　他轉身走出去後，黛西站起來朝蓋茨比走去，她拉下他的頭，往他嘴上吻了一下。

　　「我愛你，你知道的。」她輕聲地說。

　　「拜託，別忘了還有一位女士在這裡。」喬丹說。

黛西面帶懷疑地轉過頭來。

「那妳也吻尼克呀!」

「這女人真粗俗!」

「我不在乎!」黛西大聲地說,一面在磚砌的壁爐前跳了幾個舞步。後來她想起了天氣的炎熱,又乖乖地坐回沙發上。就在這個時候,一個穿著整潔的奶媽牽著一個小女孩走進來。

「親──愛──的小寶貝。」她張開雙臂溫柔地說,「來,讓媽媽好好疼疼妳。」

奶媽鬆開手之後,小孩奔過來,害羞地把頭埋進母親懷裡。

「親愛的小寶貝!媽媽的粉有沒有弄到妳這黃毛丫頭的頭上?來,站起來,跟客人說『您好』。」

蓋茨比和我先後彎下身子來拉拉那隻有些畏縮的手。之後,蓋茨比還是不停以驚訝的眼神看著小女孩。我想他從來就不相信有這個小孩的存在。

「吃午飯前我就把漂亮的衣服穿好了。」小女孩高興地轉過身對黛西說。

「那是因為媽媽要炫耀炫耀妳。」她把臉伏在女兒白皙粉嫩的小脖子後面。「妳呀，妳這個小美人，美得像夢裡的仙女。」

「是啊，」小孩老實不客氣地附和。「喬丹阿姨也穿白色衣裳。」

「妳喜不喜歡媽媽這些朋友？」黛西把她轉過來面對著蓋茨比。「妳看他們漂不漂亮？」

「爸爸呢？」

「她長得不像她父親，」黛西解釋說。「她長得像我。她的頭髮和臉型都像我。」

黛西坐回沙發上靠著。奶媽往前走了一步，伸手牽小孩。

「來，潘咪。」

「再見，寶貝！」

規矩的小女孩依依不捨地回過頭來瞥了一眼，才讓奶媽牽著她的手走出門去，正好湯姆在這時候端了四杯杜松子利克酒回來，杯子裡滿滿的冰塊叮噹作響。

蓋茨比接過一杯酒。

「看起來很冰涼。」他顯得有點緊張。

我們都大口大口地喝下冷飲。

「我在哪裡看過一篇文章，說太陽的溫度一年比一年高，」湯姆親切地說。「還有，不久地球就會掉到太陽裡去——不，我說錯了——剛好相反，太陽的溫度一年比一年還低。」

「到外面來吧，」他轉身對著蓋茨比說，「我帶你看一看這個地方。」

我跟他們一同到外面陽臺上。遙遠碧綠而悶熱的海灣裡，一艘小帆船慢慢滑向外邊比較清新的海域。蓋茨比的視線一直跟隨著它；然後他伸手指著對岸說：「我的家就在你們的正對面。」

「是啊。」

我們的眼睛掠過玫瑰花圃，掠過熱氣烘烘的草地，以及沙灘上一撮撮的亂草，只見那艘白色小船在蔚藍清新的天幕前緩緩移動。再往前看就是波光粼粼的海洋，以及許許多多宜人的小島。

「多麼好的運動，」湯姆點頭稱許，「我真想跟那艘船到海面去玩一兩個鐘頭。」

我們在餐廳裡吃午飯，裡面也遮得陰陰的，大家一面強作歡笑一面喝著冰涼的啤酒。

「今天下午我們怎麼度過？」黛西大聲說，「還有明天，以及接下來的三十年？」

「不要這麼喪氣，」喬丹說，「到了秋天天氣變得涼爽，大家不就又有生氣了？」

「可是現在實在熱得要命。」黛西還是那麼說，幾乎要哭出來的樣子，「什麼事都是亂七八糟的。我們大夥兒進城去吧！」

她的聲浪繼續在熱氣中掙扎，使勁打擊著，似乎要把毫無意識的熱氣塑出形象來。

「我只聽說過有人把馬房改成車庫，」湯姆對蓋茨比說，「但是從來沒有人像我這樣把車庫變成馬房。」

「有誰要進城去？」黛西不死心地問。蓋茨比的眼光瞟到她那邊。「哎喲，」她喊道，「你看起來很涼快。」

他們的目光相遇，彼此注視著對方，渾然忘我。過了一會兒，黛西才勉強把視線轉回餐桌上。

「你看起來總是很涼快的樣子。」她又說了一遍。

黛西剛才明明就是在表白自己對蓋茨比的愛意，湯姆·勃肯納也看到了。他目瞪口呆，不能置信，看看蓋茨比又看看黛西，好像他這才認出她是一位闊別已久的朋友。

「你的樣子好像廣告裡那個人，」她並沒有察覺到，還在對蓋茨比說，「你知道廣告裡那個人——」

「好啦，」湯姆立刻插嘴說，「我很贊成進城去。走吧，我們大家都進城去。」

他站起身來，眼光還是在蓋茨比和他老婆之間閃爍不定。誰也沒有動。

「走啊！」他有點火了。「你們到底怎麼啦，如果要進城，就走啊。」

他極力克制著，手微微發抖地將杯中剩下的啤酒送到嘴邊。黛西出聲之後，我們便起身走到外面滾燙的石子道上。

「我們就這樣去嗎？」她抗議道。「這樣就去？不讓誰先抽根煙嗎？」

「大家吃飯的時候已經抽夠了。」

「哎呀，開心一點嘛，」她央求他。「天氣這麼熱還要吵架。」

他沒有答腔。

「那就隨便你吧，」她說。「喬丹，走吧。」

　　她們上樓去準備，我們三個男人則站在那兒，用腳尖撥弄著熱得發燙的小石子。一彎銀月此刻已經掛在西邊的天空中。蓋茨比欲言又止，但是湯姆已經轉過身來等著他開口。

　　「你的馬房在這裡嗎？」蓋茨比不得已只好隨便問一句。

　　「沿著這條路下去，大概四分之一英里遠的地方。」

　　「喔。」

　　他停了半晌。

　　「我真不懂為何要進城，」湯姆怒氣沖沖地說，「女人家腦子裡老是有這麼多花樣──」

　　「要不要帶一些東西去喝？」黛西從樓上窗口往下喊。

　　「我去拿一瓶威士忌。」湯姆說著，一面走進屋子。

　　蓋茨比僵硬地轉身對我說：「老兄，在他家裡我什麼話也說不出來。」

　　「她輕率的聲音裡總是透露些什麼，」我說，「充滿了……」我遲疑了一下。

　　「她的聲音充滿了錢。」他忽然說道。

　　對了。我以前一直想不通。充滿了錢的聲音──她說話的聲音時高時低，蘊藏著無窮的吸引力，有著金錢響亮的匡噹聲……她就像白色宮殿中高高在上的公主，一個黃金女郎……。

　　湯姆從屋子裡出來，手裡拿著一瓶酒包在毛巾裡，黛西和喬丹跟在他後面，兩人都戴上窄邊緞面小帽，手臂挽著薄綢披肩。

　　「大家都坐我的車去就好了？」蓋茨比提議。他摸一摸車墊上被太陽曬得發燙的綠色皮椅。「我應該把車停在樹蔭下的。」

「你這部車是普通排擋嗎？」湯姆問。

「是的。」

「那麼，你開我的小跑車，讓我開你的車進城好了。」

蓋茨比看起來不太喜歡這項提議。

「我車裡的汽油好像沒剩多少了。」他推辭說。

「汽油還多得很。」湯姆看了看油表，粗暴地說。「而且若是用完了，可以找一個藥房停下來再加。現在的藥房什麼東西都賣。」

聽了這句無意義的話之後，大家都不出聲。黛西皺起眉頭看著湯姆，蓋茨比臉上也泛起一種曖昧的表情，這種表情既陌生又似曾相識。

「走吧，黛西。」湯姆強推著她朝蓋茨比的車子走去。「我就用這輛馬戲團的花車載妳。」

他把車門打開，但她從他的手臂裡掙脫出來。

「你載尼克和喬丹，我們開跑車在後面跟上來。」

她走近蓋茨比身邊，用手碰碰他的外套。喬丹、湯姆和我坐上了蓋茨比車子的前座，湯姆有點不熟悉地試推了幾下排擋，車子往前一衝鑽進悶熱的空氣裡，把他們遠遠地拋到視線之外了。

「你們注意到沒有？」湯姆問。

「注意到什麼？」

他目光銳利地看著我，心裡明白喬丹和我一定早已知道了。

「你們當我是個傻瓜，是不是？」他說，「也許是吧，不過有時候我有一種——一種第二感知，讓我知道該怎麼去做。你們

可能不相信這種事，但是科學……」

　　他打住不再說下去。眼前突發的現實讓他驚醒，把他從理論深淵的邊緣拉回來。

　　「我把這傢伙稍微調查了一下，」他接著說，「早知道我就調查得仔細一點……」

　　「你是說你去找靈媒？」喬丹幽默地問。

　　「什麼？」我們笑了起來，他卻一頭霧水地看著我們。「靈媒？」

　　「去問蓋茨比的事。」

　　「問蓋茨比的事？沒有，我沒有。我是說我大致調查了一下他的背景。」

　　「結果發現他是牛津大學畢業的。」喬丹很幫忙地替他說。

　　「牛津大學！」他全然不信。「他是才怪！你看他身上穿的那套粉紅色衣服。」

　　「不管怎樣他還是牛津畢業的。」

　　「恐怕是新墨西哥的牛津鎮吧，或者是這類鳥不生蛋的地方！」湯姆嗤之以鼻地說。

　　「喂，湯姆。你要是這麼勢利，為什麼還請他吃午飯呢？」喬丹不高興地問。

　　「是黛西請他來的，我們結婚前她就認識這個傢伙——天曉得他們怎麼認識的！」

　　我們發現先前喝的麥酒開始起作用了，大家都變得有點煩躁，於是便保持緘默開了好長一段路。當公路前方艾柯柏格醫師

那雙褪了色的大眼睛映入眼簾，我忽然想起蓋茲比警告過汽油可能不夠。

「夠我們開到城裡了。」湯姆說。

「反正前面就有一個汽油站，」喬丹反駁他說，「我可不想在這大太陽底下半路熄火。」

湯姆不耐煩地把煞車一踩，車子突然在威爾森的招牌下方停住，揚起一陣灰塵。過了一會兒，老闆從車行內走出來，兩眼空洞洞地瞧著我們的車子。

「幫我們加點油！」湯姆粗聲粗氣地大叫，「你以為我們停在這兒幹什麼，看風景嗎？」

「我生病了，」威爾森站在那裡動也不動了。「病了一整天。」

「怎麼了？」

「我已經累垮了。」

「那麼我要自己動手囉？」湯姆問。「剛才在電話裡聽你的

聲音，不是還挺不錯的嗎？」

威爾森費勁地從店門口陰涼的地方走出來，一面喘息一面扭下油箱的蓋子。他的臉在太陽底下顯得發青。

「我不是故意在午飯時打擾你，」他說，「但是我真的很需要錢，又不知道你打算怎麼處理你的那部舊車。」

「這輛車你覺得怎樣？」湯姆問。「我上禮拜買的。」

「很漂亮的黃色車子。」威爾森說，一面用力扭動車門的門把。

「想買嗎？」

「怎麼可能？」威爾森虛弱地笑笑。「算了吧，不過另一部我倒還能有點賺頭。」

「怎麼突然這麼需要錢？」

「我在這兒待太久了，想到其他地方去。我和我太太想搬到西部去。」

「你太太也要去？」湯姆驚訝地大叫。

「她這句話說了有十年了。」他靠在加油機旁歇了歇，用手遮著陽光。「現在不管她願不願意，我都要帶她離開這裡。」

這時那輛小跑車從旁邊急馳而過，揚起一陣塵土，車上有人向我們揮揮手。

「多少錢？」湯姆粗著嗓子問。

「前兩天我發現了一件荒唐的事，」威爾森說，「所以我才決定搬離這裡，這也是為什麼我會為了車子的事來煩你。」

「多少錢？」

「一塊兩毛。」

天氣熱得我頭昏腦脹，起先我一直很不安，後來察覺他還沒懷疑到湯姆身上。他只是發現梅朵瞞著他生活在另外一個世界裡，這個發現把他擊垮了。我看著他，再看看湯姆，因為湯姆自己不到一個小時前也有同樣的發現。我突然有個想法：男人儘管有種族的不同、智力的高下，可是最大的差別還是在於健壯與否。威爾森病得那麼嚴重，所以看起來就像幹了什麼不可饒恕的壞事，好像剛剛把一個可憐女孩的肚子搞大了。

「我會把那部車賣你。」湯姆說，「明天下午就送過來。」

這一帶地方總是令人感到不安，即使是在陽光耀眼的下午也是如此。此刻我忽然把頭掉轉過來，好像有人在警告我提防背後似的。在垃圾堆的上方，艾柯柏格醫師的巨大雙眼仍然在那裡監視著，可是過了一會兒，我發覺離我不到二十呎的地方，另外有一道強烈的目光注視著我們。

在車廠樓上，一扇窗戶的窗簾被微微拉開，梅朵·威爾森正從縫隙往下看著我們的車子。她全神貫注，並沒有察覺到有人在看著她。只見她臉上湧現一陣陣不同的表情，就像沖洗照片一樣，景物慢慢地依序出現。她的表情我覺得很眼熟──這種表情在女人臉上時常可以看到，但是出現在梅朵·威爾森的臉上似乎無法解釋，最後我才發現，她那雙睜得大大的、充滿嫉妒和惶恐的眼睛看的並不是湯姆，而是喬丹·貝克──她錯把喬丹當成湯姆的妻子了。

單純的心一旦陷入困惑便會越陷越深，當我們驅車離去之

後，湯姆覺得自己被驚恐的情緒所鞭打。一小時前，他家有嬌妻外有情婦，一切都有條不紊，如今所有的事都脫離了他的掌控。他本能地猛踩油門，一方面想趕上黛西，一方面想把威爾森拋到腦後。車子以五十英里的時速朝阿斯托利亞奔馳而去，一直追到像蜘蛛網般密布的電車鋼架之間，才看見那部逍遙自在的藍色小跑車。

「五十街附近那幾家大電影院很涼快，」喬丹建議說，「我最喜歡紐約的下午，大家都跑掉了，有種『通體舒暢』的感覺——一種熟透的感覺，好像馬上就會有各種奇奇怪怪的果子掉進你的手裡。」

「通體舒暢」這個字眼使湯姆更加的不安，可是他還沒來得及反駁，前面的小跑車突然停了下來，黛西示意我們停到他們旁邊去。

「我們要上哪兒去？」她喊著問。

「去看電影，好不好？」

「太熱了，」她抱怨道，「你們去吧，我們去兜兜風，待會兒再和你們碰頭。」她又開了個玩笑，可是這次有點勉強，「我們就約在哪個路口碰面吧，只要看見一個叨著兩根煙的傢伙，那就是我。」

「我們別在這裡爭論，」我們後面一輛卡車猛按著喇叭，湯姆不耐煩地說，「你們先跟我到中央公園南邊的『廣場飯店』前面再說。」

他好幾次轉過頭來看看他們的車子有沒有跟上來，要是被車

流隔開，他就會放慢車速等他們趕上。我想他是怕他們會忽然鑽進某條巷道，從此在他的生命中消失。

可是他們沒有這麼做。到了廣場飯店之後，我們莫名其妙地訂了一間豪華套房的客廳。

我們經歷了一連串冗長而激烈的爭辯，才進入這間客廳。究竟是為什麼我也記不得了，但是我清楚地記得，在這一段時間裡，我的內衣濕得像條蛇一樣，纏著身子慢慢往上爬，汗珠沿著背脊競相流下。開房間的主意是這樣來的，起初黛西建議我們訂下五間浴室，每人都去洗個冷水澡，後來又有人說不如「找個地方喝薄荷酒」。每個人都一再地說這種想法「太瘋狂了」——後來又七嘴八舌地搶著跟旅館掌櫃的交涉，不是裝模作樣就是自以為很搞笑⋯⋯。

那間客廳又大又悶，雖然已經是下午四點，打開窗子卻只聞得到從公園樹叢裡飄上來的一陣熱氣。黛西走到鏡子前背對著我們梳整頭髮。

「這間套房好漂亮。」喬丹恭恭敬敬地小聲說著，大家聽了都笑了起來。

「再打開另一扇窗子！」黛西命令著，頭也不回。

「已經沒有其他窗子可開了。」

「那我們最好打電話叫他們送把斧頭上來⋯⋯」

「妳最好不要再喊熱了，」湯姆不耐煩地說，「這樣一直抱怨只會讓妳覺得更熱。」

他打開毛巾，把那瓶威士忌拿出來放在桌上。

「老兄，你就隨她說吧。」蓋茨比說。「是你自己要進城的。」

有好一陣子大家都沒作聲。牆上的電話簿忽然從釘子上滑落，砰的一聲摔到地板上，喬丹輕輕說了聲：「對不起！」——可是這回卻沒有人笑。

「我去撿起來。」我說。

「讓我來。」蓋茨比查看了一下鬆掉的繩子，喃喃地「哼」的一聲，把電話簿往椅子上扔去。

「那是你的口頭禪嗎？」湯姆很不客氣地問。

「什麼？」

「開口、閉口滿嘴的『老兄』，你是從哪裡學來的？」

「你聽著，湯姆。」黛西從鏡子前轉過頭來對他說，「你要是再作人身攻擊，我馬上就離開。打個電話叫他們送點冰塊上來吧，好加在薄荷酒裡。」

湯姆拿起電話筒，壓縮的熱氣立即爆發出聲音，所有人都靜下來，聆聽著樓下傳來的孟德爾頌那莊嚴的《結婚進行曲》。

「竟然有人在這大熱天裡結婚！」喬丹說。

「當然囉……我就是在六月中結婚的。」黛西回憶著，「而且是路易維爾的六月呢！還有一位客人當場昏倒。是哪個客人昏倒了呀，湯姆？」

「畢洛克西。」他回答，怒氣未消。

「一個姓畢洛克西的，外號叫『方塊』，他是做箱子的——真的——他還是田納西州畢洛克西城的人。」

「後來他們把他抬到我家,」喬丹補充說,「因為我家離教堂只有幾步路。他一待就是三個禮拜,直到我父親下逐客令他才離開。他走後第二天我父親就死了。」她停頓了一下又說:「這兩件事並沒有關聯。」

「我以前也認識一個比爾‧畢洛克西,他是曼菲斯人。」我說。

「那是他的堂兄弟。他離開之前把整個家族史都告訴我了。他送了我一根鋁製的球棒,到現在我還在用呢。」

樓下的音樂聲停了下來,婚禮開始進行,此刻窗外傳來一陣長長的喝采,接著又是「好啊,好啊」的歡呼聲,最後響起了爵士樂,開舞了。

「我們都老了,」黛西說,「如果我們還年輕,就會跟著跳起舞了。」

「別忘了畢洛克西的教訓!」喬丹警告她。「湯姆,你是在哪裡認識他的?」

「畢洛克西?」他努力地想了一下。「我不認識他。他是黛西的朋友。」

「他才不是,」黛西否認。「我在那以前從來沒見過他。他是坐你的專車來的。」

「可是他自稱是妳的朋友。他說他是在路易維爾長大的。就在我們要出發前一分鐘,阿薩‧伯德才把他帶來,問我們車上還有沒有空位。」

喬丹微微一笑。

「他大概就這麼一路騙吃騙喝地回家。他還告訴我他是你們那屆耶魯學生會會長。」

湯姆和我茫然地互看一眼。

「你說畢洛克西？」

「別的不說，第一、我們根本沒有什麼會長──」

蓋茨比一隻腳不停地在地板上咚咚咚地敲著，湯姆突然盯著他看。

「對了，蓋茨比先生，聽說你是牛津大學畢業的。」

「也不完全是啦。」

「不必客氣了，我聽說你上過牛津大學。」

「是的……我的確在那裡讀過書。」

一陣緘默之後，湯姆以懷疑和侮辱的口吻說：「你在牛津的時候，大概就是畢洛克西上耶魯的時期吧！」

大家又是一陣緘默。一個服務生敲了敲門，手裡拿了碎薄荷和冰塊進來，當他說了聲「謝謝」並輕輕關上門之後，卻仍未打破沉寂。這個關鍵的細節終究還是要澄清的。

「我跟你說了，我上過牛津大學。」蓋茨比說。

「我聽見了，可是我想知道你是什麼時候去的。」

「一九一九年，我只在那裡唸了五個月，所以我不能說我是牛津畢業的。」

湯姆看了大家一眼，不知道我們是否也和他一樣感到懷疑。可是我們大家都看著蓋茨比。

「那是停戰以後他們為一些軍官安排的機會。」他繼續說。

「我們可以選擇英國或法國的任何大學。」

我真想過去拍拍他的背。我又和從前一樣,再度對他充滿信心。

黛西面帶微笑地站起來走到桌子前面。

「把酒打開,湯姆。」她命令道,「我替你調一杯薄荷酒。喝了酒你就不會覺得自己那麼蠢……你看這些薄荷葉子!」

「等一下,」湯姆厲聲說,「我還要問蓋茨比先生一個問題。」

「請問吧。」蓋茨比很客氣地說。

「你跑到我家裡來,到底想鬧些什麼?」

他們終於攤牌了,蓋茨比感到很滿意。

「他並沒有鬧什麼事,」黛西沮喪地看看這人又看看那人。「胡鬧的人是你,請你自制一點。」

「自制!」湯姆不敢置信地重複她的話。「難道要我眼睜睜看著一個來歷不明的小子跟自己的老婆上床,這才趕時髦嗎?這我可辦不到……這年頭的人已經完全沒有家庭觀念了,接下來他們就什麼都不管,要搞黑白通婚了!」

他激動地漲紅了臉,覺得世上唯有他獨自堅守著文明的最後防線。

「我們大家都是白人呀。」喬丹低聲說了一句。

「我知道自己不受歡迎,我也沒有舉辦過大型宴會。在這個庸俗世界裡,好像非得把自己家裡弄得像豬圈,才能交朋友!」

我雖然很生氣,我們每個人都是如此,可是每次他一開口我

就忍不住想笑。一個酒色之徒居然也這樣滿嘴自命清高。

「老兄，我也要告訴你一件事──」蓋茨比開口了，可是黛西已猜出他接下來要說什麼。

「請你不要說了！」她無助地打斷了他的話。「我們還是回去吧。大家都回家，好不好？」

「好主意。」我站起身來。「走吧，湯姆，沒有人想要喝酒了。」

「我倒要聽聽蓋茨比先生有什麼話要告訴我。」

「你太太並不愛你。」蓋茨比說。「她從來沒有愛過你。她愛的人是我。」

「你瘋啦！」湯姆衝動地說。

蓋茨比驀地跳了起來，情緒非常激動。

「她從來沒愛過你，你聽見了嗎？」他喊叫著。「她當初嫁給你只不過是因為我很窮，她累了，不想再等我了。那是她一生的大錯，但是她的心裡除了我之外，從來沒愛過任何人！」

聽到這裡，喬丹和我都想走了，可是湯姆和蓋茨比卻爭相堅持不讓我們走，好像兩人都沒有什麼好隱瞞的，也允許我們有機會分享他們內心的情感。

「黛西，妳坐下。」湯姆試著以嚴父的口吻說話，但並沒有成功。「這是怎麼回事？妳老老實實告訴我。」

「我已經告訴你是怎麼一回事了。」蓋茨比說。「已經有五年了──只是你不知道。」

湯姆忽然轉向黛西。

「妳跟這傢伙已經偷偷幽會五年了？」

「不是幽會，」蓋茨比說，「我們沒法見面。可是這段期間我們彼此愛著對方，老兄，只是你不知道。有時候我真覺得好笑。」可是他眼中並無笑意。「想到你還被蒙在鼓裡，竟然毫不知情。」

「哦，你要說的就是這些啊！」湯姆像牧師一樣把他粗粗的指頭合攏，然後往後靠在椅背上。

「你瘋了！」他忽然叫出聲。「我無法得知五年前發生的事，因為那時我還沒認識黛西，可是我猜不出你怎麼會有機會跟她接近，除非你是到後門送貨的。至於你其餘的話都是胡說八道。黛西嫁給我的時候是愛我的，現在她還是愛我。」

「不對！」蓋茨比搖著頭說。

「隨你怎麼說，反正她是愛我的，只是她偶爾會有一些傻念頭，不知道自己在做什麼。」他點點頭。「而且我也愛黛西。雖然偶爾我也會逢場作戲，鬧鬧笑話，可是我總是會回頭，我心裡始終愛著黛西。」

「你少噁心了。」黛西說。她轉身向我，聲音忽然降低一個音節，使整個屋子充滿了她對她丈夫的譏諷：「你知道我們為什麼會離開芝加哥？真奇怪，竟然沒有人把那次他逢場作戲的事告訴你。」

蓋茨比走過來站在她身邊。

「黛西，那些都過去了。」他認真地說。「現在已經無所謂了。妳老實告訴他——告訴他妳從來沒有愛過他——從此，所有

145

的事就一筆勾銷。」

她眼神空洞地看著他。「是啊，我怎麼可能愛他——怎麼可能？」

「妳從來沒有愛過他。」

她猶疑了一下。她帶著求救的眼神看著我和喬丹，好像她到現在才了解自己在做什麼事——又好像她根本沒有準備要做任何事。但是木已成舟，後悔已經太晚了。

「我從來沒愛過他。」她說，口氣很勉強。

「即使在夏威夷卡皮歐蘭尼的時候也不愛嗎？」湯姆忽然問道。

「不愛。」

樓下舞廳隱約而模糊的樂聲，隨著悶熱的空氣傳送了上來。

「為了不讓妳的鞋子弄溼，我從『酒缽號』遊艇把妳抱上岸，那時妳也不愛我嗎？」他的聲音溫柔有磁性……「黛西？」

「請你不要再說了。」她的聲音依舊冷淡，但已無怨恨。她看著蓋茨比。「唉，傑伊！」她說，她那試著要點煙的手一直抖個不停，忽然她把香煙和燃著的火柴都扔到地毯上。

「唉，你要求的太過分了！」她向蓋茨比叫道。「現在我是愛你——這還不夠嗎？過去的事我無能為力了。」她忍不住哭了起來。「我確實愛過他——但是我也愛著你。」

蓋茨比睜大了雙眼，隨後又閉上。

「妳也愛著我？」他重複了一遍。

「就連這句話也是假的。」湯姆狠狠地說。「她根本不知道

146

有你這麼一個人。告訴你──黛西跟我之間有些事你一點都不了解，我們永遠也忘不了。」

他這些話似乎刺傷了蓋茨比的心。

「我要跟黛西單獨談談。」他堅持地說。「她現在太過激動了……」

「即使跟你單獨談，我也不會說我從來沒愛過湯姆。」她坦承，「因為那不是真心話。」

「當然不是真心話。」湯姆附和道。

她轉身對著丈夫，「你說得好像你很在乎我？」

「當然在乎，從現在起我會更用心照顧妳。」

「你還是不懂，」蓋茨比心裡有點慌了。「今後你再也不必照顧她了。」

「是嗎？」湯姆睜大眼睛笑了起來。他現在已經可以控制住自己了。「這話怎麼說呢？」

「黛西要離開你了。」

「胡說。」

「我是打算這麼做。」她顯然費了好大的勁才說出口。

「她不會離開我的！」湯姆忽然對著蓋茨比大吼，「何況是為了一個庸俗的騙子，連送她的戒指也得用偷的。」

「我受不了了！」黛西大叫，「求求你，我們走吧。」

「你以為你是誰啊？」湯姆大吼。「你是梅爾‧渥夫辛的那幫狐群狗黨──這一點我很清楚。我已經把你那些事調查了一番，明天我會再進一步調查。」

「隨你高興，老兄。」蓋茨比鎮定地說。

「我知道你那些所謂的『藥房』實際上是什麼。」他轉過身來很快地對我們說，「他跟那個叫渥夫辛的在這裡和芝加哥買下許多藥房，偷偷販酒。這只是他其中的一個小把戲。我第一次看見他，就看出他是個賣私酒的，我猜得果然沒錯。」

「怎麼？」蓋茨比很有禮貌地說。「你的朋友華特・柴思是跟我們合夥的嗎？」

「結果你擺了他一道，對不對？你害他在紐澤西坐了一個月的牢！天啊，你真該聽聽華特是怎樣罵你的！」

「他來加入我們的時候是個窮光蛋，他很高興有機會賺幾個錢，老兄。」

「你別叫我『老兄』！」湯姆喊道。蓋茨比沒有應聲。「要不是渥夫辛恐嚇他，華特本來可以告你違法賭博的。」

蓋茨比的臉上再次出現那種既陌生又似曾相識的神情。

「那個開藥房的勾當不過是小意思，」湯姆慢慢地接著說，「你目前在搞什麼花樣，華特連說都不敢說。」

我望了黛西一眼，見她看著蓋茨比，又看看她丈夫，神情顯得很驚慌。我又瞥向喬丹，她抬著頭，下巴上似乎又頂著一件無形的東西。然後我又轉過頭去看蓋茨比——他的表情使我吃了一驚。他的樣子好像他「殺了人」似的——我得先聲明，我還是很鄙視在他花園裡聽到的那些謠言。然而在那一剎那，他臉上的表情卻也只能用這句話來形容。

這種表情一閃即逝，然後他開始激動地對黛西說話，他否認

一切，辯稱自己什麼都沒做，連沒有受到指責的罪狀也抵賴得一乾二淨。但是他說得越多，黛西就越畏縮，後來他只好放棄。在悄悄流逝的午後時光裡，只剩下一個沉寂的夢，還在試著觸摸那再也觸摸不到的東西，還在痛苦絕望地掙扎著，只想再聽聽屋子裡那已經消失的聲音。

那個聲音再度哀求要離開。

「湯姆，我求求你！我實在受不了啦。」

黛西驚恐的眸子透露出，不論她曾有任何意圖、任何勇氣，現在都已全然消失。

「你們兩人一起回家吧，黛西，」湯姆說。「搭蓋茨比先生的車。」

她驚懼地看著湯姆，但他十分堅持，並以一種寬大而帶著輕蔑的口氣說：「妳儘管去吧。他不會再糾纏妳了，我想他應該明白，那自不量力的愛情現在已經結束了。」

他們倆就這樣不發一語地走了，像燭光一樣熄滅了，像一件偶發事件，以後再也不會發生，也像兩具幽魂，就連我們的同情心都無從向他們表示。

過了一會兒，湯姆站起來把那瓶未開的威士忌捲進毛巾裡。

「要喝點兒嗎？喬丹？……尼克？」

我沒搭理他。

「尼克？」他又問了一遍。

「什麼？」

「要不要喝一點？」

「不要……我剛才記起來，今天是我的生日。」

我今年三十歲了。眼前即將展開的，似乎是一條未來十年坎坷不平的道路。

我們坐上湯姆的小跑車動身回長島時，已經七點了。湯姆不停地說話，看起來又得意又快活，但他的聲音對我和喬丹而言，就好像人行道兩旁的嘈雜聲和頭頂上高架鐵道的隆隆聲一樣的遙遠。人類的同情心是有限度的，我們很樂於把剛才那場爭吵隨著城市的燈火一起拋諸腦後。三十歲——眼前等待著我的可能是十年孤寂的生活，單身的朋友會逐漸變少，熱情日漸減少，自己的頭髮也一根一根地稀疏。可是我身邊有喬丹，她不像黛西那樣傻，把早已忘懷的夢想年復一年揪住不放。我們的車子駛過烏黑的鐵橋時，她那張慘白的臉龐無力地依靠在我的肩頭，她緊緊握住我的手，而我三十歲的生日，就在這溫暖的慰藉中度過了。

於是我們的車子就在微涼的暮色中，繼續朝生命終站駛去。

米可利斯是個年輕的希臘人，驗屍的時候他是主要的證人，他在垃圾堆旁邊開了一家咖啡館。那天，他午覺一直睡到五點過後熱氣散去，當他醒來閒逛到修車廠，看見喬治・威爾森在辦公室裡病懨懨的——看起來的確是很不舒服的樣子，他的臉色就像他的髮色一樣蒼白，而且渾身發抖。米可利斯勸他上床去睡一會兒，但威爾森不肯，說這樣會影響生意。這時候，樓上忽然爆出一陣吵雜聲。

「我把我老婆鎖在上面。」威爾森很冷靜地解釋說。「她得在那裡待到後天，然後我們就搬到別的地方去。」

米可利斯聽了這話頗為驚訝。他們做了四年的鄰居，他怎麼也想不出威爾森會說出這樣的話來。平時他總是精疲力竭的樣子，沒事的時候，他就坐在門口望著路上來往的人車。若是有人和他說話，他也總是無精打采地笑著附和。他凡事都聽老婆的，完全沒有一點自己的主張。

因此，米可利斯自然很想知道發生了什麼事，可是威爾森一個字也不肯說，反而用懷疑的眼光看著這位鄰居，還問他某時某日他在做些什麼。米可利斯漸漸感到不安，這時正好有幾個工人從門前經過，往他的咖啡館走去，他就趁機溜走，打算晚點兒再過來。但是他沒再回去，可能是忘記了。七點剛過不久，他又再到外面來，聽到威爾森太太在車行樓下破口大罵，才使他想起先前他和威爾森的對話。

「打我啊！」他聽見她大聲嚷著。「打呀，用力打啊，你這個沒種的東西！」

過了一會兒，她衝出門來，在黃昏的暮色中揮舞著雙手，口中大聲叫喊——他還沒來得及走出餐館的門口，一切就結束了。

那部「兇車」——第二天報紙上寫的——並沒有停下來。車子從蒼茫的暮色中突然出現，出事後稍微遲疑了一下，然後在前面轉了個彎就消失無蹤了。米可利斯連車子的顏色都沒看清楚——他告訴第一個警察說是淺綠色。另一部開往紐約方向的車子，在經過出事地點一百碼之後停了下來，駕駛人趕忙跑過來，只見梅朵·威爾森倒在路中央一命嗚呼，塵土裡混雜著她暗褐色濃稠的血。

米可利斯和這個人最先趕到她旁邊，但是他們扯開她汗濕的襯衫時，卻看見她左邊的乳房已經鬆垮下來，看來已經沒有心跳了。她的嘴巴張得大大的，嘴角有些破裂，好像要把她積蓄一輩子的精力一口氣吐出來卻被噎住一樣。

我們大老遠就看見三、四輛汽車停在那裡，四周圍站著一群人。

「出車禍了！」湯姆說。「那可好，威爾森終於有點生意做了。」

他放慢車速，可是沒有打算停車，直到我們靠近之後，看見車行門口那些人面色凝重，他才不自覺地踩了煞車。

「我們去看一下，」他覺得有點可疑。「看一下就好。」

這時我才聽見車行裡不斷傳來一陣陣空洞的哀號，我們下了車走向車行門口時，才聽清楚有人喘著氣不斷地呻吟著「喔，天啊！」

「出事了。」湯姆激動地說。

他墊起腳尖，從群眾頭上往車行望過去，只見裡頭一盞用鐵絲網罩著的黃色燈泡，在天花板上搖搖

晃晃的。他忽然大吼,接著便以他孔武有力的手臂猛力推開兩旁
的人群,擠了進去。

　　被他推開的人群馬上又靠攏過來,並發出陣陣抱怨聲。有一
陣子我什麼也看不見。後來新到來的群眾試著從外圍擠入,我和
喬丹也突然被擠了進去。

　　梅朵‧威爾森的屍體放在牆邊一張工作檯上,包裹著一層層
的毛毯,好像在這悶熱的夜晚她還覺得冷一樣,而湯姆正背對著
我們低頭看著屍體,身體一動也不動。他旁邊站著一名摩托車警
察,正忙著把相關證人的姓名抄在小本子上,一面流著汗,一面
塗塗改改。起初聽到的哀號聲在空洞的車行裡引起了許多回聲,
我一時聽不出是從哪裡來的,後來才看見威爾森站在辦公室高起
的門檻上,雙手抓著門框,身子不停地搖晃著。有一個人在跟他
低聲說話,還不時把手搭在他的肩上,可是威爾森卻彷彿又聾又
瞎一樣。他的目光從那搖晃的燈泡慢慢移到牆邊的桌上,然後又
突然轉回去看那盞燈,還不停地用尖銳、可怕的聲音喊著:
「喔,我的天啊!喔,我的天啊!喔,我的天啊!」

　　這時,湯姆猛然抬起頭來,呆呆地環顧了車行之後,對著警
察喃喃地不知說些什麼。

　　「M─A─V─」警察說,「─O─」

　　「不對,是R─」證人更正說,「M─A─V─R─O─」

　　「你聽我說!」湯姆對著警察粗暴地說。

　　「R─」警察又寫下,「O─」

　　「G─」

「Ｇ—」湯姆寬大的手掌重重地按在警察肩上，那警察才抬起頭問道：「你想幹什麼？」

「我想知道……出了什麼事？」

「她被汽車撞了，當場死亡。」

「當場死亡。」湯姆瞪著眼重複說了一遍。

「她跑到路中間。不知道哪個混蛋，車子停都沒停。」

「有兩部車子，」米可利斯說，「一部開來，一部開去，懂了嗎？」

「往哪個方向？」警察機靈地問。

「兩部車反方向。她呢——」他的手朝著毯子舉起來，但舉到一半就連忙放下。「她跑到路上，從紐約來的那部車把她撞個正著，車速大概三、四十英里那麼快。」

「這地方名叫什麼？」警察問道。

「沒有地名。」

一位皮膚不太黑、穿戴整齊的黑人走上前來。

「那部車子是黃色的。」他說，「黃顏色的大車。很新。」

「你親眼看見車禍是怎麼發生的嗎？」警察問。

「沒有，但是那部車後來超越過我的車，車速在四十英里以上，大概有五、六十英里。」

「過來這裡，我要抄下你的名字。喂，讓開點！我要把他的名字抄下來。」

剛才這段對話，一定已經傳到在辦公室門口坐立不安的威爾森耳裡，因為他的哀號中忽然出現新的內容：「你不用告訴我那

部車的樣子！我知道是什麼車！」

我看著湯姆，發現他外套底下背上的肌肉緊繃起來。他快速地走到威爾森面前，兩手緊握住他的肩膀。

「你要振作一點。」他用粗獷的聲音安慰他。

威爾森的眼光落在湯姆身上──他猛地挺直了身子，然後兩腿一軟，幾乎要跪倒下去，幸好湯姆把他扶住。

「你聽著，」湯姆搖搖他說，「我剛從紐約來到這裡，是要把那部小跑車開來給你的。今天下午我開的那部黃色車子不是我的……你聽清楚沒有？我已經一整個下午沒有看到那部車了。」

只有那個黑人和我站得夠近，才可以聽到湯姆說的話，但那個警察聽出說話的聲音有點蹊蹺，趕忙將嚴厲的目光投射過來。

「你們在說些什麼？」他質問道。

「我是他的朋友。」湯姆回過頭來，但兩手還緊緊抓住威爾森的身子。「他說他知道闖禍的車子……是一部黃色的車子。」

警察憑著直覺懷疑地看著湯姆。

「你的車子是什麼顏色？」

「藍色的，一部小跑車。」

「我們剛從紐約開到這兒。」我說。

有個人剛好開車跟在我們後面，證實了我們的話，於是警察便轉過身去。

「好，請再把你的名字清清楚楚地跟我說一遍……」

湯姆把威爾森像玩偶一樣提起來，提到辦公室裡，讓他坐在椅子上，然後自己又出來。

「有哪位能到裡邊來陪他坐一會兒。」他很權威地下命令，

一面說一面盯著站得最近的兩個人，這兩個人彼此望了一眼，才不情願地走進辦公室裡。湯姆隨後把門關上，走下臺階，眼光避開那張工作檯。他經過我身邊時低聲說：「我們出去吧。」

湯姆看起來有一點侷促不安的樣子，他又用那雙粗壯的臂膀開路，我們從人群中擠了出去，正好一位醫生拎著公事包匆匆趕來，他是半個鐘頭前大家還抱著希望時去請來的。

湯姆慢慢地將車子開走，轉了彎之後便使勁地踩著油門，小跑車在黑夜中奔馳。過了一會兒，我聽見低低的啜泣聲，接著就看見湯姆的臉上淚水縱橫。

「沒種的畜牲！」他抽噎地罵道，「竟然連車子都沒停。」

湯姆・勃肯納的別墅忽然在漆黑的樹叢中間出現在我們眼前。湯姆把車開到走廊前停下，抬頭望向二樓，爬滿藤蔓的兩扇窗子透出了光亮。

「黛西到家了。」他說。我們下車時，他看了我一眼，眉頭微微皺起。

「尼克，我剛才應該讓你在西卵下車的。今晚我們不會有什麼事可做了。」

他像變了一個人，說起話來沉著而果斷。我們走過鋪滿月光的碎石路到了陽臺，他簡單幾句話就把情況處理妥當。

「我去打電話叫一部車送你回去。等車的時候，你和喬丹先到廚房，我叫傭人給你們準備吃的——如果你們想吃點什麼。」他推開了門。「進來吧。」

「不了，謝謝。請你替我叫部車吧，我在外面等就好了。」

喬丹把她的手放在我的胳臂上。

「你不進來坐一會兒兒嗎，尼克？」

「不了，謝謝。」

我忽然覺得有點難受，很想一個人靜一靜，但是喬丹又多待了一下子。

「現在才九點半。」她說。

我是絕對不會進去的，一整天和他們在一起我受夠了，忽然間覺得連喬丹也包括在內。她大概從我臉上的表情看出了些端倪，便轉身跑上臺階進屋子裡去了。我雙手抱著頭坐了幾分鐘，後來聽見屋子裡管家打電話叫計程車的聲音，隨後我就慢慢沿著車道往外走，打算到大門口去等。

我還沒走上二十碼，就聽見有人叫著我的名字，我看見蓋茨比從兩叢矮樹中走出來。當時我一定覺得不可思議，只注意到他那件粉紅色的衣服在月光下閃閃發光。

「你在這兒做什麼？」我問。

「只是在這兒站站，老兄。」

不知怎麼的，我覺得他似乎想幹些什麼卑鄙的勾當——待會兒他大概準備進屋子裡打劫。這時要是「渥夫辛那幫人」猙獰的面孔在他後面漆黑的灌木叢中出現，我也不會感到驚訝。

「回來路上你有沒有見到什麼事故？」過一分鐘他才問我。

「看見了。」

他遲疑了一下。

「那女人死了嗎？」

157

「死了。」

「我想也是。我跟黛西說她一定死了。她早晚都要知道的，不如早些讓她有心理準備，以免一下子承受太大的打擊。我看她還挺撐得住的。」

聽他這樣說，好像黛西的反應才是唯一要緊的事。

「我們抄小路回西卵，把車子停在我的車庫裡，」他接著說。「我想應該沒有人看見我們，當然我也不是很肯定。」

這時我已經討厭他到極點了，因此覺得沒必要告訴他他的想法是錯的。

「那個女人是誰？」他問。

「姓威爾森，她丈夫是車行的老板。這件車禍到底是怎麼發生的？」

「唉，我想把方向盤轉過來──」他打住了，我才忽然猜到事情的真相。

「是黛西開的車？」

「是的，」他停了一會兒才說，「不過我當然會說開車的是我。你也知道，我們離開紐約的時候她很緊張，她覺得開車可以讓她鎮定下來……就在我們和對面開過來的車會車時，那個女人突然衝出來，她好像認識我們似的，想和我們說話。黛西先是把車頭轉開，想閃避那個女人，可是看到迎面來了一輛車，她一時緊張又轉了回來。我連忙伸手去幫她，才一碰到方向盤，我就覺得車子一震──一定當場把她撞死了。」

「她幾乎給開膛剖肚了……」

「別說了，老兄。」他畏縮了。「總之，黛西拚命踩油門。我叫她停下來，但她卻停不住，我只好把緊急煞車拉上。車子停了之後，她倒在我的腿上，我就接手繼續往前開。」

「明天她就會沒事了。」過了一會兒他又說。「我在這裡等一會兒，看湯姆會不會為了下午的事為難她。她把自己鎖在房裡，要是他動粗，黛西就會把燈熄了再開作為暗號。」

「他不會碰她的。」我說。「他目前腦子裡想的不是她。」

「我不相信這傢伙，老兄。」

「你打算等多久？」

「必要的話，我會整晚守候。至少等他們都去睡覺才行。」

我忽然有了一個新的念頭。萬一有人告訴湯姆開車的是黛西，他可能會懷疑事情並非出乎偶然──他可能會做出任何臆測。我看著別墅，樓下有兩三個窗戶亮著，二樓黛西的臥房則透出粉紅色的光。

「你在這裡等著。」我說。「我去看看有什麼動靜。」

我沿著草坪邊緣走回去，輕輕穿過碎石路，然後踮起腳尖走上臺階。客廳的窗簾是敞開的，我看了看，裡面沒有人。我穿過陽臺──就在三個月前某個六月的夜晚，我們一同在這裡用餐──走到一扇長方形的窗子前，我猜是廚房的窗子，裡面的燈也點著，雖然簾幕已經拉上，但我發現窗沿露出一條細縫。

黛西和湯姆面對面坐在餐桌前，兩人中間放著一盤冷掉的烤雞和兩瓶啤酒。他隔著桌子專注地對她說話，還把他的手擱在她的手上。她偶爾會抬起頭看他，並且點頭表示同意。

他們的樣子並不快樂，桌上的烤雞和啤酒也都沒動——可是也不能說他們不快樂。這種畫面，很明顯地流露出一種自然的親密感，任何人看了都會覺得他們在那裡一同策劃著什麼。

我躡著腳尖悄悄從陽臺上走下時，聽見計程車沿著漆黑的車道往別墅開來。我走回車道上，蓋茨比還在原地等著。

「裡面一切都安好吧？」他急切地問道。

「是的，都很平靜。」我猶疑了一下。「你還是回家去睡覺吧。」

他搖搖頭。

「我要在這兒一直等到黛西上床睡覺。再見了，老兄。」

他把兩手插進外套的口袋裡，轉過身繼續凝視著那棟房子，好像我在場有損他神聖的使命似的。我只好離開，留下他站在月光下——空守著。

第 8 章

　　我一整晚都睡不著。海灣上的霧笛不停地哀鳴，我也在怪異的現實與駭人的怪夢中輾轉反側。天快亮的時候，我聽見一輛計程車開上蓋茨比家的車道，我馬上跳下床來穿衣服——我覺得有些話想告訴他，得警告他一下，等到天亮就太遲了。

　　我穿過草坪，看見他別墅的大門還開著，他靠在穿堂裡的一張桌子旁邊，不知道是因為沮喪或失眠，他整個人顯得無精打采。

　　「什麼事都沒發生。」他懶懶地說。「我一直等到清晨四點，看見她走到窗口，站了一會兒，然後就把燈熄了。」

　　那天晚上，為了找根香煙，我們兩人走過一個又一個房間，我從來沒有想到他的別墅有這麼大。我們推開那些帳篷似的厚重帷幔，在黑暗中沿著綿延不盡的牆壁摸索著電燈開關，一度還撞到一架鬼魅般的鋼琴。不知何故，到處都積了厚厚的灰塵，每個房間都散發出一股霉味，好像已經多日沒有通風。最後我在一張似乎從未看過的桌子上找到一個煙盒，裡面還有兩根乾癟的香煙。我們把客廳的大窗戶打開，坐下來對著外面的黑夜抽菸。

　　「你應該去避避鋒頭。」我說。「他們一定會查出來是你的車子。」

「老兄，要我現在就離開嗎？」

「到大西洋城去待一個禮拜，或是到蒙特婁去。」

蓋茨比毫不考慮地拒絕。在還不知道黛西做何打算之前，他怎麼可以輕易離開她？他還抓著最後一絲希望不放，我實在不忍心搖醒他。

也就是在這天晚上，蓋茨比告訴了我他年少時跟隨丹·柯迪先生的那一段傳奇故事——他到現在才告訴我，是因為「傑伊·蓋茨比」已經像玻璃做的一樣，被湯姆無情的打擊砸得粉碎。長久以來，他賣力演出的那齣神祕而華麗的戲劇，如今也不得不落幕。我以為此刻他應該毫無保留地說出一切，不料他卻只想談關於黛西的事。

她是他生平所認識的第一位「大家閨秀」。他曾經以各種捏造的身份與這個階層的人接觸，但總覺得有一層無形的藩籬將他們隔開。而黛西卻如此令他動心。起初他是跟泰勒軍營裡的其他軍官一起到她家作客，後來就單獨前去。她的家令他驚奇不已——他從未看過這樣華麗的房子，但這棟房子之所以吸引他，主要還是因為黛西住在裡頭——這是她晨昏作息的地方，就像他在軍中住的帳篷一樣。這棟房子有一種濃厚的神祕感，讓人隱約覺得樓上還有更美麗、更涼快的臥房，穿堂裡也好像不時有宴會歡笑的聲音和熱情洋溢的氣氛，還可能有著英雄兒女的浪漫史，這些不是陳年舊事，而是新鮮的、活生生的，就像今年閃亮登場的新車，也像擺滿了豔麗鮮花的舞會。令他更興奮的是，已經有很多男人為黛西傾倒，這點更增添了她在他心目中的份量。在這

屋子裡，四處都能感覺到這些人的存在，空氣中充斥著他們的身影與回音，以及沸騰的情緒。

可是他心裡明白，他之所以能出現在黛西家裡，不過是件巧事。不管成為傑伊·蓋茨比之後他有多麼光榮，當時的他只是個沒有家世、一文不名的窮小子，為他掩飾身份的這一身軍服也隨時可能褪下來。因此，他盡可能地把握每一分每一秒，盡情地享受眼前所能得到的，狼吞虎嚥、不顧一切——終於，在十月裡一個靜寂的晚上，他佔有了黛西，佔有了她的身體，佔有她，只因為實際上他連碰一碰她的手的資格都沒有。

或許，他會因此看輕自己，畢竟他以不正當的名義佔有了她。我指的倒不是他冒充家財萬貫的富家子弟欺騙她，而是他故意使黛西有一種安全感，讓她以為他的出身背景跟她相仿——他有十足的能力可以照顧她。實際上他並沒有這樣的能力，他沒有富裕的家世作為後盾，而且在無情的政府支配之下，他隨時都有可能被派遣到天涯海角去。

可是他並沒有看輕自己，事情的發展也沒有像他想像中的那樣。起初他只想玩玩，然後一走了之，但後來他發現自己正努力追求一個夢寐以求的目標。他知道黛西很特別，但他不知道究竟一位「大家閨秀」能有多麼特別。他們道別之後，她便回到她豪華的家，返回她富麗的生活，留下蓋茨比一個人——一無所有。只是他覺得自己已經擁有了她，如此罷了。

兩天之後他們再度相遇，感到不安的還是蓋茨比，他好像有種受騙的感覺。燦爛的星光灑在她家陽臺上，當她轉過身來，讓

大亨小傳

他親吻她那可愛、奇妙的嘴唇時，籐椅也很時髦地吱吱作響。那天她著了涼，聲音變得沙啞，但也更加迷人，一時蓋茨比不勝感動，驚覺到財富中隱藏了多少的青春和神祕，驚覺到那麼多的衣裳是何其新穎華麗，更驚覺到黛西像一彎銀月安穩、驕傲地高踞天空，完全不識窮人掙扎的苦痛。

「老兄，我真的沒法向你形容我當時有多麼驚訝，發現自己愛上了她。有一段時間我甚至希望她摒棄我，可是她沒有，因為她也愛上了我。她認為我是一個見識淵博的人，因為我懂得許多她不懂的事……所以，我就是這樣陷入情網而不能自拔，把雄心壯志都忘得一乾二淨，而且忽然之間什麼都不在乎了。假使向她訴說未來的計畫就可以讓自己得到更大的快樂，又何必去做什麼轟轟烈烈的大事呢？」

在他的部隊移往海外的前一天下午，他把黛西抱在懷裡，兩人默默坐了好久。那是個寒冷的秋日，屋子裡生了火，烘得她兩頰緋紅。她不時移動身子，他的手臂也跟著稍微改換位置，有一回他低頭親吻她烏黑光亮的秀髮。那天下午他們獲得片刻的寧靜，似乎要為第二天過後就要開始的長久分離留下深刻的記憶。在他們相愛的那幾個月裡，從未有過此刻這樣的親密，也從未像此刻這樣心心相印。她靜默的嘴唇輕輕掠過他外套的肩頭，他也溫柔地碰觸她的每一個指尖，彷彿唯恐把她從睡夢中驚醒一樣。

他在軍中表現優異，還沒有上前線去就已經當到上尉。等到阿爾岡戰役之後又晉升為少校，指揮一師的機槍部隊。停戰以後他迫不及待地想回國，但不知怎麼地作業上出了問題，結果把他

送到牛津去。他非常著急，因為黛西來信的語氣顯得有些焦急和絕望。她不明白他為什麼不能即刻回來，她一直感受到外界的壓力，她需要見他，想感受到他在身邊陪著，好讓她確信自己並沒有做錯事情。

因為黛西還年輕，她的世界是天真、快樂而繁華的，充滿了舞樂的時代節奏，透過流行歌曲為逝水年華下一個註腳。薩克斯風徹夜吹奏著《畢爾街》憂鬱的藍調樂曲，伴隨著成千上百的金鞋銀履婆娑起舞。每天的午茶時刻，舞廳裡到處瀰漫著這種低沉而甜美的狂熱，讓人隨之心跳不已。女孩子們鮮豔的臉龐像一瓣瓣殘落的玫瑰，被憂傷的樂聲在舞池中吹得東飄西盪。

藉由黃昏的宴會，黛西再度隨著季節開始活躍。轉眼間她又可以每天和五、六個男人約會，到了黎明才昏昏入睡，晚禮服的薄紗和首飾，丟在睡榻旁邊的地板上，混在即將凋謝的蘭花堆裡。可是她內心卻不時有個聲音在吶喊著，要她下一個決定。她要立刻重新塑

造自己的人生 —— 但要下定決心需要憑靠一些外力 —— 愛情也好、金錢也好，總之必須是非常實際而又唾手可得的。

仲春之際，湯姆·勃肯納的出現使這股外力形成了。他相貌堂堂，家產雄厚，黛西對他的追求感到受寵若驚。毫無疑問的，黛西的內心有過一番掙扎，可是倒也總算如釋重負。她的信送達蓋茨比手中時，他還待在牛津。

長島此刻已經天亮，我們把樓下其餘的窗子都打開，讓搖曳的光線透進屋子裡來，在屋內灑下明暗交錯的光影。突然一棵大樹的影子落在外面被露水浸濕的草坪上，藏在灰藍樹葉中的鳥兒開始鳴唱。空氣緩緩流動，稱不上是風，感覺很舒服，似乎預告著這天將會是涼爽宜人的一天。

「我不認為她愛過他。」蓋茨比從一扇窗前轉過身來，目光帶著挑釁的意味。「老兄，你一定還記得吧？昨天下午她很激動，湯姆把那件事說出來的口氣嚇壞了她 —— 說得好像我只是個下流的騙子。結果弄得她幾乎不知所措。」

他悶悶不樂地坐下來。

「當然，他們剛結婚時，她也許愛過他一時半刻 —— 可是，即使是那個時候，她最愛的還是我，你懂嗎？」

忽然間他又說了一句很奇怪的話。

「總之，」他說，「這都與他人無關。」

這句話是什麼意思？應該是在暗示他對這件事情有著他人無法體會的深刻感受吧。

他從法國回來的時候，湯姆和黛西還在度蜜月，他非常傷

心，不由自主地用他僅餘的軍餉，買了車票到路易維爾去。他在那裡待了一個星期，走遍從前他倆在十一月的秋夜並肩走過的街道，又去重訪許多他倆從前開著她那部白色汽車逛過的偏僻地方。在他眼中，黛西家的豪宅還是和以前一樣，比其他的房子蘊藏著更多的神祕與歡娛；這個城市本身也是一樣，雖然她已經離開，在他看來還是瀰漫著一種抑鬱的美。

他離開的時候一直覺得，若他能再認真地去找一找，也許還能找到她——他覺得好像是自己把她拋下。他坐的是二等車——他已經身無分文了——車廂裡熱得厲害。他走到車尾的車廂外，找了一張摺疊椅坐下來，車站在他眼底逐漸遠去，一些陌生的建築物背面也在他眼簾中一幢一幢掠過。過了一會兒火車便進入春日的原野，和一列黃色電車並駛了一段路，電車上或許有些乘客一度無意間在街頭巷尾見過她那張楚楚動人的臉蛋。

火車拐了一個彎，變成是背對著太陽行駛，落日的餘暈似乎在替這個慢慢消逝的城市祝福著，這個黛西生活過的地方。他絕望地伸出一隻手，似乎想攬住一撮空氣，想留下一小塊那個因為黛西而美麗的地方。可是一幕幕的景象消逝得太快，他那模糊的眼睛來不及看清楚。他心裡明白，自己已經失去那最新最美好的一部分，永遠失去了。

我們吃完早點走到陽臺上時已經九點了。過了一夜，天氣驟然變了，空氣中顯然已有秋天的味道。蓋茨比別墅中僅存的一個老園丁走到臺階前面說：「先生，我今天打算把游泳池的水排掉。很快就會開始有落葉了，水管一不小心就會塞住的。」

「今天先不要動。」蓋茨比對他說。他帶著歉意轉身對我說:「你知道嗎,老兄,我整個夏天都沒用過那個游泳池!」

我看了看錶,站起身來。

「還有十二分鐘我那班車就要開了。」

我並不想進城,我那天簡直沒有心思做什麼工作,而更重要的是——我實在是不想丟下蓋茨比。我錯過了那班車,又錯過了第二班,然後才勉強離開。

「我再打電話給你。」我最後說。

「好的,老兄。」

「中午左右打給你。」

我們慢慢地走下臺階。

「我想黛西也會打電話來的。」他焦慮地看著我,好像希望我認同他的想法。

「我想她會的。」

「那麼,再見了。」

我們握手道別,然後我就走了。快走到樹籬的時候,突然想到了什麼,於是我掉轉身去。

「他們全都是混蛋!」我隔著草坪喊道,「他們沒有一個人比得上你。」

我一直很高興自己說了那些話。那是我唯一一次恭維他,因為自始至終我都沒認同過他這個人。他起先很禮貌地點點頭,隨後笑逐顏開向我露出會心的微笑,好像我們兩人對這件事一直都有共識。他那件粉紅色外套襯在白色的臺階上顯得特別鮮豔奪

目，令我想起三個月前我初次來他的別墅拜訪的那天晚上。那天他的草坪和車道上擠滿了客人，一個個都在揣想著他的背景是多麼不堪——而當時他就站在那臺階上向大家揮手道別，心裡蘊藏著他純潔的夢想。

我謝謝他的款待。所有的人——包括我自己——總是這麼謝他的。

「再見，蓋茨比。」我喊著，「謝謝你的早點。」

在城裡，我起先還試著整理那些不計其數的股票行情，後來實在支持不住，就在辦公椅上睡著了。快到中午的時候電話鈴響把我叫醒，我吃了一驚，額頭上冒出一片冷汗。是喬丹·貝克。她常常在這個時候打電話給我，因為她總是行蹤不定，不是在大旅館、俱樂部，就是在朋友家裡，要找到她很不容易。通常她打電話來的聲音總是很清新，就像一陣風把高爾夫球場的綠蔭送進辦公室裡來一樣，但今天早上她的聲音卻有點乾澀不悅耳。

「我已經離開黛西家了。」她說，「我在恩普斯特，下午就要到南安普敦去。」

離開黛西家是明智之舉，但我還是覺得厭煩，而她接下來的話更教我難過。

「昨晚你對我不太客氣。」

「昨晚那種情形，有什麼辦法呢？」

她沉默了一會兒後又說：

「反正，我還是想見你。」

「我也想見妳。」

「那麼我今天下午就不去南安普敦了，我到城裡去，好不好？」

「不行……我想今天下午不行。」

「那好吧。」

「今天下午真的不行。有好多事……」

我們就這樣聊了一會兒，後來突然兩人都不再言語。我也記不清是她還是我先用力掛上電話，只知道我那時毫不在乎。那天下午實在不能跟她面對面一塊喝茶聊天，即使這輩子再也不能和她說話也一樣。

幾分鐘後我打電話到蓋茨比的別墅去，但電話佔線。我一連打了四次，最後一名接線生不耐煩地告訴我說，這條線路正在等一通底特律的長途電話。我拿出火車時刻表，在三點五十分那班車上面畫了一個圈；然後我靠在椅背上試著整理一下思緒，此時才中午十二點。

我那天早上搭火車進城，車子經過垃圾堆時我故意坐到車廂的另外一邊。我想今天一整天一定還有民眾圍在那裡，好奇的小男孩在塵土中搜尋發黑的血跡，還有多嘴的閒人一遍又一遍地大談車禍的經過，一直說到連他自己都覺得不真實，說不下去了，梅朵‧威爾森的悲劇才會被人忘記。不過現在我想要追述一下前一晚在我們離開之後車行那邊的情形。

他們起初一直找不到死者的妹妹凱瑟琳。那天晚上她一定破戒喝了酒，因為她到了出事地點時已經爛醉如泥，別人告訴她救護車已開往福萊興區時，她怎麼也聽不懂。後來終於有人讓她明

白,她一聽馬上昏死過去,好像在所有發生的事當中這是她最難受的一件事。於是又有個人,也不知是出於善心或是好奇,請她坐上了車子,載著她去追趕她姊姊的屍體。

午夜已經過去多時,還有大批人潮不時湧到車行前面。喬治‧威爾森一直坐在辦公室的沙發上前後搖晃著。起先辦公室的門還敞開著,凡是進入車行的人都忍不住往裡頭瞧一眼。後來不知誰說這太過分了,才把門關上。米可利斯和幾個人陪著他,最先有四、五個人,後來剩下兩三個,到最後只剩下米可利斯和另外一個人,米可利斯只好請他再多等十五分鐘,好讓他回到自己店裡去煮一壺咖啡。最後,他便獨自陪著威爾森一直到天亮。

約莫凌晨三點左右,威爾森不再喃喃地胡言亂語,他漸漸平靜下來,又談起那部黃色的汽車。他說他有辦法找出這部黃色車子的主人。接著他突然說,幾個月前,他老婆曾經臉帶瘀血、腫著鼻子從城裡回來。

可是聽到自己這麼說時,他卻畏縮了,又開始呼天搶地哭喊起來:「我的天哪!」米可利斯想轉移他的注意力,但是方法有些笨拙。

「喬治,你結婚幾年了?好了,你安靜坐一會兒。告訴我,你結婚幾年了?」

「十二年。」

「有小孩嗎?喬治,拜託你坐好……我在問你,你有沒有小孩?」

棕色硬殼蟲繞著微弱的燈泡不停地亂飛亂撞。每次米可利斯

一聽見有車子急馳而過,他總覺得就是幾個鐘頭以前沒有停下來的那部車子。他不想走到車行去,因為那張放置過屍體的工作檯上還有一灘血漬,因此他只好在辦公室裡不安地走來走去,還沒到天亮,他已經把辦公室裡每樣東西都記得一清二楚了,不時又坐在威爾森身旁,試著安撫他的情緒。

「喬治,你有沒有上過教堂?就算已經好久沒去了也沒關係,也許我可以打電話去請一位牧師過來,讓他跟你談談,好嗎?」

「我從沒上過教堂。」

「你應該去教堂做做禮拜的,喬治,像這種時候就需要。你一定去過教堂的,難道你不是在教堂結婚的嗎?喬治,你聽我說。你不是在教堂結婚的嗎?」

「那是很久以前的事了。」

為了回答問題,把威爾森搖晃的節奏打亂了,不久,他那對無神的眼睛又恢復先前恍恍惚惚、神智不清的樣子。

「把那個抽屜打開看看。」他指著桌子說。

「哪一個抽屜?」

「那個抽屜,那邊那個。」

米可利斯打開離他手邊最近的一個抽屜。裡面空空的,只有一條狗鍊,還鑲著銀邊,看起來很昂貴,而且還很新。

「這個嗎?」他把狗鍊拿起來問道。

威爾森瞪著眼點點頭。

「那是我昨天下午發現的。她想向我解釋,但是我知道其中

173

一定有蹊蹺。」

「你是說，這是你太太買的？」

「她用紙包著放在梳妝台上。」

米可利斯不覺得這有什麼可疑之處，他隨口就說出幾十個威爾森的老婆可能買這條狗鍊的理由。也許有些理由威爾森早就從梅朵口中聽過了，所以他又開始低聲呻吟：「喔，我的天哪！」米可利斯還想到幾個可能的理由，可是見狀也就不再說了。

「他是故意用車撞死她的。」威爾森說，他的嘴巴突然張得大大的。

「誰撞死她？」

「我有辦法查出來。」

「喬治，你魔怔了。」陪著他的朋友說，「這件事對你的打擊太大了，所以才會語無倫次。你最好還是想法子安靜地坐著，等天亮再說吧。」

「他謀殺了她。」

「喬治，那是一場意外。」

威爾森搖搖頭，瞇起雙眼，咧開大嘴，還似乎帶點不屑地「哼」了一聲。

「我知道，」他肯定地說，「我一向都很信任別人，從來不曾想要傷害誰，可是只要是我知道的事情，就錯不了。就是那部車子裡的那個男人。她跑到路邊想跟他說話，但是他不肯停下來。」

米可利斯也注意到這一點，但他並未想到其中有什麼特別的

意義。他以為威爾森的老婆衝出去只是要從她丈夫身邊跑開，而不是想攔下這部汽車。

「怎麼會這樣？」

「她這個人很有心眼兒。」威爾森答非所問。「啊……」

他又開始搖晃起來。米可利斯手裡拿著狗鍊，有點不知所措。

「喬治，你有沒有什麼朋友，我幫你打電話找他們？」

他並沒有多大指望，他知道威爾森幾乎沒有什麼朋友，光是他老婆就已經讓他應付不了了。又過了一會兒，他發現屋子裡有點改變，窗外透出一些微光，他不由得高興起來，因為他知道天就快亮了。五點左右，外面的天色已經夠亮，屋子裡的燈可以關掉了。

威爾森把他那呆滯的雙眼望向窗外的垃圾堆，看見上面有幾朵奇形怪狀的灰雲，隨著晨風飄來飄去。

「我早對她說過了。」他靜默了一陣子後，語氣低沉地說，「我對她說，她也許騙得了我，可是騙不了上帝。我叫她跟我到窗口。」他掙扎著站起來，走到後面的窗子前，把臉貼在玻璃上。「然後我對她說：『妳所做的事上帝都知道，每件事祂都知道。儘管妳騙得了我，可是妳騙不了上帝！』」

米可利斯站在他背後，不由得吃了一驚，他發現威爾森正注視著艾柯柏格醫師的那雙大眼，那雙蒼白而巨大的眼睛剛從逐漸退去的夜色中顯現出來。

「上帝什麼都看得見。」威爾森又說了一遍。

大亨小傳

「那是一個廣告看板。」米可利斯想要說服他，然後不知怎麼地，他突然從窗邊轉身，把視線移回屋內。但是威爾森在那裡站了好久，他的臉緊貼著玻璃窗，朝著晨曦點著頭。

到了六點，米可利斯已經累垮了，聽見有一部車子停在門口的聲音，他心裡好欣慰。那是昨晚一起陪伴威爾森的人，他答應早上再來的。他做了三個人的早餐，但只有他和來的人一道吃。威爾森已經比較安靜了，於是米可利斯就回家睡覺。四個小時之後他醒過來，匆匆又跑回車行時，威爾森已經不在那裡了。

事後追蹤他的足跡——他一直是用徒步的——先是走到羅斯福港，然後到蓋德山，在那裡買了一個三明治和一杯咖啡，結果三明治也沒有吃。他大概已經走累了，所以走得很慢，到蓋德山時已經中午了。到目前為止，他的行蹤並不難掌握——有幾個男孩說，曾看見一個瘋瘋癲癲的人，還有幾個開車路過的人說他站在路旁神情怪異地盯著他們看。接下來的三個小時，他就不見蹤影了。警察根據他對米可利斯所說的話，說他「有辦法找出來」，猜想在這段時間裡他應該是在附近的車行遊走，打聽那部黃色汽車。可是沒有任何車行的人見他來過，所以可能他另外有更容易、更直接的方法去打聽他想知道的事。大概在下午兩點半左右，他到了西卵鎮，還向人打聽蓋茨比的住處。可見在那時他已經知道蓋茨比這個人了。

下午兩點，蓋茨比穿上泳衣，吩咐管家如果有人打電話來，就馬上到游泳池來叫他。他先到車庫去拿了一個夏天給客人們戲水的氣墊，司機幫著他充氣。然後他下了一道命令，不論發生什

176

麼事都不准把敞篷車開出去——司機覺得很奇怪，因為車子右前
方的擋泥板需要修理一下。

　　蓋茨比扛著氣墊走向游泳池。有一會兒他停下來把氣墊移動
了一下，司機問他需不需要幫忙，但他搖搖頭，過了不久就消失
在逐漸轉黃的樹叢裡。

　　電話始終沒有響，管家一直在等著，午覺也沒睡，一直等到
四點——等到那時即使有電話打來也不會有人接了。我想蓋茨比
早知道不會有電話的，也或許到了這個地步他已經不在乎了。如
果我想得沒錯，他一定覺悟到自己已經喪失了從前那個溫暖的世
界，也感覺到自己為了一個夢想而付出了很高的代價。他一定仰
著頭，透過可怕的樹葉望見一片陌生的天空而打了一個寒顫，同
時發覺玫瑰花是多麼怪異的東西，而陽光又是多麼殘酷地照在剛
冒出嫩芽的青草上。他恍然身處於一個新的世界，一個具體卻又
不真實的世界，在這裡，可憐的冤魂就像是呼吸空氣一般呼吸著
夢想，毫無目的地飄來飄去……就像這個滿身灰土的人，隱隱約
約從樹林中出現，悄悄地向他逼近。

　　司機——他是渥夫辛派來的人員之一——說他曾聽見一聲槍
聲，但當時並不以為意。我從車站僱了一部車子一路趕到蓋茨比
的別墅，聽到我慌忙的腳步聲奔上臺階時，屋子裡的人才發覺出
了什麼事。不過我相信他們早已心裡有數。司機、管家、園丁和
我，我們四個人都不發一語，匆匆奔到游泳池邊。

　　池水從一頭的出水口汩汩流向另一頭的排水口，水面上起了
微微的波動，幾乎不易察覺。那隻氣墊載著意外的負擔在水面上

不定向地漂蕩著，微風激起幾乎看不出來的漣漪，卻足以使它改變方向。後來碰到一撮落葉，氣墊開始在水上慢慢打轉，像指南針的指針不停打轉，拖曳出一絲紅圈圈。

我們幾個人抬起蓋茨比的屍體往屋子裡走去，園丁在不遠的草叢裡看見威爾森的屍體，於是這場血腥的殺戮才告落幕。

第 9 章

　　事隔兩年，在我的記憶中，那天下午、那天晚上以及第二天，就只有警察、攝影師和新聞記者不斷地進出蓋茨比家的大門，反覆地詢問和拍照。大門上圍起了繩子，一名警察看守著，不讓圍觀的民眾靠近，可是附近的小男孩不久就發現可以從我的園子繞進去，總會有幾個擠在游泳池旁，被眼前的情況嚇得目瞪口呆的。那天下午，一個頗有自信的人，也許是一名偵探，俯首檢視威爾森的屍體時，說了一聲「瘋子」，由於他的語氣頗具權威，第二天早上所有報紙就都如此報導了。

　　那些新聞報導都像在描述一場離奇、怪誕、虛構的噩夢一樣。當米可利斯接受偵訊，說出威爾森生前曾經對他老婆的懷疑時，我以為整件事會被大肆渲染，但是原本可以說些什麼的凱瑟琳，竟然一個字也沒有透露。她表現得頗為鎮定，修整過的眉毛底下那雙眼睛流露出堅毅的目光，信誓旦旦地說她姊姊從來沒見過蓋茨比，而且她姊姊和姊夫的婚姻非常美滿，從來沒有什麼逾矩的行為。她也被自己這樣的說詞說服了，同時一把眼淚一把鼻涕的，好像無法忍受別人用有色眼光看她的姊姊。因此，威爾森便成了「因憂鬱過度而精神失常」的人，這樣才不至於使案情太過複雜，而這個案子就這樣結了。

　　對我來說，這一切程序似乎都是無關緊要的。我發現自己是站在蓋茨比這一邊的，而且只有我一個人。從我打電話到西卵鎮報案開始，每一項關於他的揣測和每一個實際的問題，都會牽扯到我。起初我覺得訝異、困惑，後來，時間一分一秒地過去，而他還是冷冰冰地躺在他的別墅裡，不言不語，一動也不動，我才慢慢領悟到我必須負責，因為沒有其他人有興趣——我的意思是說，每個人死後多多少少總會有親友表示關切，而他卻一個都沒有。

　　發現他的屍體半個小時之後，我就本能地、毫不遲疑地打電話給黛西。但是當天下午稍早之前，她和湯姆已經帶著行李離開了。

　　「沒留下聯絡地址嗎？」

　　「沒有。」

　　「有沒有說什麼時候回來？」

　　「沒有。」

　　「知不知道他們可能到哪兒去？怎樣才能聯絡到他們？」

　　「不知道，說不上來。」

　　我想幫他找個人來，我甚至想走到他躺著的房間裡，向他保證：「蓋茨比，我會幫你找個人來的。你放心，一切交給我，我會幫你找個人來……」

　　電話簿裡沒有梅爾‧渥夫辛的名字。管家把他位於百老匯辦公室的地址給我，我問了查號台，但是問到號碼時早已過了五點，打過去已經沒人接聽了。

「請你再打一次好嗎？」

「我已經打了三次了。」

「這是很緊急的事。」

「對不起，我想那邊已經沒有人在了。」

　　我走回到客廳，看見屋子裡擠滿了人，我一時還以為是來了意外的訪客，後來才知道原來是調查人員。他們掀開被單，不為所動地看著蓋茨比，但我腦子裡卻聽見他一次又一次地對我說：「老兄啊，你一定要幫我找個人來。你一定要認真地找，我不能一個人孤伶伶地走啊。」

　　這時有個人突然來找我問話，我敷衍幾句便跑上樓去，倉皇地翻找著他書桌沒上鎖的抽屜──他從來沒有告訴過我他的父母是否還健在。可是我什麼都找不到，只有丹‧柯迪的肖像從牆上往下看著，象徵著遭到遺忘的暴力。

　　第二天早上，我讓管家送一封信到紐約給渥夫辛，希望他提供一些消息，並請他務必搭下一班車過來。我提出這個請求時，自覺是多此一舉，因為我相信他一看見報紙就會趕來的，我也相信中午以前就會收到黛西的電報。然而，既沒有電報，渥夫辛先生也沒有來；什麼人都沒來，只來了更多的警察、攝影師及新聞記者。等到管家帶回來渥夫辛的回信時，我開始有一種和蓋茨比同仇敵愾的感覺，我們要一起對抗所有的人。

卡拉威先生台鑒：

　　噩耗傳來有如青天霹靂，深感惋惜悲痛之

至。此人的瘋狂行為實足令人譁者。鄙人現因要務纏身，未克前來弔唁，抱歉之至。日後若有效勞之處，還望由愛德加帶信不知為荷。臨書不勝悲慟之至。

敬頌　大安

梅爾·渥夫辛敬啟

信尾又匆匆附了一句說：

再者，關於喪禮一切請告知，對於他的家屬我毫無所知。

那天下午，電話鈴響，接線生說是芝加哥來的長途電話，我想這總該是黛西了吧。但電話中傳來的卻是一個男人的聲音，聲音很細，感覺很遙遠。

「喂，我是史雷格……」

「喂？」我從來沒聽過這名字。

「那封信真是莫名其妙，你說是嗎？收到我的電報了嗎？」

「沒收到什麼電報。」

「小派克出事了，」他說得很急，「他在櫃台交割證券時被逮住了。五分鐘前他們收到紐約的公文時知道號碼的。你看多麼厲害，這種鄉下地方，想不到——」

「喂，喂！」我焦急地打斷了他的話，「你聽我說……我不是蓋茨比先生。蓋茨比先生已經去世了。」

電話那頭一陣靜默，接著傳來一聲驚叫……然後電話咯嚓一聲就掛掉了。

我記得大概是第三天，從明尼蘇達州一個小城來了一封電報，署名是亨利‧C‧蓋茲。上面只說發電報的人會立刻動身前來，要求我們將喪事延到他來再舉行。

那是蓋茨比的父親，一位神情嚴肅的老人，他看起來非常無助而且驚慌，在這樣暖和的九月天裡，他已經穿上一件又厚又長的廉價大衣。他情緒十分激動，淚水直流，我從他手裡接過行李和雨傘後，他開始用手拉扯他那稀疏花白的鬍鬚，我幾乎沒法幫他脫下大衣。他幾乎要崩潰了，我把他帶到音樂廳裡讓他坐下，又讓傭人去張羅一點吃的過來。但是他不肯吃東西，一杯牛奶拿在他顫抖不停的手裡都灑出來了。

「我在芝加哥的報紙上看到消息，」他說，「芝加哥的報紙寫得一清二楚，我就馬上動身趕來了。」

「我不知道該怎麼通知你。」

他兩眼無神，不停地向屋子裡面望來望去。

「是一個瘋子，」他說，「那個人一定是瘋了。」

「你不想喝杯咖啡嗎？」我勸他。

「我什麼都不要。我現在沒事了，你是……？」

「卡拉威。」

「沒事了，我現在好了。他們把傑米放在什麼地方？」

183

　　我把他帶到客廳裡他兒子遺體停放的地方，讓他留在那裡。幾個小男孩已經跑到臺階上，探頭探腦地往裡面張望；我告訴他們來的人是誰之後，他們才心不甘情不願地走開。

　　過了一會兒，蓋茲老先生把門打開走出來。他嘴巴半張著，臉頰微微漲紅，眼裡還噙著淚水。到了他這把年紀，死亡對他而言已經不是什麼了不起的大事了。這時他第一次向四周瞧了瞧，看見廳堂樓閣如此富麗堂皇，他在悲傷之餘也開始感到些許的驚訝和驕傲。我扶著他到樓上的一間臥室去。他脫掉了外衣和背心，我對他說一切相關事宜都延後了，就等著他來決定。

　　「我不知道你有什麼打算，蓋茨比先生……」

　　「我姓蓋茲。」

　　「哦……蓋茲先生。我想你也許會把靈柩運回西部去。」

　　他搖搖頭。

　　「傑米一直都比較喜歡東部。他也是在東部奮鬥才有今天的成就。你是我兒子的朋友吧，先生？」

　　「我們是很好的朋友。」

　　「他本來會有大好前途的，你也知道，他年紀還輕，但是他腦子裡很有東西。」

　　他用手碰碰自己的腦袋，我也點頭同意。

　　「如果他還活著，將來一定會成為一個大人物。像詹姆士·J·希爾那樣的大人物。他會對國家的建設很有貢獻的。」

　　「是啊。」我附和著，覺得有點不自在。

　　他把床上的繡花罩拉下來，然後直挺挺地躺下身去，一倒頭

便睡著了。

　　那天晚上有個人來電話，他的聲音聽起來顯得很害怕，他堅持一定要先知道我是誰，才肯說出他的姓名。

　　「我是卡拉威。」

　　「喔！」他似乎鬆了一口氣。「我是克利史賓格。」

　　我也鬆了口氣。因為我覺得可能又多了一個人可以來參加蓋茨比的葬禮。我不想在報紙上刊登訃聞，怕引來一堆看熱鬧的人，因此我就自己打了幾通電話，可是這些人真不容易找。

　　「葬禮就在明天。」我對他說，「下午三點，就在別墅裡舉行，如果有人願意來參加，希望你能轉達。」

　　「喔，我會的。」他匆忙地說，「當然了，我是不太可能會碰到什麼人，不過假使碰到的話，我會的……」

　　他的語氣讓我起了疑心。

　　「你本人一定會來吧！」

　　「嗯……我一定盡量趕到。我打電話來是要……」

　　「等一等，」我打斷他的話。「你能不能答應我一定會來？」

　　「呃，事實上……是這樣的，我現在是在格林威治的朋友家裡，他們很希望我明天能陪他們，就是去野餐什麼的。當然我走得開一定來。」

　　我忍不住「哼」了一聲，他一定聽到了，接著緊張兮兮地說：「我打電話來是因為我有一雙鞋子留在那裡。不知道能不能麻煩管家寄到這裡來給我。沒有那雙網球鞋我實在很不方便。我

的地址是康乃狄克——」

我沒有等他說完就把電話掛上了。

在這之後，我替蓋茨比感到有些難過——我又打電話給某位先生，他似乎認為蓋茨比是罪有應得的。這都怪我自己不好，不應該打電話找他的，因為當初有一些人常常藉著蓋茨比的酒裝瘋，然後對主人大肆批評，而他就是其中的一個。

出殯那天早上，我到紐約去找梅爾·渥夫辛，因為實在沒有其他方法可以找到他。依照電梯服務生的指點，我推開一扇掛著寫著「卍字控股公司」招牌的門。裡面看起來好像沒有人在，我喊了幾聲「有人在嗎」，也沒人回答，這時忽然從隔板後面傳出爭吵的聲音，不久，一個很漂亮的猶太女人從一扇門後走了出來，一雙黑色的眼睛帶有敵意地打量著我。

「沒有人在，」她回答我說，「渥夫辛先生到芝加哥去了。」

她的前半句話顯然是在撒謊，因為此時裡面傳出吹口哨的聲音，吹的是《玫瑰經》，但全走了音。

「請你告訴他，是卡拉威先生想見一見他。」

「我又不能把他從芝加哥叫回來。」

就在這時，隔壁有人喊了一聲「史黛拉！」——那是渥夫辛的聲音。

「你把名字留下來，」她趕緊說，「等他回來我會告訴他。」

「我知道他在裡面。」

她朝我面前跨了一步，兩手叉腰，顯得很生氣。

「你們這些年輕人真不懂規矩，當這裡是什麼地方啊，愛闖進來就闖進來。」她罵道，「真教人討厭！我說他在芝加哥，他就在芝加哥。」

我提了蓋茨比的名字。

「喔！」她又從頭到腳把我打量了一番。「請問……你貴姓？」

她轉眼就不見了。過了一會兒，渥夫辛很嚴肅地站在門口，兩手張得開開的。他把我拉進他的辦公室，一面用虔誠的口吻對我說，在這種時候我們大家心裡都難過，同時遞給我一支雪茄。

「我還記得當初我第一次見到他的情形。」他說，「一個剛退伍的年輕少校，胸口掛滿了勳章，他那時候窮得沒錢買便服，只好一直穿著軍服。那天他跑到四十三街韋恩伯納開的撞球店找工作，那是我第一次見到他。他已經好幾天沒吃東西了，我就說『來跟我一同吃午飯吧』。不到半個小時，他就吃了四塊多錢的東西。」

「這樣說來，是你幫助他的？」我問他。

「幫助他！是我提拔他的。」

「喔。」

「我讓他從貧民窟裡一躍升天。我看出來他相貌堂堂，很有紳士風度，當他告訴我他上過牛津，我就知道我可以重用他。我讓他加入了『美國退伍軍人協會』，他在裡面風評一直很好。接著他還幫我在奧本尼的一個客戶那裡做了點事。我們那時關係很

密切，」他伸出兩隻肥指頭做了個手勢，「做什麼事都在一起。」

我心想，不知道一九一九年世界棒球聯賽那個弊案是否也是他們兩人搭檔的成果。

「現在他死了。」隔了半晌，我說：「你是他最親近的朋友，我知道今天下午你一定會來參加他的葬禮。」

「我是很想去。」

「那就來呀。」

他的鼻毛微微顫動，眼中充滿淚水，搖了搖頭。

「我不能去……我不能牽扯進去。」他說。

「已經沒有什麼事可以牽扯的。事情都過去了。」

「只要事關人命，我就不想和整件事有任何關係，而且要離得遠遠的。我年輕的時候當然就不一樣——如果有朋友死了，不管怎樣，我總是幫忙到底，也許你會認為我意氣用事，不過我是說真的——捨命幫到底。」

我可以看出來他因為某些個人因素，是決定不參加了，於是我起身告辭。

「你是大學畢業的嗎？」他忽然問了一句。

我一時以為他要提議跟我「合夥」，不過他只是點點頭，並和我握了握手。

「我們大家都應當記住，朋友活著的時候就應該好好關心他，不要等到死掉之後才來追念他。」他建議說，「至於人死了之後，我個人的原則是少管閒事。」

　　我離開他的辦公室時天色變了，回到西卵時已經下起毛毛雨。我先回家換了衣服才到隔壁去，只見蓋茲老先生興奮地在穿堂裡走來走去。他對於兒子的事業和財產越來越感到驕傲，興沖沖地拿了一件東西給我看。

　　「你看，」他顫抖的手拿出一只皮夾，「傑米寄了這張照片給我。」

　　那是這棟別墅的照片，四角有些破損，經過很多人的手傳看，有些弄髒了。他很熱切地把照片上每個細節都指出來給我看，還頻頻說「你看！」，說完還看看我眼中有沒有讚賞之意。他顯然逢人就把這張照片拿出來炫耀，在他眼中，這張照片可能比別墅本身還要真實。

　　「這是傑米寄給我的。照得很好，很清楚。」

　　「是啊，很清楚。你前一陣子有沒有跟他見過面？」

　　「兩年以前他回來看了我一次，還幫我買下現在住的那棟房子。當然，他離開家逃跑的時候我們很傷心，但是我現在明白了，他那樣做是有道理的。他知道自己會有大好的前程，他發達之後也一直對我很好。」

　　他似乎還不想把那張照片放回去，拿在我面前希望我好好欣賞。後來他收起皮夾，又從口袋裡掏出一本破破爛爛的舊書，書名是《牛仔凱西迪》。

　　「你看，這是他小時候看的書。你看了就知道。」

　　他翻開書本的封底，倒轉過來讓我看，扉頁上工整地寫著「作息表」三個字，日期是一九零六年九月十二號。底下寫著：

大亨小傳

06:00	起床
06:15 - 06:30	啞鈴體操，爬牆練習
07:15 - 08:15	學習電腦及其他科目
08:30 - 16:30	工作
16:30 - 17:00	棒球及其他運動
17:00 - 18:00	練習演說、學習保持沉著
19:00 - 21:00	研究有用的新發明

《個人戒條》

~~不再浪費時間去沙福特或~~

不再吸煙或嚼口香糖

每兩天洗一次澡

每星期讀一本有益的書或雜誌

每星期儲蓄 ~~五元~~ 三元

對父母好一點

「我無意中發現這本書，」老人家說，「從這裡就看得出來，是不是？」

「是啊，早就看出來了。」

「我早就知道傑米會出人頭地的。他總是會這樣約束自己什麼的。你注意到沒有，他是多麼努力提升自己的內涵，他從小就有這種志氣。有一次他當面批評我吃東西像豬一樣，我還把他打

190

了一頓。」

　　他捨不得把書闔起來，他把兒子所寫的幾個項目大聲唸了一遍，然後以熱切的眼光望著我。我想他大概很希望我抄下來用以自律。

　　接近三點的時候，路德教會的牧師到了，我開始不由自主地頻頻向外望，看看有沒有其他車子到來，蓋茨比的父親也一樣。時間一分一秒過去，僕人都進到穿堂裡站著等候。他焦急地直眨眼，又說這場雨不知道要下多久，顯得很不安。牧師先生瞄了幾次手錶，我只好把他帶到一旁，請他再等半個鐘頭。可是沒有用，還是沒有人來。

　　五點鐘左右，我們一行三輛車抵達墓園，在大門旁的小雨中停了下來──第一輛是靈柩車，又黑又濕，第二輛轎車坐的是蓋茲先生、牧師和我，第三輛跟在後面的是蓋茨比的旅行車，坐著四、五名僕人和西卵鎮的郵差。大家下了車，全身都淋濕了。就在我們穿過大門走進墓園時，我聽見一輛車停下來的聲音，接著有個人踩著濡濕的草地追了上來。我回頭一看，原來是戴起眼鏡活像貓頭鷹的那個人，三個月前某天晚上，我在蓋茨比的藏書室裡發現他對真書嘆為觀止的那個人。

　　自從那晚之後我就沒再見過他。不知道他怎麼會知道葬禮的消息，我連他的姓名都不清楚。大雨落在他厚厚的眼鏡上，他摘下眼鏡擦一擦，以便看清楚我們用擋水帆布遮住的蓋茨比的墳墓和墓碑。

　　這時，我懷想起蓋茨比，可是他已經離我們太遠了。我只記

得黛西連一個字、一朵花都沒有來，然而我心中並無憤恨。隱約中，我聽見有人喃喃祈禱著：「願上帝賜福，降恩澤於死者。」然後像貓頭鷹的那位先生勇敢地附和著說：「阿門！」

我們幾個人零零散散地快步穿過雨中，跑回到停車的地方。到了大門口，貓頭鷹先生跟我說了幾句話。

「很抱歉，我沒能夠趕到別墅來弔喪。」他說。

「沒關係，誰也沒能趕來。」

「真的！」他訝異地說，「天啊！以前他的客人總是成千上百的。」

他又把眼鏡摘下來，裡裡外外都擦了一擦。

「真是可憐！」

我一生中最鮮明的記憶，就是中學以及大學時代每年聖誕節回家的情景。十二月的某

天晚上六點，那些要從芝加哥繼續往西行的學生總會聚集在老舊的聯合車站，和幾個在芝加哥下車的朋友匆匆話別，只見他們已經被過節的歡娛氣氛包圍了。我記得車站裡要從某某私立女校回家的女學生，身上穿著貂皮大衣，在寒冷的天氣裡說著話，記得大家見了熟人就高舉了手揮舞著，彼此詢問赴宴的情形：「你會去歐德偉家嗎？候希家呢？舒茲家呢？」又記得每個人手上都戴著厚厚的手套，緊握著那張長形的綠色車票。最後還記得在月臺上看見芝加哥、密爾瓦基和聖保羅鐵路的火車，那一節節模糊不清的黃色車廂，停在剪票口的軌道上，看起來同樣瀰漫著聖誕節的氣氛。

火車向寒冬的黑夜裡發動，真正的白雪，屬於我們的白雪，開始在我們身邊伸展開來，隔著窗戶閃閃發亮。威斯康辛州小車站的微弱燈火從窗前一一掠過，這時突然升起一股凜冽的寒意。從餐車吃完晚飯回到自己的座位時，我們深深地呼吸幾口冰冷的空氣。在這奇妙的一個小時裡，返鄉的意識特別強烈，我們似乎要與大自然融為一體了。

這就是我的中西部故鄉——不是充滿麥田、草原或瑞典移民的荒涼城鎮，而是我少年時代帶著激動的心返家所搭的火車，是寒夜裡的街燈和雪車的鈴響，以及窗外冬青樹映照在雪地上的影子。我也是那其中的一部分，當時的我想起漫長的冬天有一點嚴肅，想起自己生長在座落在都市幾十年屹立不搖的卡拉威家又有一點得意。我現在才明白，這一切不過就是一段西部故事——湯姆和蓋茲比、黛西和喬丹以及我自己，我們都是西部人，也許我

們都缺少了些什麼，才使我們莫名地無法適應東部的生活。

即使我對東部抱著極大的幻想，即使我曾敏銳地意識到，和俄亥俄州的城鎮比起來東部是要優越許多，因為西部城鎮不但凌亂窄小、生活無趣，而且居民視野狹隘，一天到晚對人品頭論足，只有小孩和老人倖免──即使如此，我總覺得東部的生活有一點畸形。尤其是西卵那個地方，在我許多古怪的夢中總會有它。我覺得這個小鎮就像是艾爾‧葛雷克畫筆下的一幅夜景──上百棟傳統又古怪的房子，蜷伏在陰沉沉的天空和黯然無光的月亮之下。在畫面上前方有四個穿著禮服的男人，嚴肅地抬著擔架，擔架上躺著一個身穿白色晚禮服、喝得爛醉的女人。她的一隻手垂在擔架外面晃來晃去，手上的珠寶閃耀著冰冷冷的光芒。那四個男人神情嚴肅地抬著女人走進一間房子──他們走錯了地方，並不是這棟房子。但是沒人知道這個女人叫什麼名字，也沒有人關心。

蓋茨比死後，東部在我心目中就是這樣鬼影幢幢，扭曲變形得讓我再也看不清它。因此，當空氣中揚起燃燒枯葉的藍煙，晾衣繩上的濕衣服被寒風颳得僵硬時，我就決定回家了。

離開之前還有一件事要做，一件相當尷尬、不愉快的事，也許擱著不理會好一些，但是我喜歡什麼事都處理得乾乾淨淨，不想把爛攤子丟進茫茫大海任其浮沉。於是我去見了喬丹‧貝克，和她談論了我們一起經歷的事，以及後來我所遭遇到的事。她躺在一張大沙發椅中靜靜地聽著，一動也不動。

她穿著高爾夫球裝，我記得自己曾經覺得她活像一幅美麗的

圖畫,她的下巴有點驕傲地微微抬起,頭髮有如秋葉的顏色,臉色則跟放在她膝蓋上那雙手套一樣是棕褐色的。我把話講完之後,她沒有反應,只告訴我她已經跟別人訂婚了。其實我不相信她的話,雖然我知道有好多人在追求她,只要她一點頭隨時都可以結婚的,不過我還是故意作出驚訝的表情。在那一刹那,我懷疑自己是否做錯了,可是很快地轉念一想,還是起身跟她告辭。

「總之,是你先把我甩掉的。」喬丹忽然說,「你那天在電話裡就把我甩了。我現在已經不在乎了,不過那倒是生平第一次,我難過了好一陣子。」

我們握了手。

「對了,你還記得嗎?」她又說,「有一次我們談到開車的事?」

「嗯……記不得了。」

「你對我說一個差勁的司機碰到另一個差勁的司機就會出事,記得嗎?你看,我這次不就碰上了一個差勁的司機。這要怪我自己不小心看錯了人,我起先還以為你是一個誠實、直爽的人,我還以為那是你最引以為傲的呢!」

「我已經三十歲了。」我說,「五年前也許我還會以欺騙自己為榮。」

她不作聲。我轉身離開,帶著一半惱怒、幾分不捨卻又極端的遺憾走了。

十月底的一個下午,我在第五大道上遇到湯姆 · 勃肯納。他走在我前面,還是像從前那樣敏捷,充滿活力,走起路來兩手

微微張開，好像足球比賽時要擊退對方的架勢，同時把頭忽左忽右地配合著他那不安的眼睛轉動著。我放慢腳步免得超越他，他卻停了下來，蹙著眉頭往一家珠寶店的櫥窗裡望。忽然間他看到了我，便往回走，同時伸出手來要和我握手。

「尼克，怎麼了？你不願意和我握手嗎？」

「是的。你應該知道我對你的看法。」

「你瘋了，尼克。」他急忙說，「簡直莫名其妙。我不明白你是怎麼回事。」

「湯姆，」我問道，「那天下午你對威爾森說了些什麼？」

他瞪著我不發一語，我立刻就知道威爾森失蹤的那幾個小時所發生的事果然被我猜對了。我掉頭就走，可是他緊跟上來，一把抓住我的胳臂。

「我對他說的都是實話。」他說，「他到我家的時候，我們正準備離開，我叫傭人告訴他我們不在，可是他已經闖上樓來。那時他已經失去了理智，要是我不告訴他那輛車是誰的，他一定會把我殺了。他一進到屋子裡，手中就握著一把槍……」他突然改變口吻，挑釁地說：「就算我告訴他又怎樣？那個傢伙自己找死。他欺騙了你，就像他欺騙黛西一樣，可是他也真狠，撞死梅朵就像撞死一條狗一樣，車子連停都沒停。」

我無話可說，除了心裡想說卻說不出口的一句話——事情並非如此。

「你以為我就不難過嗎……我告訴你，我去退掉那間公寓的時候，一眼就看見那盒狗餅乾還放在餐櫥上，我坐下來像個小孩

一樣哭了起來。真的，我很難受……」

我不能寬恕他，也無法喜歡他，但是我看得出來，他所做的一切，在他自己眼中絕對是合情合理的。這一切都太混亂、太隨意了。湯姆和黛西，他們同樣輕率，他們砸碎了東西、撞死了人就躲起來，躲回到他們自己的錢堆、他們的漠不關心裡，或者任何可以讓他們繼續在一起的事物背後，然後丟下爛攤子讓別人去收拾……。

於是我跟他握了握手——不和他握手似乎有點可笑，因為我忽然覺得自己像是在跟一個小孩說話。後來他走進那家珠寶店買了一串珍珠項鍊——也或許只是一副袖釦——很快地就把我這個鄉巴佬的責備都拋到腦後了。

我離開的時候，蓋茨比的別墅還是空著的，他園子裡的草已經長得跟我的一樣長了。鎮上有個計程車司機，每次載客人經過蓋茨比的大門時，總會把車子停下來朝裡頭指指點點，也許車禍那天夜裡開車送黛西和蓋茨比回東卵的就是這個司機，也許他對那件事自有一套說法，可是我卻不想聽，所以每回下了火車之後，我總是躲開他。

那幾個星期六晚上我都在紐約度過，因為蓋茨比那些五光十色、豪華熱鬧的宴會，還鮮明地印在我的腦海，彷彿依然可以聽到音樂聲和歡笑聲隱約從他園子裡不斷飄來，還有車輛在他的車道上來來去去。有一天晚上，我確實聽見汽車的聲音，也看見車燈照在他的臺階上。但是我並未走過去探問。大概是最後造訪的一個客人，由於先前遠在天邊，還不知道這裡已經曲終人散。

　　我離開前的最後一晚，在行李打包完畢，車子也賣給鎮上的雜貨店老闆之後，我走到隔壁，最後再看一次那棟龐大卻象徵著失敗的房子。白色的大理石臺階上不知道哪個頑童用瓦片寫了一個不堪入目的字，映在月光下顯得分外醒目。我用腳把它抹掉，鞋子刮在石頭上沙沙作響。後來我又走到海邊，仰天躺在沙灘上。

　　海灣一帶的大別墅現在都關閉了，四周幾乎沒有燈火，除了一盞渡船上的燈光還在移動著。當明月升到高空，地面上這些不起眼的房舍漸漸隱沒，我才慢慢認出這裡是一個古老的島岸，當年吸引荷蘭航海家的那塊林鬱蒼蒼的新大陸。昔日生長在這裡的樹木──後來為了建造蓋茨比的別墅而被砍掉──曾經低聲呢喃地應和著人類最終的目的、最大的美夢。就在那奇妙的一剎那，人們面對這個新大陸一定屏息驚異，那種大自然的美，使他們不由自主地陷入一陣莫名的沉思。那是人類最後一次面對這種值得欣賞的奇景。

　　我坐在那裡，懷念著那個古老而不可知的世界，忽然想到蓋茨比第一次認出對岸黛西家那盞綠燈的時候，必定也有著同樣的驚奇。他千里迢迢好不容易來到這片青草地上，眼看著夢想就要實現，彷彿伸手可及。但他不知道他所追求的夢想早已落到背後了，落到紐約背後那片廣袤陰暗的地方，落到那片美國的夜空下一望無際的漆黑田野中。

　　蓋茨比相信那盞綠燈，那象徵著他夢寐以求的未來，但是這個未來卻一年一年地在我們眼前逐漸遠去。未來曾經在我們的手

中溜過，但是沒關係——明天我們會跑得更快，我們的雙手會伸得更長……總有那麼一個美好的早晨——

　　因此，我們要像逆流中的扁舟，雖然不斷地被推回到過去，仍要繼續奮力向上。

The Great Gatsby
By F. Scott Fitzgerald

CHAPTER 1

In my younger and more vulnerable years my father gave me some advice that I've been turning over in my mind ever since.

"Whenever you feel like criticizing any one," he told me, "just remember that all the people in this world haven't had the advantages that you've had."

He didn't say any more but we've always been unusually communicative in a reserved way, and I understood that he meant a great deal more than that. In consequence I'm inclined to reserve all judgments, a habit that has opened up many curious natures to me and also made me the victim of not a few veteran bores. The abnormal mind is quick to detect and attach itself to this quality when it appears in a normal person, and so it came about that in college I was unjustly accused of being a politician, because I was privy to the secret griefs of wild, unknown men. Most of the confidences were unsought—frequently I have feigned sleep, preoccupation, or a hostile levity when I realized by some unmistakable sign that an intimate revelation was quivering on the horizon—for the intimate revelations of young men or at least the terms in which they express them are usually plagiaristic and marred by obvious suppressions. Reserving judgments is a matter of infinite hope. I am still a little afraid of missing something if I forget that, as my father snobbishly suggested, and I snobbishly repeat, a sense of the fundamental decencies is parcelled out unequally at birth.

And, after boasting this way of my tolerance, I come to the admission that it has a limit. Conduct may be founded on the hard rock or the wet marshes but after a certain point I don't care what it's

founded on. When I came back from the East last autumn I felt that I wanted the world to be in uniform and at a sort of moral attention forever; I wanted no more riotous excursions with privileged glimpses into the human heart. Only Gatsby, the man who gives his name to this book, was exempt from my reaction—Gatsby who represented everything for which I have an unaffected scorn. If personality is an unbroken series of successful gestures, then there was something gorgeous about him, some heightened sensitivity to the promises of life, as if he were related to one of those intricate machines that register earthquakes ten thousand miles away. This responsiveness had nothing to do with that flabby impressionability which is dignified under the name of the "creative temperament"—it was an extraordinary gift for hope, a romantic readiness such as I have never found in any other person and which it is not likely I shall ever find again. No—Gatsby turned out all right at the end; it is what preyed on Gatsby, what foul dust floated in the wake of his dreams that temporarily closed out my interest in the abortive sorrows and short-winded elations of men.

My family have been prominent, well-to-do people in this middle-western city for three generations. The Carraways are something of a clan and we have a tradition that we're descended from the Dukes of Buccleuch, but the actual founder of my line was my grandfather's brother who came here in fifty-one, sent a substitute to the Civil War and started the wholesale hardware business that my father carries on today.

I never saw this great-uncle but I'm supposed to look like him—with special reference to the rather hard-boiled painting that hangs in Father's office. I graduated from New Haven in 1915, just a quarter of a century after my father, and a little later I participated in that delayed Teutonic migration known as the Great War. I enjoyed the counter-raid so thoroughly that I came back restless. Instead of being the warm center of the world the middle-west now seemed like the ragged edge of the

universe—so I decided to go east and learn the bond business. Everybody I knew was in the bond business so I supposed it could support one more single man. All my aunts and uncles talked it over as if they were choosing a prep-school for me and finally said, "Why—ye-es" with very grave, hesitant faces. Father agreed to finance me for a year and after various delays I came east, permanently, I thought, in the spring of twenty-two.

The practical thing was to find rooms in the city but it was a warm season and I had just left a country of wide lawns and friendly trees, so when a young man at the office suggested that we take a house together in a commuting town it sounded like a great idea. He found the house, a weather beaten cardboard bungalow at eighty a month, but at the last minute the firm ordered him to Washington and I went out to the country alone. I had a dog, at least I had him for a few days until he ran away, and an old Dodge and a Finnish woman who made my bed and cooked breakfast and muttered Finnish wisdom to herself over the electric stove.

It was lonely for a day or so until one morning some man, more recently arrived than I, stopped me on the road.

"How do you get to West Egg village?" he asked helplessly.

I told him. And as I walked on I was lonely no longer. I was a guide, a pathfinder, an original settler. He had casually conferred on me the freedom of the neighborhood.

And so with the sunshine and the great bursts of leaves growing on the trees—just as things grow in fast movies—I had that familiar conviction that life was beginning over again with the summer.

There was so much to read for one thing and so much fine health to be pulled down out of the young breath-giving air. I bought a dozen volumes on banking and credit and investment securities and they stood on my shelf in red and gold like new money from the mint, promising to unfold the shining secrets that only Midas and Morgan and Maecenas

knew. And I had the high intention of reading many other books besides. I was rather literary in college—one year I wrote a series of very solemn and obvious editorials for the "Yale News"—and now I was going to bring back all such things into my life and become again that most limited of all specialists, the "well-rounded man." This isn't just an epigram—life is much more successfully looked at from a single window, after all.

It was a matter of chance that I should have rented a house in one of the strangest communities in North America. It was on that slender riotous island which extends itself due east of New York and where there are, among other natural curiosities, two unusual formations of land. Twenty miles from the city a pair of enormous eggs, identical in contour and separated only by a courtesy bay, jut out into the most domesticated body of salt water in the Western Hemisphere, the great wet barnyard of Long Island Sound. They are not perfect ovals—like the egg in the Columbus story they are both crushed flat at the contact end—but their physical resemblance must be a source of perpetual confusion to the gulls that fly overhead. To the wingless a more arresting phenomenon is their dissimilarity in every particular except shape and size.

I lived at West Egg, the—well, the less fashionable of the two, though this is a most superficial tag to express the bizarre and not a little sinister contrast between them. My house was at the very tip of the egg, only fifty yards from the Sound, and squeezed between two huge places that rented for twelve or fifteen thousand a season. The one on my right was a colossal affair by any standard—it was a factual imitation of some Hôtel de Ville in Normandy, with a tower on one side, spanking new under a thin beard of raw ivy, and a marble swimming pool and more than forty acres of lawn and garden. It was Gatsby's mansion. Or rather, as I didn't know Mr. Gatsby it was a mansion inhabited by a gentleman of that name. My own house was an eye-sore, but it was a small eye-sore, and it had been overlooked, so

I had a view of the water, a partial view of my neighbor's lawn, and the consoling proximity of millionaires—all for eighty dollars a month.

Across the courtesy bay the white palaces of fashionable East Egg glittered along the water, and the history of the summer really begins on the evening I drove over there to have dinner with the Tom Buchanans. Daisy was my second cousin once removed and I'd known Tom in college. And just after the war I spent two days with them in Chicago.

Her husband, among various physical accomplishments, had been one of the most powerful ends that ever played football at New Haven—a national figure in a way, one of those men who reach such an acute limited excellence at twenty-one that everything afterward savors of anticlimax. His family were enormously wealthy—even in college his freedom with money was a matter for reproach—but now he'd left Chicago and come east in a fashion that rather took your breath away: for instance he'd brought down a string of polo ponies from Lake Forest. It was hard to realize that a man in my own generation was wealthy enough to do that.

Why they came east I don't know. They had spent a year in France, for no particular reason, and then drifted here and there unrestfully wherever people played polo and were rich together. This was a permanent move, said Daisy over the telephone, but I didn't believe it—I had no sight into Daisy's heart but I felt that Tom would drift on forever seeking a little wistfully for the dramatic turbulence of some irrecoverable football game.

And so it happened that on a warm windy evening I drove over to East Egg to see two old friends whom I scarcely knew at all. Their house was even more elaborate than I expected, a cheerful red and white Georgian Colonial mansion overlooking the bay. The lawn started at the beach and ran toward the front door for a quarter of a mile, jumping over sun-dials and brick walks and burning gardens—finally when it reached the house drifting up the side in bright vines as

though from the momentum of its run. The front was broken by a line of French windows, glowing now with reflected gold, and wide open to the warm windy afternoon, and Tom Buchanan in riding clothes was standing with his legs apart on the front porch.

He had changed since his New Haven years. Now he was a sturdy, straw haired man of thirty with a rather hard mouth and a supercilious manner. Two shining, arrogant eyes had established dominance over his face and gave him the appearance of always leaning aggressively forward. Not even the effeminate swank of his riding clothes could hide the enormous power of that body—he seemed to fill those glistening boots until he strained the top lacing and you could see a great pack of muscle shifting when his shoulder moved under his thin coat. It was a body capable of enormous leverage—a cruel body.

His speaking voice, a gruff husky tenor, added to the impression of fractiousness he conveyed. There was a touch of paternal contempt in it, even toward people he liked—and there were men at New Haven who had hated his guts.

"Now, don't think my opinion on these matters is final," he seemed to say, "just because I'm stronger and more of a man than you are." We were in the same Senior Society, and while we were never intimate I always had the impression that he approved of me and wanted me to like him with some harsh, defiant wistfulness of his own.

We talked for a few minutes on the sunny porch.

"I've got a nice place here," he said, his eyes flashing about restlessly.

Turning me around by one arm he moved a broad flat hand along the front vista, including in its sweep a sunken Italian garden, a half acre of deep pungent roses and a snub-nosed motor boat that bumped the tide off shore.

"It belonged to Demaine the oil man." He turned me around again, politely and abruptly. "We'll go inside."

We walked through a high hallway into a bright rosy-colored space, fragilely bound into the house by French windows at either end. The windows were ajar and gleaming white against the fresh grass outside that seemed to grow a little way into the house. A breeze blew through the room, blew curtains in at one end and out the other like pale flags, twisting them up toward the frosted wedding cake of the ceiling—and then rippled over the wine-colored rug, making a shadow on it as wind does on the sea.

The only completely stationary object in the room was an enormous couch on which two young women were buoyed up as though upon an anchored balloon. They were both in white and their dresses were rippling and fluttering as if they had just been blown back in after a short flight around the house. I must have stood for a few moments listening to the whip and snap of the curtains and the groan of a picture on the wall. Then there was a boom as Tom Buchanan shut the rear windows and the caught wind died out about the room and the curtains and the rugs and the two young women ballooned slowly to the floor.

The younger of the two was a stranger to me. She was extended full length at her end of the divan, completely motionless and with her chin raised a little as if she were balancing something on it which was quite likely to fall. If she saw me out of the corner of her eyes she gave no hint of it—indeed, I was almost surprised into murmuring an apology for having disturbed her by coming in.

The other girl, Daisy, made an attempt to rise—she leaned slightly forward with a conscientious expression—then she laughed, an absurd, charming little laugh, and I laughed too and came forward into the room.

"I'm p-paralyzed with happiness."

She laughed again, as if she said something very witty, and held my hand for a moment, looking up into my face, promising that there was no one in the world she so much wanted to see. That was a way she had.

She hinted in a murmur that the surname of the balancing girl was Baker. (I've heard it said that Daisy's murmur was only to make people lean toward her; an irrelevant criticism that made it no less charming.)

At any rate Miss Baker's lips fluttered, she nodded at me almost imperceptibly and then quickly tipped her head back again—the object she was balancing had obviously tottered a little and given her something of a fright. Again a sort of apology arose to my lips. Almost any exhibition of complete self sufficiency draws a stunned tribute from me.

I looked back at my cousin who began to ask me questions in her low, thrilling voice. It was the kind of voice that the ear follows up and down as if each speech is an arrangement of notes that will never be played again. Her face was sad and lovely with bright things in it, bright eyes and a bright passionate mouth—but there was an excitement in her voice that men who had cared for her found difficult to forget: a singing compulsion, a whispered "Listen," a promise that she had done gay, exciting things just a while since and that there were gay, exciting things hovering in the next hour.

I told her how I had stopped off in Chicago for a day on my way east and how a dozen people had sent their love through me.

"Do they miss me?" she cried ecstatically.

"The whole town is desolate. All the cars have the left rear wheel painted black as a mourning wreath and there's a persistent wail all night along the North Shore."

"How gorgeous! Let's go back, Tom. Tomorrow!" Then she added irrelevantly, "You ought to see the baby."

"I'd like to."

"She's asleep. She's two years old. Haven't you ever seen her?"

"Never."

"Well, you ought to see her. She's—"

Tom Buchanan who had been hovering restlessly about the room

stopped and rested his hand on my shoulder.

"What you doing, Nick?"

"I'm a bond man."

"Who with?"

I told him.

"Never heard of them," he remarked decisively.

This annoyed me.

"You will," I answered shortly. "You will if you stay in the East."

"Oh, I'll stay in the East, don't you worry," he said, glancing at Daisy and then back at me, as if he were alert for something more. "I'd be a God Damned fool to live anywhere else."

At this point Miss Baker said "Absolutely!" with such suddenness that I started—it was the first word she uttered since I came into the room. Evidently it surprised her as much as it did me, for she yawned and with a series of rapid, deft movements stood up into the room.

"I'm stiff," she complained, "I've been lying on that sofa for as long as I can remember."

"Don't look at me," Daisy retorted. "I've been trying to get you to New York all afternoon."

"No, thanks," said Miss Baker to the four cocktails just in from the pantry, "I'm absolutely in training."

Her host looked at her incredulously.

"You are!" He took down his drink as if it were a drop in the bottom of a glass. "How you ever get anything done is beyond me."

I looked at Miss Baker wondering what it was she "got done." I enjoyed looking at her. She was a slender, small-breasted girl, with an erect carriage which she accentuated by throwing her body backward at the shoulders like a young cadet. Her grey sun-strained eyes looked back at me with polite reciprocal curiosity out of a wan, charming discontented face. It occurred to me now that I had seen her, or a

picture of her, somewhere before.

"You live in West Egg," she remarked contemptuously. "I know somebody there."

"I don't know a single–"

"You must know Gatsby."

"Gatsby?" demanded Daisy. "What Gatsby?"

Before I could reply that he was my neighbor dinner was announced; wedging his tense arm imperatively under mine Tom Buchanan compelled me from the room as though he were moving a checker to another square.

Slenderly, languidly, their hands set lightly on their hips the two young women preceded us out onto a rosy-colored porch open toward the sunset where four candles flickered on the table in the diminished wind.

"Why candles?" objected Daisy, frowning. She snapped them out with her fingers. "In two weeks it'll be the longest day in the year." She looked at us all radiantly. "Do you always watch for the longest day of the year and then miss it? I always watch for the longest day in the year and then miss it."

"We ought to plan something," yawned Miss Baker, sitting down at the table as if she were getting into bed.

"All right," said Daisy. "What'll we plan?" She turned to me helplessly. "What do people plan?"

Before I could answer her eyes fastened with an awed expression on her little finger.

"Look!" she complained. "I hurt it."

We all looked–the knuckle was black and blue.

"You did it, Tom," she said accusingly. "I know you didn't mean to but you did do it. That's what I get for marrying a brute of a man, a great big hulking physical specimen of a–"

"I hate that word hulking," objected Tom crossly, "even in kidding."

"Hulking," insisted Daisy.

Sometimes she and Miss Baker talked at once, unobtrusively and with a bantering inconsequence that was never quite chatter, that was as cool as their white dresses and their impersonal eyes in the absence of all desire. They were here—and they accepted Tom and me, making only a polite pleasant effort to entertain or to be entertained. They knew that presently dinner would be over and a little later the evening too would be over and casually put away. It was sharply different from the West where an evening was hurried from phase to phase toward its close in a continually disappointed anticipation or else in sheer nervous dread of the moment itself.

"You make me feel uncivilized, Daisy," I confessed on my second glass of corky but rather impressive claret. "Can't you talk about crops or something?"

I meant nothing in particular by this remark but it was taken up in an unexpected way.

"Civilization's going to pieces," broke out Tom violently. "I've gotten to be a terrible pessimist about things. Have you read 'The Rise of the Coloured Empires' by this man Goddard?"

"Why, no," I answered, rather surprised by his tone.

"Well, it's a fine book, and everybody ought to read it. The idea is if we don't look out the white race will be—will be utterly submerged. It's all scientific stuff; it's been proved."

"Tom's getting very profound," said Daisy with an expression of unthoughtful sadness. "He reads deep books with long words in them. What was that word we—"

"Well, these books are all scientific," insisted Tom, glancing at her impatiently. "This fellow has worked out the whole thing. It's up to us who are the dominant race to watch out or these other races will have control of things."

"We've got to beat them down," whispered Daisy, winking ferociously toward the fervent sun.

"You ought to live in California–" began Miss Baker but Tom interrupted her by shifting heavily in his chair.

"This idea is that we're Nordics. I am, and you are and you are and–" After an infinitesimal hesitation he included Daisy with a slight nod and she winked at me again. "–and we've produced all the things that go to make civilization–oh, science and art and all that. Do you see?"

There was something pathetic in his concentration as if his complacency, more acute than of old, was not enough to him any more. When, almost immediately, the telephone rang inside and the butler left the porch Daisy seized upon the momentary interruption and leaned toward me.

"I'll tell you a family secret," she whispered enthusiastically. "It's about the butler's nose. Do you want to hear about the butler's nose?"

"That's why I came over tonight."

"Well, he wasn't always a butler; he used to be the silver polisher for some people in New York that had a silver service for two hundred people. He had to polish it from morning till night until finally it began to affect his nose–"

"Things went from bad to worse," suggested Miss Baker.

"Yes. Things went from bad to worse until finally he had to give up his position."

For a moment the last sunshine fell with romantic affection upon her glowing face; her voice compelled me forward breathlessly as I listened–then the glow faded, each light deserting her with lingering regret like children leaving a pleasant street at dusk.

The butler came back and murmured something close to Tom's ear whereupon Tom frowned, pushed back his chair and without a word went inside. As if his absence quickened something within her

Daisy leaned forward again, her voice glowing and singing.

"I love to see you at my table, Nick. You remind me of a–of a rose, an absolute rose. Doesn't he?" She turned to Miss Baker for confirmation. "An absolute rose?"

This was untrue. I am not even faintly like a rose. She was only extemporizing but a stirring warmth flowed from her as if her heart was trying to come out to you concealed in one of those breathless, thrilling words. Then suddenly she threw her napkin on the table and excused herself and went into the house.

Miss Baker and I exchanged a short glance consciously devoid of meaning. I was about to speak when she sat up alertly and said "Sh!" in a warning voice. A subdued impassioned murmur was audible in the room beyond and Miss Baker leaned forward, unashamed, trying to hear. The murmur trembled on the verge of coherence, sank down, mounted excitedly, and then ceased altogether.

"This Mr. Gatsby you spoke of is my neighbor–" I said.

"Don't talk. I want to hear what happens."

"Is something happening?" I inquired innocently.

"You mean to say you don't know?" said Miss Baker, honestly surprised. "I thought everybody knew."

"I don't."

"Why–" she said hesitantly, "Tom's got some woman in New York."

"Got some woman?" I repeated blankly.

Miss Baker nodded.

"She might have the decency not to telephone him at dinner-time. Don't you think?"

Almost before I had grasped her meaning there was the flutter of a dress and the crunch of leather boots and Tom and Daisy were back at the table.

"It couldn't be helped!" cried Daisy with tense gayety.

She sat down, glanced searchingly at Miss Baker and then at me and continued: "I looked outdoors for a minute and it's very romantic outdoors. There's a bird on the lawn that I think must be a nightingale come over on the Cunard or White Star Line. He's singing away–" her voice sang "–It's romantic, isn't it, Tom?"

"Very romantic," he said, and then miserably to me: "If it's light enough after dinner I want to take you down to the stables."

The telephone rang inside, startlingly, and as Daisy shook her head decisively at Tom the subject of the stables, in fact all subjects, vanished into air. Among the broken fragments of the last five minutes at table I remember the candles being lit again, pointlessly, and I was conscious of wanting to look squarely at every one and yet to avoid all eyes. I couldn't guess what Daisy and Tom were thinking but I doubt if even Miss Baker who seemed to have mastered a certain hardy skepticism was able utterly to put this fifth guest's shrill metallic urgency out of mind. To a certain temperament the situation might have seemed intriguing–my own instinct was to telephone immediately for the police.

The horses, needless to say, were not mentioned again. Tom and Miss Baker, with several feet of twilight between them strolled back into the library, as if to a vigil beside a perfectly tangible body, while trying to look pleasantly interested and a little deaf I followed Daisy around a chain of connecting verandas to the porch in front. In its deep gloom we sat down side by side on a wicker settee.

Daisy took her face in her hands, as if feeling its lovely shape, and her eyes moved gradually out into the velvet dusk. I saw that turbulent emotions possessed her, so I asked what I thought would be some sedative questions about her little girl.

"We don't know each other very well, Nick," she said suddenly. "Even if we are cousins. You didn't come to my wedding."

"I wasn't back from the war."

"That's true." She hesitated. "Well, I've had a very bad time, Nick, and I'm pretty cynical about everything."

Evidently she had reason to be. I waited but she didn't say any more, and after a moment I returned rather feebly to the subject of her daughter.

"I suppose she talks, and—eats, and everything."

"Oh, yes." She looked at me absently. "Listen, Nick; let me tell you what I said when she was born. Would you like to hear?"

"Very much."

"It'll show you how I've gotten to feel about—things. Well, she was less than an hour old and Tom was God knows where. I woke up out of the ether with an utterly abandoned feeling and asked the nurse right away if it was a boy or a girl. She told me it was a girl, and so I turned my head away and wept. 'All right,' I said, 'I'm glad it's a girl. And I hope she'll be a fool—that's the best thing a girl can be in this world, a beautiful little fool.'"

"You see I think everything's terrible anyhow," she went on in a convinced way. "Everybody thinks so—the most advanced people. And I know. I've been everywhere and seen everything and done everything." Her eyes flashed around her in a defiant way, rather like Tom's, and she laughed with thrilling scorn. "Sophisticated—God, I'm sophisticated!"

The instant her voice broke off, ceasing to compel my attention, my belief, I felt the basic insincerity of what she had said. It made me uneasy, as though the whole evening had been a trick of some sort to exact a contributory emotion from me. I waited, and sure enough, in a moment she looked at me with an absolute smirk on her lovely face as if she had asserted her membership in a rather distinguished secret society to which she and Tom belonged.

Inside, the crimson room bloomed with light. Tom and Miss Baker sat at either end of the long couch and she read aloud to him from the "Saturday Evening Post"—the words, murmurous and uninflected,

running together in a soothing tune. The lamp-light, bright on his boots and dull on the autumn-leaf yellow of her hair, glinted along the paper as she turned a page with a flutter of slender muscles in her arms.

When we came in she held us silent for a moment with a lifted hand.

"To be continued," she said, tossing the magazine on the table, "in our very next issue."

Her body asserted itself with a restless movement of her knee, and she stood up.

"Ten o'clock," she remarked, apparently finding the time on the ceiling. "Time for this good girl to go to bed."

"Jordan's going to play in the tournament tomorrow," explained Daisy, "over at Westchester."

"Oh,—you're Jordan Baker."

I knew now why her face was familiar—its pleasing contemptuous expression had looked out at me from many rotogravure pictures of the sporting life at Asheville and Hot Springs and Palm Beach. I had heard some story of her too, a critical, unpleasant story, but what it was I had forgotten long ago.

"Good night," she said softly. "Wake me at eight, won't you."

"If you'll get up."

"I will. Good night, Mr. Carraway. See you anon."

"Of course you will," confirmed Daisy. "In fact I think I'll arrange a marriage. Come over often, Nick, and I'll sort of—oh—fling you together. You know—lock you up accidentally in linen closets and push you out to sea in a boat, and all that sort of thing—"

"Good night," called Miss Baker from the stairs. "I haven't heard a word."

"She's a nice girl," said Tom after a moment. "They oughtn't to let her run around the country this way."

"Who oughtn't to?" inquired Daisy coldly.

"Her family."

"Her family is one aunt about a thousand years old. Besides, Nick's going to look after her, aren't you, Nick? She's going to spend lots of week-ends out here this summer. I think the home influence will be very good for her."

Daisy and Tom looked at each other for a moment in silence.

"Is she from New York?" I asked quickly.

"From Louisville. Our white girlhood was passed together there. Our beautiful white–"

"Did you give Nick a little heart to heart talk on the veranda?" demanded Tom suddenly.

"Did I?" She looked at me. "I can't seem to remember, but I think we talked about the Nordic race. Yes, I'm sure we did. It sort of crept up on us and first thing you know–"

"Don't believe everything you hear, Nick," he advised me.

I said lightly that I had heard nothing at all, and a few minutes later I got up to go home. They came to the door with me and stood side by side in a cheerful square of light. As I started my motor Daisy peremptorily called "Wait!

"I forgot to ask you something, and it's important. We heard you were engaged to a girl out West."

"That's right," corroborated Tom kindly. "We heard that you were engaged."

"It's libel. I'm too poor."

"But we heard it," insisted Daisy, surprising me by opening up again in a flower-like way. "We heard it from three people so it must be true."

Of course I knew what they were referring to, but I wasn't even vaguely engaged. The fact that gossip had published the banns was one of the reasons I had come east. You can't stop going with an old friend on account of rumors and on the other hand I had no intention

of being rumored into marriage.

Their interest rather touched me and made them less remotely rich—nevertheless, I was confused and a little disgusted as I drove away. It seemed to me that the thing for Daisy to do was to rush out of the house, child in arms—but apparently there were no such intentions in her head. As for Tom, the fact that he "had some woman in New York" was really less surprising than that he had been depressed by a book. Something was making him nibble at the edge of stale ideas as if his sturdy physical egotism no longer nourished his peremptory heart.

Already it was deep summer on roadhouse roofs and in front of wayside garages, where new red gas-pumps sat out in pools of light, and when I reached my estate at West Egg I ran the car under its shed and sat for a while on an abandoned grass roller in the yard. The wind had blown off, leaving a loud bright night with wings beating in the trees and a persistent organ sound as the full bellows of the earth blew the frogs full of life. The silhouette of a moving cat wavered across the moonlight and turning my head to watch it I saw that I was not alone—fifty feet away a figure had emerged from the shadow of my neighbor's mansion and was standing with his hands in his pockets regarding the silver pepper of the stars. Something in his leisurely movements and the secure position of his feet upon the lawn suggested that it was Mr. Gatsby himself, come out to determine what share was his of our local heavens.

I decided to call to him. Miss Baker had mentioned him at dinner, and that would do for an introduction. But I didn't call to him for he gave a sudden intimation that he was content to be alone—he stretched out his arms toward the dark water in a curious way, and far as I was from him I could have sworn he was trembling. Involuntarily I glanced seaward—and distinguished nothing except a single green light, minute and far away, that might have been the end of a dock. When I looked once more for Gatsby he had vanished, and I was alone again in the unquiet darkness.

CHAPTER 2

About half way between West Egg and New York the motor-road hastily joins the railroad and runs beside it for a quarter of a mile, so as to shrink away from a certain desolate area of land. This is a valley of ashes—a fantastic farm where ashes grow like wheat into ridges and hills and grotesque gardens where ashes take the forms of houses and chimneys and rising smoke and finally, with a transcendent effort, of men who move dimly and already crumbling through the powdery air. Occasionally a line of grey cars crawls along an invisible track, gives out a ghastly creak and comes to rest, and immediately the ash-grey men swarm up with leaden spades and stir up an impenetrable cloud which screens their obscure operations from your sight.

But above the grey land and the spasms of bleak dust which drift endlessly over it, you perceive, after a moment, the eyes of Doctor T. J. Eckleburg. The eyes of Doctor T. J. Eckleburg are blue and gigantic—their retinas are one yard high. They look out of no face but, instead, from a pair of enormous yellow spectacles which pass over a nonexistent nose. Evidently some wild wag of an oculist set them there to fatten his practice in the borough of Queens, and then sank down himself into eternal blindness or forgot them and moved away. But his eyes, dimmed a little by many paintless days under sun and rain, brood on over the solemn dumping ground.

The valley of ashes is bounded on one side by a small foul river, and when the drawbridge is up to let barges through, the passengers on waiting trains can stare at the dismal scene for as long as half an hour. There is always a halt there of at least a minute and it was

because of this that I first met Tom Buchanan's mistress.

The fact that he had one was insisted upon wherever he was known. His acquaintances resented the fact that he turned up in popular restaurants with her and, leaving her at a table, sauntered about, chatting with whomsoever he knew. Though I was curious to see her I had no desire to meet her–but I did. I went up to New York with Tom on the train one afternoon and when we stopped by the ashheaps he jumped to his feet and taking hold of my elbow literally forced me from the car.

"We're getting off!" he insisted. "I want you to meet my girl."

I think he'd tanked up a good deal at luncheon and his determination to have my company bordered on violence. The supercilious assumption was that on Sunday afternoon I had nothing better to do.

I followed him over a low white-washed railroad fence and we walked back a hundred yards along the road under Doctor Eckleburg's persistent stare. The only building in sight was a small block of yellow brick sitting on the edge of the waste land, a sort of compact Main Street ministering to it and contiguous to absolutely nothing. One of the three shops it contained was for rent and another was an all-night restaurant approached by a trail of ashes; the third was a garage–Repairs. GEORGE B. WILSON. Cars Bought and Sold–and I followed Tom inside.

The interior was unprosperous and bare; the only car visible was the dust-covered wreck of a Ford which crouched in a dim corner. It had occurred to me that this shadow of a garage must be a blind and that sumptuous and romantic apartments were concealed overhead when the proprietor himself appeared in the door of an office, wiping his hands on a piece of waste. He was a blonde, spiritless man, anaemic, and faintly handsome. When he saw us a damp gleam of hope sprang into his light blue eyes.

"Hello, Wilson, old man," said Tom, slapping him jovially on the shoulder. "How's business?"

"I can't complain," answered Wilson unconvincingly. "When are you going to sell me that car?"

"Next week; I've got my man working on it now."

"Works pretty slow, don't he?"

"No, he doesn't," said Tom coldly. "And if you feel that way about it, maybe I'd better sell it somewhere else after all."

"I don't mean that," explained Wilson quickly. "I just meant—"

His voice faded off and Tom glanced impatiently around the garage. Then I heard footsteps on a stairs and in a moment the thickish figure of a woman blocked out the light from the office door. She was in the middle thirties, and faintly stout, but she carried her surplus flesh sensuously as some women can. Her face, above a spotted dress of dark blue crepe-de-chine, contained no facet or gleam of beauty but there was an immediately perceptible vitality about her as if the nerves of her body were continually smouldering. She smiled slowly and walking through her husband as if he were a ghost shook hands with Tom, looking him flush in the eye. Then she wet her lips and without turning around spoke to her husband in a soft, coarse voice:

"Get some chairs, why don't you, so somebody can sit down."

"Oh, sure," agreed Wilson hurriedly and went toward the little office, mingling immediately with the cement color of the walls. A white ashen dust veiled his dark suit and his pale hair as it veiled everything in the vicinity—except his wife, who moved close to Tom.

"I want to see you," said Tom intently. "Get on the next train."

"All right."

"I'll meet you by the news-stand on the lower level."

She nodded and moved away from him just as George Wilson emerged with two chairs from his office door.

We waited for her down the road and out of sight. It was a few days before the Fourth of July, and a grey, scrawny Italian child was

setting torpedoes in a row along the railroad track.

"Terrible place, isn't it," said Tom, exchanging a frown with Doctor Eckleburg.

"Awful."

"It does her good to get away."

"Doesn't her husband object?"

"Wilson? He thinks she goes to see her sister in New York. He's so dumb he doesn't know he's alive."

So Tom Buchanan and his girl and I went up together to New York—or not quite together, for Mrs. Wilson sat discreetly in another car. Tom deferred that much to the sensibilities of those East Eggers who might be on the train.

She had changed her dress to a brown figured muslin which stretched tight over her rather wide hips as Tom helped her to the platform in New York. At the news-stand she bought a copy of "Town Tattle" and a moving-picture magazine and, in the station drug store, some cold cream and a small flask of perfume. Upstairs, in the solemn echoing drive she let four taxi cabs drive away before she selected a new one, lavender-colored with grey upholstery, and in this we slid out from the mass of the station into the glowing sunshine. But immediately she turned sharply from the window and leaning forward tapped on the front glass.

"I want to get one of those dogs," she said earnestly. "I want to get one for the apartment. They're nice to have—a dog."

We backed up to a grey old man who bore an absurd resemblance to John D. Rockefeller. In a basket, swung from his neck, cowered a dozen very recent puppies of an indeterminate breed.

"What kind are they?" asked Mrs. Wilson eagerly as he came to the taxi-window.

"All kinds. What kind do you want, lady?"

"I'd like to get one of those police dogs; I don't suppose you got

223

that kind?"

The man peered doubtfully into the basket, plunged in his hand and drew one up, wriggling, by the back of the neck.

"That's no police dog," said Tom.

"No, it's not exactly a police dog," said the man with disappointment in his voice. "It's more of an airedale." He passed his hand over the brown wash-rag of a back. "Look at that coat. Some coat. That's a dog that'll never bother you with catching cold."

"I think it's cute," said Mrs. Wilson enthusiastically. "How much is it?"

"That dog?" He looked at it admiringly. "That dog will cost you ten dollars."

The airedale—undoubtedly there was an airedale concerned in it somewhere though its feet were startlingly white—changed hands and settled down into Mrs. Wilson's lap, where she fondled the weather-proof coat with rapture.

"Is it a boy or a girl?" she asked delicately.

"That dog? That dog's a boy."

"It's a bitch," said Tom decisively. "Here's your money. Go and buy ten more dogs with it."

We drove over to Fifth Avenue, so warm and soft, almost pastoral, on the summer Sunday afternoon that I wouldn't have been surprised to see a great flock of white sheep turn the corner.

"Hold on," I said, "I have to leave you here."

"No, you don't," interposed Tom quickly. "Myrtle'll be hurt if you don't come up to the apartment. Won't you, Myrtle?"

"Come on," she urged. "I'll telephone my sister Catherine. She's said to be very beautiful by people who ought to know."

"Well, I'd like to, but—"

We went on, cutting back again over the Park toward the West

Hundreds. At 158th Street the cab stopped at one slice in a long white cake of apartment houses. Throwing a regal homecoming glance around the neighborhood, Mrs. Wilson gathered up her dog and her other purchases and went haughtily in.

"I'm going to have the McKees come up," she announced as we rose in the elevator. "And of course I got to call up my sister, too."

The apartment was on the top floor—a small living room, a small dining room, a small bedroom and a bath. The living room was crowded to the doors with a set of tapestried furniture entirely too large for it so that to move about was to stumble continually over scenes of ladies swinging in the gardens of Versailles. The only picture was an over-enlarged photograph, apparently a hen sitting on a blurred rock. Looked at from a distance however the hen resolved itself into a bonnet and the countenance of a stout old lady beamed down into the room. Several old copies of "Town Tattle" lay on the table together with a copy of "Simon Called Peter" and some of the small scandal magazines of Broadway. Mrs. Wilson was first concerned with the dog. A reluctant elevator boy went for a box full of straw and some milk to which he added on his own initiative a tin of large hard dog biscuits—one of which decomposed apathetically in the saucer of milk all afternoon. Meanwhile Tom brought out a bottle of whiskey from a locked bureau door.

I have been drunk just twice in my life and the second time was that afternoon so everything that happened has a dim hazy cast over it although until after eight o'clock the apartment was full of cheerful sun. Sitting on Tom's lap Mrs. Wilson called up several people on the telephone; then there were no cigarettes and I went out to buy some at the drug store on the corner. When I came back they had disappeared so I sat down discreetly in the living room and read a chapter of "Simon Called Peter"—either it was terrible stuff or the whiskey distorted things because it didn't make any sense to me.

Just as Tom and Myrtle—after the first drink Mrs. Wilson and I called each other by our first names—reappeared, company commenced to arrive at the apartment door.

The sister, Catherine, was a slender, worldly girl of about thirty with a solid sticky bob of red hair and a complexion powdered milky white. Her eyebrows had been plucked and then drawn on again at a more rakish angle but the efforts of nature toward the restoration of the old alignment gave a blurred air to her face. When she moved about there was an incessant clicking as innumerable pottery bracelets jingled up and down upon her arms. She came in with such a proprietary haste and looked around so possessively at the furniture that I wondered if she lived here. But when I asked her she laughed immoderately, repeated my question aloud and told me she lived with a girl friend at a hotel.

Mr. McKee was a pale feminine man from the flat below. He had just shaved for there was a white spot of lather on his cheekbone and he was most respectful in his greeting to everyone in the room. He informed me that he was in the "artistic game" and I gathered later that he was a photographer and had made the dim enlargement of Mrs. Wilson's mother which hovered like an ectoplasm on the wall. His wife was shrill, languid, handsome and horrible. She told me with pride that her husband had photographed her a hundred and twenty-seven times since they had been married.

Mrs. Wilson had changed her costume some time before and was now attired in an elaborate afternoon dress of cream colored chiffon, which gave out a continual rustle as she swept about the room. With the influence of the dress her personality had also undergone a change. The intense vitality that had been so remarkable in the garage was converted into impressive hauteur. Her laughter, her gestures, her assertions became more violently affected moment by moment and as she expanded the room grew smaller around her until she seemed to

be revolving on a noisy, creaking pivot through the smoky air.

"My dear," she told her sister in a high mincing shout, "most of these fellas will cheat you every time. All they think of is money. I had a woman up here last week to look at my feet and when she gave me the bill you'd of thought she had my appendicitus out."

"What was the name of the woman?" asked Mrs. McKee.

"Mrs. Eberhardt. She goes around looking at people's feet in their own homes."

"I like your dress," remarked Mrs. McKee, "I think it's adorable."

Mrs. Wilson rejected the compliment by raising her eyebrow in disdain.

"It's just a crazy old thing," she said. "I just slip it on sometimes when I don't care what I look like."

"But it looks wonderful on you, if you know what I mean," pursued Mrs. McKee. "If Chester could only get you in that pose I think he could make something of it."

We all looked in silence at Mrs. Wilson who removed a strand of hair from over her eyes and looked back at us with a brilliant smile. Mr. McKee regarded her intently with his head on one side and then moved his hand back and forth slowly in front of his face.

"I should change the light," he said after a moment. "I'd like to bring out the modelling of the features. And I'd try to get hold of all the back hair."

"I wouldn't think of changing the light," cried Mrs. McKee. "I think it's—"

Her husband said "Sh!" and we all looked at the subject again whereupon Tom Buchanan yawned audibly and got to his feet.

"You McKees have something to drink," he said. "Get some more ice and mineral water, Myrtle, before everybody goes to sleep."

"I told that boy about the ice." Myrtle raised her eyebrows in

despair at the shiftlessness of the lower orders. "These people! You have to keep after them all the time."

She looked at me and laughed pointlessly. Then she flounced over to the dog, kissed it with ecstasy and swept into the kitchen, implying that a dozen chefs awaited her orders there.

"I've done some nice things out on Long Island," asserted Mr. McKee.

Tom looked at him blankly.

"Two of them we have framed downstairs."

"Two what?" demanded Tom.

"Two studies. One of them I call 'Montauk Point—the Gulls,' and the other I call 'Montauk Point—the Sea.' "

The sister Catherine sat down beside me on the couch.

"Do you live down on Long Island, too?" she inquired.

"I live at West Egg."

"Really? I was down there at a party about a month ago. At a man named Gatsby's. Do you know him?"

"I live next door to him."

"Well, they say he's a nephew or a cousin of Kaiser Wilhelm's. That's where all his money comes from."

"Really?"

She nodded.

"I'm scared of him. I'd hate to have him get anything on me."

This absorbing information about my neighbor was interrupted by Mrs. McKee's pointing suddenly at Catherine:

"Chester, I think you could do something with her," she broke out, but Mr. McKee only nodded in a bored way and turned his attention to Tom.

"I'd like to do more work on Long Island if I could get the entry. All I ask is that they should give me a start."

"Ask Myrtle," said Tom, breaking into a short shout of laughter as Mrs. Wilson entered with a tray. "She'll give you a letter of introduction, won't you, Myrtle?"

"Do what?" she asked, startled.

"You'll give McKee a letter of introduction to your husband, so he can do some studies of him." His lips moved silently for a moment as he invented. " 'George B. Wilson at the Gasoline Pump,' or something like that."

Catherine leaned close to me and whispered in my ear: "Neither of them can stand the person they're married to."

"Can't they?"

"Can't stand them." She looked at Myrtle and then at Tom. "What I say is, why go on living with them if they can't stand them? If I was them I'd get a divorce and get married to each other right away."

"Doesn't she like Wilson either?"

The answer to this was unexpected. It came from Myrtle who had overheard the question and it was violent and obscene.

"You see?" cried Catherine triumphantly. She lowered her voice again. "It's really his wife that's keeping them apart. She's a Catholic and they don't believe in divorce."

Daisy was not a Catholic and I was a little shocked at the elaborateness of the lie.

"When they do get married," continued Catherine, "they're going west to live for a while until it blows over."

"It'd be more discreet to go to Europe."

"Oh, do you like Europe?" she exclaimed surprisingly. "I just got back from Monte Carlo."

"Really."

"Just last year. I went over there with another girl."

"Stay long?"

"No, we just went to Monte Carlo and back. We went by way of Marseilles. We had over twelve hundred dollars when we started but we got gypped out of it all in two days in the private rooms. We had an awful time getting back, I can tell you. God, how I hated that town!"

The late afternoon sky bloomed in the window for a moment like the blue honey of the Mediterranean—then the shrill voice of Mrs. McKee called me back into the room.

"I almost made a mistake, too," she declared vigorously. "I almost married a little kyke who'd been after me for years. I knew he was below me. Everybody kept saying to me: 'Lucille, that man's way below you!' But if I hadn't met Chester, he'd of got me sure."

"Yes, but listen," said Myrtle Wilson, nodding her head up and down, "at least you didn't marry him."

"I know I didn't."

"Well, I married him," said Myrtle, ambiguously. "And that's the difference between your case and mine."

"Why did you, Myrtle?" demanded Catherine. "Nobody forced you to."

Myrtle considered.

"I married him because I thought he was a gentleman," she said finally. "I thought he knew something about breeding, but he wasn't fit to lick my shoe."

"You were crazy about him for a while," said Catherine.

"Crazy about him!" cried Myrtle incredulously. "Who said I was crazy about him? I never was any more crazy about him than I was about that man there."

She pointed suddenly at me, and every one looked at me accusingly. I tried to show by my expression that I had played no part in her past.

"The only crazy I was was when I married him. I knew right away I made a mistake. He borrowed somebody's best suit to get married in

and never even told me about it, and the man came after it one day when he was out." She looked around to see who was listening: " 'Oh, is that your suit?' I said. 'This is the first I ever heard about it.' But I gave it to him and then I lay down and cried to beat the band all afternoon."

"She really ought to get away from him," resumed Catherine to me. "They've been living over that garage for eleven years. And Tom's the first sweetie she ever had."

The bottle of whiskey—a second one—was now in constant demand by all present, excepting Catherine who "felt just as good on nothing at all." Tom rang for the janitor and sent him for some celebrated sandwiches, which were a complete supper in themselves. I wanted to get out and walk eastward toward the park through the soft twilight but each time I tried to go I became entangled in some wild strident argument which pulled me back, as if with ropes, into my chair. Yet high over the city our line of yellow windows must have contributed their share of human secrecy to the casual watcher in the darkening streets, and I was him too, looking up and wondering. I was within and without, simultaneously enchanted and repelled by the inexhaustible variety of life.

Myrtle pulled her chair close to mine, and suddenly her warm breath poured over me the story of her first meeting with Tom.

"It was on the two little seats facing each other that are always the last ones left on the train. I was going up to New York to see my sister and spend the night. He had on a dress suit and patent leather shoes and I couldn't keep my eyes off him but every time he looked at me I had to pretend to be looking at the advertisement over his head. When we came into the station he was next to me and his white shirt-front pressed against my arm—and so I told him I'd have to call a policeman, but he knew I lied. I was so excited that when I got into a taxi with him I didn't hardly know I wasn't getting into a subway train. All I kept thinking

about, over and over, was 'You can't live forever, you can't live forever.' "

She turned to Mrs. McKee and the room rang full of her artificial laughter.

"My dear," she cried, "I'm going to give you this dress as soon as I'm through with it. I've got to get another one tomorrow. I'm going to make a list of all the things I've got to get. A massage and a wave and a collar for the dog and one of those cute little ash-trays where you touch a spring, and a wreath with a black silk bow for mother's grave that'll last all summer. I got to write down a list so I won't forget all the things I got to do."

It was nine o'clock—almost immediately afterward I looked at my watch and found it was ten. Mr. McKee was asleep on a chair with his fists clenched in his lap, like a photograph of a man of action. Taking out my handkerchief I wiped from his cheek the remains of the spot of dried lather that had worried me all the afternoon.

The little dog was sitting on the table looking with blind eyes through the smoke and from time to time groaning faintly. People disappeared, reappeared, made plans to go somewhere, and then lost each other, searched for each other, found each other a few feet away. Some time toward midnight Tom Buchanan and Mrs. Wilson stood face to face discussing in impassioned voices whether Mrs. Wilson had any right to mention Daisy's name.

"Daisy! Daisy! Daisy!" shouted Mrs. Wilson. "I'll say it whenever I want to! Daisy! Dai—"

Making a short deft movement Tom Buchanan broke her nose with his open hand.

Then there were bloody towels upon the bathroom floor, and women's voices scolding, and high over the confusion a long broken wail of pain. Mr. McKee awoke from his doze and started in a daze toward the door. When he had gone half way he turned around and stared at the scene—his wife and Catherine scolding and consoling as

The Great Gatsby

they stumbled here and there among the crowded furniture with articles of aid, and the despairing figure on the couch bleeding fluently and trying to spread a copy of "Town Tattle" over the tapestry scenes of Versailles. Then Mr. McKee turned and continued on out the door. Taking my hat from the chandelier I followed.

"Come to lunch some day," he suggested, as we groaned down in the elevator.

"Where?"

"Anywhere."

"Keep your hands off the lever," snapped the elevator boy.

"I beg your pardon," said Mr. McKee with dignity, "I didn't know I was touching it."

"All right," I agreed, "I'll be glad to."

I was standing beside his bed and he was sitting up between the sheets, clad in his underwear, with a great portfolio in his hands.

"Beauty and the Beast...Loneliness...Old Grocery Horse... Brook'n Bridge..."

Then I was lying half asleep in the cold lower level of the Pennsylvania Station, staring at the morning "Tribune" and waiting for the four o'clock train.

CHAPTER 3

There was music from my neighbor's house through the summer nights. In his blue gardens men and girls came and went like moths among the whisperings and the champagne and the stars. At high tide in the afternoon I watched his guests diving from the tower of his raft or taking the sun on the hot sand of his beach while his two motorboats slit the waters of the Sound, drawing aquaplanes over cataracts of foam. On week-ends his Rolls-Royce became an omnibus, bearing parties to and from the city, between nine in the morning and long past midnight, while his station wagon scampered like a brisk yellow bug to meet all trains. And on Mondays eight servants including an extra gardener toiled all day with mops and scrubbing-brushes and hammers and garden-shears, repairing the ravages of the night before.

Every Friday five crates of oranges and lemons arrived from a fruiterer in New York—every Monday these same oranges and lemons left his back door in a pyramid of pulpless halves. There was a machine in the kitchen which could extract the juice of two hundred oranges in half an hour, if a little button was pressed two hundred times by a butler's thumb.

At least once a fortnight a corps of caterers came down with several hundred feet of canvas and enough colored lights to make a Christmas tree of Gatsby's enormous garden. On buffet tables, garnished with glistening hors-d'oeuvre, spiced baked hams crowded against salads of harlequin designs and pastry pigs and turkeys bewitched to a dark gold. In the main hall a bar with a real brass rail was set up, and stocked with gins and liquors and with cordials so long

forgotten that most of his female guests were too young to know one from another.

By seven o'clock the orchestra has arrived—no thin five-piece affair but a whole pitful of oboes and trombones and saxophones and viols and cornets and piccolos and low and high drums. The last swimmers have come in from the beach now and are dressing upstairs; the cars from New York are parked five deep in the drive, and already the halls and salons and verandas are gaudy with primary colors and hair shorn in strange new ways and shawls beyond the dreams of Castile. The bar is in full swing and floating rounds of cocktails permeate the garden outside until the air is alive with chatter and laughter and casual innuendo and introductions forgotten on the spot and enthusiastic meetings between women who never knew each other's names.

The lights grow brighter as the earth lurches away from the sun and now the orchestra is playing yellow cocktail music and the opera of voices pitches a key higher. Laughter is easier, minute by minute, spilled with prodigality, tipped out at a cheerful word. The groups change more swiftly, swell with new arrivals, dissolve and form in the same breath—already there are wanderers, confident girls who weave here and there among the stouter and more stable, become for a sharp, joyous moment the center of a group and then excited with triumph glide on through the sea-change of faces and voices and color under the constantly changing light.

Suddenly one of these gypsies in trembling opal, seizes a cocktail out of the air, dumps it down for courage and moving her hands like Frisco dances out alone on the canvas platform. A momentary hush; the orchestra leader varies his rhythm obligingly for her and there is a burst of chatter as the erroneous news goes around that she is Gilda Gray's understudy from the "Follies." The party has begun.

The Great Gatsby

I believe that on the first night I went to Gatsby's house I was one of the few guests who had actually been invited. People were not invited–they went there. They got into automobiles which bore them out to Long Island and somehow they ended up at Gatsby's door. Once there they were introduced by somebody who knew Gatsby and after that they conducted themselves according to the rules of behavior associated with amusement parks. Sometimes they came and went without having met Gatsby at all, came for the party with a simplicity of heart that was its own ticket of admission.

I had been actually invited. A chauffeur in a uniform of robin's egg blue crossed my lawn early that Saturday morning with a surprisingly formal note from his employer–the honor would be entirely Gatsby's, it said, if I would attend his "little party" that night. He had seen me several times and had intended to call on me long before but a peculiar combination of circumstances had prevented it– signed Jay Gatsby in a majestic hand.

Dressed up in white flannels I went over to his lawn a little after seven and wandered around rather ill-at-ease among swirls and eddies of people I didn't know–though here and there was a face I had noticed on the commuting train. I was immediately struck by the number of young Englishmen dotted about; all well dressed, all looking a little hungry and all talking in low earnest voices to solid and prosperous Americans. I was sure that they were selling something: bonds or insurance or automobiles. They were, at least, agonizingly aware of the easy money in the vicinity and convinced that it was theirs for a few words in the right key.

As soon as I arrived I made an attempt to find my host but the two or three people of whom I asked his whereabouts stared at me in such an amazed way and denied so vehemently any knowledge of his movements that I slunk off in the direction of the cocktail table–the

only place in the garden where a single man could linger without looking purposeless and alone.

I was on my way to get roaring drunk from sheer embarrassment when Jordan Baker came out of the house and stood at the head of the marble steps, leaning a little backward and looking with contemptuous interest down into the garden.

Welcome or not, I found it necessary to attach myself to someone before I should begin to address cordial remarks to the passers-by.

"Hello!" I roared, advancing toward her. My voice seemed unnaturally loud across the garden.

"I thought you might be here," she responded absently as I came up. "I remembered you lived next door to—"

She held my hand impersonally, as a promise that she'd take care of me in a minute, and gave ear to two girls in twin yellow dresses who stopped at the foot of the steps.

"Hello!" they cried together. "Sorry you didn't win."

That was for the golf tournament. She had lost in the finals the week before.

"You don't know who we are," said one of the girls in yellow, "but we met you here about a month ago."

"You've dyed your hair since then," remarked Jordan, and I started but the girls had moved casually on and her remark was addressed to the premature moon, produced like the supper, no doubt, out of a caterer's basket. With Jordan's slender golden arm resting in mine we descended the steps and sauntered about the garden. A tray of cocktails floated at us through the twilight and we sat down at a table with the two girls in yellow and three men, each one introduced to us as Mr. Mumble.

"Do you come to these parties often?" inquired Jordan of the girl

beside her.

"The last one was the one I met you at," answered the girl, in an alert, confident voice. She turned to her companion: "Wasn't it for you, Lucille?"

It was for Lucille, too.

"I like to come," Lucille said. "I never care what I do, so I always have a good time. When I was here last I tore my gown on a chair, and he asked me my name and address—inside of a week I got a package from Croirier's with a new evening gown in it."

"Did you keep it?" asked Jordan.

"Sure I did. I was going to wear it tonight, but it was too big in the bust and had to be altered. It was gas blue with lavender beads. Two hundred and sixty-five dollars."

"There's something funny about a fellow that'll do a thing like that," said the other girl eagerly. "He doesn't want any trouble with anybody."

"Who doesn't?" I inquired.

"Gatsby. Somebody told me—"

The two girls and Jordan leaned together confidentially.

"Somebody told me they thought he killed a man once."

A thrill passed over all of us. The three Mr. Mumbles bent forward and listened eagerly.

"I don't think it's so much that," argued Lucille skeptically; "it's more that he was a German spy during the war."

One of the men nodded in confirmation.

"I heard that from a man who knew all about him, grew up with him in Germany," he assured us positively.

"Oh, no," said the first girl, "it couldn't be that, because he was in the American army during the war." As our credulity switched back to her she leaned forward with enthusiasm. "You look at him sometimes

when he thinks nobody's looking at him. I'll bet he killed a man."

She narrowed her eyes and shivered. Lucille shivered. We all turned and looked around for Gatsby. It was testimony to the romantic speculation he inspired that there were whispers about him from those who found little that it was necessary to whisper about in this world.

The first supper—there would be another one after midnight—was now being served, and Jordan invited me to join her own party who were spread around a table on the other side of the garden. There were three married couples and Jordan's escort, a persistent undergraduate given to violent innuendo and obviously under the impression that sooner or later Jordan was going to yield him up her person to a greater or lesser degree. Instead of rambling this party had preserved a dignified homogeneity, and assumed to itself the function of representing the staid nobility of the countryside—East Egg condescending to West Egg, and carefully on guard against its spectroscopic gayety.

"Let's get out," whispered Jordan, after a somehow wasteful and inappropriate half hour. "This is much too polite for me."

We got up, and she explained that we were going to find the host—I had never met him, she said, and it was making me uneasy. The undergraduate nodded in a cynical, melancholy way.

The bar, where we glanced first, was crowded but Gatsby was not there. She couldn't find him from the top of the steps, and he wasn't on the veranda. On a chance we tried an important-looking door, and walked into a high Gothic library, panelled with carved English oak, and probably transported complete from some ruin overseas.

A stout, middle-aged man with enormous owl-eyed spectacles was sitting somewhat drunk on the edge of a great table, staring with unsteady concentration at the shelves of books. As we entered he

wheeled excitedly around and examined Jordan from head to foot.

"What do you think?" he demanded impetuously.

"About what?"

He waved his hand toward the book-shelves.

"About that. As a matter of fact you needn't bother to ascertain. I ascertained. They're real."

"The books?"

He nodded.

"Absolutely real—have pages and everything. I thought they'd be a nice durable cardboard. Matter of fact, they're absolutely real. Pages and—Here! Lemme show you."

Taking our skepticism for granted, he rushed to the bookcases and returned with Volume One of the "Stoddard Lectures."

"See!" he cried triumphantly. "It's a bona fide piece of printed matter. It fooled me. This fella's a regular Belasco. It's a triumph. What thoroughness! What realism! Knew when to stop too—didn't cut the pages. But what do you want? What do you expect?"

He snatched the book from me and replaced it hastily on its shelf muttering that if one brick was removed the whole library was liable to collapse.

"Who brought you?" he demanded. "Or did you just come? I was brought. Most people were brought."

Jordan looked at him alertly, cheerfully without answering.

"I was brought by a woman named Roosevelt," he continued. "Mrs. Claud Roosevelt. Do you know her? I met her somewhere last night. I've been drunk for about a week now, and I thought it might sober me up to sit in a library."

"Has it?"

"A little bit, I think. I can't tell yet. I've only been here an hour. Did I tell you about the books? They're real. They're—"

"You told us."

We shook hands with him gravely and went back outdoors.

There was dancing now on the canvas in the garden, old men pushing young girls backward in eternal graceless circles, superior couples holding each other tortuously, fashionably and keeping in the corners–and a great number of single girls dancing individualistically or relieving the orchestra for a moment of the burden of the banjo or the traps. By midnight the hilarity had increased. A celebrated tenor had sung in Italian and a notorious contralto had sung in jazz and between the numbers people were doing "stunts" all over the garden, while happy vacuous bursts of laughter rose toward the summer sky. A pair of stage "twins"–who turned out to be the girls in yellow–did a baby act in costume and champagne was served in glasses bigger than finger bowls. The moon had risen higher, and floating in the Sound was a triangle of silver scales, trembling a little to the stiff, tinny drip of the banjoes on the lawn.

I was still with Jordan Baker. We were sitting at a table with a man of about my age and a rowdy little girl who gave way upon the slightest provocation to uncontrollable laughter. I was enjoying myself now. I had taken two finger bowls of champagne and the scene had changed before my eyes into something significant, elemental and profound.

At a lull in the entertainment the man looked at me and smiled.

"Your face is familiar," he said, politely. "Weren't you in the Third Division during the war?"

"Why, yes. I was in the Ninth Machine-Gun Battalion."

"I was in the Seventh Infantry until June nineteen-eighteen. I knew I'd seen you somewhere before."

We talked for a moment about some wet, grey little villages in France. Evidently he lived in this vicinity for he told me that he had

just bought a hydroplane and was going to try it out in the morning.

"Want to go with me, old sport? Just near the shore along the Sound."

"What time?"

"Any time that suits you best."

It was on the tip of my tongue to ask his name when Jordan looked around and smiled.

"Having a gay time now?" she inquired.

"Much better." I turned again to my new acquaintance. "This is an unusual party for me. I haven't even seen the host. I live over there–" I waved my hand at the invisible hedge in the distance, "and this man Gatsby sent over his chauffeur with an invitation."

For a moment he looked at me as if he failed to understand.

"I'm Gatsby," he said suddenly.

"What!" I exclaimed. "Oh, I beg your pardon."

"I thought you knew, old sport. I'm afraid I'm not a very good host."

He smiled understandingly–much more than understandingly. It was one of those rare smiles with a quality of eternal reassurance in it, that you may come across four or five times in life. It faced–or seemed to face–the whole external world for an instant, and then concentrated on you with an irresistible prejudice in your favor. It understood you just so far as you wanted to be understood, believed in you as you would like to believe in yourself and assured you that it had precisely the impression of you that, at your best, you hoped to convey. Precisely at that point it vanished–and I was looking at an elegant young rough-neck, a year or two over thirty, whose elaborate formality of speech just missed being absurd. Some time before he introduced himself I'd got a strong impression that he was picking his words with care.

Almost at the moment when Mr. Gatsby identified himself a butler hurried toward him with the information that Chicago was calling him on the wire. He excused himself with a small bow that included each of us in turn.

"If you want anything just ask for it, old sport," he urged me. "Excuse me. I will rejoin you later."

When he was gone I turned immediately to Jordan—constrained to assure her of my surprise. I had expected that Mr. Gatsby would be a florid and corpulent person in his middle years.

"Who is he?" I demanded. "Do you know?"

"He's just a man named Gatsby."

"Where is he from, I mean? And what does he do?"

"Now you're started on the subject," she answered with a wan smile. "Well,—he told me once he was an Oxford man."

A dim background started to take shape behind him but at her next remark it faded away.

"However, I don't believe it."

"Why not?"

"I don't know," she insisted, "I just don't think he went there."

Something in her tone reminded me of the other girl's "I think he killed a man," and had the effect of stimulating my curiosity. I would have accepted without question the information that Gatsby sprang from the swamps of Louisiana or from the lower East Side of New York. That was comprehensible. But young men didn't—at least in my provincial inexperience I believed they didn't—drift coolly out of nowhere and buy a palace on Long Island Sound.

"Anyhow he gives large parties," said Jordan, changing the subject with an urbane distaste for the concrete. "And I like large parties. They're so intimate. At small parties there isn't any privacy."

There was the boom of a bass drum, and the voice of the

orchestra leader rang out suddenly above the echolalia of the garden.

"Ladies and gentlemen," he cried. "At the request of Mr. Gatsby we are going to play for you Mr. Vladimir Tostoff's latest work which attracted so much attention at Carnegie Hall last May. If you read the papers you know there was a big sensation." He smiled with jovial condescension and added "Some sensation!" whereupon everybody laughed.

"The piece is known," he concluded lustily, "as 'Vladimir Tostoff's Jazz History of the World.' "

The nature of Mr. Tostoff's composition eluded me, because just as it began my eyes fell on Gatsby, standing alone on the marble steps and looking from one group to another with approving eyes. His tanned skin was drawn attractively tight on his face and his short hair looked as though it were trimmed every day. I could see nothing sinister about him. I wondered if the fact that he was not drinking helped to set him off from his guests, for it seemed to me that he grew more correct as the fraternal hilarity increased. When the "Jazz History of the World" was over girls were putting their heads on men's shoulders in a puppyish, convivial way, girls were swooning backward playfully into men's arms, even into groups knowing that some one would arrest their falls—but no one swooned backward on Gatsby and no French bob touched Gatsby's shoulder and no singing quartets were formed with Gatsby's head for one link.

"I beg your pardon."

Gatsby's butler was suddenly standing beside us.

"Miss Baker?" he inquired. "I beg your pardon but Mr. Gatsby would like to speak to you alone."

"With me?" she exclaimed in surprise.

"Yes, madame."

She got up slowly, raising her eyebrows at me in astonishment,

and followed the butler toward the house. I noticed that she wore her evening dress, all her dresses, like sports clothes – there was a jauntiness about her movements as if she had first learned to walk upon golf courses on clean, crisp mornings.

I was alone and it was almost two. For some time confused and intriguing sounds had issued from a long many-windowed room which overhung the terrace. Eluding Jordan's undergraduate who was now engaged in an obstetrical conversation with two chorus girls, and who implored me to join him, I went inside.

The large room was full of people. One of the girls in yellow was playing the piano and beside her stood a tall, red haired young lady from a famous chorus, engaged in song. She had drunk a quantity of champagne and during the course of her song she had decided ineptly that everything was very very sad – she was not only singing, she was weeping too. Whenever there was a pause in the song she filled it with gasping broken sobs and then took up the lyric again in a quavering soprano. The tears coursed down her cheeks – not freely, however, for when they came into contact with her heavily beaded eyelashes they assumed an inky color, and pursued the rest of their way in slow black rivulets. A humorous suggestion was made that she sing the notes on her face whereupon she threw up her hands, sank into a chair and went off into a deep vinous sleep.

"She had a fight with a man who says he's her husband," explained a girl at my elbow.

I looked around. Most of the remaining women were now having fights with men said to be their husbands. Even Jordan's party, the quartet from East Egg, were rent asunder by dissension. One of the men was talking with curious intensity to a young actress, and his wife after attempting to laugh at the situation in a dignified and indifferent way broke down entirely and resorted to flank attacks – at intervals she

appeared suddenly at his side like an angry diamond, and hissed "You promised!" into his ear.

The reluctance to go home was not confined to wayward men. The hall was at present occupied by two deplorably sober men and their highly indignant wives. The wives were sympathizing with each other in slightly raised voices.

"Whenever he sees I'm having a good time he wants to go home."

"Never heard anything so selfish in my life."

"We're always the first ones to leave."

"So are we."

"Well, we're almost the last tonight," said one of the men sheepishly. "The orchestra left half an hour ago."

In spite of the wives' agreement that such malevolence was beyond credibility, the dispute ended in a short struggle, and both wives were lifted kicking into the night.

As I waited for my hat in the hall the door of the library opened and Jordan Baker and Gatsby came out together. He was saying some last word to her but the eagerness in his manner tightened abruptly into formality as several people approached him to say goodbye.

Jordan's party were calling impatiently to her from the porch but she lingered for a moment to shake hands.

"I've just heard the most amazing thing," she whispered. "How long were we in there?"

"Why,–about an hour."

"It was–simply amazing," she repeated abstractedly. "But I swore I wouldn't tell it and here I am tantalizing you." She yawned gracefully in my face. "Please come and see me...Phone book... Under the name of Mrs. Sigourney Howard...My aunt..." She was hurrying off as she talked–her brown hand waved a jaunty salute as she melted into her

party at the door.

Rather ashamed that on my first appearance I had stayed so late, I joined the last of Gatsby's guests who were clustered around him. I wanted to explain that I'd hunted for him early in the evening and to apologize for not having known him in the garden.

"Don't mention it," he enjoined me eagerly. "Don't give it another thought, old sport." The familiar expression held no more familiarity than the hand which reassuringly brushed my shoulder. "And don't forget we're going up in the hydroplane tomorrow morning at nine o'clock."

Then the butler, behind his shoulder:

"Philadelphia wants you on the phone, sir."

"All right, in a minute. Tell them I'll be right there...good night."

"Good night."

"Good night." He smiled—and suddenly there seemed to be a pleasant significance in having been among the last to go, as if he had desired it all the time. "Good night, old sport...Good night."

But as I walked down the steps I saw that the evening was not quite over. Fifty feet from the door a dozen headlights illuminated a bizarre and tumultuous scene. In the ditch beside the road, right side up but violently shorn of one wheel, rested a new coupé which had left Gatsby's drive not two minutes before. The sharp jut of a wall accounted for the detachment of the wheel which was now getting considerable attention from half a dozen curious chauffeurs. However, as they had left their cars blocking the road a harsh discordant din from those in the rear had been audible for some time and added to the already violent confusion of the scene.

A man in a long duster had dismounted from the wreck and now stood in the middle of the road, looking from the car to the tire and from the tire to the observers in a pleasant, puzzled way.

"See!" he explained. "It went in the ditch."

The fact was infinitely astonishing to him—and I recognized first the unusual quality of wonder and then the man—it was the late patron of Gatsby's library.

"How'd it happen?"

He shrugged his shoulders.

"I know nothing whatever about mechanics," he said decisively.

"But how did it happen? Did you run into the wall?"

"Don't ask me," said Owl Eyes, washing his hands of the whole matter. "I know very little about driving—next to nothing. It happened, and that's all I know."

"Well, if you're a poor driver you oughtn't to try driving at night."

"But I wasn't even trying," he explained indignantly, "I wasn't even trying."

An awed hush fell upon the bystanders.

"Do you want to commit suicide?"

"You're lucky it was just a wheel! A bad driver and not even trying!"

"You don't understand," explained the criminal. "I wasn't driving. There's another man in the car."

The shock that followed this declaration found voice in a sustained "Ah-h-h!" as the door of the coupé swung slowly open. The crowd—it was now a crowd—stepped back involuntarily and when the door had opened wide there was a ghostly pause. Then, very gradually, part by part, a pale dangling individual stepped out of the wreck, pawing tentatively at the ground with a large uncertain dancing shoe.

Blinded by the glare of the headlights and confused by the incessant groaning of the horns the apparition stood swaying for a moment before he perceived the man in the duster.

"Wha's matter?" he inquired calmly. "Did we run outa gas?"

"Look!"

Half a dozen fingers pointed at the amputated wheel—he stared at it for a moment and then looked upward as though he suspected that it had dropped from the sky.

"It came off," some one explained.

He nodded.

"At first I din' notice we'd stopped."

A pause. Then, taking a long breath and straightening his shoulders he remarked in a determined voice:

"Wonder'ff tell me where there's a gas'line station?"

At least a dozen men, some of them little better off than he was, explained to him that wheel and car were no longer joined by any physical bond.

"Back out," he suggested after a moment. "Put her in reverse."

"But the wheel's off!"

He hesitated.

"No harm in trying," he said.

The caterwauling horns had reached a crescendo and I turned away and cut across the lawn toward home. I glanced back once. A wafer of a moon was shining over Gatsby's house, making the night fine as before and surviving the laughter and the sound of his still glowing garden. A sudden emptiness seemed to flow now from the windows and the great doors, endowing with complete isolation the figure of the host who stood on the porch, his hand up in a formal gesture of farewell.

Reading over what I have written so far I see I have given the impression that the events of three nights several weeks apart were all that absorbed me. On the contrary they were merely casual events in a crowded summer and, until much later, they absorbed me infinitely less than my personal affairs.

Most of the time I worked. In the early morning the sun threw my shadow westward as I hurried down the white chasms of lower New York to the Probity Trust. I knew the other clerks and young bond-salesmen by their first names and lunched with them in dark crowded restaurants on little pig sausages and mashed potatoes and coffee. I even had a short affair with a girl who lived in Jersey City and worked in the accounting department, but her brother began throwing mean looks in my direction so when she went on her vacation in July I let it blow quietly away.

I took dinner usually at the Yale Club—for some reason it was the gloomiest event of my day—and then I went upstairs to the library and studied investments and securities for a conscientious hour. There were generally a few rioters around but they never came into the library so it was a good place to work. After that, if the night was mellow I strolled down Madison Avenue past the old Murray Hill Hotel and over Thirty-third Street to the Pennsylvania Station.

I began to like New York, the racy, adventurous feel of it at night and the satisfaction that the constant flicker of men and women and machines gives to the restless eye. I liked to walk up Fifth Avenue and pick out romantic women from the crowd and imagine that in a few minutes I was going to enter into their lives, and no one would ever know or disapprove. Sometimes, in my mind, I followed them to their apartments on the corners of hidden streets, and they turned and smiled back at me before they faded through a door into warm darkness. At the enchanted metropolitan twilight I felt a haunting loneliness sometimes, and felt it in others—poor young clerks who loitered in front of windows waiting until it was time for a solitary restaurant dinner—young clerks in the dusk, wasting the most poignant moments of night and life.

Again at eight o'clock, when the dark lanes of the Forties were

five deep with throbbing taxi cabs, bound for the theatre district, I felt a sinking in my heart. Forms leaned together in the taxis as they waited, and voices sang, and there was laughter from unheard jokes, and lighted cigarettes outlined unintelligible gestures inside. Imagining that I, too, was hurrying toward gayety and sharing their intimate excitement, I wished them well.

For a while I lost sight of Jordan Baker, and then in midsummer I found her again. At first I was flattered to go places with her because she was a golf champion and every one knew her name. Then it was something more. I wasn't actually in love, but I felt a sort of tender curiosity. The bored haughty face that she turned to the world concealed something-most affectations conceal something eventually, even though they don't in the beginning-and one day I found what it was. When we were on a house-party together up in Warwick, she left a borrowed car out in the rain with the top down, and then lied about it-and suddenly I remembered the story about her that had eluded me that night at Daisy's. At her first big golf tournament there was a row that nearly reached the newspapers-a suggestion that she had moved her ball from a bad lie in the semi-final round. The thing approached the proportions of a scandal-then died away. A caddy retracted his statement and the only other witness admitted that he might have been mistaken. The incident and the name had remained together in my mind.

Jordan Baker instinctively avoided clever, shrewd men, and now I saw that this was because she felt safer on a plane where any divergence from a code would be thought impossible. She was incurably dishonest. She wasn't able to endure being at a disadvantage, and given this unwillingness, I suppose she had begun dealing in subterfuges when she was very young in order to keep that cool, insolent smile turned to the world and yet satisfy the demands of her

hard jaunty body.

It made no difference to me. Dishonesty in a woman is a thing you never blame deeply—I was casually sorry, and then I forgot. It was on that same house party that we had a curious conversation about driving a car. It started because she passed so close to some workmen that our fender flicked a button on one man's coat.

"You're a rotten driver," I protested. "Either you ought to be more careful or you oughtn't to drive at all."

"I am careful."

"No, you're not."

"Well, other people are," she said lightly.

"What's that got to do with it?"

"They'll keep out of my way," she insisted. "It takes two to make an accident."

"Suppose you met somebody just as careless as yourself."

"I hope I never will," she answered. "I hate careless people. That's why I like you."

Her grey, sun-strained eyes stared straight ahead, but she had deliberately shifted our relations, and for a moment I thought I loved her. But I am slow-thinking and full of interior rules that act as brakes on my desires, and I knew that first I had to get myself definitely out of that tangle back home. I'd been writing letters once a week and signing them: "Love, Nick," and all I could think of was how, when that certain girl played tennis, a faint mustache of perspiration appeared on her upper lip. Nevertheless there was a vague understanding that had to be tactfully broken off before I was free.

Every one suspects himself of at least one of the cardinal virtues, and this is mine: I am one of the few honest people that I have ever known.

CHAPTER 4

On Sunday morning while church bells rang in the villages along shore the world and its mistress returned to Gatsby's house and twinkled hilariously on his lawn.

"He's a bootlegger," said the young ladies, moving somewhere between his cocktails and his flowers. "One time he killed a man who had found out that he was nephew to von Hindenburg and second cousin to the devil. Reach me a rose, honey, and pour me a last drop into that there crystal glass."

Once I wrote down on the empty spaces of a time-table the names of those who came to Gatsby's house that summer. It is an old time-table now, disintegrating at its folds and headed "This schedule in effect July 5th, 1922." But I can still read the grey names and they will give you a better impression than my generalities of those who accepted Gatsby's hospitality and paid him the subtle tribute of knowing nothing whatever about him.

From East Egg, then, came the Chester Beckers and the Leeches and a man named Bunsen whom I knew at Yale and Doctor Webster Civet who was drowned last summer up in Maine. And the Hornbeams and the Willie Voltaires and a whole clan named Blackbuck who always gathered in a corner and flipped up their noses like goats at whosoever came near. And the Ismays and the Chrysties (or rather Hubert Auerbach and Mr. Chrystie's wife) and Edgar Beaver, whose hair they say turned cotton-white one winter afternoon for no good reason at all.

Clarence Endive was from East Egg, as I remember. He came

only once, in white knickerbockers, and had a fight with a bum named Etty in the garden. From farther out on the Island came the Cheadles and the O. R. P. Schraeders and the Stonewall Jackson Abrams of Georgia and the Fishguards and the Ripley Snells. Snell was there three days before he went to the penitentiary, so drunk out on the gravel drive that Mrs. Ulysses Swett's automobile ran over his right hand. The Dancies came too and S. B. Whitebait, who was well over sixty, and Maurice A. Flink and the Hammerheads and Beluga the tobacco importer and Beluga's girls.

From West Egg came the Poles and the Mulreadys and Cecil Roebuck and Cecil Schoen and Gulick the state senator and Newton Orchid who controlled Films Par Excellence and Eckhaust and Clyde Cohen and Don S. Schwartze (the son) and Arthur McCarty, all connected with the movies in one way or another. And the Catlips and the Bembergs and G. Earl Muldoon, brother to that Muldoon who afterward strangled his wife. Da Fontano the promoter came there, and Ed Legros and James B. ("Rot-Gut") Ferret and the De Jongs and Ernest Lilly–they came to gamble and when Ferret wandered into the garden it meant he was cleaned out and Associated Traction would have to fluctuate profitably next day.

A man named Klipspringer was there so often and so long that he became known as "the boarder"–I doubt if he had any other home. Of theatrical people there were Gus Waize and Horace O'Donavan and Lester Meyer and George Duckweed and Francis Bull. Also from New York were the Chromes and the Backhyssons and the Dennickers and Russel Betty and the Corrigans and the Kellehers and the Dewars and the Scullys and S. W. Belcher and the Smirkes and the young Quinns, divorced now, and Henry L. Palmetto who killed himself by jumping in front of a subway train in Times Square.

Benny McClenahan arrived always with four girls. They were never quite the same ones in physical person but they were so identical one with another that it inevitably seemed they had been there before. I have forgotten their names—Jaqueline, I think, or else Consuela or Gloria or Judy or June, and their last names were either the melodious names of flowers and months or the sterner ones of the great American capitalists whose cousins, if pressed, they would confess themselves to be.

In addition to all these I can remember that Faustina O'Brien came there at least once and the Baedeker girls and young Brewer who had his nose shot off in the war and Mr. Albrucksburger and Miss Haag, his fiancée, and Ardita Fitz-Peters, and Mr. P. Jewett, once head of the American Legion, and Miss Claudia Hip with a man reputed to be her chauffeur, and a prince of something whom we called Duke and whose name, if I ever knew it, I have forgotten.

All these people came to Gatsby's house in the summer.

At nine o'clock, one morning late in July Gatsby's gorgeous car lurched up the rocky drive to my door and gave out a burst of melody from its three noted horn. It was the first time he had called on me though I had gone to two of his parties, mounted in his hydroplane, and, at his urgent invitation, made frequent use of his beach.

"Good morning, old sport. You're having lunch with me today and I thought we'd ride up together."

He was balancing himself on the dashboard of his car with that resourcefulness of movement that is so peculiarly American—that comes, I suppose, with the absence of lifting work or rigid sitting in youth and, even more, with the formless grace of our nervous, sporadic games. This quality was continually breaking through his punctilious manner in the shape of restlessness. He was never quite still; there was always a tapping foot somewhere or the impatient

opening and closing of a hand.

He saw me looking with admiration at his car.

"It's pretty, isn't it, old sport." He jumped off to give me a better view. "Haven't you ever seen it before?"

I'd seen it. Everybody had seen it. It was a rich cream color, bright with nickel, swollen here and there in its monstrous length with triumphant hatboxes and supper-boxes and tool-boxes, and terraced with a labyrinth of windshields that mirrored a dozen suns. Sitting down behind many layers of glass in a sort of green leather conservatory we started to town.

I had talked with him perhaps half a dozen times in the past month and found, to my disappointment, that he had little to say. So my first impression, that he was a person of some undefined consequence, had gradually faded and he had become simply the proprietor of an elaborate roadhouse next door.

And then came that disconcerting ride. We hadn't reached West Egg village before Gatsby began leaving his elegant sentences unfinished and slapping himself indecisively on the knee of his caramel-colored suit.

"Look here, old sport," he broke out surprisingly. "What's your opinion of me, anyhow?"

A little overwhelmed, I began the generalized evasions which that question deserves.

"Well, I'm going to tell you something about my life," he interrupted. "I don't want you to get a wrong idea of me from all these stories you hear."

So he was aware of the bizarre accusations that flavored conversation in his halls.

"I'll tell you God's truth." His right hand suddenly ordered divine retribution to stand by. "I am the son of some wealthy people in the

middle-west—all dead now. I was brought up in America but educated at Oxford because all my ancestors have been educated there for many years. It is a family tradition."

He looked at me sideways—and I knew why Jordan Baker had believed he was lying. He hurried the phrase "educated at Oxford," or swallowed it or choked on it as though it had bothered him before. And with this doubt his whole statement fell to pieces and I wondered if there wasn't something a little sinister about him after all.

"What part of the middle-west?" I inquired casually.

"San Francisco."

"I see."

"My family all died and I came into a good deal of money."

His voice was solemn as if the memory of that sudden extinction of a clan still haunted him. For a moment I suspected that he was pulling my leg but a glance at him convinced me otherwise.

"After that I lived like a young rajah in all the capitals of Europe—Paris, Venice, Rome—collecting jewels, chiefly rubies, hunting big game, painting a little, things for myself only, and trying to forget something very sad that had happened to me long ago."

With an effort I managed to restrain my incredulous laughter. The very phrases were worn so threadbare that they evoked no image except that of a turbaned "character" leaking sawdust at every pore as he pursued a tiger through the Bois de Boulogne.

"Then came the war, old sport. It was a great relief and I tried very hard to die but I seemed to bear an enchanted life. I accepted a commission as first lieutenant when it began. In the Argonne Forest I took two machine-gun detachments so far forward that there was a half mile gap on either side of us where the infantry couldn't advance. We stayed there two days and two nights, a hundred and thirty men with sixteen Lewis guns, and when the infantry came up at last they

257

found the insignia of three German divisions among the piles of dead. I was promoted to be a major and every Allied government gave me a decoration—even Montenegro, little Montenegro down on the Adriatic Sea!"

Little Montenegro! He lifted up the words and nodded at them—with his smile. The smile comprehended Montenegro's troubled history and sympathized with the brave struggles of the Montenegrin people. It appreciated fully the chain of national circumstances which had elicited this tribute from Montenegro's warm little heart. My incredulity was submerged in fascination now; it was like skimming hastily through a dozen magazines.

He reached in his pocket and a piece of metal, slung on a ribbon, fell into my palm.

"That's the one from Montenegro."

To my astonishment, the thing had an authentic look.

Orderi di Danilo, ran the circular legend, Montenegro, Nicolas Rex.

"Turn it."

Major Jay Gatsby, I read, For Valour Extraordinary.

"Here's another thing I always carry. A souvenir of Oxford days. It was taken in Trinity Quad—the man on my left is now the Earl of Dorcaster."

It was a photograph of half a dozen young men in blazers loafing in an archway through which were visible a host of spires. There was Gatsby, looking a little, not much, younger—with a cricket bat in his hand.

Then it was all true. I saw the skins of tigers flaming in his palace on the Grand Canal; I saw him opening a chest of rubies to ease, with their crimson-lighted depths, the gnawings of his broken heart.

"I'm going to make a big request of you today," he said,

pocketing his souvenirs with satisfaction, "so I thought you ought to know something about me. I didn't want you to think I was just some nobody. You see, I usually find myself among strangers because I drift here and there trying to forget the sad thing that happened to me." He hesitated. "You'll hear about it this afternoon."

"At lunch?"

"No, this afternoon. I happened to find out that you're taking Miss Baker to tea."

"Do you mean you're in love with Miss Baker?"

"No, old sport, I'm not. But Miss Baker has kindly consented to speak to you about this matter."

I hadn't the faintest idea what "this matter" was, but I was more annoyed than interested. I hadn't asked Jordan to tea in order to discuss Mr. Jay Gatsby. I was sure the request would be something utterly fantastic and for a moment I was sorry I'd ever set foot upon his overpopulated lawn.

He wouldn't say another word. His correctness grew on him as we neared the city. We passed Port Roosevelt, where there was a glimpse of red-belted ocean-going ships, and sped along a cobbled slum lined with the dark, undeserted saloons of the faded gilt nineteen-hundreds. Then the valley of ashes opened out on both sides of us, and I had a glimpse of Mrs. Wilson straining at the garage pump with panting vitality as we went by.

With fenders spread like wings we scattered light through half Astoria—only half, for as we twisted among the pillars of the elevated I heard the familiar "jug—jug—spat!" of a motor cycle, and a frantic policeman rode alongside.

"All right, old sport," called Gatsby. We slowed down. Taking a white card from his wallet he waved it before the man's eyes.

"Right you are," agreed the policeman, tipping his cap. "Know

you next time, Mr. Gatsby. Excuse me!"

"What was that?" I inquired. "The picture of Oxford?"

"I was able to do the commissioner a favor once, and he sends me a Christmas card every year."

Over the great bridge, with the sunlight through the girders making a constant flicker upon the moving cars, with the city rising up across the river in white heaps and sugar lumps all built with a wish out of non-olfactory money. The city seen from the Queensboro Bridge is always the city seen for the first time, in its first wild promise of all the mystery and the beauty in the world.

A dead man passed us in a hearse heaped with blooms, followed by two carriages with drawn blinds and by more cheerful carriages for friends. The friends looked out at us with the tragic eyes and short upper lips of south-eastern Europe, and I was glad that the sight of Gatsby's splendid car was included in their somber holiday. As we crossed Blackwell's Island a limousine passed us, driven by a white chauffeur, in which sat three modish Negroes, two bucks and a girl. I laughed aloud as the yolks of their eyeballs rolled toward us in haughty rivalry.

"Anything can happen now that we've slid over this bridge," I thought; "anything at all..."

Even Gatsby could happen, without any particular wonder.

Roaring noon. In a well-fanned Forty-second Street cellar I met Gatsby for lunch. Blinking away the brightness of the street outside my eyes picked him out obscurely in the anteroom, talking to another man.

"Mr. Carraway this is my friend Mr. Wolfshiem."

A small, flat-nosed Jew raised his large head and regarded me with two fine growths of hair which luxuriated in either nostril. After a moment I discovered his tiny eyes in the half darkness.

"—so I took one look at him—" said Mr. Wolfshiem, shaking my

hand earnestly, "–and what do you think I did?"

"What?" I inquired politely.

But evidently he was not addressing me for he dropped my hand and covered Gatsby with his expressive nose.

"I handed the money to Katspaugh and I sid, 'All right, Katspaugh, don't pay him a penny till he shuts his mouth.' He shut it then and there."

Gatsby took an arm of each of us and moved forward into the restaurant whereupon Mr. Wolfshiem swallowed a new sentence he was starting and lapsed into a somnambulatory abstraction.

"Highballs?" asked the head waiter.

"This is a nice restaurant here," said Mr. Wolfshiem looking at the Presbyterian nymphs on the ceiling. "But I like across the street better!"

"Yes, highballs," agreed Gatsby, and then to Mr. Wolfshiem: "It's too hot over there."

"Hot and small–yes," said Mr. Wolfshiem, "but full of memories."

"What place is that?" I asked.

"The old Metropole.

"The old Metropole," brooded Mr. Wolfshiem gloomily. "Filled with faces dead and gone. Filled with friends gone now forever. I can't forget so long as I live the night they shot Rosy Rosenthal there. It was six of us at the table and Rosy had eat and drunk a lot all evening. When it was almost morning the waiter came up to him with a funny look and says somebody wants to speak to him outside. 'All right,' says Rosy and begins to get up and I pulled him down in his chair.

" 'Let the bastards come in here if they want you, Rosy, but don't you, so help me, move outside this room.'

"It was four o'clock in the morning then, and if we'd of raised the blinds we'd of seen daylight."

"Did he go?" I asked innocently.

"Sure he went,"—Mr. Wolfshiem's nose flashed at me indignantly—"He turned around in the door and says, 'Don't let that waiter take away my coffee!' Then he went out on the sidewalk and they shot him three times in his full belly and drove away."

"Four of them were electrocuted," I said, remembering.

"Five with Becker." His nostrils turned to me in an interested way. "I understand you're looking for a business gonnegtion."

The juxtaposition of these two remarks was startling. Gatsby answered for me:

"Oh, no," he exclaimed, "this isn't the man!"

"No?" Mr. Wolfshiem seemed disappointed.

"This is just a friend. I told you we'd talk about that some other time."

"I beg your pardon," said Mr. Wolfshiem, "I had a wrong man."

A succulent hash arrived, and Mr. Wolfshiem, forgetting the more sentimental atmosphere of the old Metropole, began to eat with ferocious delicacy. His eyes, meanwhile, roved very slowly all around the room—he completed the arc by turning to inspect the people directly behind. I think that, except for my presence, he would have taken one short glance beneath our own table.

"Look here, old sport," said Gatsby, leaning toward me, "I'm afraid I made you a little angry this morning in the car."

There was the smile again, but this time I held out against it.

"I don't like mysteries," I answered. "And I don't understand why you won't come out frankly and tell me what you want. Why has it all got to come through Miss Baker?"

"Oh, it's nothing underhand," he assured me. "Miss Baker's a great sportswoman, you know, and she'd never do anything that wasn't all right."

Suddenly he looked at his watch, jumped up and hurried from the room leaving me with Mr. Wolfshiem at the table.

"He has to telephone," said Mr. Wolfshiem, following him with his eyes. "Fine fellow, isn't he? Handsome to look at and a perfect gentleman."

"Yes."

"He's an Oggsford man."

"Oh!"

"He went to Oggsford College in England. You know Oggsford College?"

"I've heard of it."

"It's one of the most famous colleges in the world."

"Have you known Gatsby for a long time?" I inquired.

"Several years," he answered in a gratified way. "I made the pleasure of his acquaintance just after the war. But I knew I had discovered a man of fine breeding after I talked with him an hour. I said to myself: 'There's the kind of man you'd like to take home and introduce to your mother and sister.' " He paused. "I see you're looking at my cuff buttons."

I hadn't been looking at them, but I did now. They were composed of oddly familiar pieces of ivory.

"Finest specimens of human molars," he informed me.

"Well!" I inspected them. "That's a very interesting idea."

"Yeah." He flipped his sleeves up under his coat. "Yeah, Gatsby's very careful about women. He would never so much as look at a friend's wife."

When the subject of this instinctive trust returned to the table and sat down Mr. Wolfshiem drank his coffee with a jerk and got to his feet.

"I have enjoyed my lunch," he said, "and I'm going to run off

from you two young men before I outstay my welcome."

"Don't hurry, Meyer," said Gatsby, without enthusiasm. Mr. Wolfshiem raised his hand in a sort of benediction.

"You're very polite but I belong to another generation," he announced solemnly. "You sit here and discuss your sports and your young ladies and your–" He supplied an imaginary noun with another wave of his hand–"As for me, I am fifty years old, and I won't impose myself on you any longer."

As he shook hands and turned away his tragic nose was trembling. I wondered if I had said anything to offend him.

"He becomes very sentimental sometimes," explained Gatsby. "This is one of his sentimental days. He's quite a character around New York–a denizen of Broadway."

"Who is he anyhow–an actor?"

"No."

"A dentist?"

"Meyer Wolfshiem? No, he's a gambler." Gatsby hesitated, then added coolly: "He's the man who fixed the World's Series back in 1919."

"Fixed the World's Series?" I repeated.

The idea staggered me. I remembered of course that the World's Series had been fixed in 1919 but if I had thought of it at all I would have thought of it as a thing that merely happened, the end of some inevitable chain. It never occurred to me that one man could start to play with the faith of fifty million people–with the single-mindedness of a burglar blowing a safe.

"How did he happen to do that?" I asked after a minute.

"He just saw the opportunity."

"Why isn't he in jail?"

"They can't get him, old sport. He's a smart man."

I insisted on paying the check. As the waiter brought my change I caught sight of Tom Buchanan across the crowded room.

"Come along with me for a minute," I said. "I've got to say hello to someone."

When he saw us Tom jumped up and took half a dozen steps in our direction.

"Where've you been?" he demanded eagerly. "Daisy's furious because you haven't called up."

"This is Mr. Gatsby, Mr. Buchanan."

They shook hands briefly and a strained, unfamiliar look of embarrassment came over Gatsby's face.

"How've you been, anyhow?" demanded Tom of me. "How'd you happen to come up this far to eat?"

"I've been having lunch with Mr. Gatsby."

I turned toward Mr. Gatsby, but he was no longer there.

One October day in nineteen-seventeen–(said Jordan Baker that afternoon, sitting up very straight on a straight chair in the tea-garden at the Plaza Hotel)–I was walking along from one place to another half on the sidewalks and half on the lawns. I was happier on the lawns because I had on shoes from England with rubber nobs on the soles that bit into the soft ground. I had on a new plaid skirt also that blew a little in the wind and whenever this happened the red, white and blue banners in front of all the houses stretched out stiff and said tut-tut-tut-tut in a disapproving way.

The largest of the banners and the largest of the lawns belonged to Daisy Fay's house. She was just eighteen, two years older than me, and by far the most popular of all the young girls in Louisville. She dressed in white, and had a little white roadster and all day long the telephone rang in her house and excited young officers from Camp Taylor demanded the privilege of monopolizing her that night,

"anyways, for an hour!"

When I came opposite her house that morning her white roadster was beside the curb, and she was sitting in it with a lieutenant I had never seen before. They were so engrossed in each other that she didn't see me until I was five feet away.

"Hello Jordan," she called unexpectedly. "Please come here."

I was flattered that she wanted to speak to me, because of all the older girls I admired her most. She asked me if I was going to the Red Cross and make bandages. I was. Well, then, would I tell them that she couldn't come that day? The officer looked at Daisy while she was speaking, in a way that every young girl wants to be looked at sometime, and because it seemed romantic to me I have remembered the incident ever since. His name was Jay Gatsby and I didn't lay eyes on him again for over four years—even after I'd met him on Long Island I didn't realize it was the same man.

That was nineteen-seventeen. By the next year I had a few beaux myself, and I began to play in tournaments, so I didn't see Daisy very often. She went with a slightly older crowd—when she went with anyone at all. Wild rumors were circulating about her—how her mother had found her packing her bag one winter night to go to New York and say goodbye to a soldier who was going overseas. She was effectually prevented, but she wasn't on speaking terms with her family for several weeks. After that she didn't play around with the soldiers any more but only with a few flat-footed, short-sighted young men in town who couldn't get into the army at all.

By the next autumn she was gay again, gay as ever. She had a debut after the Armistice, and in February she was presumably engaged to a man from New Orleans. In June she married Tom Buchanan of Chicago with more pomp and circumstance than Louisville ever knew before. He came down with a hundred people in

four private cars and hired a whole floor of the Seelbach Hotel, and the day before the wedding he gave her a string of pearls valued at three hundred and fifty thousand dollars.

I was bridesmaid. I came into her room half an hour before the bridal dinner, and found her lying on her bed as lovely as the June night in her flowered dress–and as drunk as a monkey. She had a bottle of sauterne in one hand and a letter in the other.

" 'Gratulate me," she muttered. "Never had a drink before but oh, how I do enjoy it."

"What's the matter, Daisy?"

I was scared, I can tell you; I'd never seen a girl like that before.

"Here, dearis." She groped around in a waste-basket she had with her on the bed and pulled out the string of pearls. "Take 'em downstairs and give 'em back to whoever they belong to. Tell 'em all Daisy's change' her mine. Say 'Daisy's change' her mine!'."

She began to cry–she cried and cried. I rushed out and found her mother's maid and we locked the door and got her into a cold bath. She wouldn't let go of the letter. She took it into the tub with her and squeezed it up into a wet ball, and only let me leave it in the soap dish when she saw that it was coming to pieces like snow.

But she didn't say another word. We gave her spirits of ammonia and put ice on her forehead and hooked her back into her dress and half an hour later when we walked out of the room the pearls were around her neck and the incident was over. Next day at five o'clock she married Tom Buchanan without so much as a shiver and started off on a three months' trip to the South Seas.

I saw them in Santa Barbara when they came back and I thought I'd never seen a girl so mad about her husband. If he left the room for a minute she'd look around uneasily and say "Where's Tom gone?" and wear the most abstracted expression until she saw him coming in

the door. She used to sit on the sand with his head in her lap by the hour rubbing her fingers over his eyes and looking at him with unfathomable delight. It was touching to see them together—it made you laugh in a hushed, fascinated way. That was in August. A week after I left Santa Barbara Tom ran into a wagon on the Ventura road one night and ripped a front wheel off his car. The girl who was with him got into the papers too because her arm was broken—she was one of the chambermaids in the Santa Barbara Hotel.

The next April Daisy had her little girl and they went to France for a year. I saw them one spring in Cannes and later in Deauville and then they came back to Chicago to settle down. Daisy was popular in Chicago, as you know. They moved with a fast crowd, all of them young and rich and wild, but she came out with an absolutely perfect reputation. Perhaps because she doesn't drink. It's a great advantage not to drink among hard-drinking people. You can hold your tongue and, moreover, you can time any little irregularity of your own so that everybody else is so blind that they don't see or care. Perhaps Daisy never went in for amour at all—and yet there's something in that voice of hers...

Well, about six weeks ago, she heard the name Gatsby for the first time in years. It was when I asked you—do you remember?—if you knew Gatsby in West Egg. After you had gone home she came into my room and woke me up, and said "What Gatsby?" and when I described him—I was half asleep—she said in the strangest voice that it must be the man she used to know. It wasn't until then that I connected this Gatsby with the officer in her white car.

When Jordan Baker had finished telling all this we had left the Plaza for half an hour and were driving in a Victoria through Central Park. The sun had gone down behind the tall apartments of the movie stars in the West Fifties and the clear voices of girls, already gathered

like crickets on the grass, rose through the hot twilight:

I'm the Sheik of Araby,
Your love belongs to me.
At night when you're asleep,
Into your tent I'll creep—

"It was a strange coincidence," I said.

"But it wasn't a coincidence at all."

"Why not?"

"Gatsby bought that house so that Daisy would be just across the bay."

Then it had not been merely the stars to which he had aspired on that June night. He came alive to me, delivered suddenly from the womb of his purposeless splendor.

"He wants to know–" continued Jordan "–if you'll invite Daisy to your house some afternoon and then let him come over."

The modesty of the demand shook me. He had waited five years and bought a mansion where he dispensed starlight to casual moths so that he could "come over" some afternoon to a stranger's garden.

"Did I have to know all this before he could ask such a little thing?"

"He's afraid. He's waited so long. He thought you might be offended. You see he's a regular tough underneath it all."

Something worried me.

"Why didn't he ask you to arrange a meeting?"

"He wants her to see his house," she explained. "And your house is right next door."

"Oh!"

"I think he half expected her to wander into one of his parties, some night," went on Jordan, "but she never did. Then he began asking people casually if they knew her, and I was the first one he found. It was

that night he sent for me at his dance, and you should have heard the elaborate way he worked up to it. Of course, I immediately suggested a luncheon in New York—and I thought he'd go mad:

" 'I don't want to do anything out of the way!' he kept saying. 'I want to see her right next door.'

"When I said you were a particular friend of Tom's he started to abandon the whole idea. He doesn't know very much about Tom, though he says he's read a Chicago paper for years just on the chance of catching a glimpse of Daisy's name."

It was dark now, and as we dipped under a little bridge I put my arm around Jordan's golden shoulder and drew her toward me and asked her to dinner. Suddenly I wasn't thinking of Daisy and Gatsby any more but of this clean, hard, limited person who dealt in universal skepticism and who leaned back jauntily just within the circle of my arm. A phrase began to beat in my ears with a sort of heady excitement: "There are only the pursued, the pursuing, the busy and the tired."

"And Daisy ought to have something in her life," murmured Jordan to me.

"Does she want to see Gatsby?"

"She's not to know about it. Gatsby doesn't want her to know. You're just supposed to invite her to tea."

We passed a barrier of dark trees, and then the facade of Fifty-ninth Street, a block of delicate pale light, beamed down into the park. Unlike Gatsby and Tom Buchanan I had no girl whose disembodied face floated along the dark cornices and blinding signs and so I drew up the girl beside me, tightening my arms. Her wan, scornful mouth smiled and so I drew her up again, closer, this time to my face.

CHAPTER 5

When I came home to West Egg that night I was afraid for a moment that my house was on fire. Two o'clock and the whole corner of the peninsula was blazing with light which fell unreal on the shrubbery and made thin elongating glints upon the roadside wires. Turning a corner I saw that it was Gatsby's house, lit from tower to cellar.

At first I thought it was another party, a wild rout that had resolved itself into "hide-and-go-seek" or "sardines-in-the-box" with all the house thrown open to the game. But there wasn't a sound. Only wind in the trees which blew the wires and made the lights go off and on again as if the house had winked into the darkness. As my taxi groaned away I saw Gatsby walking toward me across his lawn.

"Your place looks like the world's fair," I said.

"Does it?" He turned his eyes toward it absently. "I have been glancing into some of the rooms. Let's go to Coney Island, old sport. In my car."

"It's too late."

"Well, suppose we take a plunge in the swimming pool? I haven't made use of it all summer."

"I've got to go to bed."

"All right."

He waited, looking at me with suppressed eagerness.

"I talked with Miss Baker," I said after a moment. "I'm going to call up Daisy tomorrow and invite her over here to tea."

"Oh, that's all right," he said carelessly. "I don't want to put you to any trouble."

"What day would suit you?"

"What day would suit you?" he corrected me quickly. "I don't want to put you to any trouble, you see."

"How about the day after tomorrow?" He considered for a moment. Then, with reluctance:

"I want to get the grass cut," he said.

We both looked at the grass–there was a sharp line where my ragged lawn ended and the darker, well-kept expanse of his began. I suspected that he meant my grass.

"There's another little thing," he said uncertainly, and hesitated.

"Would you rather put it off for a few days?" I asked.

"Oh, it isn't about that. At least–" He fumbled with a series of beginnings. "Why, I thought–why, look here, old sport, you don't make much money, do you?"

"Not very much."

This seemed to reassure him and he continued more confidently.

"I thought you didn't, if you'll pardon my–you see, I carry on a little business on the side, a sort of sideline, you understand. And I thought that if you don't make very much–You're selling bonds, aren't you, old sport?"

"Trying to."

"Well, this would interest you. It wouldn't take up much of your time and you might pick up a nice bit of money. It happens to be a rather confidential sort of thing."

I realize now that under different circumstances that conversation might have been one of the crises of my life. But, because the offer was obviously and tactlessly for a service to be rendered, I had no choice except to cut him off there.

"I've got my hands full," I said. "I'm much obliged but I couldn't take on any more work."

"You wouldn't have to do any business with Wolfshiem." Evidently he thought that I was shying away from the "gonnegtion" mentioned at lunch, but I assured him he was wrong. He waited a moment longer, hoping I'd begin a conversation, but I was too absorbed to be responsive, so he went unwillingly home.

The evening had made me light-headed and happy; I think I walked into a deep sleep as I entered my front door. So I didn't know whether or not Gatsby went to Coney Island or for how many hours he "glanced into rooms" while his house blazed gaudily on. I called up Daisy from the office next morning and invited her to come to tea.

"Don't bring Tom," I warned her.

"What?"

"Don't bring Tom."

"Who is 'Tom'?" she asked innocently.

The day agreed upon was pouring rain. At eleven o'clock a man in a raincoat dragging a lawn-mower tapped at my front door and said that Mr. Gatsby had sent him over to cut my grass. This reminded me that I had forgotten to tell my Finn to come back so I drove into West Egg Village to search for her among soggy white-washed alleys and to buy some cups and lemons and flowers.

The flowers were unnecessary, for at two o'clock a greenhouse arrived from Gatsby's, with innumerable receptacles to contain it. An hour later the front door opened nervously, and Gatsby in a white flannel suit, silver shirt and gold-colored tie hurried in. He was pale and there were dark signs of sleeplessness beneath his eyes.

"Is everything all right?" he asked immediately.

"The grass looks fine, if that's what you mean."

"What grass?" he inquired blankly. "Oh, the grass in the yard." He looked out the window at it, but judging from his expression I don't believe he saw a thing.

"Looks very good," he remarked vaguely. "One of the papers said they thought the rain would stop about four. I think it was 'The Journal.' Have you got everything you need in the shape of—of tea?"

I took him into the pantry where he looked a little reproachfully at the Finn. Together we scrutinized the twelve lemon cakes from the delicatessen shop.

"Will they do?" I asked.

"Of course, of course! They're fine!" and he added hollowly, " ...old sport."

The rain cooled about half-past three to a damp mist through which occasional thin drops swam like dew. Gatsby looked with vacant eyes through a copy of Clay's "Economics," starting at the Finnish tread that shook the kitchen floor and peering toward the bleared windows from time to time as if a series of invisible but alarming happenings were taking place outside. Finally he got up and informed me in an uncertain voice that he was going home.

"Why's that?"

"Nobody's coming to tea. It's too late!" He looked at his watch as if there was some pressing demand on his time elsewhere. "I can't wait all day."

"Don't be silly; it's just two minutes to four."

He sat down, miserably, as if I had pushed him, and simultaneously there was the sound of a motor turning into my lane. We both jumped up and, a little harrowed myself, I went out into the yard.

Under the dripping bare lilac trees a large open car was coming up the drive. It stopped. Daisy's face, tipped sideways beneath a three-cornered lavender hat, looked out at me with a bright ecstatic smile.

"Is this absolutely where you live, my dearest one?"

The exhilarating ripple of her voice was a wild tonic in the rain. I had to follow the sound of it for a moment, up and down, with my

ear alone before any words came through. A damp streak of hair lay like a dash of blue paint across her cheek and her hand was wet with glistening drops as I took it to help her from the car.

"Are you in love with me," she said low in my ear. "Or why did I have to come alone?"

"That's the secret of Castle Rackrent. Tell your chauffeur to go far away and spend an hour."

"Come back in an hour, Ferdie." Then in a grave murmur, "His name is Ferdie."

"Does the gasoline affect his nose?"

"I don't think so," she said innocently. "Why?"

We went in. To my overwhelming surprise the living room was deserted.

"Well, that's funny!" I exclaimed.

"What's funny?"

She turned her head as there was a light, dignified knocking at the front door. I went out and opened it. Gatsby, pale as death, with his hands plunged like weights in his coat pockets, was standing in a puddle of water glaring tragically into my eyes.

With his hands still in his coat pockets he stalked by me into the hall, turned sharply as if he were on a wire and disappeared into the living room. It wasn't a bit funny. Aware of the loud beating of my own heart I pulled the door to against the increasing rain.

For half a minute there wasn't a sound. Then from the living room I heard a sort of choking murmur and part of a laugh followed by Daisy's voice on a clear artificial note.

"I certainly am awfully glad to see you again."

A pause; it endured horribly. I had nothing to do in the hall so I went into the room.

Gatsby, his hands still in his pockets, was reclining against the

mantelpiece in a strained counterfeit of perfect ease, even of boredom. His head leaned back so far that it rested against the face of a defunct mantelpiece clock and from this position his distraught eyes stared down at Daisy who was sitting frightened but graceful on the edge of a stiff chair.

"We've met before," muttered Gatsby. His eyes glanced momentarily at me and his lips parted with an abortive attempt at a laugh. Luckily the clock took this moment to tilt dangerously at the pressure of his head, whereupon he turned and caught it with trembling fingers and set it back in place. Then he sat down, rigidly, his elbow on the arm of the sofa and his chin in his hand.

"I'm sorry about the clock," he said.

My own face had now assumed a deep tropical burn. I couldn't muster up a single commonplace out of the thousand in my head.

"It's an old clock," I told them idiotically.

I think we all believed for a moment that it had smashed in pieces on the floor.

"We haven't met for many years," said Daisy, her voice as matter-of-fact as it could ever be.

"Five years next November."

The automatic quality of Gatsby's answer set us all back at least another minute. I had them both on their feet with the desperate suggestion that they help me make tea in the kitchen when the demoniac Finn brought it in on a tray.

Amid the welcome confusion of cups and cakes a certain physical decency established itself. Gatsby got himself into a shadow and while Daisy and I talked looked conscientiously from one to the other of us with tense unhappy eyes. However, as calmness wasn't an end in itself I made an excuse at the first possible moment and got to my feet.

"Where are you going?" demanded Gatsby in immediate alarm.

"I'll be back."

"I've got to speak to you about something before you go."

He followed me wildly into the kitchen, closed the door and whispered: "Oh, God!" in a miserable way.

"What's the matter?"

"This is a terrible mistake," he said, shaking his head from side to side, "a terrible, terrible mistake."

"You're just embarrassed, that's all," and luckily I added: "Daisy's embarrassed too."

"She's embarrassed?" he repeated incredulously.

"Just as much as you are."

"Don't talk so loud."

"You're acting like a little boy," I broke out impatiently. "Not only that but you're rude. Daisy's sitting in there all alone."

He raised his hand to stop my words, looked at me with unforgettable reproach and opening the door cautiously went back into the other room.

I walked out the back way—just as Gatsby had when he had made his nervous circuit of the house half an hour before—and ran for a huge black knotted tree whose massed leaves made a fabric against the rain. Once more it was pouring and my irregular lawn, well-shaved by Gatsby's gardener, abounded in small muddy swamps and prehistoric marshes. There was nothing to look at from under the tree except Gatsby's enormous house, so I stared at it, like Kant at his church steeple, for half an hour. A brewer had built it early in the "period" craze, a decade before, and there was a story that he'd agreed to pay five years' taxes on all the neighboring cottages if the owners would have their roofs thatched with straw. Perhaps their refusal took the heart out of his plan to Found a Family—he went into an immediate decline. His children sold his house with the black wreath still on the door. Americans, while occasionally

willing to be serfs, have always been obstinate about being peasantry.

After half an hour the sun shone again and the grocer's automobile rounded Gatsby's drive with the raw material for his servants' dinner—I felt sure he wouldn't eat a spoonful. A maid began opening the upper windows of his house, appeared momentarily in each, and, leaning from a large central bay, spat meditatively into the garden. It was time I went back. While the rain continued it had seemed like the murmur of their voices, rising and swelling a little, now and then, with gusts of emotion. But in the new silence I felt that silence had fallen within the house too.

I went in—after making every possible noise in the kitchen short of pushing over the stove—but I don't believe they heard a sound. They were sitting at either end of the couch looking at each other as if some question had been asked or was in the air, and every vestige of embarrassment was gone. Daisy's face was smeared with tears and when I came in she jumped up and began wiping at it with her handkerchief before a mirror. But there was a change in Gatsby that was simply confounding. He literally glowed; without a word or a gesture of exultation a new well-being radiated from him and filled the little room.

"Oh, hello, old sport," he said, as if he hadn't seen me for years. I thought for a moment he was going to shake hands.

"It's stopped raining."

"Has it?" When he realized what I was talking about, that there were twinkle-bells of sunshine in the room, he smiled like a weather man, like an ecstatic patron of recurrent light, and repeated the news to Daisy. "What do you think of that? It's stopped raining."

"I'm glad, Jay." Her throat, full of aching, grieving beauty, told only of her unexpected joy.

"I want you and Daisy to come over to my house," he said, "I'd like to show her around."

"You're sure you want me to come?"

"Absolutely, old sport."

Daisy went upstairs to wash her face–too late I thought with humiliation of my towels–while Gatsby and I waited on the lawn.

"My house looks well, doesn't it?" he demanded. "See how the whole front of it catches the light."

I agreed that it was splendid.

"Yes." His eyes went over it, every arched door and square tower. "It took me just three years to earn the money that bought it."

"I thought you inherited your money."

"I did, old sport," he said automatically, "but I lost most of it in the big panic–the panic of the war."

I think he hardly knew what he was saying, for when I asked him what business he was in he answered "That's my affair," before he realized that it wasn't the appropriate reply.

"Oh, I've been in several things," he corrected himself. "I was in the drug business and then I was in the oil business. But I'm not in either one now." He looked at me with more attention. "Do you mean you've been thinking over what I proposed the other night?"

Before I could answer, Daisy came out of the house and two rows of brass buttons on her dress gleamed in the sunlight.

"That huge place there?" she cried pointing.

"Do you like it?"

"I love it, but I don't see how you live there all alone."

"I keep it always full of interesting people, night and day. People who do interesting things. Celebrated people."

Instead of taking the short cut along the Sound we went down the road and entered by the big postern. With enchanting murmurs Daisy admired this aspect or that of the feudal silhouette against the sky, admired the gardens, the sparkling odor of jonquils and the frothy odor of hawthorn and plum blossoms and the pale gold odor of kiss-

me-at-the-gate. It was strange to reach the marble steps and find no stir of bright dresses in and out the door, and hear no sound but bird voices in the trees.

And inside as we wandered through Marie Antoinette music rooms and Restoration salons I felt that there were guests concealed behind every couch and table, under orders to be breathlessly silent until we had passed through. As Gatsby closed the door of "the Merton College Library" I could have sworn I heard the owl-eyed man break into ghostly laughter.

We went upstairs, through period bedrooms swathed in rose and lavender silk and vivid with new flowers, through dressing rooms and poolrooms, and bathrooms with sunken baths—intruding into one chamber where a dishevelled man in pajamas was doing liver exercises on the floor. It was Mr. Klipspringer, the "boarder." I had seen him wandering hungrily about the beach that morning. Finally we came to Gatsby's own apartment, a bedroom and a bath and an Adam study, where we sat down and drank a glass of some Chartreuse he took from a cupboard in the wall.

He hadn't once ceased looking at Daisy and I think he revalued everything in his house according to the measure of response it drew from her well-loved eyes. Sometimes, too, he stared around at his possessions in a dazed way as though in her actual and astounding presence none of it was any longer real. Once he nearly toppled down a flight of stairs.

His bedroom was the simplest room of all—except where the dresser was garnished with a toilet set of pure dull gold. Daisy took the brush with delight and smoothed her hair, whereupon Gatsby sat down and shaded his eyes and began to laugh.

"It's the funniest thing, old sport," he said hilariously. "I can't—when I try to—"

He had passed visibly through two states and was entering upon a third. After his embarrassment and his unreasoning joy he was consumed with wonder at her presence. He had been full of the idea so long, dreamed it right through to the end, waited with his teeth set, so to speak, at an inconceivable pitch of intensity. Now, in the reaction, he was running down like an overwound clock.

Recovering himself in a minute he opened for us two hulking patent cabinets which held his massed suits and dressing-gowns and ties, and his shirts, piled like bricks in stacks a dozen high.

"I've got a man in England who buys me clothes. He sends over a selection of things at the beginning of each season, spring and fall."

He took out a pile of shirts and began throwing them, one by one before us, shirts of sheer linen and thick silk and fine flannel which lost their folds as they fell and covered the table in many-colored disarray. While we admired he brought more and the soft rich heap mounted higher—shirts with stripes and scrolls and plaids in coral and apple-green and lavender and faint orange with monograms of Indian blue. Suddenly with a strained sound, Daisy bent her head into the shirts and began to cry stormily.

"They're such beautiful shirts," she sobbed, her voice muffled in the thick folds. "It makes me sad because I've never seen such—such beautiful shirts before."

After the house, we were to see the grounds and the swimming pool, and the hydroplane and the midsummer flowers—but outside Gatsby's window it began to rain again so we stood in a row looking at the corrugated surface of the Sound.

"If it wasn't for the mist we could see your home across the bay," said Gatsby. "You always have a green light that burns all night at the end of your dock."

Daisy put her arm through his abruptly but he seemed absorbed

in what he had just said. Possibly it had occurred to him that the colossal significance of that light had now vanished forever. Compared to the great distance that had separated him from Daisy it had seemed very near to her, almost touching her. It had seemed as close as a star to the moon. Now it was again a green light on a dock. His count of enchanted objects had diminished by one.

I began to walk about the room, examining various indefinite objects in the half darkness. A large photograph of an elderly man in yachting costume attracted me, hung on the wall over his desk.

"Who's this?"

"That? That's Mr. Dan Cody, old sport."

The name sounded faintly familiar.

"He's dead now. He used to be my best friend years ago."

There was a small picture of Gatsby, also in yachting costume, on the bureau—Gatsby with his head thrown back defiantly—taken apparently when he was about eighteen.

"I adore it!" exclaimed Daisy. "The pompadour! You never told me you had a pompadour—or a yacht."

"Look at this," said Gatsby quickly. "Here's a lot of clippings—about you."

They stood side by side examining it. I was going to ask to see the rubies when the phone rang and Gatsby took up the receiver.

"Yes...Well, I can't talk now...I can't talk now, old sport...I said a small town...He must know what a small town is...Well, he's no use to us if Detroit is his idea of a small town..."

He rang off.

"Come here quick!" cried Daisy at the window.

The rain was still falling, but the darkness had parted in the west, and there was a pink and golden billow of foamy clouds above the sea.

"Look at that," she whispered, and then after a moment: "I'd like

to just get one of those pink clouds and put you in it and push you around."

I tried to go then, but they wouldn't hear of it; perhaps my presence made them feel more satisfactorily alone.

"I know what we'll do," said Gatsby, "we'll have Klipspringer play the piano."

He went out of the room calling "Ewing!" and returned in a few minutes accompanied by an embarrassed, slightly worn young man with shell-rimmed glasses and scanty blonde hair. He was now decently clothed in a "sport shirt" open at the neck, sneakers and duck trousers of a nebulous hue.

"Did we interrupt your exercises?" inquired Daisy politely.

"I was asleep," cried Mr. Klipspringer, in a spasm of embarrassment. "That is, I'd been asleep. Then I got up..."

"Klipspringer plays the piano," said Gatsby, cutting him off. "Don't you, Ewing, old sport?"

"I don't play well. I don't—I hardly play at all. I'm all out of prac—"

"We'll go downstairs," interrupted Gatsby. He flipped a switch. The grey windows disappeared as the house glowed full of light.

In the music room Gatsby turned on a solitary lamp beside the piano. He lit Daisy's cigarette from a trembling match, and sat down with her on a couch far across the room where there was no light save what the gleaming floor bounced in from the hall.

When Klipspringer had played "The Love Nest" he turned around on the bench and searched unhappily for Gatsby in the gloom.

"I'm all out of practice, you see. I told you I couldn't play. I'm all out of prac—"

"Don't talk so much, old sport," commanded Gatsby. "Play!"

In the morning,
In the evening,

Ain't we got fun—

Outside the wind was loud and there was a faint flow of thunder along the Sound. All the lights were going on in West Egg now; the electric trains, men-carrying, were plunging home through the rain from New York. It was the hour of a profound human change, and excitement was generating on the air.

One thing's sure and nothing's surer
The rich get richer and the poor get—children.
In the meantime,
In between time—

As I went over to say goodbye I saw that the expression of bewilderment had come back into Gatsby's face, as though a faint doubt had occurred to him as to the quality of his present happiness. Almost five years! There must have been moments even that afternoon when Daisy tumbled short of his dreams—not through her own fault but because of the colossal vitality of his illusion. It had gone beyond her, beyond everything. He had thrown himself into it with a creative passion, adding to it all the time, decking it out with every bright feather that drifted his way. No amount of fire or freshness can challenge what a man will store up in his ghostly heart.

As I watched him he adjusted himself a little, visibly. His hand took hold of hers and as she said something low in his ear he turned toward her with a rush of emotion. I think that voice held him most with its fluctuating, feverish warmth because it couldn't be over-dreamed—that voice was a deathless song.

They had forgotten me, but Daisy glanced up and held out her hand; Gatsby didn't know me now at all. I looked once more at them and they looked back at me, remotely, possessed by intense life. Then I went out of the room and down the marble steps into the rain, leaving them there together.

CHAPTER 6

About this time an ambitious young reporter from New York arrived one morning at Gatsby's door and asked him if he had anything to say.

"Anything to say about what?" inquired Gatsby politely.

"Why,—any statement to give out."

It transpired after a confused five minutes that the man had heard Gatsby's name around his office in a connection which he either wouldn't reveal or didn't fully understand. This was his day off and with laudable initiative he had hurried out "to see."

It was a random shot, and yet the reporter's instinct was right. Gatsby's notoriety, spread about by the hundreds who had accepted his hospitality and so become authorities on his past, had increased all summer until he fell just short of being news. Contemporary legends such as the "underground pipe-line to Canada" attached themselves to him, and there was one persistent story that he didn't live in a house at all, but in a boat that looked like a house and was moved secretly up and down the Long Island shore. Just why these inventions were a source of satisfaction to James Gatz of North Dakota, isn't easy to say.

James Gatz—that was really, or at least legally, his name. He had changed it at the age of seventeen and at the specific moment that witnessed the beginning of his career—when he saw Dan Cody's yacht drop anchor over the most insidious flat on Lake Superior. It was James Gatz who had been loafing along the beach that afternoon in a torn green jersey and a pair of canvas pants, but it was already Jay Gatsby who borrowed a row-boat, pulled out to the Tuolomee and informed Cody that a wind might catch him and break him up in half an hour.

I suppose he'd had the name ready for a long time, even then. His parents were shiftless and unsuccessful farm people—his imagination had never really accepted them as his parents at all. The truth was that Jay Gatsby, of West Egg, Long Island, sprang from his Platonic conception of himself. He was a son of God—a phrase which, if it means anything, means just that—and he must be about His Father's Business, the service of a vast, vulgar and meretricious beauty. So he invented just the sort of Jay Gatsby that a seventeen-year-old boy would be likely to invent, and to this conception he was faithful to the end.

For over a year he had been beating his way along the south shore of Lake Superior as a clam digger and a salmon fisher or in any other capacity that brought him food and bed. His brown, hardening body lived naturally through the half fierce, half lazy work of the bracing days. He knew women early and since they spoiled him he became contemptuous of them, of young virgins because they were ignorant, of the others because they were hysterical about things which in his overwhelming self-absorption he took for granted.

But his heart was in a constant, turbulent riot. The most grotesque and fantastic conceits haunted him in his bed at night. A universe of ineffable gaudiness spun itself out in his brain while the clock ticked on the wash-stand and the moon soaked with wet light his tangled clothes upon the floor. Each night he added to the pattern of his fancies until drowsiness closed down upon some vivid scene with an oblivious embrace. For a while these reveries provided an outlet for his imagination; they were a satisfactory hint of the unreality of reality, a promise that the rock of the world was founded securely on a fairy's wing.

An instinct toward his future glory had led him, some months before, to the small Lutheran college of St. Olaf in southern Minnesota. He stayed there two weeks, dismayed at its ferocious indifference to the drums of his destiny, to destiny itself, and despising the janitor's work

with which he was to pay his way through. Then he drifted back to Lake Superior, and he was still searching for something to do on the day that Dan Cody's yacht dropped anchor in the shallows along shore.

Cody was fifty years old then, a product of the Nevada silver fields, of the Yukon, of every rush for metal since Seventy-five. The transactions in Montana copper that made him many times a millionaire found him physically robust but on the verge of soft-mindedness, and, suspecting this an infinite number of women tried to separate him from his money. The none too savory ramifications by which Ella Kaye, the newspaper woman, played Madame de Maintenon to his weakness and sent him to sea in a yacht, were common knowledge to the turgid journalism of 1902. He had been coasting along all too hospitable shores for five years when he turned up as James Gatz's destiny at Little Girl Bay.

To the young Gatz, resting on his oars and looking up at the railed deck, the yacht represented all the beauty and glamor in the world. I suppose he smiled at Cody—he had probably discovered that people liked him when he smiled. At any rate Cody asked him a few questions (one of them elicited the brand new name) and found that he was quick, and extravagantly ambitious. A few days later he took him to Duluth and bought him a blue coat, six pair of white duck trousers and a yachting cap. And when the Tuolomee left for the West Indies and the Barbary Coast Gatsby left too.

He was employed in a vague personal capacity—while he remained with Cody he was in turn steward, mate, skipper, secretary, and even jailor, for Dan Cody sober knew what lavish doings Dan Cody drunk might soon be about and he provided for such contingencies by reposing more and more trust in Gatsby. The arrangement lasted five years during which the boat went three times around the continent. It might have lasted indefinitely except for the fact that Ella Kaye came on board one night in Boston and a week later Dan Cody inhospitably died.

I remember the portrait of him up in Gatsby's bedroom, a grey, florid man with a hard empty face—the pioneer debauchee who during one phase of American life brought back to the eastern seaboard the savage violence of the frontier brothel and saloon. It was indirectly due to Cody that Gatsby drank so little. Sometimes in the course of gay parties women used to rub champagne into his hair; for himself he formed the habit of letting liquor alone.

And it was from Cody that he inherited money—a legacy of twenty-five thousand dollars. He didn't get it. He never understood the legal device that was used against him but what remained of the millions went intact to Ella Kaye. He was left with his singularly appropriate education; the vague contour of Jay Gatsby had filled out to the substantiality of a man.

He told me all this very much later, but I've put it down here with the idea of exploding those first wild rumors about his antecedents, which weren't even faintly true. Moreover he told it to me at a time of confusion, when I had reached the point of believing everything and nothing about him. So I take advantage of this short halt, while Gatsby, so to speak, caught his breath, to clear this set of misconceptions away.

It was a halt, too, in my association with his affairs. For several weeks I didn't see him or hear his voice on the phone—mostly I was in New York, trotting around with Jordan and trying to ingratiate myself with her senile aunt—but finally I went over to his house one Sunday afternoon. I hadn't been there two minutes when somebody brought Tom Buchanan in for a drink. I was startled, naturally, but the really surprising thing was that it hadn't happened before.

They were a party of three on horseback—Tom and a man named Sloane and a pretty woman in a brown riding habit who had been there previously.

"I'm delighted to see you," said Gatsby standing on his porch. "I'm delighted that you dropped in."

As though they cared!

"Sit right down. Have a cigarette or a cigar." He walked around the room quickly, ringing bells. "I'll have something to drink for you in just a minute."

He was profoundly affected by the fact that Tom was there. But he would be uneasy anyhow until he had given them something, realizing in a vague way that that was all they came for. Mr. Sloane wanted nothing. A lemonade? No, thanks. A little champagne? Nothing at all, thanks...I'm sorry—

"Did you have a nice ride?"

"Very good roads around here."

"I suppose the automobiles—"

"Yeah."

Moved by an irresistible impulse, Gatsby turned to Tom who had accepted the introduction as a stranger.

"I believe we've met somewhere before, Mr. Buchanan."

"Oh, yes," said Tom, gruffly polite but obviously not remembering. "So we did. I remember very well."

"About two weeks ago."

"That's right. You were with Nick here."

"I know your wife," continued Gatsby, almost aggressively.

"That so?"

Tom turned to me.

"You live near here, Nick?"

"Next door."

"That so?"

Mr. Sloane didn't enter into the conversation but lounged back haughtily in his chair; the woman said nothing either—until unexpectedly, after two highballs, she became cordial.

"We'll all come over to your next party, Mr. Gatsby," she

suggested. "What do you say?"

"Certainly. I'd be delighted to have you."

"Be ver' nice," said Mr. Sloane, without gratitude. "Well—think ought to be starting home."

"Please don't hurry," Gatsby urged them. He had control of himself now and he wanted to see more of Tom. "Why don't you— why don't you stay for supper? I wouldn't be surprised if some other people dropped in from New York."

"You come to supper with me," said the lady enthusiastically. "Both of you."

This included me. Mr. Sloane got to his feet.

"Come along," he said—but to her only.

"I mean it," she insisted. "I'd love to have you. Lots of room."

Gatsby looked at me questioningly. He wanted to go and he didn't see that Mr. Sloane had determined he shouldn't.

"I'm afraid I won't be able to," I said.

"Well, you come," she urged, concentrating on Gatsby.

Mr. Sloane murmured something close to her ear.

"We won't be late if we start now," she insisted aloud.

"I haven't got a horse," said Gatsby. "I used to ride in the army but I've never bought a horse. I'll have to follow you in my car. Excuse me for just a minute."

The rest of us walked out on the porch, where Sloane and the lady began an impassioned conversation aside.

"My God, I believe the man's coming," said Tom. "Doesn't he know she doesn't want him?"

"She says she does want him."

"She has a big dinner party and he won't know a soul there." He frowned. "I wonder where in the devil he met Daisy. By God, I may be old-fashioned in my ideas, but women run around too much these

days to suit me. They meet all kinds of crazy fish."

Suddenly Mr. Sloane and the lady walked down the steps and mounted their horses.

"Come on," said Mr. Sloane to Tom, "we're late. We've got to go." And then to me: "Tell him we couldn't wait, will you?"

Tom and I shook hands, the rest of us exchanged a cool nod and they trotted quickly down the drive, disappearing under the August foliage just as Gatsby with hat and light overcoat in hand came out the front door.

Tom was evidently perturbed at Daisy's running around alone, for on the following Saturday night he came with her to Gatsby's party. Perhaps his presence gave the evening its peculiar quality of oppressiveness—it stands out in my memory from Gatsby's other parties that summer. There were the same people, or at least the same sort of people, the same profusion of champagne, the same many-colored, many-keyed commotion, but I felt an unpleasantness in the air, a pervading harshness that hadn't been there before. Or perhaps I had merely grown used to it, grown to accept West Egg as a world complete in itself, with its own standards and its own great figures, second to nothing because it had no consciousness of being so, and now I was looking at it again, through Daisy's eyes. It is invariably saddening to look through new eyes at things upon which you have expended your own powers of adjustment.

They arrived at twilight and as we strolled out among the sparkling hundreds Daisy's voice was playing murmurous tricks in her throat.

"These things excite me so," she whispered. "If you want to kiss me any time during the evening, Nick, just let me know and I'll be glad to arrange it for you. Just mention my name. Or present a green card. I'm giving out green—"

"Look around," suggested Gatsby.

"I'm looking around. I'm having a marvelous—"

"You must see the faces of many people you've heard about."

Tom's arrogant eyes roamed the crowd.

"We don't go around very much," he said. "In fact I was just thinking I don't know a soul here."

"Perhaps you know that lady." Gatsby indicated a gorgeous, scarcely human orchid of a woman who sat in state under a white plum tree. Tom and Daisy stared, with that peculiarly unreal feeling that accompanies the recognition of a hitherto ghostly celebrity of the movies.

"She's lovely," said Daisy.

"The man bending over her is her director."

He took them ceremoniously from group to group:

"Mrs. Buchanan...and Mr. Buchanan—" After an instant's hesitation he added: "the polo player."

"Oh no," objected Tom quickly, "Not me."

But evidently the sound of it pleased Gatsby for Tom remained "the polo player" for the rest of the evening.

"I've never met so many celebrities!" Daisy exclaimed. "I liked that man—what was his name?—with the sort of blue nose."

Gatsby identified him, adding that he was a small producer.

"Well, I liked him anyhow."

"I'd a little rather not be the polo player," said Tom pleasantly, "I'd rather look at all these famous people in—in oblivion."

Daisy and Gatsby danced. I remember being surprised by his graceful, conservative fox-trot—I had never seen him dance before. Then they sauntered over to my house and sat on the steps for half an hour while at her request I remained watchfully in the garden: "In case there's a fire or a flood," she explained, "or any act of God."

Tom appeared from his oblivion as we were sitting down to supper together. "Do you mind if I eat with some people over here?" he said. "A fellow's getting off some funny stuff."

"Go ahead," answered Daisy genially, "And if you want to take

down any addresses here's my little gold pencil..." She looked around after a moment and told me the girl was "common but pretty," and I knew that except for the half hour she'd been alone with Gatsby she wasn't having a good time.

We were at a particularly tipsy table. That was my fault–Gatsby had been called to the phone and I'd enjoyed these same people only two weeks before. But what had amused me then turned septic on the air now.

"How do you feel, Miss Baedeker?"

The girl addressed was trying, unsuccessfully, to slump against my shoulder. At this inquiry she sat up and opened her eyes.

"Wha?"

A massive and lethargic woman, who had been urging Daisy to play golf with her at the local club tomorrow, spoke in Miss Baedeker's defence:

"Oh, she's all right now. When she's had five or six cocktails she always starts screaming like that. I tell her she ought to leave it alone."

"I do leave it alone," affirmed the accused hollowly.

"We heard you yelling, so I said to Doc Civet here: 'There's somebody that needs your help, Doc.' "

"She's much obliged, I'm sure," said another friend, without gratitude. "But you got her dress all wet when you stuck her head in the pool."

"Anything I hate is to get my head stuck in a pool," mumbled Miss Baedeker. "They almost drowned me once over in New Jersey."

"Then you ought to leave it alone," countered Doctor Civet.

"Speak for yourself!" cried Miss Baedeker violently. "Your hand shakes. I wouldn't let you operate on me!"

It was like that. Almost the last thing I remember was standing with Daisy and watching the moving picture director and his Star. They were still under the white plum tree and their faces were touching except for a pale thin ray of moonlight between. It occurred to me that he had been very

slowly bending toward her all evening to attain this proximity, and even while I watched I saw him stoop one ultimate degree and kiss at her cheek.

"I like her," said Daisy, "I think she's lovely."

But the rest offended her—and inarguably, because it wasn't a gesture but an emotion. She was appalled by West Egg, this unprecedented "place" that Broadway had begotten upon a Long Island fishing village—appalled by its raw vigor that chafed under the old euphemisms and by the too obtrusive fate that herded its inhabitants along a short cut from nothing to nothing. She saw something awful in the very simplicity she failed to understand.

I sat on the front steps with them while they waited for their car. It was dark here in front: only the bright door sent ten square feet of light volleying out into the soft black morning. Sometimes a shadow moved against a dressing-room blind above, gave way to another shadow, an indefinite procession of shadows, who rouged and powdered in an invisible glass.

"Who is this Gatsby anyhow?" demanded Tom suddenly. "Some big bootlegger?"

"Where'd you hear that?" I inquired.

"I didn't hear it. I imagined it. A lot of these newly rich people are just big bootleggers, you know."

"Not Gatsby," I said shortly.

He was silent for a moment. The pebbles of the drive crunched under his feet.

"Well, he certainly must have strained himself to get this menagerie together."

A breeze stirred the grey haze of Daisy's fur collar.

"At least they're more interesting than the people we know," she said with an effort.

"You didn't look so interested."

"Well, I was."

Tom laughed and turned to me.

"Did you notice Daisy's face when that girl asked her to put her under a cold shower?"

Daisy began to sing with the music in a husky, rhythmic whisper, bringing out a meaning in each word that it had never had before and would never have again. When the melody rose, her voice broke up sweetly, following it, in a way contralto voices have, and each change tipped out a little of her warm human magic upon the air.

"Lots of people come who haven't been invited," she said suddenly. "That girl hadn't been invited. They simply force their way in and he's too polite to object."

"I'd like to know who he is and what he does," insisted Tom. "And I think I'll make a point of finding out."

"I can tell you right now," she answered. "He owned some drug stores, a lot of drug stores. He built them up himself."

The dilatory limousine came rolling up the drive.

"Good night, Nick," said Daisy.

Her glance left me and sought the lighted top of the steps where "Three o'clock in the Morning," a neat, sad little waltz of that year, was drifting out the open door. After all, in the very casualness of Gatsby's party there were romantic possibilities totally absent from her world. What was it up there in the song that seemed to be calling her back inside? What would happen now in the dim incalculable hours? Perhaps some unbelievable guest would arrive, a person infinitely rare and to be marvelled at, some authentically radiant young girl who with one fresh glance at Gatsby, one moment of magical encounter, would blot out those five years of unwavering devotion.

I stayed late that night. Gatsby asked me to wait until he was free and I lingered in the garden until the inevitable swimming party had

run up, chilled and exalted, from the black beach, until the lights were extinguished in the guest rooms overhead. When he came down the steps at last the tanned skin was drawn unusually tight on his face, and his eyes were bright and tired.

"She didn't like it," he said immediately.

"Of course she did."

"She didn't like it," he insisted. "She didn't have a good time."

He was silent and I guessed at his unutterable depression.

"I feel far away from her," he said. "It's hard to make her understand."

"You mean about the dance?"

"The dance?" He dismissed all the dances he had given with a snap of his fingers. "Old sport, the dance is unimportant."

He wanted nothing less of Daisy than that she should go to Tom and say: "I never loved you." After she had obliterated three years with that sentence they could decide upon the more practical measures to be taken. One of them was that, after she was free, they were to go back to Louisville and be married from her house–just as if it were five years ago.

"And she doesn't understand," he said. "She used to be able to understand. We'd sit for hours–"

He broke off and began to walk up and down a desolate path of fruit rinds and discarded favors and crushed flowers.

"I wouldn't ask too much of her," I ventured. "You can't repeat the past."

"Can't repeat the past?" he cried incredulously. "Why of course you can!"

He looked around him wildly, as if the past were lurking here in the shadow of his house, just out of reach of his hand.

"I'm going to fix everything just the way it was before," he said, nodding determinedly. "She'll see."

He talked a lot about the past and I gathered that he wanted to recover something, some idea of himself perhaps, that had gone into loving Daisy. His life had been confused and disordered since then, but if he could once return to a certain starting place and go over it all slowly, he could find out what that thing was...

One autumn night, five years before, they had been walking down the street when the leaves were falling, and they came to a place where there were no trees and the sidewalk was white with moonlight. They stopped here and turned toward each other. Now it was a cool night with that mysterious excitement in it which comes at the two changes of the year. The quiet lights in the houses were humming out into the darkness and there was a stir and bustle among the stars. Out of the corner of his eye Gatsby saw that the blocks of the sidewalk really formed a ladder and mounted to a secret place above the trees—he could climb to it, if he climbed alone, and once there he could suck on the pap of life, gulp down the incomparable milk of wonder.

His heart beat faster and faster as Daisy's white face came up to his own. He knew that when he kissed this girl, and forever wed his unutterable visions to her perishable breath, his mind would never romp again like the mind of God. So he waited, listening for a moment longer to the tuning fork that had been struck upon a star. Then he kissed her. At his lips' touch she blossomed for him like a flower and the incarnation was complete.

Through all he said, even through his appalling sentimentality, I was reminded of something—an elusive rhythm, a fragment of lost words, that I had heard somewhere a long time ago. For a moment a phrase tried to take shape in my mouth and my lips parted like a dumb man's, as though there was more struggling upon them than a wisp of startled air. But they made no sound and what I had almost remembered was uncommunicable forever.

CHAPTER 7

It was when curiosity about Gatsby was at its highest that the lights in his house failed to go on one Saturday night—and, as obscurely as it had begun, his career as Trimalchio was over.

Only gradually did I become aware that the automobiles which turned expectantly into his drive stayed for just a minute and then drove sulkily away. Wondering if he were sick I went over to find out—an unfamiliar butler with a villainous face squinted at me suspiciously from the door.

"Is Mr. Gatsby sick?"

"Nope." After a pause he added "sir" in a dilatory, grudging way.

"I hadn't seen him around, and I was rather worried. Tell him Mr. Carraway came over."

"Who?" he demanded rudely.

"Carraway."

"Carraway. All right, I'll tell him." Abruptly he slammed the door.

My Finn informed me that Gatsby had dismissed every servant in his house a week ago and replaced them with half a dozen others, who never went into West Egg Village to be bribed by the tradesmen, but ordered moderate supplies over the telephone. The grocery boy reported that the kitchen looked like a pigsty, and the general opinion in the village was that the new people weren't servants at all.

Next day Gatsby called me on the phone.

"Going away?" I inquired.

"No, old sport."

"I hear you fired all your servants."

"I wanted somebody who wouldn't gossip. Daisy comes over quite often—in the afternoons."

So the whole caravansary had fallen in like a card house at the disapproval in her eyes.

"They're some people Wolfshiem wanted to do something for. They're all brothers and sisters. They used to run a small hotel."

"I see."

He was calling up at Daisy's request—would I come to lunch at her house tomorrow? Miss Baker would be there. Half an hour later Daisy herself telephoned and seemed relieved to find that I was coming. Something was up. And yet I couldn't believe that they would choose this occasion for a scene—especially for the rather harrowing scene that Gatsby had outlined in the garden.

The next day was broiling, almost the last, certainly the warmest, of the summer. As my train emerged from the tunnel into sunlight, only the hot whistles of the National Biscuit Company broke the simmering hush at noon. The straw seats of the car hovered on the edge of combustion; the woman next to me perspired delicately for a while into her white shirtwaist, and then, as her newspaper dampened under her fingers, lapsed despairingly into deep heat with a desolate cry. Her pocket-book slapped to the floor.

"Oh, my!" she gasped.

I picked it up with a weary bend and handed it back to her, holding it at arm's length and by the extreme tip of the corners to indicate that I had no designs upon it—but every one near by, including the woman, suspected me just the same.

"Hot!" said the conductor to familiar faces. "Some weather! Hot! Hot! Hot! Is it hot enough for you? Is it hot? Is it...?"

My commutation ticket came back to me with a dark stain from his hand. That any one should care in this heat whose flushed lips he

kissed, whose head made damp the pajama pocket over his heart!

Through the hall of the Buchanans' house blew a faint wind, carrying the sound of the telephone bell out to Gatsby and me as we waited at the door.

"The master's body!" roared the butler into the mouthpiece. "I'm sorry, madame, but we can't furnish it—it's far too hot to touch this noon!"

What he really said was: "Yes...yes...I'll see."

He set down the receiver and came toward us, glistening slightly, to take our stiff straw hats.

"Madame expects you in the salon!" he cried, needlessly indicating the direction. In this heat every extra gesture was an affront to the common store of life.

The room, shadowed well with awnings, was dark and cool. Daisy and Jordan lay upon an enormous couch, like silver idols, weighing down their own white dresses against the singing breeze of the fans.

"We can't move," they said together.

Jordan's fingers, powdered white over their tan, rested for a moment in mine.

"And Mr. Thomas Buchanan, the athlete?" I inquired.

Simultaneously I heard his voice, gruff, muffled, husky, at the hall telephone.

Gatsby stood in the center of the crimson carpet and gazed around with fascinated eyes. Daisy watched him and laughed, her sweet, exciting laugh; a tiny gust of powder rose from her bosom into the air.

"The rumor is," whispered Jordan, "that that's Tom's girl on the telephone."

We were silent. The voice in the hall rose high with annoyance. "Very well, then, I won't sell you the car at all...I'm under no obligations to you at all...And as for your bothering me about it at lunch time I won't stand that at all!"

"Holding down the receiver," said Daisy cynically.

"No, he's not," I assured her. "It's a bona fide deal. I happen to know about it."

Tom flung open the door, blocked out its space for a moment with his thick body, and hurried into the room.

"Mr. Gatsby!" He put out his broad, flat hand with well-concealed dislike. "I'm glad to see you, sir...Nick..."

"Make us a cold drink," cried Daisy.

As he left the room again she got up and went over to Gatsby and pulled his face down kissing him on the mouth.

"You know I love you," she murmured.

"You forget there's a lady present," said Jordan.

Daisy looked around doubtfully.

"You kiss Nick too."

"What a low, vulgar girl!"

"I don't care!" cried Daisy and began to clog on the brick fireplace. Then she remembered the heat and sat down guiltily on the couch just as a freshly laundered nurse leading a little girl came into the room.

"Bles-sed pre-cious," she crooned, holding out her arms. "Come to your own mother that loves you."

The child, relinquished by the nurse, rushed across the room and rooted shyly into her mother's dress.

"The Bles-sed pre-cious! Did mother get powder on your old yellowy hair? Stand up now, and say How-de-do."

Gatsby and I in turn leaned down and took the small reluctant hand. Afterward he kept looking at the child with surprise. I don't think he had ever really believed in its existence before.

"I got dressed before luncheon," said the child, turning eagerly to Daisy.

"That's because your mother wanted to show you off." Her face

bent into the single wrinkle of the small white neck. "You dream, you. You absolute little dream."

"Yes," admitted the child calmly. "Aunt Jordan's got on a white dress too."

"How do you like mother's friends?" Daisy turned her around so that she faced Gatsby. "Do you think they're pretty?"

"Where's Daddy?"

"She doesn't look like her father," explained Daisy. "She looks like me. She's got my hair and shape of the face."

Daisy sat back upon the couch. The nurse took a step forward and held out her hand.

"Come, Pammy."

"Goodbye, sweetheart!"

With a reluctant backward glance the well-disciplined child held to her nurse's hand and was pulled out the door, just as Tom came back, preceding four gin rickeys that clicked full of ice.

Gatsby took up his drink.

"They certainly look cool," he said, with visible tension.

We drank in long greedy swallows.

"I read somewhere that the sun's getting hotter every year," said Tom genially. "It seems that pretty soon the earth's going to fall into the sun—or wait a minute—it's just the opposite—the sun's getting colder every year.

"Come outside," he suggested to Gatsby, "I'd like you to have a look at the place."

I went with them out to the veranda. On the green Sound, stagnant in the heat, one small sail crawled slowly toward the fresher sea. Gatsby's eyes followed it momentarily; he raised his hand and pointed across the bay.

"I'm right across from you."

"So you are."

Our eyes lifted over the rosebeds and the hot lawn and the weedy refuse of the dog days along shore. Slowly the white wings of the boat moved against the blue cool limit of the sky. Ahead lay the scalloped ocean and the abounding blessed isles.

"There's sport for you," said Tom, nodding. "I'd like to be out there with him for about an hour."

We had luncheon in the dining-room, darkened, too, against the heat, and drank down nervous gayety with the cold ale.

"What'll we do with ourselves this afternoon," cried Daisy, "and the day after that, and the next thirty years?"

"Don't be morbid," Jordan said. "Life starts all over again when it gets crisp in the fall."

"But it's so hot," insisted Daisy, on the verge of tears, "And everything's so confused. Let's all go to town!"

Her voice struggled on through the heat, beating against it, moulding its senselessness into forms.

"I've heard of making a garage out of a stable," Tom was saying to Gatsby, "but I'm the first man who ever made a stable out of a garage."

"Who wants to go to town?" demanded Daisy insistently. Gatsby's eyes floated toward her. "Ah," she cried, "you look so cool."

Their eyes met, and they stared together at each other, alone in space. With an effort she glanced down at the table.

"You always look so cool," she repeated.

She had told him that she loved him, and Tom Buchanan saw. He was astounded. His mouth opened a little and he looked at Gatsby and then back at Daisy as if he had just recognized her as some one he knew a long time ago.

"You resemble the advertisement of the man," she went on innocently. "You know the advertisement of the man—"

"All right," broke in Tom quickly, "I'm perfectly willing to go to town. Come on—we're all going to town."

He got up, his eyes still flashing between Gatsby and his wife. No one moved.

"Come on!" His temper cracked a little. "What's the matter, anyhow? If we're going to town let's start."

His hand, trembling with his effort at self control, bore to his lips the last of his glass of ale. Daisy's voice got us to our feet and out on to the blazing gravel drive.

"Are we just going to go?" she objected. "Like this? Aren't we going to let any one smoke a cigarette first?"

"Everybody smoked all through lunch."

"Oh, let's have fun," she begged him. "It's too hot to fuss."

He didn't answer.

"Have it your own way," she said. "Come on, Jordan."

They went upstairs to get ready while we three men stood there shuffling the hot pebbles with our feet. A silver curve of the moon hovered already in the western sky. Gatsby started to speak, changed his mind, but not before Tom wheeled and faced him expectantly.

"Have you got your stables here?" asked Gatsby with an effort.

"About a quarter of a mile down the road."

"Oh."

A pause.

"I don't see the idea of going to town," broke out Tom savagely. "Women get these notions in their heads—"

"Shall we take anything to drink?" called Daisy from an upper window.

"I'll get some whiskey," answered Tom. He went inside.

Gatsby turned to me rigidly:

"I can't say anything in his house, old sport."

"She's got an indiscreet voice," I remarked. "It's full of—"
I hesitated.

"Her voice is full of money," he said suddenly.

That was it. I'd never understood before. It was full of money—
that was the inexhaustible charm that rose and fell in it, the jingle of
it, the cymbals' song of it...High in a white palace the king's daughter,
the golden girl...

Tom came out of the house wrapping a quart bottle in a towel,
followed by Daisy and Jordan wearing small tight hats of metallic
cloth and carrying light capes over their arms.

"Shall we all go in my car?" suggested Gatsby. He felt the hot,
green leather of the seat. "I ought to have left it in the shade."

"Is it standard shift?" demanded Tom.

"Yes."

"Well, you take my coupé and let me drive your car to town."

The suggestion was distasteful to Gatsby.

"I don't think there's much gas," he objected.

"Plenty of gas," said Tom boisterously. He looked at the gauge.
"And if it runs out I can stop at a drug store. You can buy anything at
a drug store nowadays."

A pause followed this apparently pointless remark. Daisy looked
at Tom frowning and an indefinable expression, at once definitely
unfamiliar and vaguely recognizable, as if I had only heard it described
in words, passed over Gatsby's face.

"Come on, Daisy," said Tom, pressing her with his hand toward
Gatsby's car. "I'll take you in this circus wagon."

He opened the door but she moved out from the circle of his arm.

"You take Nick and Jordan. We'll follow you in the coupé."

She walked close to Gatsby, touching his coat with her hand.
Jordan and Tom and I got into the front seat of Gatsby's car, Tom

pushed the unfamiliar gears tentatively and we shot off into the oppressive heat leaving them out of sight behind.

"Did you see that?" demanded Tom.

"See what?"

He looked at me keenly, realizing that Jordan and I must have known all along.

"You think I'm pretty dumb, don't you?" he suggested. "Perhaps I am, but I have a–almost a second sight, sometimes, that tells me what to do. Maybe you don't believe that, but science–"

He paused. The immediate contingency overtook him, pulled him back from the edge of the theoretical abyss.

"I've made a small investigation of this fellow," he continued. "I could have gone deeper if I'd known–"

"Do you mean you've been to a medium?" inquired Jordan humorously.

"What?" Confused, he stared at us as we laughed. "A medium?"

"About Gatsby."

"About Gatsby! No, I haven't. I said I'd been making a small investigation of his past."

"And you found he was an Oxford man," said Jordan helpfully.

"An Oxford man!" He was incredulous. "Like hell he is! He wears a pink suit."

"Nevertheless he's an Oxford man."

"Oxford, New Mexico," snorted Tom contemptuously, "or something like that."

"Listen, Tom. If you're such a snob, why did you invite him to lunch?" demanded Jordan crossly.

"Daisy invited him; she knew him before we were married–God knows where!"

We were all irritable now with the fading ale and, aware of it, we

drove for a while in silence. Then as Doctor T. J. Eckleburg's faded
eyes came into sight down the road, I remembered Gatsby's caution
about gasoline.

"We've got enough to get us to town," said Tom.

"But there's a garage right here," objected Jordan. "I don't want
to get stalled in this baking heat."

Tom threw on both brakes impatiently and we slid to an abrupt
dusty stop under Wilson's sign. After a moment the proprietor emerged
from the interior of his establishment and gazed hollow-eyed at the car.

"Let's have some gas!" cried Tom roughly. "What do you think
we stopped for–to admire the view?"

"I'm sick," said Wilson without moving. "I been sick all day."

"What's the matter?"

"I'm all run down."

"Well, shall I help myself?" Tom demanded. "You sounded well
enough on the phone."

With an effort Wilson left the shade and support of the doorway
and, breathing hard, unscrewed the cap of the tank. In the sunlight his
face was green.

"I didn't mean to interrupt your lunch," he said. "But I need
money pretty bad and I was wondering what you were going to do
with your old car."

"How do you like this one?" inquired Tom. "I bought it last week."

"It's a nice yellow one," said Wilson, as he strained at the handle.

"Like to buy it?"

"Big chance," Wilson smiled faintly. "No, but I could make some
money on the other."

"What do you want money for, all of a sudden?"

"I've been here too long. I want to get away. My wife and I want
to go west."

"Your wife does!" exclaimed Tom, startled.

"She's been talking about it for ten years." He rested for a moment against the pump, shading his eyes. "And now she's going whether she wants to or not. I'm going to get her away."

The coupé flashed by us with a flurry of dust and the flash of a waving hand.

"What do I owe you?" demanded Tom harshly.

"I just got wised up to something funny the last two days," remarked Wilson. "That's why I want to get away. That's why I been bothering you about the car."

"What do I owe you?"

"Dollar twenty."

The relentless beating heat was beginning to confuse me and I had a bad moment there before I realized that so far his suspicions hadn't alighted on Tom. He had discovered that Myrtle had some sort of life apart from him in another world and the shock had made him physically sick. I stared at him and then at Tom, who had made a parallel discovery less than an hour before–and it occurred to me that there was no difference between men, in intelligence or race, so profound as the difference between the sick and the well. Wilson was so sick that he looked guilty, unforgivably guilty–as if he had just got some poor girl with child.

"I'll let you have that car," said Tom. "I'll send it over tomorrow afternoon."

That locality was always vaguely disquieting, even in the broad glare of afternoon, and now I turned my head as though I had been warned of something behind. Over the ashheaps the giant eyes of Doctor T. J. Eckleburg kept their vigil but I perceived, after a moment, that other eyes were regarding us with peculiar intensity from less than twenty feet away.

In one of the windows over the garage the curtains had been moved aside a little and Myrtle Wilson was peering down at the car. So engrossed was she that she had no consciousness of being observed and one emotion after another crept into her face like objects into a slowly developing picture. Her expression was curiously familiar—it was an expression I had often seen on women's faces but on Myrtle Wilson's face it seemed purposeless and inexplicable until I realized that her eyes, wide with jealous terror, were fixed not on Tom, but on Jordan Baker, whom she took to be his wife.

There is no confusion like the confusion of a simple mind, and as we drove away Tom was feeling the hot whips of panic. His wife and his mistress, until an hour ago secure and inviolate, were slipping precipitately from his control. Instinct made him step on the accelerator with the double purpose of overtaking Daisy and leaving Wilson behind, and we sped along toward Astoria at fifty miles an hour, until, among the spidery girders of the elevated, we came in sight of the easygoing blue coupé.

"Those big movies around Fiftieth Street are cool," suggested Jordan. "I love New York on summer afternoons when every one's away. There's something very sensuous about it—overripe, as if all sorts of funny fruits were going to fall into your hands."

The word "sensuous" had the effect of further disquieting Tom but before he could invent a protest the coupé came to a stop and Daisy signalled us to draw up alongside.

"Where are we going?" she cried.

"How about the movies?"

"It's so hot," she complained. "You go. We'll ride around and meet you after." With an effort her wit rose faintly, "We'll meet you on some corner. I'll be the man smoking two cigarettes."

"We can't argue about it here," Tom said impatiently as a truck

gave out a cursing whistle behind us. "You follow me to the south side of Central Park, in front of the Plaza."

Several times he turned his head and looked back for their car, and if the traffic delayed them he slowed up until they came into sight. I think he was afraid they would dart down a side street and out of his life forever.

But they didn't. And we all took the less explicable step of engaging the parlor of a suite in the Plaza Hotel.

The prolonged and tumultuous argument that ended by herding us into that room eludes me, though I have a sharp physical memory that, in the course of it, my underwear kept climbing like a damp snake around my legs and intermittent beads of sweat raced cool across my back. The notion originated with Daisy's suggestion that we hire five bathrooms and take cold baths, and then assumed more tangible form as "a place to have a mint julep." Each of us said over and over that it was a "crazy idea"—we all talked at once to a baffled clerk and thought, or pretended to think, that we were being very funny...

The room was large and stifling, and, though it was already four o'clock, opening the windows admitted only a gust of hot shrubbery from the Park. Daisy went to the mirror and stood with her back to us, fixing her hair.

"It's a swell suite," whispered Jordan respectfully and every one laughed.

"Open another window," commanded Daisy, without turning around.

"There aren't any more."

"Well, we'd better telephone for an axe—"

"The thing to do is to forget about the heat," said Tom impatiently. "You make it ten times worse by crabbing about it."

He unrolled the bottle of whiskey from the towel and put it on the table.

"Why not let her alone, old sport?" remarked Gatsby. "You're the one that wanted to come to town."

There was a moment of silence. The telephone book slipped from its nail and splashed to the floor, whereupon Jordan whispered "Excuse me"–but this time no one laughed.

"I'll pick it up," I offered.

"I've got it." Gatsby examined the parted string, muttered "Hum!" in an interested way, and tossed the book on a chair.

"That's a great expression of yours, isn't it?" said Tom sharply.

"What is?"

"All this 'old sport' business. Where'd you pick that up?"

"Now see here, Tom," said Daisy, turning around from the mirror, "if you're going to make personal remarks I won't stay here a minute. Call up and order some ice for the mint julep."

As Tom took up the receiver the compressed heat exploded into sound and we were listening to the portentous chords of Mendelssohn's Wedding March from the ballroom below.

"Imagine marrying anybody in this heat!" cried Jordan dismally.

"Still–I was married in the middle of June," Daisy remembered, "Louisville in June! Somebody fainted. Who was it fainted, Tom?"

"Biloxi," he answered shortly.

"A man named Biloxi. 'Blocks' Biloxi, and he made boxes–that's a fact–and he was from Biloxi, Tennessee."

"They carried him into my house," appended Jordan, "because we lived just two doors from the church. And he stayed three weeks, until Daddy told him he had to get out. The day after he left Daddy died." After a moment she added as if she might have sounded irreverent, "There wasn't any connection."

"I used to know a Bill Biloxi from Memphis," I remarked.

"That was his cousin. I knew his whole family history before he left. He gave me an aluminum putter that I use today."

The music had died down as the ceremony began and now a long cheer floated in at the window, followed by intermittent cries of "Yea—ea—ea!" and finally by a burst of jazz as the dancing began.

"We're getting old," said Daisy. "If we were young we'd rise and dance."

"Remember Biloxi," Jordan warned her. "Where'd you know him, Tom?"

"Biloxi?" He concentrated with an effort. "I didn't know him. He was a friend of Daisy's."

"He was not," she denied. "I'd never seen him before. He came down in the private car."

"Well, he said he knew you. He said he was raised in Louisville. Asa Bird brought him around at the last minute and asked if we had room for him."

Jordan smiled.

"He was probably bumming his way home. He told me he was president of your class at Yale."

Tom and I looked at each other blankly.

"Biloxi?"

"First place, we didn't have any president—"

Gatsby's foot beat a short, restless tattoo and Tom eyed him suddenly.

"By the way, Mr. Gatsby, I understand you're an Oxford man."

"Not exactly."

"Oh, yes, I understand you went to Oxford."

"Yes—I went there."

A pause. Then Tom's voice, incredulous and insulting:

"You must have gone there about the time Biloxi went to New Haven."

Another pause. A waiter knocked and came in with crushed mint and ice but the silence was unbroken by his "Thank you" and the soft closing of the door. This tremendous detail was to be cleared up at last.

"I told you I went there," said Gatsby.

"I heard you, but I'd like to know when."

"It was in nineteen-nineteen, I only stayed five months. That's why I can't really call myself an Oxford man."

Tom glanced around to see if we mirrored his unbelief. But we were all looking at Gatsby.

"It was an opportunity they gave to some of the officers after the Armistice," he continued. "We could go to any of the universities in England or France."

I wanted to get up and slap him on the back. I had one of those renewals of complete faith in him that I'd experienced before.

Daisy rose, smiling faintly, and went to the table.

"Open the whiskey, Tom," she ordered. "And I'll make you a mint julep. Then you won't seem so stupid to yourself...Look at the mint!"

"Wait a minute," snapped Tom, "I want to ask Mr. Gatsby one more question."

"Go on," Gatsby said politely.

"What kind of a row are you trying to cause in my house anyhow?"

They were out in the open at last and Gatsby was content.

"He isn't causing a row." Daisy looked desperately from one to the other. "You're causing a row. Please have a little self control."

"Self control!" repeated Tom incredulously. "I suppose the latest thing is to sit back and let Mr. Nobody from Nowhere make love to your wife. Well, if that's the idea you can count me out... Nowadays people begin by sneering at family life and family institutions and next

they'll throw everything overboard and have intermarriage between black and white."

Flushed with his impassioned gibberish he saw himself standing alone on the last barrier of civilization.

"We're all white here," murmured Jordan.

"I know I'm not very popular. I don't give big parties. I suppose you've got to make your house into a pigsty in order to have any friends—in the modern world."

Angry as I was, as we all were, I was tempted to laugh whenever he opened his mouth. The transition from libertine to prig was so complete.

"I've got something to tell you, old sport,—" began Gatsby. But Daisy guessed at his intention.

"Please don't!" she interrupted helplessly. "Please let's all go home. Why don't we all go home?"

"That's a good idea." I got up. "Come on, Tom. Nobody wants a drink."

"I want to know what Mr. Gatsby has to tell me."

"Your wife doesn't love you," said Gatsby. "She's never loved you. She loves me."

"You must be crazy!" exclaimed Tom automatically.

Gatsby sprang to his feet, vivid with excitement.

"She never loved you, do you hear?" he cried. "She only married you because I was poor and she was tired of waiting for me. It was a terrible mistake, but in her heart she never loved any one except me!"

At this point Jordan and I tried to go but Tom and Gatsby insisted with competitive firmness that we remain—as though neither of them had anything to conceal and it would be a privilege to partake vicariously of their emotions.

"Sit down Daisy." Tom's voice groped unsuccessfully for the paternal note. "What's been going on? I want to hear all about it."

"I told you what's been going on," said Gatsby. "Going on for five years—and you didn't know."

Tom turned to Daisy sharply.

"You've been seeing this fellow for five years?"

"Not seeing," said Gatsby. "No, we couldn't meet. But both of us loved each other all that time, old sport, and you didn't know. I used to laugh sometimes—"but there was no laughter in his eyes, "to think that you didn't know."

"Oh—that's all." Tom tapped his thick fingers together like a clergyman and leaned back in his chair.

"You're crazy!" he exploded. "I can't speak about what happened five years ago, because I didn't know Daisy then—and I'll be damned if I see how you got within a mile of her unless you brought the groceries to the back door. But all the rest of that's a God Damned lie. Daisy loved me when she married me and she loves me now."

"No," said Gatsby, shaking his head.

"She does, though. The trouble is that sometimes she gets foolish ideas in her head and doesn't know what she's doing." He nodded sagely. "And what's more, I love Daisy too. Once in a while I go off on a spree and make a fool of myself, but I always come back, and in my heart I love her all the time."

"You're revolting," said Daisy. She turned to me, and her voice, dropping an octave lower, filled the room with thrilling scorn: "Do you know why we left Chicago? I'm surprised that they didn't treat you to the story of that little spree."

Gatsby walked over and stood beside her.

"Daisy, that's all over now," he said earnestly. "It doesn't matter any more. Just tell him the truth—that you never loved him—and it's all wiped out forever."

She looked at him blindly. "Why,—how could I love him—possibly?"

"You never loved him."

She hesitated. Her eyes fell on Jordan and me with a sort of appeal, as though she realized at last what she was doing—and as though she had never, all along, intended doing anything at all. But it was done now. It was too late.

"I never loved him," she said, with perceptible reluctance.

"Not at Kapiolani?" demanded Tom suddenly.

"No."

From the ballroom beneath, muffled and suffocating chords were drifting up on hot waves of air.

"Not that day I carried you down from the Punch Bowl to keep your shoes dry?" There was a husky tenderness in his tone. "...Daisy?"

"Please don't." Her voice was cold, but the rancour was gone from it. She looked at Gatsby. "There, Jay," she said—but her hand as she tried to light a cigarette was trembling. Suddenly she threw the cigarette and the burning match on the carpet.

"Oh, you want too much!" she cried to Gatsby. "I love you now—isn't that enough? I can't help what's past." She began to sob helplessly. "I did love him once—but I loved you too."

Gatsby's eyes opened and closed.

"You loved me too?" he repeated.

"Even that's a lie," said Tom savagely. "She didn't know you were alive. Why,—there're things between Daisy and me that you'll never know, things that neither of us can ever forget."

The words seemed to bite physically into Gatsby.

"I want to speak to Daisy alone," he insisted. "She's all excited now—"

"Even alone I can't say I never loved Tom," she admitted in a pitiful voice. "It wouldn't be true."

"Of course it wouldn't," agreed Tom.

She turned to her husband.

"As if it mattered to you," she said.

"Of course it matters. I'm going to take better care of you from now on."

"You don't understand," said Gatsby, with a touch of panic. "You're not going to take care of her any more."

"I'm not?" Tom opened his eyes wide and laughed. He could afford to control himself now. "Why's that?"

"Daisy's leaving you."

"Nonsense."

"I am, though," she said with a visible effort.

"She's not leaving me!" Tom's words suddenly leaned down over Gatsby. "Certainly not for a common swindler who'd have to steal the ring he put on her finger."

"I won't stand this!" cried Daisy. "Oh, please let's get out."

"Who are you, anyhow?" broke out Tom. "You're one of that bunch that hangs around with Meyer Wolfshiem—that much I happen to know. I've made a little investigation into your affairs—and I'll carry it further tomorrow."

"You can suit yourself about that, old sport." said Gatsby steadily.

"I found out what your 'drug stores' were." He turned to us and spoke rapidly. "He and this Wolfshiem bought up a lot of side-street drug stores here and in Chicago and sold grain alcohol over the counter. That's one of his little stunts. I picked him for a bootlegger the first time I saw him and I wasn't far wrong."

"What about it?" said Gatsby politely. "I guess your friend Walter Chase wasn't too proud to come in on it."

"And you left him in the lurch, didn't you? You let him go to jail for a month over in New Jersey. God! You ought to hear Walter on the subject of you."

"He came to us dead broke. He was very glad to pick up some money, old sport."

"Don't you call me 'old sport'!" cried Tom. Gatsby said nothing. "Walter could have you up on the betting laws too, but Wolfshiem scared him into shutting his mouth."

That unfamiliar yet recognizable look was back again in Gatsby's face.

"That drug store business was just small change," continued Tom slowly, "but you've got something on now that Walter's afraid to tell me about."

I glanced at Daisy who was staring terrified between Gatsby and her husband and at Jordan who had begun to balance an invisible but absorbing object on the tip of her chin. Then I turned back to Gatsby–and was startled at his expression. He looked–and this is said in all contempt for the babbled slander of his garden–as if he had "killed a man." For a moment the set of his face could be described in just that fantastic way.

It passed, and he began to talk excitedly to Daisy, denying everything, defending his name against accusations that had not been made. But with every word she was drawing further and further into herself, so he gave that up and only the dead dream fought on as the afternoon slipped away, trying to touch what was no longer tangible, struggling unhappily, undespairingly, toward that lost voice across the room.

The voice begged again to go.

"Please, Tom! I can't stand this any more."

Her frightened eyes told that whatever intentions, whatever courage she had had, were definitely gone.

"You two start on home, Daisy," said Tom. "In Mr. Gatsby's car."

She looked at Tom, alarmed now, but he insisted with magnanimous scorn.

"Go on. He won't annoy you. I think he realizes that his presumptuous little flirtation is over."

They were gone, without a word, snapped out, made accidental, isolated, like ghosts even from our pity.

After a moment Tom got up and began wrapping the unopened bottle of whiskey in the towel.

"Want any of this stuff? Jordan? ...Nick?"

I didn't answer.

"Nick?" He asked again.

"What?"

"Want any?"

"No...I just remembered that today's my birthday."

I was thirty. Before me stretched the portentous menacing road of a new decade.

It was seven o'clock when we got into the coupé with him and started for Long Island. Tom talked incessantly, exulting and laughing, but his voice was as remote from Jordan and me as the foreign clamor on the sidewalk or the tumult of the elevated overhead. Human sympathy has its limits and we were content to let all their tragic arguments fade with the city lights behind. Thirty–the promise of a decade of loneliness, a thinning list of single men to know, a thinning brief-case of enthusiasm, thinning hair. But there was Jordan beside me who, unlike Daisy, was too wise ever to carry well-forgotten dreams from age to age. As we passed over the dark bridge her wan face fell lazily against my coat's shoulder and the formidable stroke of thirty died away with the reassuring pressure of her hand.

So we drove on toward death through the cooling twilight.

The young Greek, Michaelis, who ran the coffee joint beside the ashheaps was the principal witness at the inquest. He had slept through the heat until after five, when he strolled over to the garage and found

George Wilson sick in his office—really sick, pale as his own pale hair and shaking all over. Michaelis advised him to go to bed but Wilson refused, saying that he'd miss a lot of business if he did. While his neighbor was trying to persuade him a violent racket broke out overhead.

"I've got my wife locked in up there," explained Wilson calmly. "She's going to stay there till the day after tomorrow and then we're going to move away."

Michaelis was astonished; they had been neighbors for four years and Wilson had never seemed faintly capable of such a statement. Generally he was one of these worn-out men: when he wasn't working he sat on a chair in the doorway and stared at the people and the cars that passed along the road. When any one spoke to him he invariably laughed in an agreeable, colorless way. He was his wife's man and not his own.

So naturally Michaelis tried to find out what had happened, but Wilson wouldn't say a word—instead he began to throw curious, suspicious glances at his visitor and ask him what he'd been doing at certain times on certain days. Just as the latter was getting uneasy some workmen came past the door bound for his restaurant and Michaelis took the opportunity to get away, intending to come back later. But he didn't. He supposed he forgot to, that's all. When he came outside again a little after seven he was reminded of the conversation because he heard Mrs. Wilson's voice, loud and scolding, downstairs in the garage.

"Beat me!" he heard her cry. "Throw me down and beat me, you dirty little coward!"

A moment later she rushed out into the dusk, waving her hands and shouting; before he could move from his door the business was over.

The "death car" as the newspapers called it, didn't stop; it came out of the gathering darkness, wavered tragically for a moment and then disappeared around the next bend. Michaelis wasn't even sure of its color—he told the first policeman that it was light green. The other

car, the one going toward New York, came to rest a hundred yards beyond, and its driver hurried back to where Myrtle Wilson, her life violently extinguished, knelt in the road and mingled her thick, dark blood with the dust.

Michaelis and this man reached her first but when they had torn open her shirtwaist still damp with perspiration, they saw that her left breast was swinging loose like a flap and there was no need to listen for the heart beneath. The mouth was wide open and ripped at the corners as though she had choked a little in giving up the tremendous vitality she had stored so long.

We saw the three or four automobiles and the crowd when we were still some distance away.

"Wreck!" said Tom. "That's good. Wilson'll have a little business at last."

He slowed down, but still without any intention of stopping until, as we came nearer, the hushed intent faces of the people at the garage door made him automatically put on the brakes.

"We'll take a look," he said doubtfully, "just a look."

I became aware now of a hollow, wailing sound which issued incessantly from the garage, a sound which as we got out of the coupé and walked toward the door resolved itself into the words "Oh, my God!" uttered over and over in a gasping moan.

"There's some bad trouble here," said Tom excitedly.

He reached up on tiptoes and peered over a circle of heads into the garage which was lit only by a yellow light in a swinging wire basket overhead. Then he made a harsh sound in his throat and with a violent thrusting movement of his powerful arms pushed his way through.

The circle closed up again with a running murmur of expostulation; it was a minute before I could see anything at all. Then new arrivals disarranged the line and Jordan and I were pushed suddenly inside.

Myrtle Wilson's body wrapped in a blanket and then in another blanket as though she suffered from a chill in the hot night lay on a work table by the wall and Tom, with his back to us, was bending over it, motionless. Next to him stood a motorcycle policeman taking down names with much sweat and correction in a little book. At first I couldn't find the source of the high, groaning words that echoed clamorously through the bare garage—then I saw Wilson standing on the raised threshold of his office, swaying back and forth and holding to the doorposts with both hands. Some man was talking to him in a low voice and attempting from time to time to lay a hand on his shoulder, but Wilson neither heard nor saw. His eyes would drop slowly from the swinging light to the laden table by the wall and then jerk back to the light again and he gave out incessantly his high horrible call.

"O, my Ga-od! O, my Ga-od! Oh, Ga-od! Oh, my Ga-od!"

Presently Tom lifted his head with a jerk and after staring around the garage with glazed eyes addressed a mumbled incoherent remark to the policeman.

"M-a-v—" the policeman was saying, "—o—"

"No,—r—" corrected the man, "M-a-v-r-o—"

"Listen to me!" muttered Tom fiercely.

"r—" said the policeman, "o—"

"g—"

"g—" He looked up as Tom's broad hand fell sharply on his shoulder. "What you want, fella?"

"What happened—that's what I want to know!"

"Auto hit her. Ins'antly killed."

"Instantly killed," repeated Tom, staring.

"She ran out ina road. Son-of-a-bitch didn't even stopus car."

"There was two cars," said Michaelis, "one comin', one goin', see?"

"Going where?" asked the policeman keenly.

"One goin' each way. Well, she–" His hand rose toward the blankets but stopped half way and fell to his side, "–she ran out there an' the one comin' from N'York knock right into her goin' thirty or forty miles an hour."

"What's the name of this place here?" demanded the officer.

"Hasn't got any name."

A pale, well-dressed Negro stepped near.

"It was a yellow car," he said, "big yellow car. New."

"See the accident?" asked the policeman.

"No, but the car passed me down the road, going faster'n forty. Going fifty, sixty."

"Come here and let's have your name. Look out now. I want to get his name."

Some words of this conversation must have reached Wilson swaying in the office door, for suddenly a new theme found voice among his gasping cries.

"You don't have to tell me what kind of car it was! I know what kind of car it was!"

Watching Tom I saw the wad of muscle back of his shoulder tighten under his coat. He walked quickly over to Wilson and standing in front of him seized him firmly by the upper arms.

"You've got to pull yourself together," he said with soothing gruffness.

Wilson's eyes fell upon Tom; he started up on his tiptoes and then would have collapsed to his knees had not Tom held him upright.

"Listen," said Tom, shaking him a little. "I just got here a minute ago, from New York. I was bringing you that coupé we've been talking about. That yellow car I was driving this afternoon wasn't mine, do you hear? I haven't seen it all afternoon."

Only the Negro and I were near enough to hear what he said but

the policeman caught something in the tone and looked over with truculent eyes.

"What's all that?" he demanded.

"I'm a friend of his." Tom turned his head but kept his hands firm on Wilson's body. "He says he knows the car that did it...It was a yellow car."

Some dim impulse moved the policeman to look suspiciously at Tom.

"And what color's your car?"

"It's a blue car, a coupé."

"We've come straight from New York," I said.

Some one who had been driving a little behind us confirmed this and the policeman turned away.

"Now, if you'll let me have that name again correct—"

Picking up Wilson like a doll Tom carried him into the office, set him down in a chair and came back.

"If somebody'll come here and sit with him!" he snapped authoritatively. He watched while the two men standing closest glanced at each other and went unwillingly into the room. Then Tom shut the door on them and came down the single step, his eyes avoiding the table. As he passed close to me he whispered "Let's get out."

Self consciously, with his authoritative arms breaking the way, we pushed through the still gathering crowd, passing a hurried doctor, case in hand, who had been sent for in wild hope half an hour ago.

Tom drove slowly until we were beyond the bend—then his foot came down hard and the coupé raced along through the night. In a little while I heard a low husky sob and saw that the tears were overflowing down his face.

"The God Damn coward!" he whimpered. "He didn't even stop his car."

The Buchanans' house floated suddenly toward us through the dark rustling trees. Tom stopped beside the porch and looked up at the second floor where two windows bloomed with light among the vines.

"Daisy's home," he said. As we got out of the car he glanced at me and frowned slightly.

"I ought to have dropped you in West Egg, Nick. There's nothing we can do tonight."

A change had come over him and he spoke gravely, and with decision. As we walked across the moonlight gravel to the porch he disposed of the situation in a few brisk phrases.

"I'll telephone for a taxi to take you home, and while you're waiting you and Jordan better go in the kitchen and have them get you some supper–if you want any." He opened the door. "Come in."

"No thanks. But I'd be glad if you'd order me the taxi. I'll wait outside."

Jordan put her hand on my arm.

"Won't you come in, Nick?"

"No thanks."

I was feeling a little sick and I wanted to be alone. But Jordan lingered for a moment more.

"It's only half past nine," she said.

I'd be damned if I'd go in; I'd had enough of all of them for one day and suddenly that included Jordan too. She must have seen something of this in my expression for she turned abruptly away and ran up the porch steps into the house. I sat down for a few minutes with my head in my hands, until I heard the phone taken up inside and the butler's voice calling a taxi. Then I walked slowly down the drive away from the house intending to wait by the gate.

I hadn't gone twenty yards when I heard my name and Gatsby stepped from between two bushes into the path. I must have felt

pretty weird by that time because I could think of nothing except the luminosity of his pink suit under the moon.

"What are you doing?" I inquired.

"Just standing here, old sport."

Somehow, that seemed a despicable occupation. For all I knew he was going to rob the house in a moment; I wouldn't have been surprised to see sinister faces, the faces of "Wolfshiem's people," behind him in the dark shrubbery.

"Did you see any trouble on the road?" he asked after a minute.

"Yes."

He hesitated.

"Was she killed?"

"Yes."

"I thought so; I told Daisy I thought so. It's better that the shock should all come at once. She stood it pretty well."

He spoke as if Daisy's reaction was the only thing that mattered.

"I got to West Egg by a side road," he went on, "and left the car in my garage. I don't think anybody saw us but of course I can't be sure."

I disliked him so much by this time that I didn't find it necessary to tell him he was wrong.

"Who was the woman?" he inquired.

"Her name was Wilson. Her husband owns the garage. How the devil did it happen?"

"Well, I tried to swing the wheel—" He broke off, and suddenly I guessed at the truth.

"Was Daisy driving?"

"Yes," he said after a moment, "but of course I'll say I was. You see, when we left New York she was very nervous and she thought it would steady her to drive—and this woman rushed out at us just as we were passing a car coming the other way. It all happened in a minute but it

seemed to me that she wanted to speak to us, thought we were somebody she knew. Well, first Daisy turned away from the woman toward the other car, and then she lost her nerve and turned back. The second my hand reached the wheel I felt the shock—it must have killed her instantly."

"It ripped her open—"

"Don't tell me, old sport." He winced. "Anyhow—Daisy stepped on it. I tried to make her stop, but she couldn't so I pulled on the emergency brake. Then she fell over into my lap and I drove on.

"She'll be all right tomorrow," he said presently. "I'm just going to wait here and see if he tries to bother her about that unpleasantness this afternoon. She's locked herself into her room and if he tries any brutality she's going to turn the light out and on again."

"He won't touch her," I said. "He's not thinking about her."

"I don't trust him, old sport."

"How long are you going to wait?"

"All night if necessary. Anyhow till they all go to bed."

A new point of view occurred to me. Suppose Tom found out that Daisy had been driving. He might think he saw a connection in it—he might think anything. I looked at the house: there were two or three bright windows downstairs and the pink glow from Daisy's room on the second floor.

"You wait here," I said. "I'll see if there's any sign of a commotion."

I walked back along the border of the lawn, traversed the gravel softly and tiptoed up the veranda steps. The drawing-room curtains were open, and I saw that the room was empty. Crossing the porch where we had dined that June night three months before I came to a small rectangle of light which I guessed was the pantry window. The blind was drawn but I found a rift at the sill.

Daisy and Tom were sitting opposite each other at the kitchen table with a plate of cold fried chicken between them and two bottles

of ale. He was talking intently across the table at her and in his earnestness his hand had fallen upon and covered her own. Once in a while she looked up at him and nodded in agreement.

They weren't happy, and neither of them had touched the chicken or the ale—and yet they weren't unhappy either. There was an unmistakable air of natural intimacy about the picture and anybody would have said that they were conspiring together.

As I tiptoed from the porch I heard my taxi feeling its way along the dark road toward the house. Gatsby was waiting where I had left him in the drive.

"Is it all quiet up there?" he asked anxiously.

"Yes, it's all quiet." I hesitated. "You'd better come home and get some sleep."

He shook his head.

"I want to wait here till Daisy goes to bed. Good night, old sport."

He put his hands in his coat pockets and turned back eagerly to his scrutiny of the house, as though my presence marred the sacredness of the vigil. So I walked away and left him standing there in the moonlight—watching over nothing.

CHAPTER 8

I couldn't sleep all night; a fog-horn was groaning incessantly on the Sound, and I tossed half-sick between grotesque reality and savage frightening dreams. Toward dawn I heard a taxi go up Gatsby's drive and immediately I jumped out of bed and began to dress—I felt that I had something to tell him, something to warn him about and morning would be too late.

Crossing his lawn I saw that his front door was still open and he was leaning against a table in the hall, heavy with dejection or sleep.

"Nothing happened," he said wanly. "I waited, and about four o'clock she came to the window and stood there for a minute and then turned out the light."

His house had never seemed so enormous to me as it did that night when we hunted through the great rooms for cigarettes. We pushed aside curtains that were like pavilions and felt over innumerable feet of dark wall for electric light switches—once I tumbled with a sort of splash upon the keys of a ghostly piano. There was an inexplicable amount of dust everywhere and the rooms were musty as though they hadn't been aired for many days. I found the humidor on an unfamiliar table with two stale dry cigarettes inside. Throwing open the French windows of the drawing-room we sat smoking out into the darkness.

"You ought to go away," I said. "It's pretty certain they'll trace your car."

"Go away now, old sport?"

"Go to Atlantic City for a week, or up to Montreal."

He wouldn't consider it. He couldn't possibly leave Daisy until he

knew what she was going to do. He was clutching at some last hope and I couldn't bear to shake him free.

It was this night that he told me the strange story of his youth with Dan Cody—told it to me because "Jay Gatsby" had broken up like glass against Tom's hard malice and the long secret extravaganza was played out. I think that he would have acknowledged anything, now, without reserve, but he wanted to talk about Daisy.

She was the first "nice" girl he had ever known. In various unrevealed capacities he had come in contact with such people but always with indiscernible barbed wire between. He found her excitingly desirable. He went to her house, at first with other officers from Camp Taylor, then alone. It amazed him—he had never been in such a beautiful house before. But what gave it an air of breathless intensity was that Daisy lived there—it was as casual a thing to her as his tent out at camp was to him. There was a ripe mystery about it, a hint of bedrooms upstairs more beautiful and cool than other bedrooms, of gay and radiant activities taking place through its corridors and of romances that were not musty and laid away already in lavender but fresh and breathing and redolent of this year's shining motor cars and of dances whose flowers were scarcely withered. It excited him too that many men had already loved Daisy—it increased her value in his eyes. He felt their presence all about the house, pervading the air with the shades and echoes of still vibrant emotions.

But he knew that he was in Daisy's house by a colossal accident. However glorious might be his future as Jay Gatsby, he was at present a penniless young man without a past, and at any moment the invisible cloak of his uniform might slip from his shoulders. So he made the most of his time. He took what he could get, ravenously and unscrupulously—eventually he took Daisy one still October night, took her because he had no real right to touch her hand.

He might have despised himself, for he had certainly taken her under false pretenses. I don't mean that he had traded on his phantom millions, but he had deliberately given Daisy a sense of security; he let her believe that he was a person from much the same stratum as herself—that he was fully able to take care of her. As a matter of fact he had no such facilities—he had no comfortable family standing behind him and he was liable at the whim of an impersonal government to be blown anywhere about the world.

But he didn't despise himself and it didn't turn out as he had imagined. He had intended, probably, to take what he could and go—but now he found that he had committed himself to the following of a grail. He knew that Daisy was extraordinary but he didn't realize just how extraordinary a "nice" girl could be. She vanished into her rich house, into her rich, full life, leaving Gatsby—nothing. He felt married to her, that was all.

When they met again two days later it was Gatsby who was breathless, who was somehow betrayed. Her porch was bright with the bought luxury of star-shine; the wicker of the settee squeaked fashionably as she turned toward him and he kissed her curious and lovely mouth. She had caught a cold and it made her voice huskier and more charming than ever and Gatsby was overwhelmingly aware of the youth and mystery that wealth imprisons and preserves, of the freshness of many clothes and of Daisy, gleaming like silver, safe and proud above the hot struggles of the poor.

"I can't describe to you how surprised I was to find out I loved her, old sport. I even hoped for a while that she'd throw me over, but she didn't, because she was in love with me too. She thought I knew a lot because I knew different things from her...Well, there I was, way off my ambitions, getting deeper in love every minute, and all of a sudden I didn't care. What was the use of doing great things if I could

have a better time telling her what I was going to do?"

On the last afternoon before he went abroad he sat with Daisy in his arms for a long, silent time. It was a cold fall day with fire in the room and her cheeks flushed. Now and then she moved and he changed his arm a little and once he kissed her dark shining hair. The afternoon had made them tranquil for a while as if to give them a deep memory for the long parting the next day promised. They had never been closer in their month of love nor communicated more profoundly one with another than when she brushed silent lips against his coat's shoulder or when he touched the end of her fingers, gently, as though she were asleep.

He did extraordinarily well in the war. He was a captain before he went to the front and following the Argonne battles he got his majority and the command of the divisional machine guns. After the Armistice he tried frantically to get home but some complication or misunderstanding sent him to Oxford instead. He was worried now— there was a quality of nervous despair in Daisy's letters. She didn't see why he couldn't come. She was feeling the pressure of the world outside and she wanted to see him and feel his presence beside her and be reassured that she was doing the right thing after all.

For Daisy was young and her artificial world was redolent of orchids and pleasant, cheerful snobbery and orchestras which set the rhythm of the year, summing up the sadness and suggestiveness of life in new tunes. All night the saxophones wailed the hopeless comment of the "Beale Street Blues" while a hundred pairs of golden and silver slippers shuffled the shining dust. At the grey tea hour there were always rooms that throbbed incessantly with this low sweet fever, while fresh faces drifted here and there like rose petals blown by the sad horns around the floor.

Through this twilight universe Daisy began to move again with the season; suddenly she was again keeping half a dozen dates a day with half a dozen men and drowsing asleep at dawn with the beads

and chiffon of an evening dress tangled among dying orchids on the floor beside her bed. And all the time something within her was crying for a decision. She wanted her life shaped now, immediately–and the decision must be made by some force–of love, of money, of unquestionable practicality–that was close at hand.

That force took shape in the middle of spring with the arrival of Tom Buchanan. There was a wholesome bulkiness about his person and his position and Daisy was flattered. Doubtless there was a certain struggle and a certain relief. The letter reached Gatsby while he was still at Oxford.

It was dawn now on Long Island and we went about opening the rest of the windows downstairs, filling the house with grey turning, gold turning light. The shadow of a tree fell abruptly across the dew and ghostly birds began to sing among the blue leaves. There was a slow pleasant movement in the air, scarcely a wind, promising a cool lovely day.

"I don't think she ever loved him." Gatsby turned around from a window and looked at me challengingly. "You must remember, old sport, she was very excited this afternoon. He told her those things in a way that frightened her–that made it look as if I was some kind of cheap sharper. And the result was she hardly knew what she was saying."

He sat down gloomily.

"Of course she might have loved him, just for a minute, when they were first married–and loved me more even then, do you see?"

Suddenly he came out with a curious remark:

"In any case," he said, "it was just personal."

What could you make of that, except to suspect some intensity in his conception of the affair that couldn't be measured?

He came back from France when Tom and Daisy were still on their wedding trip, and made a miserable but irresistible journey to Louisville on the last of his army pay. He stayed there a week, walking the streets

where their footsteps had clicked together through the November night and revisiting the out-of-the-way places to which they had driven in her white car. Just as Daisy's house had always seemed to him more mysterious and gay than other houses so his idea of the city itself, even though she was gone from it, was pervaded with a melancholy beauty.

He left feeling that if he had searched harder he might have found her—that he was leaving her behind. The day-coach—he was penniless now—was hot. He went out to the open vestibule and sat down on a folding-chair, and the station slid away and the backs of unfamiliar buildings moved by. Then out into the spring fields, where a yellow trolley raced them for a minute with people in it who might once have seen the pale magic of her face along the casual street.

The track curved and now it was going away from the sun which, as it sank lower, seemed to spread itself in benediction over the vanishing city where she had drawn her breath. He stretched out his hand desperately as if to snatch only a wisp of air, to save a fragment of the spot that she had made lovely for him. But it was all going by too fast now for his blurred eyes and he knew that he had lost that part of it, the freshest and the best, forever.

It was nine o'clock when we finished breakfast and went out on the porch. The night had made a sharp difference in the weather and there was an autumn flavor in the air. The gardener, the last one of Gatsby's former servants, came to the foot of the steps.

"I'm going to drain the pool today, Mr. Gatsby. Leaves'll start falling pretty soon and then there's always trouble with the pipes."

"Don't do it today," Gatsby answered. He turned to me apologetically. "You know, old sport, I've never used that pool all summer?"

I looked at my watch and stood up.

"Twelve minutes to my train."

I didn't want to go to the city. I wasn't worth a decent stroke of work but it was more than that—I didn't want to leave Gatsby. I missed that train, and then another, before I could get myself away.

"I'll call you up," I said finally.

"Do, old sport."

"I'll call you about noon."

We walked slowly down the steps.

"I suppose Daisy'll call too." He looked at me anxiously as if he hoped I'd corroborate this.

"I suppose so."

"Well—goodbye."

We shook hands and I started away. Just before I reached the hedge I remembered something and turned around.

"They're a rotten crowd," I shouted across the lawn. "You're worth the whole damn bunch put together."

I've always been glad I said that. It was the only compliment I ever gave him, because I disapproved of him from beginning to end. First he nodded politely, and then his face broke into that radiant and understanding smile, as if we'd been in ecstatic cahoots on that fact all the time. His gorgeous pink rag of a suit made a bright spot of color against the white steps and I thought of the night when I first came to his ancestral home three months before. The lawn and drive had been crowded with the faces of those who guessed at his corruption—and he had stood on those steps, concealing his incorruptible dream, as he waved them goodbye.

I thanked him for his hospitality. We were always thanking him for that—I and the others.

"Goodbye," I called. "I enjoyed breakfast, Gatsby."

Up in the city I tried for a while to list the quotations on an interminable amount of stock, then I fell asleep in my swivel-chair.

Just before noon the phone woke me and I started up with sweat breaking out on my forehead. It was Jordan Baker; she often called me up at this hour because the uncertainty of her own movements between hotels and clubs and private houses made her hard to find in any other way. Usually her voice came over the wire as something fresh and cool as if a divot from a green golf links had come sailing in at the office window but this morning it seemed harsh and dry.

"I've left Daisy's house," she said. "I'm at Hempstead and I'm going down to Southampton this afternoon."

Probably it had been tactful to leave Daisy's house, but the act annoyed me and her next remark made me rigid.

"You weren't so nice to me last night."

"How could it have mattered then?"

Silence for a moment. Then—

"However—I want to see you."

"I want to see you too."

"Suppose I don't go to Southampton, and come into town this afternoon?"

"No—I don't think this afternoon."

"Very well."

"It's impossible this afternoon. Various—"

We talked like that for a while and then abruptly we weren't talking any longer. I don't know which of us hung up with a sharp click but I know I didn't care. I couldn't have talked to her across a tea-table that day if I never talked to her again in this world.

I called Gatsby's house a few minutes later, but the line was busy. I tried four times; finally an exasperated central told me the wire was being kept open for long distance from Detroit. Taking out my time-table I drew a small circle around the three-fifty train. Then I leaned back in my chair and tried to think. It was just noon.

When I passed the ashheaps on the train that morning I had crossed deliberately to the other side of the car. I suppose there'd be a curious crowd around there all day with little boys searching for dark spots in the dust and some garrulous man telling over and over what had happened until it became less and less real even to him and he could tell it no longer and Myrtle Wilson's tragic achievement was forgotten. Now I want to go back a little and tell what happened at the garage after we left there the night before.

They had difficulty in locating the sister, Catherine. She must have broken her rule against drinking that night for when she arrived she was stupid with liquor and unable to understand that the ambulance had already gone to Flushing. When they convinced her of this she immediately fainted as if that was the intolerable part of the affair. Someone kind or curious took her in his car and drove her in the wake of her sister's body.

Until long after midnight a changing crowd lapped up against the front of the garage while George Wilson rocked himself back and forth on the couch inside. For a while the door of the office was open and everyone who came into the garage glanced irresistibly through it. Finally someone said it was a shame and closed the door. Michaelis and several other men were with him—first four or five men, later two or three men. Still later Michaelis had to ask the last stranger to wait there fifteen minutes longer while he went back to his own place and made a pot of coffee. After that he stayed there alone with Wilson until dawn.

About three o'clock the quality of Wilson's incoherent muttering changed—he grew quieter and began to talk about the yellow car. He announced that he had a way of finding out whom the yellow car belonged to, and then he blurted out that a couple of months ago his wife had come from the city with her face bruised and her nose swollen.

But when he heard himself say this, he flinched and began to cry

"Oh, my God!" again in his groaning voice. Michaelis made a clumsy attempt to distract him.

"How long have you been married, George? Come on there, try and sit still a minute and answer my question. How long have you been married?"

"Twelve years."

"Ever had any children? Come on, George, sit still—I asked you a question. Did you ever have any children?"

The hard brown beetles kept thudding against the dull light and whenever Michaelis heard a car go tearing along the road outside it sounded to him like the car that hadn't stopped a few hours before. He didn't like to go into the garage because the work bench was stained where the body had been lying so he moved uncomfortably around the office—he knew every object in it before morning—and from time to time sat down beside Wilson trying to keep him more quiet.

"Have you got a church you go to sometimes, George? Maybe even if you haven't been there for a long time? Maybe I could call up the church and get a priest to come over and he could talk to you, see?"

"Don't belong to any."

"You ought to have a church, George, for times like this. You must have gone to church once. Didn't you get married in a church? Listen, George, listen to me. Didn't you get married in a church?"

"That was a long time ago."

The effort of answering broke the rhythm of his rocking—for a moment he was silent. Then the same half knowing, half bewildered look came back into his faded eyes.

"Look in the drawer there," he said, pointing at the desk.

"Which drawer?"

"That drawer—that one."

Michaelis opened the drawer nearest his hand. There was nothing

in it but a small expensive dog leash made of leather and braided silver. It was apparently new.

"This?" he inquired, holding it up.

Wilson stared and nodded.

"I found it yesterday afternoon. She tried to tell me about it but I knew it was something funny."

"You mean your wife bought it?"

"She had it wrapped in tissue paper on her bureau."

Michaelis didn't see anything odd in that and he gave Wilson a dozen reasons why his wife might have bought the dog leash. But conceivably Wilson had heard some of these same explanations before, from Myrtle, because he began saying "Oh, my God!" again in a whisper—his comforter left several explanations in the air.

"Then he killed her," said Wilson. His mouth dropped open suddenly.

"Who did?"

"I have a way of finding out."

"You're morbid, George," said his friend. "This has been a strain to you and you don't know what you're saying. You'd better try and sit quiet till morning."

"He murdered her."

"It was an accident, George."

Wilson shook his head. His eyes narrowed and his mouth widened slightly with the ghost of a superior "Hm!"

"I know," he said definitely, "I'm one of these trusting fellas and I don't think any harm to nobody, but when I get to know a thing I know it. It was the man in that car. She ran out to speak to him and he wouldn't stop."

Michaelis had seen this too but it hadn't occurred to him that there was any special significance in it. He believed that Mrs. Wilson

had been running away from her husband, rather than trying to stop any particular car.

"How could she of been like that?"

"She's a deep one," said Wilson, as if that answered the question. "Ah-h-h—"

He began to rock again and Michaelis stood twisting the leash in his hand.

"Maybe you got some friend that I could telephone for, George?"

This was a forlorn hope—he was almost sure that Wilson had no friend: there was not enough of him for his wife. He was glad a little later when he noticed a change in the room, a blue quickening by the window, and realized that dawn wasn't far off. About five o'clock it was blue enough outside to snap off the light.

Wilson's glazed eyes turned out to the ashheaps, where small grey clouds took on fantastic shape and scurried here and there in the faint dawn wind.

"I spoke to her," he muttered, after a long silence. «I told her she might fool me but she couldn't fool God. I took her to the window—" With an effort he got up and walked to the rear window and leaned with his face pressed against it, "—and I said 'God knows what you've been doing, everything you've been doing. You may fool me but you can't fool God!' "

Standing behind him Michaelis saw with a shock that he was looking at the eyes of Doctor T. J. Eckleburg which had just emerged pale and enormous from the dissolving night.

"God sees everything," repeated Wilson.

"That's an advertisement," Michaelis assured him. Something made him turn away from the window and look back into the room. But Wilson stood there a long time, his face close to the window pane, nodding into the twilight.

By six o'clock Michaelis was worn out and grateful for the sound of a car stopping outside. It was one of the watchers of the night before who had promised to come back so he cooked breakfast for three which he and the other man ate together. Wilson was quieter now and Michaelis went home to sleep; when he awoke four hours later and hurried back to the garage Wilson was gone.

His movements—he was on foot all the time—were afterward traced to Port Roosevelt and then to Gad's Hill where he bought a sandwich that he didn't eat and a cup of coffee. He must have been tired and walking slowly for he didn't reach Gad's Hill until noon. Thus far there was no difficulty in accounting for his time—there were boys who had seen a man "acting sort of crazy" and motorists at whom he stared oddly from the side of the road. Then for three hours he disappeared from view. The police, on the strength of what he said to Michaelis, that he "had a way of finding out," supposed that he spent that time going from garage to garage thereabouts inquiring for a yellow car. On the other hand no garage man who had seen him ever came forward—and perhaps he had an easier, surer way of finding out what he wanted to know. By half past two he was in West Egg where he asked someone the way to Gatsby's house. So by that time he knew Gatsby's name.

At two o'clock Gatsby put on his bathing suit and left word with the butler that if any one phoned word was to be brought to him at the pool. He stopped at the garage for a pneumatic mattress that had amused his guests during the summer, and the chauffeur helped him pump it up. Then he gave instructions that the open car wasn't to be taken out under any circumstances—and this was strange because the front right fender needed repair.

Gatsby shouldered the mattress and started for the pool. Once he stopped and shifted it a little, and the chauffeur asked him if he needed help, but he shook his head and in a moment disappeared

among the yellowing trees.

No telephone message arrived but the butler went without his sleep and waited for it until four o'clock—until long after there was any one to give it to if it came. I have an idea that Gatsby himself didn't believe it would come and perhaps he no longer cared. If that was true he must have felt that he had lost the old warm world, paid a high price for living too long with a single dream. He must have looked up at an unfamiliar sky through frightening leaves and shivered as he found what a grotesque thing a rose is and how raw the sunlight was upon the scarcely created grass. A new world, material without being real, where poor ghosts, breathing dreams like air, drifted fortuitously about...like that ashen, fantastic figure gliding toward him through the amorphous trees.

The chauffeur—he was one of Wolfshiem's protégés—heard the shots—afterward he could only say that he hadn't thought anything much about them. I drove from the station directly to Gatsby's house and my rushing anxiously up the front steps was the first thing that alarmed any one. But they knew then, I firmly believe. With scarcely a word said, four of us, the chauffeur, butler, gardener and I, hurried down to the pool.

There was a faint, barely perceptible movement of the water as the fresh flow from one end urged its way toward the drain at the other. With little ripples that were hardly the shadows of waves, the laden mattress moved irregularly down the pool. A small gust of wind that scarcely corrugated the surface was enough to disturb its accidental course with its accidental burden. The touch of a cluster of leaves revolved it slowly, tracing, like the leg of compass, a thin red circle in the water.

It was after we started with Gatsby toward the house that the gardener saw Wilson's body a little way off in the grass, and the holocaust was complete.

CHAPTER 9

After two years I remember the rest of that day, and that night and the next day, only as an endless drill of police and photographers and newspaper men in and out of Gatsby's front door. A rope stretched across the main gate and a policeman by it kept out the curious, but little boys soon discovered that they could enter through my yard and there were always a few of them clustered open-mouthed about the pool. Someone with a positive manner, perhaps a detective, used the expression "mad man" as he bent over Wilson's body that afternoon, and the adventitious authority of his voice set the key for the newspaper reports next morning.

Most of those reports were a nightmare—grotesque, circumstantial, eager and untrue. When Michaelis's testimony at the inquest brought to light Wilson's suspicions of his wife I thought the whole tale would shortly be served up in racy pasquinade—but Catherine, who might have said anything, didn't say a word. She showed a surprising amount of character about it too—looked at the coroner with determined eyes under that corrected brow of hers and swore that her sister had never seen Gatsby, that her sister was completely happy with her husband, that her sister had been into no mischief whatever. She convinced herself of it and cried into her handkerchief as if the very suggestion was more than she could endure. So Wilson was reduced to a man "deranged by grief" in order that the case might remain in its simplest form. And it rested there.

But all this part of it seemed remote and unessential. I found myself on Gatsby's side, and alone. From the moment I telephoned news of the catastrophe to West Egg village, every surmise about him,

and every practical question, was referred to me. At first I was surprised and confused; then, as he lay in his house and didn't move or breathe or speak hour upon hour it grew upon me that I was responsible, because no one else was interested—interested, I mean, with that intense personal interest to which every one has some vague right at the end.

I called up Daisy half an hour after we found him, called her instinctively and without hesitation. But she and Tom had gone away early that afternoon, and taken baggage with them.

"Left no address?"

"No."

"Say when they'd be back?"

"No."

"Any idea where they are? How I could reach them?"

"I don't know. Can't say."

I wanted to get somebody for him. I wanted to go into the room where he lay and reassure him: "I'll get somebody for you, Gatsby. Don't worry. Just trust me and I'll get somebody for you—"

Meyer Wolfshiem's name wasn't in the phone book. The butler gave me his office address on Broadway and I called Information, but by the time I had the number it was long after five and no one answered the phone.

"Will you ring again?"

"I've rung them three times."

"It's very important."

"Sorry. I'm afraid no one's there."

I went back to the drawing room and thought for an instant that they were chance visitors, all these official people who suddenly filled it. But as they drew back the sheet and looked at Gatsby with unmoved eyes, his protest continued in my brain.

"Look here, old sport, you've got to get somebody for me.

You've got to try hard. I can't go through this alone."

Some one started to ask me questions but I broke away and going upstairs looked hastily through the unlocked parts of his desk– he'd never told me definitely that his parents were dead. But there was nothing–only the picture of Dan Cody, a token of forgotten violence staring down from the wall.

Next morning I sent the butler to New York with a letter to Wolfshiem which asked for information and urged him to come out on the next train. That request seemed superfluous when I wrote it. I was sure he'd start when he saw the newspapers, just as I was sure there'd be a wire from Daisy before noon–but neither a wire nor Mr. Wolfshiem arrived, no one arrived except more police and photographers and newspaper men. When the butler brought back Wolfshiem's answer I began to have a feeling of defiance, of scornful solidarity between Gatsby and me against them all.

Dear Mr. Carraway.

This has been one of the most terrible shocks of my life to me I hardly can believe it that it is true at all. Such a mad act as that man did should make us all think. I cannot come down now as I am tied up in some very important business and cannot get mixed up in this thing now. If there is anything I can do a little later let me know in a letter by Edgar. I hardly know where I am when I hear about a thing like this and am completely knocked down and out.

Yours truly

MEYER WOLFSHIEM

and then hasty addenda beneath:

Let me know about the funeral etc do not know his family at all.

When the phone rang that afternoon and Long Distance said

Chicago was calling I thought this would be Daisy at last. But the connection came through as a man's voice, very thin and far away.

"This is Slagle speaking..."

"Yes?" The name was unfamiliar.

"Hell of a note, isn't it? Get my wire?"

"There haven't been any wires."

"Young Parke's in trouble," he said rapidly. "They picked him up when he handed the bonds over the counter. They got a circular from New York giving 'em the numbers just five minutes before. What d'you know about that, hey? You never can tell in these hick towns—"

"Hello!" I interrupted breathlessly. "Look here—this isn't Mr. Gatsby. Mr. Gatsby's dead."

There was a long silence on the other end of the wire, followed by an exclamation...then a quick squawk as the connection was broken.

I think it was on the third day that a telegram signed Henry C. Gatz arrived from a town in Minnesota. It said only that the sender was leaving immediately and to postpone the funeral until he came.

It was Gatsby's father, a solemn old man very helpless and dismayed, bundled up in a long cheap ulster against the warm September day. His eyes leaked continuously with excitement and when I took the bag and umbrella from his hands he began to pull so incessantly at his sparse grey beard that I had difficulty in getting off his coat. He was on the point of collapse so I took him into the music room and made him sit down while I sent for something to eat. But he wouldn't eat and the glass of milk spilled from his trembling hand.

"I saw it in the Chicago newspaper," he said. "It was all in the Chicago newspaper. I started right away."

"I didn't know how to reach you."

His eyes, seeing nothing, moved ceaselessly about the room.

"It was a mad man," he said. "He must have been mad."

"Wouldn't you like some coffee?" I urged him.

"I don't want anything. I'm all right now, Mr.–"

"Carraway."

"Well, I'm all right now. Where have they got Jimmy?"

I took him into the drawing-room, where his son lay, and left him there. Some little boys had come up on the steps and were looking into the hall; when I told them who had arrived they went reluctantly away.

After a little while Mr. Gatz opened the door and came out, his mouth ajar, his face flushed slightly, his eyes leaking isolated and unpunctual tears. He had reached an age where death no longer has the quality of ghastly surprise, and when he looked around him now for the first time and saw the height and splendor of the hall and the great rooms opening out from it into other rooms his grief began to be mixed with an awed pride. I helped him to a bedroom upstairs; while he took off his coat and vest I told him that all arrangements had been deferred until he came.

"I didn't know what you'd want, Mr. Gatsby–"

"Gatz is my name."

"–Mr. Gatz. I thought you might want to take the body west."

He shook his head.

"Jimmy always liked it better down East. He rose up to his position in the East. Were you a friend of my boy's, Mr.–?"

"We were close friends."

"He had a big future before him, you know. He was only a young man but he had a lot of brain power here."

He touched his head impressively and I nodded.

"If he'd of lived he'd of been a great man. A man like James J. Hill. He'd of helped build up the country."

"That's true," I said, uncomfortably.

He fumbled at the embroidered coverlet, trying to take it from

the bed, and lay down stiffly—was instantly asleep.

That night an obviously frightened person called up and demanded to know who I was before he would give his name.

"This is Mr. Carraway," I said.

"Oh—" He sounded relieved. "This is Klipspringer."

I was relieved too for that seemed to promise another friend at Gatsby's grave. I didn't want it to be in the papers and draw a sightseeing crowd so I'd been calling up a few people myself. They were hard to find.

"The funeral's tomorrow," I said. "Three o'clock, here at the house. I wish you'd tell anybody who'd be interested."

"Oh, I will," he broke out hastily. "Of course I'm not likely to see anybody, but if I do."

His tone made me suspicious.

"Of course you'll be there yourself."

"Well, I'll certainly try. What I called up about is—"

"Wait a minute," I interrupted. "How about saying you'll come?"

"Well, the fact is—the truth of the matter is that I'm staying with some people up here in Greenwich and they rather expect me to be with them tomorrow. In fact there's a sort of picnic or something. Of course I'll do my very best to get away."

I ejaculated an unrestrained "Huh!" and he must have heard me for he went on nervously:

"What I called up about was a pair of shoes I left there. I wonder if it'd be too much trouble to have the butler send them on. You see they're tennis shoes and I'm sort of helpless without them. My address is care of B. F.—"

I didn't hear the rest of the name because I hung up the receiver.

After that I felt a certain shame for Gatsby—one gentleman to whom I telephoned implied that he had got what he deserved. However, that was my fault, for he was one of those who used to

sneer most bitterly at Gatsby on the courage of Gatsby's liquor and I should have known better than to call him.

The morning of the funeral I went up to New York to see Meyer Wolfshiem; I couldn't seem to reach him any other way. The door that I pushed open on the advice of an elevator boy was marked "The Swastika Holding Company" and at first there didn't seem to be any one inside. But when I'd shouted "Hello" several times in vain an argument broke out behind a partition and presently a lovely Jewess appeared at an interior door and scrutinized me with black hostile eyes.

"Nobody's in," she said. "Mr. Wolfshiem's gone to Chicago."

The first part of this was obviously untrue for someone had begun to whistle "The Rosary," tunelessly, inside.

"Please say that Mr. Carraway wants to see him."

"I can't get him back from Chicago, can I?"

At this moment a voice, unmistakably Wolfshiem's called "Stella!" from the other side of the door.

"Leave your name on the desk," she said quickly. "I'll give it to him when he gets back."

"But I know he's there."

She took a step toward me and began to slide her hands indignantly up and down her hips.

"You young men think you can force your way in here any time," she scolded. "We're getting sickantired of it. When I say he's in Chicago, he's in Chicago."

I mentioned Gatsby.

"Oh–h!" She looked at me over again. "Will you just–what was your name?"

She vanished. In a moment Meyer Wolfshiem stood solemnly in the doorway, holding out both hands. He drew me into his office, remarking in a reverent voice that it was a sad time for all of us, and

offered me a cigar.

"My memory goes back to when I first met him," he said. "A young major just out of the army and covered over with medals he got in the war. He was so hard up he had to keep on wearing his uniform because he couldn't buy some regular clothes. First time I saw him was when he come into Winebrenner's poolroom at Forty-third Street and asked for a job. He hadn't eat anything for a couple of days. 'Come on have some lunch with me,' I sid. He ate more than four dollars' worth of food in half an hour."

"Did you start him in business?" I inquired.

"Start him! I made him."

"Oh."

"I raised him up out of nothing, right out of the gutter. I saw right away he was a fine appearing, gentlemanly young man, and when he told me he was an Oggsford I knew I could use him good. I got him to join up in the American Legion and he used to stand high there. Right off he did some work for a client of mine up to Albany. We were so thick like that in everything–" He held up two bulbous fingers "–always together."

I wondered if this partnership had included the World's Series transaction in 1919.

"Now he's dead," I said after a moment. "You were his closest friend, so I know you'll want to come to his funeral this afternoon."

"I'd like to come."

"Well, come then."

The hair in his nostrils quivered slightly and as he shook his head his eyes filled with tears.

"I can't do it–I can't get mixed up in it," he said.

"There's nothing to get mixed up in. It's all over now."

"When a man gets killed I never like to get mixed up in it in any

way. I keep out. When I was a young man it was different—if a friend of mine died, no matter how, I stuck with them to the end. You may think that's sentimental but I mean it—to the bitter end."

I saw that for some reason of his own he was determined not to come, so I stood up.

"Are you a college man?" he inquired suddenly.

For a moment I thought he was going to suggest a "gonnegtion" but he only nodded and shook my hand.

"Let us learn to show our friendship for a man when he is alive and not after he is dead," he suggested. "After that my own rule is to let everything alone."

When I left his office the sky had turned dark and I got back to West Egg in a drizzle. After changing my clothes I went next door and found Mr. Gatz walking up and down excitedly in the hall. His pride in his son and in his son's possessions was continually increasing and now he had something to show me.

"Jimmy sent me this picture." He took out his wallet with trembling fingers. "Look there."

It was a photograph of the house, cracked in the corners and dirty with many hands. He pointed out every detail to me eagerly. "Look there!" and then sought admiration from my eyes. He had shown it so often that I think it was more real to him now than the house itself.

"Jimmy sent it to me. I think it's a very pretty picture. It shows up well."

"Very well. Had you seen him lately?"

"He come out to see me two years ago and bought me the house I live in now. Of course we was broke up when he run off from home but I see now there was a reason for it. He knew he had a big future in front of him. And ever since he made a success he was very generous with me."

He seemed reluctant to put away the picture, held it for another

minute, lingeringly, before my eyes. Then he returned the wallet and pulled from his pocket a ragged old copy of a book called "Hopalong Cassidy."

"Look here, this is a book he had when he was a boy. It just shows you."

He opened it at the back cover and turned it around for me to see. On the last fly-leaf was printed the word SCHEDULE, and the date September 12th, 1906. And underneath:

Rise from bed . . . . 6.00 A.M.

Dumbbell exercise and wall-scaling . . . . 6.15-6.30 A.M.

Study electricity, etc. . . . . 7.15-8.15 A.M.

Work . . . . 8.30-4.30 P.M.

Baseball and sports . . . . 4.30-5.00 P.M.

Practice elocution, poise and how to attain it . . . . . . 5.00-6.00 P.M.

Study needed inventions . . . . 7.00-9.00 P.M.

GENERAL RESOLVES

No wasting time at Shafters or

No more smokeing or chewing

Bath every other day

Read one improving book or magazine per week

Save $5.00 $3.00 per week

Be better to parents

"I come across this book by accident," said the old man. "It just shows you, don't it?"

"It just shows you."

"Jimmy was bound to get ahead. He always had some resolves like this or something. Do you notice what he's got about improving his mind? He was always great for that. He told me I et like a hog once and I beat him for it."

He was reluctant to close the book, reading each item aloud and then looking eagerly at me. I think he rather expected me to copy down the list for my own use.

A little before three the Lutheran minister arrived from Flushing and I began to look involuntarily out the windows for other cars. So did Gatsby's father. And as the time passed and the servants came in and stood waiting in the hall, his eyes began to blink anxiously and he spoke of the rain in a worried uncertain way. The minister glanced several times at his watch so I took him aside and asked him to wait for half an hour. But it wasn't any use. Nobody came.

About five o'clock our procession of three cars reached the cemetery and stopped in a thick drizzle beside the gate—first a motor hearse, horribly black and wet, then Mr. Gatz and the minister and I in the limousine, and, a little later, four or five servants and the postman from West Egg in Gatsby's station wagon, all wet to the skin. As we started through the gate into the cemetery I heard a car stop and then the sound of someone splashing after us over the soggy ground. I looked around. It was the man with owl-eyed glasses whom I had found marvelling over Gatsby's books in the library one night three months before.

I'd never seen him since then. I don't know how he knew about the funeral or even his name. The rain poured down his thick glasses and he took them off and wiped them to see the protecting canvas unrolled from Gatsby's grave.

I tried to think about Gatsby then for a moment but he was already too far away and I could only remember, without resentment,

that Daisy hadn't sent a message or a flower. Dimly I heard someone murmur "Blessed are the dead that the rain falls on," and then the owl-eyed man said "Amen to that," in a brave voice.

We straggled down quickly through the rain to the cars. Owl-Eyes spoke to me by the gate.

"I couldn't get to the house," he remarked.

"Neither could anybody else."

"Go on!" He started. "Why, my God! they used to go there by the hundreds."

He took off his glasses and wiped them again outside and in.

"The poor son-of-a-bitch," he said.

One of my most vivid memories is of coming back west from prep school and later from college at Christmas time. Those who went farther than Chicago would gather in the old dim Union Station at six o'clock of a December evening with a few Chicago friends already caught up into their own holiday gayeties to bid them a hasty goodbye. I remember the fur coats of the girls returning from Miss This or That's and the chatter of frozen breath and the hands waving overhead as we caught sight of old acquaintances and the matchings of invitations: "Are you going to the Ordways᾿ ? the Herseys᾿ ? the Schultzes᾿ ?" and the long green tickets clasped tight in our gloved hands. And last the murky yellow cars of the Chicago Milwaukee and St. Paul Railroad looking cheerful as Christmas itself on the tracks beside the gate.

When we pulled out into the winter night and the real snow, our snow, began to stretch out beside us and twinkle against the windows, and the dim lights of small Wisconsin stations moved by, a sharp wild brace came suddenly into the air. We drew in deep breaths of it as we walked back from dinner through the cold vestibules, unutterably aware of our identity with this country for one strange hour before we melted indistinguishably into it again.

That's my middle west—not the wheat or the prairies or the lost Swede towns but the thrilling, returning trains of my youth and the street lamps and sleigh bells in the frosty dark and the shadows of holly wreaths thrown by lighted windows on the snow. I am part of that, a little solemn with the feel of those long winters, a little complacent from growing up in the Carraway house in a city where dwellings are still called through decades by a family's name. I see now that this has been a story of the West, after all—Tom and Gatsby, Daisy and Jordan and I, were all Westerners, and perhaps we possessed some deficiency in common which made us subtly unadaptable to Eastern life.

Even when the East excited me most, even when I was most keenly aware of its superiority to the bored, sprawling, swollen towns beyond the Ohio, with their interminable inquisitions which spared only the children and the very old—even then it had always for me a quality of distortion. West Egg especially still figures in my more fantastic dreams. I see it as a night scene by El Greco: a hundred houses, at once conventional and grotesque, crouching under a sullen, overhanging sky and a lustreless moon. In the foreground four solemn men in dress suits are walking along the sidewalk with a stretcher on which lies a drunken woman in a white evening dress. Her hand, which dangles over the side, sparkles cold with jewels. Gravely the men turn in at a house—the wrong house. But no one knows the woman's name, and no one cares.

After Gatsby's death the East was haunted for me like that, distorted beyond my eyes' power of correction. So when the blue smoke of brittle leaves was in the air and the wind blew the wet laundry stiff on the line I decided to come back home.

There was one thing to be done before I left, an awkward, unpleasant thing that perhaps had better have been let alone. But I wanted to leave things in order and not just trust that obliging and indifferent sea to sweep my refuse away. I saw Jordan Baker and talked over and around

what had happened to us together and what had happened afterward to me, and she lay perfectly still listening in a big chair.

She was dressed to play golf and I remember thinking she looked like a good illustration, her chin raised a little, jauntily, her hair the color of an autumn leaf, her face the same brown tint as the fingerless glove on her knee. When I had finished she told me without comment that she was engaged to another man. I doubted that though there were several she could have married at a nod of her head but I pretended to be surprised. For just a minute I wondered if I wasn't making a mistake, then I thought it all over again quickly and got up to say goodbye.

"Nevertheless you did throw me over," said Jordan suddenly. "You threw me over on the telephone. I don't give a damn about you now but it was a new experience for me and I felt a little dizzy for a while."

We shook hands.

"Oh, and do you remember—" she added, "—a conversation we had once about driving a car?"

"Why—not exactly."

"You said a bad driver was only safe until she met another bad driver? Well, I met another bad driver, didn't I? I mean it was careless of me to make such a wrong guess. I thought you were rather an honest, straightforward person. I thought it was your secret pride."

"I'm thirty," I said. "I'm five years too old to lie to myself and call it honor."

She didn't answer. Angry, and half in love with her, and tremendously sorry, I turned away.

One afternoon late in October I saw Tom Buchanan. He was walking ahead of me along Fifth Avenue in his alert, aggressive way, his hands out a little from his body as if to fight off interference, his head moving sharply here and there, adapting itself to his restless eyes. Just as I slowed up to avoid overtaking him he stopped and began

frowning into the windows of a jewelry store. Suddenly he saw me and walked back holding out his hand.

"What's the matter, Nick? Do you object to shaking hands with me?"

"Yes. You know what I think of you."

"You're crazy, Nick," he said quickly. "Crazy as hell. I don't know what's the matter with you."

"Tom," I inquired, "what did you say to Wilson that afternoon?"

He stared at me without a word and I knew I had guessed right about those missing hours. I started to turn away but he took a step after me and grabbed my arm.

"I told him the truth," he said. "He came to the door while we were getting ready to leave and when I sent down word that we weren't in he tried to force his way upstairs. He was crazy enough to kill me if I hadn't told him who owned the car. His hand was on a revolver in his pocket every minute he was in the house—" He broke off defiantly. "What if I did tell him? That fellow had it coming to him. He threw dust into your eyes just like he did in Daisy's but he was a tough one. He ran over Myrtle like you'd run over a dog and never even stopped his car."

There was nothing I could say, except the one unutterable fact that it wasn't true.

"And if you think I didn't have my share of suffering—look here, when I went to give up that flat and saw that damn box of dog biscuits sitting there on the sideboard I sat down and cried like a baby. By God it was awful—"

I couldn't forgive him or like him but I saw that what he had done was, to him, entirely justified. It was all very careless and confused. They were careless people, Tom and Daisy—they smashed up things and creatures and then retreated back into their money or their vast carelessness or whatever it was that kept them together, and let other people clean up the mess they had made...

I shook hands with him; it seemed silly not to, for I felt suddenly as though I were talking to a child. Then he went into the jewelry store to buy a pearl necklace—or perhaps only a pair of cuff buttons—rid of my provincial squeamishness forever.

Gatsby's house was still empty when I left—the grass on his lawn had grown as long as mine. One of the taxi drivers in the village never took a fare past the entrance gate without stopping for a minute and pointing inside; perhaps it was he who drove Daisy and Gatsby over to East Egg the night of the accident and perhaps he had made a story about it all his own. I didn't want to hear it and I avoided him when I got off the train.

I spent my Saturday nights in New York because those gleaming, dazzling parties of his were with me so vividly that I could still hear the music and the laughter faint and incessant from his garden and the cars going up and down his drive. One night I did hear a material car there and saw its lights stop at his front steps. But I didn't investigate. Probably it was some final guest who had been away at the ends of the earth and didn't know that the party was over.

On the last night, with my trunk packed and my car sold to the grocer, I went over and looked at that huge incoherent failure of a house once more. On the white steps an obscene word, scrawled by some boy with a piece of brick, stood out clearly in the moonlight and I erased it, drawing my shoe raspingly along the stone. Then I wandered down to the beach and sprawled out on the sand.

Most of the big shore places were closed now and there were hardly any lights except the shadowy, moving glow of a ferryboat across the Sound. And as the moon rose higher the inessential houses began to melt away until gradually I became aware of the old island here that flowered once for Dutch sailors' eyes—a fresh, green breast of the new world. Its vanished trees, the trees that had made way for Gatsby's house, had once pandered in whispers to the last and greatest of all human

dreams; for a transitory enchanted moment man must have held his breath in the presence of this continent, compelled into an aesthetic contemplation he neither understood nor desired, face to face for the last time in history with something commensurate to his capacity for wonder.

And as I sat there brooding on the old, unknown world, I thought of Gatsby's wonder when he first picked out the green light at the end of Daisy's dock. He had come a long way to this blue lawn and his dream must have seemed so close that he could hardly fail to grasp it. He did not know that it was already behind him, somewhere back in that vast obscurity beyond the city, where the dark fields of the republic rolled on under the night.

Gatsby believed in the green light, the orgastic future that year by year recedes before us. It eluded us then, but that's no matter—tomorrow we will run faster, stretch out our arms farther...And one fine morning—

So we beat on, boats against the current, borne back ceaselessly into the past.

The End

國家圖書館出版品預行編目資料

大亨小傳（中英雙語典藏版）/ 史考特‧費茲傑羅
（F. Scott Fitzgerald）著；成惠英繪；邱淑娟譯. --
臺中市：晨星，2021.07
面； 公分. --（愛藏本；096）

譯自：The Great Gatsby

ISBN 978-986-5582-95-1（精裝）

874.57   110009089

愛藏本：96

大亨小傳（中英雙語典藏版）
The Great Gatsby

作　　者｜史考特‧費茲傑羅（F. Scott Fitzgerald）
繪　　者｜成惠英
譯　　者｜邱淑娟

責任編輯｜謝宜真
封面設計｜鐘文君
美術編輯｜黃偵瑜
文字校潤｜呂曉婕、謝宜真、蔡雅莉

填寫線上回函，立刻享有
晨星網路書店50元購書金

創 辦 人｜陳銘民
發 行 所｜晨星出版有限公司
　　　　　台中市 407 工業區 30 路 1 號 1 樓
　　　　　TEL:(04)23595820　FAX:(04)23550581
　　　　　http://star.morningstar.com.tw
　　　　　行政院新聞局局版台業字第 2500 號
法律顧問｜陳思成律師

初版日期｜2002 年 09 月 01 日
二版日期｜2021 年 07 月 01 日
　　ISBN｜978-986-5582-95-1
　　定價｜新台幣 330 元

讀者服務專線｜TEL:（02）23672044 /（04）23595819#230
讀者傳真專線｜FAX:（02）23635741 /（04）23595493
讀者專用信箱｜service@morningstar.com.tw
　　網路書店｜http://www.morningstar.com.tw
　　郵政劃撥｜15060393（知己圖書股份有限公司）

印　　刷｜上好印刷股份有限公司